It was far t

"I'll be off then_____rol as he could mus_____ee, but…"

She gave a nervous laugh. "Yeah, I know. Thank you for coming over and checking the hot water for me."

"No problem. If you like, I can call in tomorrow and show you how to use the espresso machine."

'I'd like that," she replied, following him as he went out the front door.

She stayed there on the front verandah, her hands shoved into the pockets of her jeans, watching while he executed a neat turn and headed down the drive.

A sense of anticipation stole over him. Getting to know Tamsyn Masters better was proving to be more challenging than he'd expected.

And more appealing. Far, far more appealing.

* * *

The High Price of Secrets
is part of The Master Vinters series:

Tangled vines, tangled lives.

THE HIGH PRICE OF SECRETS

BY
YVONNE LINDSAY

Published in Great Britain 2013
by Mills & Boon, an imprint of Harlequin (UK) Limited,
Eton House, 18-24 Paradise Road, Richmond, Surrey TW9 1SR

© Dolce Vita Trust 2013

ISBN: 978 0 263 90495 6

51-1213

Harlequin (UK) policy is to use papers that are natural, renewable and recyclable products and made from wood grown in sustainable forests. The logging and manufacturing processes conform to the legal environmental regulations of the country of origin.

Printed and bound in Spain
by Blackprint CPI, Barcelona

New Zealand born, to Dutch immigrant parents, **Yvonne Lindsay** became an avid romance reader at the age of thirteen. Now, married to her "blind date" and with two fabulous children, she remains a firm believer in the power of romance. Yvonne feels privileged to be able to bring to her readers the stories of her heart. In her spare time, when not writing, she can be found with her nose firmly in a book, reliving the power of love in all walks of life. She can be contacted via her website, www.yvonnelindsay.com.

This book is dedicated to my wonderful readers and fans who give me a reason for writing every single day. Please know I appreciate you all.

One

"What do you mean you quit? It's only four and a half weeks to Christmas! We're so busy with guests and functions that we can barely move. Look, let's talk about it. If you're not happy, we can work around that. Find you something else to do."

Tamsyn sighed inwardly. Find her something else to do. Sure, that would solve how she felt right now—not. She couldn't blame her brother, Ethan, for wanting to make things right for her. He'd done it all her life, after all. But this situation was beyond his fixing. That was why she'd needed to get away.

A holiday was something she'd been thinking about for a while. Working at The Masters, which in addition to being their family home was a vineyard and winery with luxury cottage accommodation on the outskirts of Adelaide in South Australia, hadn't given her any satisfaction for a very long time. She'd been restless, feeling as if she didn't really fit in anymore—at work, at home, in her family, even in her engagement.

The debacle of the night before had only proven just how right she was.

"Ethan, I can't talk about it. I'm in New Zealand."

"*You're in New Zealand?* I thought you were staying here in Adelaide with Trent last night," Ethan's incredulity was clear as it transmitted through the hands-free kit in her rental car.

Tamsyn counted slowly to ten, letting her brother continue to let off steam before replying.

"I've ended our engagement."

There was the briefest of silences as her words sunk in.

"You what?" Ethan sounded as if he wasn't certain he'd heard her correctly.

"Long story." She swallowed against the pain that had lessened to a persistent dull throb deep in her chest.

"I have ears."

"Not now, Ethan. I c-can't." Her voice broke and tears spilled uncontrolled down her cheeks.

"I'm going to hurt him," Ethan growled from far across the Tasman Sea with his characteristic brotherly protectiveness.

"No, don't. He's not worth it."

Her brother sighed and she could feel his concern and frustration in that single huff of air. "When are you coming back?"

"I…I don't know. It's kind of up in the air at the moment." She didn't think that now was a good time to tell him she'd only bought a one-way ticket.

"Well, at least you trained your assistant to take over when needed. Is Zac up to date with everything?"

Even though she knew he couldn't see her, Tamsyn shook her head and bit her lip.

"Tam?"

"Um, no. I fired him."

"You wh—?" Ethan fell silent as he started to put two and two together, coming up with his usual four. Even so, he couldn't keep the incredulity from his voice. "Zac and Trent?"

"Yup," she said, her throat almost paralyzed and strangling the single word.

"Will you be okay? I'll come over. Just tell me where you are."

"No, don't. I'll be fine—eventually. I just need…" She drew in a shuddering breath. She couldn't even find the words to say what she really needed—she had to simply tell him something he'd understand. "I just need some time alone. Some space so I can think things out. I'm sorry about leaving like this. Everything is in my computer, you know the password, and the bookings are all duplicated on the wall planner as well. Worse comes to worst, they can phone me if they need to."

"We'll take care of it, don't worry."

Her big brother's firm conviction wasn't as good as being right there with him, but in terms of comfort it came close.

"Thanks, Ethan."

"No problem, but Tam? Who's going to take care of you?"

"*I* will," she said firmly.

"I really think you should come home."

"No, I know what I need to do. It's important to me, now more than ever." This part, she had to share with him—even though she knew he wouldn't like it. "I'm going to find her, Ethan."

Silence, then another sigh. "Are you sure now is the best time to go searching for our mother?"

It had already been a few months now, but the shock of discovering their mother—who they'd long been told was dead—was alive and living in New Zealand still reverberated through her mind almost every moment of every day. Learning after his death that their father had lied to them all this time was one thing, discovering the rest of their family had supported him in the lie was another—but realizing that their mother had chosen to remain apart from them, to never even try to make contact, well, that had raised so many questions in Tamsyn's mind they'd begun to define everything about the way she saw herself.

Tamsyn grimaced and shook her head slightly. "Can't think of a better time than now, can you?"

"Yeah, actually, I can. You're hurt, you're vulnerable. I don't want you to get let down again. Come home. Let me put an investigator on to it so that you know what you're going into when they find her."

She could picture him right now, the frown on his forehead, the thinned line of his lips as he worried from afar.

"I want to do this myself. I need to. Look, I'm not far from that address you gave me a couple of months ago. I'd better go," she said, checking the distance on the screen of her GPS.

"You're just going to show up, no warning?"

"Why not?"

"Tam, be sensible. You can't just arrive on someone's doorstep claiming to be their long-lost child."

"Except I'm not *lost,* am I? She knew where *we* were all along. She's the one who left and didn't come back."

She couldn't hide the hurt in the words. A hurt that warred with resentment and anger and sorrow and so many unanswered questions that Tamsyn had hardly had a full night's sleep since she'd heard the news that her mother still lived. That the woman she'd quietly fantasized about, a mother who'd loved her and cared for her too much to ever leave her behind, didn't exist. She had so many questions and she had convinced herself that she was strong enough now to face the answers. She needed to so she could move forward with her life, because what she'd believed up until now had been based on lies and fabrication. Trent's betrayal was the final straw. She didn't even know who she was anymore. But she was ready to find out. Ethan's voice broke into her thoughts.

"Do me a favor, find a motel or somewhere and sleep on it before you do anything you might regret. We can talk in the morning."

"I'll let you know how it goes," Tamsyn replied, ignoring her brother's plea. "I'll call you in a few days."

She disconnected the phone before Ethan could say another word and listened carefully as the disembodied voice on the GPS carefully enunciated that her turn was coming up in five hundred meters. Tamsyn's gut clenched tight. She had to do this. As irrational and out of character as it was for her, the woman who usually planned everything out to the finest degree, she *needed* to do this.

Carefully, Tamsyn turned in at the imposing stone-wall-lined entrance to a long driveway. She drew the car to a halt and closed her eyes for a moment. This was it—soon she could be face-to-face with her mother for the first time since she was three years old. A shudder passed through her body as her adrenaline levels kicked up a notch.

The past twenty-four hours had been a roller-coaster ride. One that had alternately left her giddy with anticipation or sick to her stomach. Tamsyn opened her eyes and took her foot off the brake. The car began inching forward, rumbling loudly over the cattle guard beneath the tires and along the long straight stretch of driveway that gently inclined up the hill.

To the left and the right of her, regimented lines of grapevines grew, their foliage lush and green and the early signs of fruit could be seen hanging on the vines. Considering it was only late November, Tamsyn's experienced eye could see that this vineyard was in for a bumper crop.

She continued along the long driveway. It snaked up a steep incline until finally, after a particularly tight hairpin turn, she saw the house ahead of her. The sprawling two-story building, crafted in stone and cedar, dominated the crest of the hill. Her lips set in a firm line of disapproval. So it clearly hadn't been a lack of money that had kept her mother from staying in touch, she thought cynically. Was this how Ellen Masters had used the money her husband had sent her for the past twenty-odd years?

Tamsyn used that cynicism to propel her out of her car and toward the front door. It was now or never. Taking a deep breath, she reached for the iron door knocker and lifted it, only to let it drop with a solid clang. A short time later she heard footsteps echo from inside. Her stomach tied in knots as every last ounce of her resolve suddenly fled.

What the hell was she doing here?

Finn Gallagher opened his front door and had to force himself not to take a step back. He recognized the woman standing in front of him with a surety that went soul deep. Ellen's daughter.

So the little princess from Australia had finally decided to visit. Too little, too late, as far as he was concerned. Far too late.

The pictures he'd seen of her over the years, hadn't done her justice, though he had the sense he wasn't seeing her at her best. His sweeping gaze took in the mussed long dark brown hair that cascaded over her shoulders and the dark bruises of tiredness that stained porcelain skin under wide-spaced brown eyes. Eyes that reminded him so much of her mother. The woman who, together with her partner, Lorenzo, had mothered him when his own family had disintegrated.

Her clothes were creased but still stylish, and clung to her curves in a way that drew his eye to the opening of her blouse and especially to the tempting swell of creamy skin exposed there. Her skirt skimmed her hips and down her slender thighs to end just above the knee. Not long enough to be dowdy and not so short as to be inappropriate, but somehow still enticing.

It all spoke to the privileged upbringing she'd enjoyed. He found it difficult not to feel bitter when he knew how hard her mother had scraped and worked for a decent life. Clearly the Masters family had looked after their own—they just didn't look after those who walked away from them. Those who didn't conform.

His gaze drifted back to her face where he noticed her full lips tremble slightly before pulling into a nervous smile.

"H-hello, I was wondering if Ellen Masters lives here?" she said.

Her voice was tight, as if her throat was constricted and in the late-afternoon sun that slanted across her face he could see telltale signs of tear tracks. Natural curiosity rose from inside him but he quelled it with his usual determination.

"And you are…?" he asked, knowing full well what the answer would be.

"Oh, I'm sorry." She held out a delicate hand. "I'm Tamsyn Masters. I'm looking for my mother, Ellen."

He took her hand in his, noting instantly the coolness of her touch, the fragility in the bones of her fingers as his larger, stronger ones closed around hers. He struggled against the instinct to go into protection mode. There was something very not right in Tamsyn Masters's world right now, but, he reminded himself, that wasn't his problem.

Keeping her away from Ellen was.

Two

"There's no Ellen Masters here," he replied, letting go of her hand. "Was your mother expecting you?"

She had the grace to look shamefaced. "No, I kind of hoped to surprise her."

Surprise her? Yeah, he just bet she did. Without sparing a thought to whether or not her mother would, or could, see her. How typical of her type, he thought angrily. Pampered, spoiled and thinking the world spun for her delectation. He knew the type well—unfortunately. Too well. They were the kind who'd always expect more, no matter how much you gave. People like Briana, his ex. Beautiful, seemingly compassionate, born into a life of opportunity—but in the cold light of day as grasping and as single-minded as Fagin in *Oliver Twist*.

"Are you sure you have the right address?" he asked, tamping his fury down.

"Well…I thought…" She reached into her handbag and pulled out a crumpled sheet of paper and read off the address. "That's right, isn't it? I'm at the right place."

"That is my address, but there's no Ellen Masters here. I'm sorry. It looks like you've had a wasted trip."

Before his eyes, every particle in her body slumped. Her eyes suddenly brimmed with unshed tears and a stricken look froze her delicate features into a mask of sadness. Again that urge to protect her welled within him—along with the compulsion to tell her of the well-concealed and unsealed driveway she'd have passed on the road here. The one that led to the cottage where Ellen and Lorenzo had lived for the past twenty-five years or so—but he just as determinedly pushed the impulse back.

He knew for a fact Tamsyn Masters had legally been an adult for ten years. What whim had finally driven her to seek out Ellen now? And, more important, why hadn't she reached out to her mother sooner, when it could possibly still have made a difference to the other woman's happiness?

"I—oh, well, I'm sorry to have bothered you. My information can't have been correct."

She reached into her handbag for an oversize pair of sunglasses and shoved them none too elegantly onto her face, hiding her tortured gaze from view. As she did so, he caught sight of the white band of skin on the ring finger of her left hand. Had the engagement he'd read of over a year ago come to an end? Had that been the catalyst to send her searching for her mother?

Whatever it was, it was none of his business.

"No problem," he answered and watched as she walked back to her car and turned it around to drive back down the driveway.

Finn didn't waste another second before reaching for his cell phone and punching in a number. It went straight to voice mail and he uttered a short sharp epithet in frustration while listening to the disembodied voice asking him to leave a message.

"Lorenzo, call me. There's been a complication here at home."

He slid his phone back in his pocket and closed the front door of his house. Somehow, though, he had the feeling he hadn't completely closed the door on Tamsyn Masters.

As Tamsyn steered down the driveway, disappointment crashed through her with the force of a wrecking ball. The tears she'd battled to hold back while talking to the stranger now fell rapidly down her cheeks. She sniffed unevenly, trying to hold in the emotion that had been bubbling so close to the surface ever since she'd left Adelaide last night.

Why on earth had she thought it would be simple? She should have known better. Should have listened to Ethan, even, and tackled this another time—another day when she was in a stronger frame of mind. Well, she'd done it now, she'd gone to the address her late father's solicitor had used to send her mother all those payments through the years and it had been the wrong one.

Disappointment had a nasty bitter taste, she'd discovered—not just once, but twice now in the past twenty-four hours. It just went to prove, that for her, acting out of character was the wrong thing to do. She wasn't made to be impulsive. All her life she had weighed things up long and carefully before doing anything. Now she fully understood why she'd always been that way. It was safer. You didn't get hurt. Sure, you didn't have the thrill of taking a risk either, but was the pain you suffered when things went wrong worth it? Not in her book.

Tamsyn thought about the man who'd opened his door to her at the top of the hill. Over six feet, she'd been forced to look up at him. He'd had presence—being the kind of guy who turned heads just by entering a room. A broad forehead and straight brows had shadowed clear gray eyes the color of the schist rock used on the side of the house that was very definitely his castle. A light stubble had stippled his strong square jaw, but his smile, while polite, had lacked warmth.

There'd been something in his gaze when he'd looked at her. As if…no, she was just being fanciful. He couldn't have known her because she knew full well she'd never met him before in her life. She would most definitely have remembered.

The sun was sinking in the sky and weariness pulled at every muscle in her body as all her activity, not to mention crossing time zones, over the past day took its toll. She needed to find somewhere to stay before she did something stupid like drive off the road and into a ditch.

Tamsyn pulled the car to the side of the road and consulted the GPS for accommodation options nearby. Thankfully there was a boutique hotel that provided meals on request about a fifteen-minute drive away. She keyed the phone number into her mobile phone and was relieved to find that while the room rate was on a par with the accommodation at The Masters, yes, they had a room available for the next few nights. Booking made, Tamsyn pressed the appropriate section of the GPS screen and followed the computerized instructions, eventually pulling up outside a quaint-looking early-1900s single-story building.

With the golden rays of the early-evening sun caressing its creamy paintwork, it looked warm and inviting. Just what she needed.

Finn paced his office, unable to settle back down to the plans that were sprawled across his wide desk. Plans that were going to go to hell in a handbasket if he couldn't buy the easement necessary to gain access to the tract of land he wanted to use for this special project. He shoved a hand through his short hair, mussing it even more than usual.

The chirp of his phone was a happy distraction.

"Gallagher."

"Finn, is there a problem?"

"Lorenzo, I'm glad you called." Finn settled in his chair and swiveled it around to face the window, allowing the vista spread before him to fill his mind and relax his thoughts into a semblance of order. Thoughts that had been distracted all too thoroughly by his earlier visitor.

"What is it, my boy?"

Despite Lorenzo's years in Australia, followed by the past couple of decades in New Zealand, his voice still held the lilt of his native Italian tongue.

"First, how is Ellen?"

The older man sighed. "Not good, she is having a bad day today."

After Ellen began to show signs of kidney and liver failure, she and Lorenzo had relocated to Wellington, where she could receive the specialized care her advancing dementia required.

"I'm sorry to hear that."

He could almost hear Lorenzo shrug in acceptance. "It is what it is. I have asked Alexis to make plans to return from Italy."

"Ellen's that bad?"

Alexis was Lorenzo and Ellen's only child and had been working overseas for the past year. Currently, she was visiting with Lorenzo's family still living in Tuscany.

"*Si,* she has no fight left in her anymore. If she recognizes me at all it is a good day, but they are few."

Finn could hear the pain echoing in the older man's voice before Lorenzo took another deep breath and continued.

"Now, what did you call me for?"

Choosing blunt statement over trying to find an easy way to say what he had to, Finn said, "Tamsyn Masters showed up here today wanting to see Ellen."

"So, it has finally happened."

"I told her Ellen Masters doesn't live here and sent her on her way."

Lorenzo gave a short laugh, the sound crackling like autumn leaves. "But you didn't tell her that Ellen *Fabrini* does, I assume?"

"No," Finn admitted. He hadn't told an outright lie when he'd spoken to Tamsyn. Though Lorenzo and Ellen had never formalized their union, she'd always been known as his wife and had gone by his last name the whole time they'd lived in New Zealand.

"You say she left again?"

"Yes, hopefully to return to Australia."

"Hmm, but what if she doesn't leave?"

Finn's lips firmed in a line as he considered Lorenzo's statement. "What are you thinking?"

"You know I have no love for that family after what they did to my Ellen. I lost count of the hours she spent crying over letters she wrote to those children. It broke her heart a little more every single time. And did they ever write back, or even try to contact her when they were older? No. Yet as much as I would wish them all to Dante's inferno, I know how much Ellen loved them and if she was to stabilize, if her mind was to clear just a little, she might benefit from a visit from her daughter."

Finn fought to keep the incredulity from his voice. "You want me to keep her from going home?"

"Do not chase her away just yet. But, if you can, keep her in the dark about where Ellen is—about all of us, if you can. With things the way they are…" His voice cracked and he took a moment to recover.

"I understand," Finn soothed.

His heart broke for the man who'd stepped into the role of father figure when Finn's own father had died, and his mother suffered a complete nervous breakdown. Finn had been only twelve and Lorenzo, his father's business partner, and Ellen had taken him into their hearts and their home. The couple had been his rock through his turbulent adolescence and his teens. Their unwavering support, together with their careful guardianship of the land his father had owned, had ensured stability and, eventually, a good living for them all. Finn owed them everything.

"I'll take care of things. Don't worry," he assured Lorenzo as they completed their call.

Exactly *how* he was going to take care of things was another matter. First, he had to find out whether Tamsyn had left the area. Given how exhausted she'd looked hovering on his doorstep, he doubted she'd have gone far. It only took a few calls to find her and he wasn't at all surprised to discover the Aussie princess had chosen one of the most expensive accommodation providers in the area.

Okay, so now he knew where she was, what was he going to do next? Finn leaned back in his chair and steepled his fingers under his chin, rocking the leather chair back and forth slightly as he stared back out the window again.

Encroaching twilight began to obscure the Kaikoura ranges in the far distance, narrowing his world to the acres that surrounded him. His acres. His land. His home. A home he wouldn't have today but for the determination of Lorenzo and Ellen all those years ago. What was he going to do? Whatever they needed him to—even if it meant befriending the woman who'd caused Ellen so much suffering over the years.

Growing up, he'd heard occasional tales about Ellen's other children—the ones she'd been forced to leave behind once her marriage had irretrievably broken down. Even then, he'd seen the pain that abandoning her children had caused her, how she'd sought solace in alcohol that had eventually led to her current illness, and over the intervening years he'd wondered about the children themselves and why they hadn't done a thing to try to get in touch with the mother who'd loved them with all her heart.

As soon as he'd been old enough, and computer savvy enough, he'd done a little research and discovered the favored lives Ethan and Tamsyn Masters lived on their family vineyard estate, The Masters. They'd grown up wanting for nothing and had had every opportunity to excel presented to them on a platter. Not for them the hard graft of after-school jobs and backbreaking weekend work, just to get ahead. Not for them the millstone of student loans and expenses.

Finn didn't mind admitting he'd felt some resentment toward Ellen's other family, they'd had it so easy while she, on the other hand, had made do with so little—secure only in the love of the man she'd walked away from her husband and children with.

A man who continued to stay by her side as she'd battled her alcoholism and as eventually her body and mind broke down around her. Ellen's health was so precarious right now that Finn feared that even if she recognized Tamsyn, should she manage to track her mother down, at the sight of her, Ellen could slide into a place in her mind from which she would never return.

After all, hadn't his own mother's death occurred after he had finally been allowed to visit her following her breakdown? Hadn't seeing him been a reminder of what she'd given up on when the sudden death of her husband had forced her to retreat into the supposedly safe reaches of her mind? And hadn't her shame pushed her deeper into her mind, never to emerge again? Even now, those memories had the power to hurt. He pushed them forcibly away.

Tamsyn Masters—she should be the focus of his thoughts right now, and his plans to get her to stay in the area without letting her find out the truth about Ellen. Finn thought again what he knew about the young woman who'd turned up at his house today. She was twenty-eight years old, five years younger than himself. Last he'd heard, she was engaged to marry some up-and-coming lawyer in Adelaide. Clearly she hadn't been wearing her ring today. It could mean anything. Maybe she had taken it off to get it cleaned or resized. Or maybe she'd taken it off when she'd washed her hands and had forgotten to put it back on again.

Another idea occurred to him. One that sparked his interest. Maybe, just maybe, it meant she might be in the market for a bit of rebound romance. A bit of light flirtation perhaps—some enticement to stay in the Marlborough district? If she was as shallow as he'd found her type to be in the past it would be all good fun—no chance of emotional involvement or hurt feelings, just an opportunity to keep her very carefully under observation while making sure she found out nothing about Ellen.

It would take some doing, sure, but he was confident he could handle it. A buzz of anticipation hummed through his body. Yeah, he was definitely the man to do it, and along the way he'd find out as much as he could about the perplexing Ms. Tamsyn Masters.

Three

Voices echoed down the wide paneled hallway of the hotel as Tamsyn walked toward the dining room. She still felt a little tired, but last night's light meal, warm bath and a comfortable night in a good bed, had all gone a long way toward restoring her equilibrium.

Last night she'd all but decided to head to the airport this morning and book a flight back to Auckland. But she'd woken filled with a new sense of purpose—more determined than ever to make the most of her time here. Her mother had to be in the area somewhere. As far as she and Ethan were aware, checks were still being sent to her from their father's estate—and none of the checks had ever been returned to sender. Last night she'd been too tired and too disheartened to remember that vital detail. Today was another matter entirely and she was thinking far more clearly. A call to Ethan would confirm the address her father's lawyers used.

First order of the day though, after breakfast, was a trip to Blenheim to purchase some new clothes and luggage. She'd left Adelaide in such an all-fired hurry she'd arrived here in New Zealand with only the clothes she stood in and her handbag. Despite making use of the iron and ironing board stashed in her room's wardrobe, her clothing was definitely looking the worse for wear.

She couldn't wait to rid herself of her underwear, either—the pieces so carefully chosen to titillate and entice her then fiancé. Despite the fact she'd had to rinse out, dry and then rewear them twice now, she wouldn't be happy until she'd seen them thrown into the trash.

They were yet another reminder of how foolishly naive she'd been—and how the people she'd trusted had let her down. Bile rose in her throat as she remembered how eager she'd been to surprise Trent just two nights ago. How she'd planned a romantic dinner and evening for two culminating in the slow and sexy removal of said lingerie. But the surprise had been all hers when she'd discovered him in bed with someone else—her personal assistant, Zac.

Once the hurt had begun to recede she'd felt such a fool. What kind of woman didn't know her fiancé was gay? Worse, that he'd been prepared to marry her and simply string her along as a mask of respectability so he could continue his steady rise through the ranks of the old-school law firm he worked for.

She'd known that she only had to go home to have her family surrounding her, consoling her—but the thought had failed to comfort her. Her family had lied to her, too, had hidden things from her that she'd had the right to know. Her father, her uncle and aunts—they'd all known that her mother was alive, and they'd kept it from her. Even Ethan had hidden the truth from her once he found out, after their father's death. Suddenly desperate to get away from the secrets, the evasions and the betrayals, she'd headed to the airport, determined not to return until she found some answers for a change.

So far, it was going dreadfully.

She swallowed against the burning sensation in her throat. Maybe breakfast wasn't such a good idea after all.

"Here she is," the voice of her hostess, Penny, greeted her as she reached the doorway of the dining room. Penny rose from a small table set in the bay window that looked out over a delightfully old-fashioned garden. "Good morning, Ms. Masters, I trust you slept well?"

"Oh, call me Tamsyn, please. And yes, my room is very comfortable, thank you."

Tamsyn's eyes flicked to the man who sat opposite Penny and who now rose to his feet in welcome. The man from yesterday—and absolutely the last man she had expected to see this morning. Courtesy demanded she acknowledge his presence and she gave him a short nod, just the barest inclination of her head.

He stepped forward and held out his hand in a greeting. "We didn't get to exchanging names yesterday. Finn Gallagher. Pleased to see you again."

She gave him a weak smile and briefly shook his hand. The warmth of his broad palm permeated her skin, sending a curl of awareness winding up her arm and through her body. She pulled her hand free.

"Really, Mr. Gallagher? I had the impression yesterday you were only too pleased to see the back of me."

Amusement lit his cool slate-colored eyes. "Ah, you caught me at a bad time, I'm afraid. I'm here to apologize."

Tamsyn's mind scattered in a hundred directions. How had he tracked her down?

"Isn't that a bit stalkerish?" she said without thinking.

"We're a close-knit bunch around here," he explained with an apologetic smile that made Tamsyn's stomach do a tiny loop-the-loop. "I was concerned after you left. You looked tired, and being unfamiliar with the area...well, let's just say tourists have a bad habit of wandering off the road here and there. I called around a few places and I was relieved when Penny assured me you'd arrived safely."

It all sounded plausible, she thought, but it didn't explain what he was doing here right now. As if he could read her mind, he continued speaking.

"I didn't want to leave you with the impression that we're rude around here and thought I'd offer to show you around, if you'd like. Take you on a tour of the district. You will be staying a few days now you're here, won't you?"

He said the last few words with subtle emphasis, almost as if he was willing her to stick around.

"Yes, I will," she admitted, reluctant to tell him that her time here had no specific expiry. "But there's no need for you to show me around. I can make my own way." Besides, she wasn't really here for the sights. She just wanted to find her mother.

"Please, at least allow me to take you to lunch or dinner to make up for my abruptness yesterday."

An ember of warmth lit deep in her belly. Maybe she was being overly suspicious. He certainly seemed sincere enough. She studied him briefly, taking in the short spiky hair, the clear gray eyes that appeared to be imploring her to give in to his politely put demand. His body language was open, nonthreatening, and dressed as he was in a pair of jeans and a tight-fitting T-shirt, he clearly wasn't hiding any weapons. Except his charisma. She couldn't deny he exuded oodles of magnetism, today at least, and there was no doubting that he was one beautifully put-together piece of manhood. What would be the harm in enjoying his company for a few hours? Despite what she'd just been through with Trent, Finn Gallagher was pinging her receptors. And then there was that smile that played around Finn's lips, the expression on his face that suggested he found her attractive and actually wanted to spend time with her. Something her fiancé had not been so wont to do. The thought was like water on a drought-stricken land.

Penny interrupted her thoughts. "If you're worried about Finn, I can vouch for the fact that he's a complete gentleman. He's also a much-loved local-born philanthropist. Honestly, you couldn't be in better hands."

"I…"

Tamsyn's eyes dropped to those very hands, eyeing his broad palms and long tapered fingers. The ember flared to a flame and spread, her breasts suddenly feeling full, her nipples tight, as she involuntarily imagined those hands touching her. With a sharply indrawn breath, she dragged her eyes up to his face, where he clearly awaited her response.

"I don't want to be any trouble," she said lamely, feeling a flush of color heat her cheeks. "Besides, I have plans to do some shopping today—I came a little underprepared for this trip."

Underprepared. As if that wasn't the understatement of the year, she thought scathingly.

"No problem. Why don't you do your shopping this morning, Penny will be able to direct you to where you need to go, and I'll pick you up around lunchtime, say one o'clock, back here? Then I can show you around a bit and deliver you back this evening."

She couldn't refuse. He'd made the plan sound so reasonable. Penny had given her approval as well, and somehow Tamsyn knew the older woman wouldn't have been so forthcoming if she hadn't been certain Tamsyn would be safe with Finn.

"Then, thank you, I'd like that."

"Excellent. I'll leave you to your breakfast and I'll see you later today. Thanks for the coffee, Penny."

"You're always welcome, Finn. I'll see you out. Tamsyn, please help yourself to the breakfast buffet. If there's anything else you'd like, just ring the bell on the sideboard and one of the kitchen staff will be along to take your order."

Penny smiled and then preceded Finn from the room. Finn gave Tamsyn a wink before following.

"I'm looking forward to this afternoon," he said, his voice lowered for her hearing only and sending a shiver of anticipation down Tamsyn's spine.

She smiled in response, a nervous, almost involuntary action, and then he was gone. Tamsyn stepped over to the chafing dishes on the antique sideboard and lifted the lids. Nerves danced like butterflies in her stomach. What had she let herself in for? she wondered as she took a small serving of scrambled egg with a few fried button mushrooms and half a grilled tomato.

She placed her plate on a table and turned back to the sideboard to pour a cup of coffee from the silver carafe warmed by a single candle in a holder beneath it. Everything here was modern and comfortable yet still exuded old-world charm with these touches of elegance from a bygone era. Much like back at home, at The Masters.

For just an instant she was almost overwhelmed by a wave of homesickness, by the desire to quit this search of hers and go home and pick up where she'd left off. But she couldn't go back, not yet. Not until she'd gotten some answers. After everything that had happened, she felt so lost, as if she didn't know who she was anymore. She needed this trip, this quest, to help her find herself again.

Tamsyn forced herself to lift her fork and spear a mushroom, bringing the morsel to her mouth. The burst of flavor on her tongue reminded her that she might be down, but she wasn't out yet. Not when there were still things in this life to enjoy, to savor. Things that proved life went on as surely as the sun rose each day.

"Ah, excellent, you've helped yourself," Penny said, walking briskly back into the room. "Is everything to your liking? Perhaps there's something else I can get for you?"

"Everything is lovely, thank you. I'm fine for now."

"I'm glad," the other woman said, bustling over to clear the table where she and Finn had been sitting when Tamsyn had come into the dining room. "Finn seems quite taken with you. You can't go wrong there. He'll show you a wonderful time."

Was it Tamsyn's imagination or was there a hefty dose of double entendre seasoning Penny's words?

"You didn't mention you met him yesterday," Penny probed.

"I'd been given an address to go to. It turned out to be his and not the person I was seeking."

"Well, if anyone around here can help you find someone local it'll be Finn," Penny said with a warm smile. "Come and see me in my office before you head out to the shops and tell me what you're looking for, and I'll point you in the right direction."

What she was looking for? Well, there was an opening she couldn't ignore. Finn himself had said they were a close-knit community. Surely her mother had to be known by someone.

"Actually, now that you mention it, I was wondering… have you ever heard of an Ellen Masters?"

Penny halted midstride and the cups she'd just cleared from the table wobbled a little in their saucers.

"Ellen Masters, you say?" She pulled her mouth down into a small frown for a second before reverting to a bright smile that didn't feel quite as genuine as it had a moment before. "No, can't say I've ever heard that name. Well, I'll leave you to your breakfast. Remember to ring if you need anything else."

Tamsyn watched as Penny left the dining room. She must be getting overly sensitive because for a minute there she thought she'd seen a spark of something on Penny's face. Tamsyn took another sip of her coffee and shook her head slightly. She was probably just jet-lagged and perhaps a little overtired still. Imagining things that weren't there simply because she wanted them to be.

Still, she refused to be cowed. Someone in the district had to know where her mother was and as soon as she crossed paths with that someone, she would know, too. A person didn't just disappear off the grid without leaving a trace somewhere, did they?

Four

After her shopping expedition into Blenheim, where she found all the basics she needed, as well as a few things she didn't but were fun to buy anyway, Tamsyn continued back toward her accommodations. Certain she could navigate her way without her GPS, she was surprised when a wrong turn brought her out into a small but bustling township.

She wondered briefly, as she pulled up to halt on a street peppered with cafés and boutiques and art stores, why Penny hadn't directed her here first for her shopping. With a shrug she got out of the car and locked it before strolling the length of the main street down one side and back up the other before going into one of the clothing boutiques to browse.

"Hello, are you looking for a special outfit?" the older woman behind the counter asked with a welcoming smile.

"Not particularly, but I love this," Tamsyn said, pulling out a sleeveless dress in vibrant hues of purple and blue for a better look.

"That would look lovely on you with your coloring. The fitting room is just to your left if you'd like to try it on."

"Oh, I don't think…" About to refuse, Tamsyn hesitated. Why shouldn't she indulge herself? This morning's shopping had been mostly about function—jeans, T-shirts, a pair of shorts and a few sets of underwear, together with some trainers. Her hand stroked the fabric, relishing the texture of the hand-painted silk. It would feel divine on. "Okay, I'll try it," she said before she could change her mind.

A few minutes later she turned this way and that in front of the dressing-room mirror. The dress was perfect, as if it had been made for her. If only she had the right shoes to go with it, she'd be able to wear it to lunch with Finn. Not that she was setting out to try and attract him or anything but a girl needed her armor, didn't she? And the way this dress made her look and made her feel was armor indeed.

"How does it feel on?" a disembodied voice asked from outside the curtain.

"Fantastic but I don't have the right shoes with me."

"Oh, maybe we have something here. We carry a few styles and sizes. You're what, a size seven?"

When Tamsyn murmured her assent the woman replied, "I'll be right back."

Tamsyn took a minute to study her reflection again. She loved the dress, loved the softness of the silk as it fell around her legs, as it caressed her body. It made her feel feminine, desirable.

Was that what her need for armor was all about? Had Trent's betrayal left her feeling so unappealing? Questioning her femininity so much? Not surprising, given how he'd deliberately misled her throughout their relationship. The sting still smarted. And looking at her reflection now, thoughts of her former fiancé made her angry, too. Her reflection in the mirror looked beautiful and sexy—why had she let Trent make her feel any different? Why had she agreed to marry a man who never made her feel irresistible?

Tamsyn was more certain than ever that this trip was exactly what she needed. She had to get away from the perceptions and expectations everyone had of her back home and figure out who she really wanted to be. She just hoped her mother would want to be part of that—part of her life.

"Here we are!"

Tamsyn pulled aside the curtain.

"Oh, my," the assistant said, "that dress is really you. You look wonderful. Here, try these on with it."

She held out a pair of sandals in shades of purple, blue

and pink, and with a ridiculously high heel. They were perfect, Tamsyn thought as she slid off the trainers and socks she'd been wearing and slipped her feet into the sandals, bending down to fasten the dainty ankle strap.

"Come on out into the store, we have a full-length mirror just over by the counter. You'll have more room to twirl," the woman said with a wink.

Tamsyn couldn't help but smile in response. She actually felt like twirling when she saw her reflection in the larger mirror.

"I'll take it," she said impulsively. "The dress and the shoes. Do you mind if I wear them now?"

"Why would I mind?" The assistant smiled in response. "You're the perfect walking advertisement for one of our local designers—Alexis Fabrini."

"I love what she's done with this dress, do you have more of her clothes here? I'd really like to come back when I have more time."

The assistant just smiled and spread her arm to encompass an entire wall of garments. "Take your pick," she said, smiling. "Let me bag up your other things and take off those price tags and you'll be good to go."

Tamsyn paid for her purchases just as a Shania Twain song came onto the speakers in the store. She smiled to herself, agreeing with the lyrics. She really felt like a woman right now and was actually looking forward to lunch with the enigmatic Finn Gallagher more than she realized.

"Are you just passing through town?" asked the store clerk. Tamsyn looked at her, suddenly struck by the realization that the woman was probably around the same age as her mother. In fact, there were so many people around—on the street, in the shops—who were all around that age. Surely, amongst them, would be some of her mother's friends.

"I'm here a few days at least, although I might stay longer

if I can. I'm…" She hesitated a moment and then decided, in for a penny, in for a pound. If she didn't start asking every person she met if they knew her mom, she'd never find out, would she? "I'm looking for my mother. Ellen Masters. Do you know her?"

The other woman shook her head slowly and pursed her lips. "Hmm, Ellen Masters…no. Can't say I've met anyone by that name around here, but I'm fairly new in the region and I'm still getting to know all the locals."

"Never mind," Tamsyn said pasting a smile over the pang of disappointment that tugged at her heart. It was a numbers game. Eventually she'd find someone who knew her. Didn't New Zealanders pride themselves on the fact that there were only two degrees of separation between them and a fellow Kiwi? "It was a wild shot."

"Well, good luck finding her and do come back soon!"

Tamsyn gathered her things and started to walk back to her car. Even with this small latest setback she still felt more positive. Just before she reached her car she stopped and perused the window of a real estate office that appeared to double as a letting agency and an idea occurred to her. If she found a place to rent she could set herself up more permanently here and could use the property as a base from which to widen her search. She scanned the listings in the window and an address caught her eye. It was on the same road as Finn Gallagher's property, fairly close, too, if the street number was any indicator.

A coil of something she couldn't quite identify curled tight in her stomach as she read the details. It was a short-term lease on a week-by-week basis. She could see why it was still available. Not many people would want the insecurity of week-by-week rental, but it suited her just perfectly and as a bonus it was fully furnished. All she'd need to do was feed the cat and the chickens on the property. She could do that. She pushed open the door to the agency, coming out twenty minutes later with an agreement in one hand, a key in the other and an excitement roiling in her she barely knew how to contain.

A late-model Porsche Cayenne, a Turbo S model, she noted with some appreciation, stood in the driveway when she returned to the hotel. No doubt Finn's, she thought as she took a quick look at the dashboard clock on her rental. The side trip to the property agency had made her late, but right now she didn't care. From tomorrow she had somewhere of her own to stay. Things were falling into place and who knew? Maybe the next person she saw would be someone who could tell her where to find her mother.

Finn watched from the office window as Tamsyn alighted from her car. Even from here he could tell she was excited. There was a light and energy about her now that had been missing yesterday and this morning. It served to make her even more beautiful.

He tamped down on the shiver of desire that threatened to ripple through his body. If he was going to control this situation he'd have to start by controlling himself. Errant physical attractions would only complicate things. And as complications went, getting a call from the leasing agent handling Lorenzo and Ellen's cottage to say a certain princess from Australia was interested in taking up the short-term leasing option was a big one.

As tempting as it had been to say an absolute and re-sounding no when the agent had queried him about the lease, especially as the leasee had no references, he'd been mindful of Lorenzo's wish to keep Tamsyn close for Ellen's sake. How much easier would it be to keep an eye on her if she was just down the hill from where he lived?

Of course, he reminded himself, there was the bonus of him not having to feed Ellen's man-eating black cat, Lucy—short for Lucifer. A singularly appropriate moniker Finn had always privately thought. He hadn't had a morning yet where the feisty feline hadn't delivered him a scathing hiss or a barbed paw.

Plus, he knew for a fact that Lorenzo and Ellen's personal effects and identifying items had all been packed away in Alexis's old bedroom and a new lock put on the door to ensure that while renters made use of the house, their private things remained just that, private. He'd done it himself after Lorenzo had accompanied Ellen to Wellington. What harm could come from having Tamsyn literally under his eye?

"Looks like she's been shopping," he commented as he watched Tamsyn pull several shopping bags and a small wheeled suitcase from the trunk of her car.

"And not just in Blenheim. That pink bag, that's from a local store," Penny commented from behind him.

"Damn. I thought you directed her to Blenheim for what she needed."

"I did, but honestly, Finn, you can't expect to control her every movement."

Oh, can't I? "More's the pity," he growled, stepping away from the window before Tamsyn could see her spying on him.

Penny laughed. "She obviously found our nearby center all on her own, and from the look of things she's boosted the local economy in the bargain. I'm pretty sure that's one of Alexis's designs she's wearing right now and you and I both know they don't come cheap."

Finn stifled a groan. What were the odds that Tamsyn Masters would walk out the door here this morning and come back wearing a dress designed by her half sister? A sister she didn't even know she had—and probably wouldn't, ever, if he succeeded in keeping Tamsyn in the dark as he'd promised. He needed to hold it together, for Lorenzo's sake. The man had stepped in and helped him when his whole world shattered apart when he was only twelve years old. Now Lorenzo's world was imploding and it was up to Finn to return the favor.

At the sound of her heels clicking on the polished wooden hall floor he spun away from the window and went out to greet her.

"Oh, hello!" Tamsyn said, coming to an abrupt halt as he exited the office right in front of her.

A waft of her fragrance drifted around him. Something with flowers, fruit and a hint of spice. Something that sent reason fleeing from his mind and a crazy desire to lean forward and inhale more deeply driving through his body.

"Sorry I'm late," she continued, oblivious to the tug-of-war going on in Finn's mind, not to mention the tug of something else far lower down in his body. "I'll only be a minute. Just let me put these things in my room and I'm all yours."

All his? Somehow he doubted that. But it certainly promised to be interesting finding out, he thought with a smile as he watched her graceful departure.

Gone was the wounded creature who had been at his front door last night. Gone was the troubled but determined young woman who'd arrived in the dining room this morning. In her place was charming, confident sex on legs, and very beautiful legs they were, too, he admitted as he admired the slim turn of her ankle and the slender, yet shapely, calf muscles heading in the opposite direction on a pair of colored icepicks that defied logic and gravity in one, literally, easy step.

He shook himself out of his daze as she disappeared from view. Just as well, he thought, or he might even have been tempted to follow her.

True to her word, she was back in only a few minutes, delivering him a shy smile as she returned.

"All ready?" he asked, his mouth drying as he studied her anew.

The purple of the dress did something striking to her

brown eyes, reminding him of pansies. Bold, yet fragile at the same time. *God,* he groaned inwardly. What the hell was wrong with him? Next he'd be acting like some crush-struck teenager.

"I certainly am," she replied, falling in alongside him as he headed for the door. "Where are we going?"

He named a vineyard and winery that was only a fifteen-minute drive away. "Their restaurant is immensely popular for lunches and their wines are world renowned."

Tamsyn rubbed her flat tummy and laughed. "I certainly hope you're right. I'm famished after all that shopping this morning."

"You won't be disappointed," he assured her.

He kept up a bland running commentary on the surrounding countryside and their destination, to fill in time as they drove to the vineyard.

"This place sounds a lot like home," Tamsyn commented. "We run a similar operation with cellar door, restaurant and winery. It'll be fun seeing how they do things. I could almost tell myself it was work if—" Her voice broke off.

"If?" he coaxed.

"If I hadn't resigned and walked away from it all," she said with a brittle smile that didn't quite reach her eyes.

"Oh? Sick of the daily drudge?" he probed, curious to know her answer.

If she was the spoiled princess he'd always imagined her to be, then his guess would fit right in with that. He used that thought to quell his firing libido.

"Something like that," she answered noncommittally and turned her head to stare out the window.

Something like that. Huh. What he wouldn't give to find out what that "something" was. Then maybe he could resolve his conflicted feelings. On the surface, Tamsyn Masters had proven true to form. She'd turned up at his doorstep unannounced, which, if it had been Ellen's home, could have had devastating consequences. She spent money like water, which made him wonder if she'd ever had to work hard for a single thing. And, by her own admission, she'd simply walked away from the family business and whatever responsibilities had been hers while she was there.

All in all, her actions made her appear to be an unappealing package—a package not unlike Briana had proven to be.

So why on earth did he find her anything but?

Five

Tamsyn woke the next morning filled with a renewed vigor to face the day. Lunch with Finn had been delightful, far better than she'd anticipated, although the setting had sharpened her homesickness for The Masters. Her host, however, seemed to read her mood instinctively and had distracted her with his knowledge of the immediate district. It was obvious he cared about the area and the people within it, and several other diners had stopped by their table at the restaurant to give their regards.

While Finn had introduced her politely to each and every person who had spoken with him, he'd made it subtly clear at the same time that he didn't want additional company. She'd been a little surprised by how efficiently he'd closed people out. She'd also been frustrated as she'd wanted to ask each of them if they'd heard of her mother. Despite that, by the time they were enjoying their coffee and a shared apple tarte tatin for dessert Tamsyn had begun to feel more relaxed than she had in a very long time.

And there was something else. She'd felt protected, almost cherished, which was weird considering she'd only just met Finn, but his behavior toward her was caring and solicitous. She'd thrived under his undivided attention. It was a luxury she couldn't remember experiencing in a very long time.

After a delicious leisurely lunch, their sightseeing had taken them well off the beaten track and away from populated areas. Tamsyn had fallen in love with the amazing vistas that looked out over the Marlborough Sounds and then the stunning valleys and hills on the journey home that led them back to the river plains and her hotel.

As lovely as yesterday afternoon had been, today promised a different and perhaps more challenging agenda. Moving into the cottage. She understood it had been vacant for a couple of weeks. Hopefully that didn't mean it would be musty and in need of heavy cleaning when she arrived.

"Are you all set?" Penny asked as Tamsyn wheeled her new gleaming blue suitcase containing her recently acquired possessions toward the front door.

Tamsyn had told her hostess last night that she'd be checking out in the morning. Penny hadn't been able to keep the surprise from her eyes when Tamsyn had told her where she'd be staying but had swiftly covered that with an offer to provide her with some food supplies to take with her.

"Yes, I am, and thank you so much for a lovely stay."

"You're welcome, any time," the other woman smiled. "Are you sure you want to go out to a place on your own? You'll be a bit isolated there."

"You know, my life has been so frenetic lately, I think I'm going to relish the peace and quiet of being on my own. To be honest, I don't think I've ever just had to bear my own company. I'm actually looking forward to it."

"Well, don't be a stranger, feel free to pop in for a cuppa if you're passing," Penny invited.

Tamsyn drove to the address the letting agent had given her, missing the entrance completely the first time. After executing a U-turn she inched back along the road until she saw the slightly overgrown access to the driveway. It was obviously a good place to go when you didn't really want to be found, she thought as she drove up the dusty unsealed track and toward a small cottage nestled at the bottom of the hill. The very hill, in fact, that was crowned by Finn Gallagher's opulent stone-and-cedar palace.

She hadn't realized she'd be this close. She could hop a

fence and walk through the vineyard that stretched up the hill and be at his place in little more than a vigorous ten- to fifteen-minute walk. It was both unsettling and reassuring at the same time. At least knowing someone was close in case she needed help was a bonus...but Finn Gallagher?

As attractive as he was, and as immediate as her reaction was to him, he still unnerved her on some levels. His attentive behavior since their not-so-friendly first meeting definitely was appealing, as was the way he looked at her as if she was all woman, but coming so close on the heels of her broken engagement she still felt nervy, distrustful. And while it was flattering at the time that he'd obviously wanted to keep her company all to himself yesterday, when she'd thought about it late last night she'd started to get the niggling feeling that he had some ulterior motive for doing so.

Maybe she was just overreacting. After all, it wasn't every day a woman had to accept that she'd been efficiently lied to for the better part of two years by a man she'd trusted enough to want to marry. The dull ache that seemed to permanently reside in her chest intensified.

In the clothing store, wearing a beautiful dress and anticipating an afternoon with a handsome man, it had been easy to lay the mess of their shattered engagement entirely on Trent's shoulders...but deep down she felt it had to be her fault. How could she not have seen Trent and Zac's interest in one another? How could she never have suspected a thing? Sure, her relationship with Trent had been cool, their sex life minimal, but she'd put that down to the type of man he was. And she'd loved him—believed they had a future together. Just went to show what a rotten judge of character she really was, she told herself with a rueful glance in her rearview mirror.

She pulled her car to a halt outside the front of an old detached garage next to the cottage and got out. Maybe she was just being paranoid. Actually, more than maybe and that wasn't necessarily a bad thing. Her experience with Trent had been a rude and very unpleasant awakening. It wouldn't do her any harm at all to be a little less eager to salve her mortally wounded pride with the company of a handsome man, even if he did have the power to make her heart skip.

The cottage was old, probably circa early 1900s, but very well maintained by the look of things. A large deep veranda stretched invitingly along the front of the house and around to one side. She hoped the interior was as appealing. Tamsyn grabbed the plastic bags Penny had enthusiastically filled with what she'd deemed to be the essentials to see her through the next day or so. Tam had been overwhelmed by the other woman's generosity, even more so when Penny had refused any payment for the items. As a result, Tamsyn doubted she'd need to make her way into town for supplies for several days, given the fresh meat, milk, eggs and other items the hotelier had given her.

The key slid smoothly into the front door lock and turned easily. Feeling almost as if she was trespassing, Tamsyn stepped inside.

Dust motes floated on the gilded rays of morning sun that streamed in through windows to her left, but aside from that, the place looked well kept. Almost as if the owners had stepped outside for only a moment.

"Prrrrp." She jumped at the sound as a sleek black cat followed in through the front door behind her, eyeing her carefully with its golden eyes before winding in and out of her legs and purring.

"Well, hello," Tamsyn said, bending down to stroke the cat. "I guess you're one of my responsibilities while I'm here, hmm? What a shame no one thought to tell me your name."

The letting agent had mentioned that a neighbor had been caring for the animals at the house, but that they'd be her responsibility for the duration of the tenancy. How hard could it be, right? A few chickens, a cat. It wasn't rocket science.

The cat looked up at her and blinked slowly before lithely jumping up onto the windowsill and grooming itself in the sun. For some reason, the animal's presence made Tamsyn feel more at home. She took her supplies through to the compact and slightly old-fashioned kitchen and put them in the refrigerator. Through the window over the kitchen counter she could see a vast, somewhat overgrown, vegetable garden.

She wrapped her arms around herself and squeezed tight. It shouldn't be so exciting to have this—temporary—home of her own. After all, she'd grown up on an amazing estate. But it was her *family's* estate, never solely hers. She'd never truly been on her own. It was surprising how much she liked it. She really was pretty self-sufficient for the next few days. If she didn't want to, she needn't go anywhere. But how would she find her mother if she didn't keep going out into the community and asking around?

Tamsyn groaned aloud as another thought came to her. The internet. Of course. Why hadn't she thought of that?

Because her mind had been too distracted with other thoughts—thoughts of Trent and, more so, thoughts of the tall, enigmatic man who lived at the top of the hill—she'd completely discounted using her smartphone to do an internet search for her mother. As soon as she'd unpacked she'd get right onto it.

Tamsyn turned on her heel and nearly screamed when something brushed against her leg. The cat. Oh, God, her heart was racing. Living on her own, albeit with a resident feline, was going to take some getting used to.

The cat rubbed against her, twining in a figure eight between her legs and purring loudly before stalking toward a cupboard with its tail in the air. Sitting in front of the cupboard, it began to scratch.

"Oh, no, don't do that," Tamsyn said, hastening over.

She pushed the cat away from the door, but it determinedly moved back in front and began scratching again. Curious, and not a little fearful that perhaps there might be a mouse inside, she opened the cupboard. A sigh of relief flooded through her when she saw the bag of dried cat food sitting on the bottom shelf of what was obviously a pantry.

"You're hungry, that's what it is, isn't it, Puss?"

She looked around for a bowl and spied a small plastic mat on the floor near a glass-paned door, an empty bowl and a water dish sitting side by side. The cat purred its obvious approval as she collected the empty dishes and rinsed them out at the kitchen sink before drying them and refilling them with cat biscuits and water.

"There you go," she said, putting them back on the little mat and running her hand down the cat's black furry back.

Feeling well-satisfied with herself, Tamsyn went back out to her car and grabbed her suitcase. This time, she turned to her right as she came back in. The bedrooms had to be down this way, she thought as she tried each door as she got to it. There were two bedrooms to choose from, one bathroom and one door that was locked. Tamsyn chose the smaller of the two bedrooms and unpacked her meager belongings. It was hardly worth the bother, she thought as she hung up the couple of things she'd bought and stuffed her small collection of underwear into a drawer. Compared with her walk-in closet at home, she had majorly downsized.

Home. Another wave of homesickness washed over her. She should call her brother, reassure him she was okay and tell him of her plans. Before she could talk herself out of it, she pressed the quick dial for his mobile number.

"I was beginning to think I'd have to send out a search party for you," he answered.

While there was a teasing note in his voice, Tamsyn could hear the underlying concern.

"I did say I'd call in few days. I'm fine, by the way," she assured him. "Thanks for asking."

"Ready to come home yet?"

"Not anywhere near it, Ethan. How are you managing without me?"

"We're coping surprisingly well. Aunt Cynthia has really come into her own taking over for you, you'd be impressed."

Tamsyn felt his words like a physical blow. Sure, she'd walked out on them, but couldn't they have missed her—even just a little bit? Nobody had missed her, it seemed. She hadn't even had so much as a text or email from Trent. Not that she wanted to hear from him, but they'd been engaged over a year and had gone out for several months before that. Surely she'd warranted something from him, some explanation, *anything*. She quashed the thought. She'd walked away from him and his lover, and everything associated with them. That was her choice, as was her mission to find her mother. It was time to stop looking back and to keep her sights firmly fixed on her new future.

Forcing a smile to her lips, she said, "Hey, can you check something for me?"

"Name it."

"The address Mom's checks are sent to—can you give that to me again?"

"Sure, just give me a minute to find the email," her brother replied.

In the background she could hear him using his usual hunt-and-peck keyboard skills to pull up the information. She smiled to herself. Computers were a necessary evil in Ethan's book—he'd much rather be blending his world-famous wines and watching over their production as if they were his children heading out to a first day at school. While he was busy, Tamsyn scrabbled in her handbag for a pen and notebook.

"Found it," he said a moment later. He rattled off the address.

"That's weird," Tamsyn replied, chewing on the end of her pen. "That's the address I went to on Saturday, but the man there said he hadn't heard of Mom."

"Let me check with Dad's solicitor and get back to you. Could be someone made a mistake somewhere."

Or it could be that someone was lying to her. The thought echoed around in her mind. Could Finn be deliberately keeping information about her mother from her? Surely not. What would be the point? It's not as if he stood to gain anything by it.

"Okay, thanks. Send me a text or email when you know, okay? In the meantime, I've decided to take a short-term lease on a cottage here. I want to spend more time poking around, see if I can bump into anyone who might know her and how I can find her."

"Tam, are you sure you're doing the right thing? Maybe if she's hard to find it's because she doesn't want to be."

"It's not about what she wants anymore," Tamsyn said with uncharacteristic firmness. "This time it's about what she owes me. I deserve to know why she left us, Ethan. I *need* to know."

She heard her brother sigh in frustration. "By the way," Ethan said, "I talked to Trent. He told me what happened."

Tamsyn felt as if a fist had closed around her heart and her lungs burned, reminding her to draw in a breath.

"R-really? Ev-everything?" she stuttered.

"With a little coaxing." The steel in Ethan's voice left her in no doubt that her brother had not been his usual urbane self when approaching her ex-fiancé. He continued before she could gather her thoughts together. "I don't blame you for needing some time out. He duped us all, Tam. Led us all to believe he'd love you the way you deserved to be loved. He was promising something he couldn't deliver. No matter his orientation, what he did to you was wrong on every level. You deserved better than that and you still do. Isobel's so mad I had to physically restrain her from heading into town to deal with him. I just wanted you to know, we're in your corner. Whatever you need from us right now, it's yours."

Tears throbbed at the back of Tamsyn's eyes and she stared up at the ceiling in a vain attempt to force them back. If she let go now, she didn't know if she'd be able to stop, and if Ethan heard her crying he'd be here faster than she could blink. This was her mission, her goal. She had to do it for herself. For once in her life she wasn't doing something to please someone else, this was all about her.

She focused, instead, on the idea of Ethan's fiancée, Isobel, and the very idea of the tiny blonde going head to head with Trent in a fight. It was enough to calm her—to almost make her smile.

"Thank you," she managed to whisper then drew in a steadying breath, one that made her voice stronger. "I'll be in touch when I learn anything, okay?"

"It'll have to be okay," Ethan conceded. "And I'll check that address and get back to you later today."

Tamsyn said goodbye and severed the connection, feeling a little as if she'd cut off a lifeline. She was grateful for the distraction when the sound of tires on the graveled driveway drew her attention out the window. She watched as a now-familiar SUV pulled in next to her rental. An all new tightness replaced the pain that had been in her chest only moments ago as Finn stepped down from the vehicle and started toward the house.

Ignoring her body's sudden and unsettling awareness of him, she examined the question that now hovered foremost in her mind. Did some of the answers she sought lie with Finn Gallager?

Six

Finn approached the open front door not entirely sure what he was doing here. Lorenzo had asked for updates, but even that wasn't enough of a reason to be virtually stalking Tamsyn Masters the way he was.

She moved into the doorway just as he raised his hand to the frame to knock. Today she was dressed simply in strategically faded, snug blue jeans and a deep V-necked white T-shirt that hinted at the shell-pink bra she wore beneath. The soft swells of her breasts pushed against the fine cotton above the cups of her bra.

Finn forced his eyes upward to her face. With her hair pulled back into a ponytail she looked younger, the dark marks under her eyes were a little more faded than they'd been the day before.

"Hi," he said. "I was just passing and thought I'd see if you needed anything in town."

A slow sweet smile pulled at Tamsyn's lips.

"That was thoughtful of you, but Penny's actually given me quite a few things to take care of me for the next few days."

"Okay, great. That was good of her." He searched for something else he could say to prolong the conversation. "Oh, and I thought I'd give you my number in case you need any help with anything around the house."

He yanked his card holder from the back of his jeans pocket and slid out a business card, handing it to her. She took it carefully, but her fingers still lightly grazed his. A flare of sudden and instant heat burned up his arm at her touch.

"Thank you, although on first glance around here I don't think I'll need help with anything. Your neighbors appear to have been very self-sufficient."

"Yes, they are."

"Have you been the one feeding the animals?" she asked.

"Yeah, the chickens are easier than that feline monster."

The monster in question padded down the hallway and sat down at Tamsyn's feet, eyeing him with a baleful glare.

"This one?" she asked, bending down to tickle it behind the ears. "Do you know its name?"

"Lucy, short for Lucifer. In name and in nature. They thought she was a boy when they first got her and had to shorten her name when they discovered she was carrying a litter."

Finn watched in surprise as the wretched animal began to purr and nudge its head against Tamsyn's hand.

"Lucifer? For this cutie?" Tamsyn laughed. "That's a touch harsh, don't you think?"

Maybe he'd misjudged the animal. It had only ever barely tolerated him. He bent down to give it a pat only to have Lucy's ears flare back and her teeth bare as she hissed her displeasure at his presumption.

"Nope, not harsh at all. Funny that she's so tolerant of you. She usually only lets her owner and her daughter touch her."

As soon as the words were out of his mouth Finn wished them back. Of course Lucy would connect with Tamsyn. She was Ellen's daughter, too.

"Maybe she just prefers female company," Tamsyn commented, oblivious to Finn's discomfort.

"That's probably it."

"Did you want to stop in for a cup of coffee or something? I'm not quite sure where everything is yet, but I'm sure I can find it all."

Should he? Sure, why not. It was neighborly, after all.

"That'd be great. While I'm here I can check the hot water is turned on for you. I know the property manager was going to take care of it, but they may not have gotten around to it yet."

"Oh, would you? That would be wonderful. I'd love nothing better than a long soak in that fabulous old bath tonight."

Finn's body hardened at the visual image that flooded his mind. It took no stretch of the imagination to envisage the drape of her lean arms along the sides of the old clawfooted tub he knew resided in the bathroom. Or the delicate curve of her shoulders and the sweep of her collarbone glistening with scented bath oil.

"Right," he said, pulling himself together abruptly. "I'll get onto it then."

"I'll go and put the jug on," she replied, stepping back from the doorway and ushering him inside.

Lucy gave another short hiss at him before springing away and settling herself on the windowsill of the large front bay window.

"The cylinder is in the old laundry off the back porch," Finn said by way of explanation as he followed her through to the kitchen.

He unlocked the back door and stepped through the small porch to the door on the other side, reaching above the door frame for the key. He was as familiar with this house as he was with his own face in the mirror each morning. Lorenzo and Ellen had provided him a home here and despite his offers to build them something newer and more comfortable, they'd insisted they were happy in their small cottage, especially now that Alexis's business was taking off, leading her to spend much of her time working from overseas.

By the time he'd checked the cylinder he could hear the jug beginning to boil, the sound accompanied by Tamsyn's light humming as she moved around the kitchen finding coffee and mugs.

"You just have your coffee black, right?"

He was impressed she'd both noticed and remembered. Her attention to detail was good—he needed to remind himself of that, and not to slip up the way he had earlier when he'd nearly mentioned Ellen and Alexis by name.

"That's right," he answered, locking the laundry door behind him and returning the key to its spot.

"You seem to know your way around here pretty well."

"We've been neighbors a long time. Plus, I've been watching the animals the past few weeks."

She gave a short laugh. "It's a good thing that Lucy could tolerate you feeding her then."

"Cupboard love," he commented in response. "Cats are well known for it."

"I wouldn't know," Tamsyn replied as she added sugar and milk to her coffee. "We never had pets growing up."

"Not at all?"

"No, our father didn't think they had a place in our household. Occasionally a feral cat would have kittens on the property, but Dad always made sure they were rehomed before we could adopt any of them."

Finn thought of the farm dogs his father had always had, even after he'd downsized the stock running on the farm and begun to change his primary business over to growing grapevines. The animals had been as much of an extension of his life as Lorenzo and Ellen had been after his father died. Add to that his mother's and Ellen's procession of cats over the years and he couldn't imagine growing up without a pet. He'd always imagined he'd have a couple of dogs when he finished building the house, but Briana had insisted she was allergic and since her departure, a year ago, he'd been too busy to do anything about it.

"So where did you grow up that pets weren't considered a necessary part of family life?" he asked, forcing a smile to try to soften his words.

"It's a property similar to where we lunched yesterday, although possibly a bit bigger. We have a vineyard and winery, restaurant and wedding venue, plus luxury cottage accommodation. Of course, when I was little it was just the vineyard and winery and on a much smaller scale. Dad's family were still working really hard to reestablish what they'd lost after a devastating bushfire when he was in his early twenties. The whole family had to start from scratch."

"Sounds like hard work."

"I guess it was. We didn't know any different, though, growing up. And all of us, my brother and my cousins, we all knew we'd be a part of it one day. Each of us has had their place in the family business basically grow around them and their interests."

What she said didn't quite gel with the image he'd always had of her. He'd imagined her living off the luxury, not working hard to be a part of bringing it about. It roused his curiosity even further.

"And you? What about your place and your interests?"

Tamsyn picked up her spoon and began absently stirring her coffee.

"That doesn't matter now," she said, her voice empty of emotion.

Clearly she didn't want to talk about it, which only served to make Finn all the more determined to find out why. Even he knew when not to push, though. Softly, softly would be the best approach, he decided, taking a sip of the instant brew Tamsyn had poured for him.

He pulled a face. "Remind me to show you how to use the espresso machine," he said.

"It's bad, isn't it?" she admitted with an uncharacteristic giggle. "I'm not even sure it's coffee."

"If you don't mind, I'm going to tip this out," Finn said, brushing past her on the way to the kitchen sink.

She'd moved toward the sink at the same time and his

arm grazed the side of her breast. Not a deliberate move on his part but he wasn't sorry, especially not when he saw her nipples pebble behind the lacy bra she was wearing and thrust against her shirt. This close to her, he heard her breath catch in her throat. Knowing she was just as affected by his touch as he was by hers was gratifying.

Her eyes were dark pools of confusion, her mouth still slightly parted on that gasp. It would only take a second to lean forward and capture those lips with his. To test their softness, to tease a response from her. The air thickened between them. Outside, he was aware of the rasp of cicadas in the garden, the lazy buzz of bees around the flower beds. Inside, he could hear nothing but his rapid heartbeat whooshing in his ears.

Too soon. It was far too soon. She was a timid thing. Tentative, almost wounded. She needed to be drawn in slowly, to be tempted to take him as bait. He took one step back, then another, his body instantly mourning the nearness of hers.

"I'll be off then," he said with as much control as he could muster. "I'd say thanks for the coffee, but…"

She gave a nervous laugh. "Yeah, I know. Thank you for coming over and checking the hot water for me."

"No problem. If you like, I can call in tomorrow and show you how to use the espresso machine."

"I'd like that," she replied, following him as he went out the front door.

She stayed there on the front veranda, her hands shoved into the pockets at the front of her jeans, watching while he executed a neat turn and headed down the driveway. A sense of anticipation stole over him. Getting to know Tamsyn Masters better was proving to be more challenging than he'd anticipated. And more appealing. Far, far more appealing.

Seven

Tamsyn waited until Finn's car was out of view before turning and going back into the cottage. The place felt still and empty without his presence. She chided herself for being fanciful as she went around the house opening windows to let in fresh air. Lucy had disappeared again, clearly off on an agenda of her own, which pretty much left Tamsyn to her own devices.

Speaking of devices, she retrieved her mobile from her handbag and, after pouring herself a glass of water, she settled down on the front porch in a sagging wicker arm chair to see if her mother's name came up in any local searches.

An hour later she was feeling intensely frustrated. The only search information she'd turned up to date all related back to when her mother still lived in Adelaide, the most recent being her wedding announcement way back over thirty years ago, together with a grainy photo of her parents standing in the entrance to the church, followed by brief birth announcements in the newspaper when Ethan and Tamsyn were born. After that, nothing. Tamsyn stared at the wedding photo on her cell phone screen. The quality of the photo was poor, blurring their features into near obscurity. A bit like the dearth of information about Ellen Masters since. It was truly bizarre. Almost as if, in marrying John Masters, Ellen had dropped out of society and circulation and ceased to exist.

Tamsyn scoured her memories for any hint of her mother that went past a vaguely remembered cuddle. The best she could muster was the sound of peals of laughter infused with the scent of freshly cut grass and the heat of summer sun. She gave up with a curse that startled the birds that had been pecking at the lawn. They lifted to the nearby trees with a flurry of wings and squawks of indignation.

This was hopeless, she decided, closing the applications on her phone and picking up her glass to take it back inside. Clearly she needed a face-to-face approach. She wondered if there was somewhere local where she could view an electoral roll or something like that. Perhaps the nearby town's information center might be able to head her in the right direction.

Tamsyn went back into the house and grabbed her keys. Eschewing closing all the windows again, she locked the front door and headed for her car.

The drive into town was quiet; in fact, she hardly saw another vehicle on the road until she got within town limits. She eased her car into a space on a side street, near the boutique where she'd shopped yesterday, and got out. She vaguely remembered seeing an information center sign posted near the end of the main street and she struck out in that direction.

It looked as if she was headed toward a small town hall. This was probably the hub of the immediate district's social life in its day. Judging by the activity milling around there now—a mixed age group of people wearing loose clothing and carrying yoga mats, spilling out the front door—it was still equally well used. A large notice board out front attracted her attention and Tamsyn was surprised to see the list of activities available on various days. A bright notice stuck to one side caught her eye. It was an advertisement for a volunteer seniors' activities coordinator to provide temporary cover one day a week in the lead-up to Christmas. Applicants were bidden to apply at the office.

Tamsyn mulled over the notice. Once a week for five weeks? She could easily commit to that. It might take her that long to find her mother at this rate. Even if she found her sooner, she'd certainly want to spend time with her before going back to Adelaide.

If she went back at all.

The thought wasn't as unsettling as it should have been. Instead, a kernel of excitement began to cautiously unfurl within her at the thought of truly starting over fresh. She reached out to take the notice from the board and walked up the steps leading to the front of the hall. Nerves assailed her as she lifted her hand to knock at the door marked Office. This was the first job she'd ever actually applied for. In the past she'd always worked at The Masters in one field or another. Odd jobs while she was at school, and subsequently, during her semester breaks while she was at university. Once she graduated, she took over developing and managing the accommodation cottages, eventually expanding to special events and weddings. She'd never once had to face rejection in the course of her work.

What if she applied for the job and they said no?

She swallowed against the fear that threatened to paralyze her. She'd never had to second-guess herself before. Trent's lies and subterfuge had totally done a number on her head, she realized. Especially coming on the heels of discovering the secret her family had been keeping from her. Now she was so shaken up she was second-guessing her ability to apply for a casual position doing something she knew in her heart she could do virtually blindfolded.

She forced herself to knock on the door before she could give in to the anxiety.

"Come in if you're good looking!" a gravelly voice answered.

The words brought a smile to her face and she opened the door.

"I'm here about the coordinator's job?" she said as she stepped into the chaos that was the hall's office.

Papers were strewn on every available surface, together

with an array of multicolored empty coffee cups. Behind the desk sat a woman who was probably anywhere in age between fifty and eighty. Her wiry hair stuck out in all directions and an unlit cigarette hung from her lips as she looked up in response.

"An Aussie, huh? What makes you think you can do the job?" she barked.

Tamsyn fought to keep her face impassive. She took a deep breath. "I have a degree in communication, majoring in event management, and I've worked the past seven years coordinating events on both small and large scales, from company dinners and product launches, to weddings and anniversary celebrations."

"The job's not paid."

"I'm aware of that. Money isn't an issue."

"Hmmph. Nice for some. You know it's only for five weeks—only four probably because no one will want to come on Christmas Eve."

"Five weeks is fine."

"Damn-fool woman who normally does it tripped backward last week over a carpet bowling ball and broke her leg. I guess you'll give the old codgers something new to look at. You're hired."

Tamsyn looked at the woman in surprise. "Just like that? Don't you want references?"

"Do I look like I need references?" The woman peered at Tamsyn over her half-lens glasses. "What I need is a cigarette, but we're not allowed to smoke in a council-affiliated building anymore."

Just privately, Tamsyn thought that given the tsunami of paper throughout the small office, it was a good thing the woman wasn't allowed to light up.

"Okay, when do I start?"

"Next session is Wednesday this week. Runs from ten-thirty until one. People bring their own lunch. Here's the ring binder with the weeks' activities set and the roster of who does what. Don't lose it."

"Thank you. I'm Tamsyn Masters, by the way."

"Gladys. I run this joint because no one else can. Got any questions, ask me. Just not now. Damn bingo caller for tomorrow night has laryngitis and I need to get someone else. I don't suppose…?" Gladys looked at Tamsyn who firmly shook her head. "Hmmph, you better give me your number in case I need to call you."

Tamsyn gave her cell phone number. "Okay if I take a look around?"

"Feel free. And don't lose that binder, whatever you do."

"I won't," she promised, tucking the item firmly under one arm and walking back out of the office.

Well, she thought as she carried on into the main hall, that had to be the shortest job interview in history. She laughed out loud. What on earth had she been worried about? She stopped and looked around.

Sash windows with half-lowered black-out blinds lined the hall on both sides. A raised stage stood at one end with ancient dark red velvet drapes hanging on either side. Tamsyn felt as if she'd stepped into a time warp. As if she could just close her eyes and reopen them to a wartime dance, or a seventies disco.

Folding tables were slanted against the wall on one side, stacking chairs on the other. Tamsyn pulled out one of the stacking chairs and sat down to study the folder she'd been given. Despite Gladys's curt demeanor and seeming disorganization, everything in here was neatly compiled and ordered. Activities were basically the same each week, with an occasional out-of-town trip organized to see a movie in Blenheim or to visit a restaurant.

Basically, all she had to do was oversee each week and ensure that the door takings, a gold coin per member each meeting, were given to Gladys to bank by the end of each session. It'd be a walk in the park. Even so, the prospect left her feeling more enthused than she'd felt in a very long time. She itched to share her news with someone. Finn, maybe?

She put a clamp on her wayward thoughts. Tomorrow would be soon enough to tell him, when he came to show her how to use the espresso machine. It wasn't as if they were friends or anything.

Tamsyn thought back to this morning's meeting, to that moment when she'd thought he might kiss her. He'd been so close, his gray eyes—dark as storm clouds before torrential rain—fixed on her lips. Her whole body had gone on high alert from the instant he'd brushed against her, all her feminine sensors pinging at that merest of touches. She lifted her fingers to her lips. What would it have felt like, she wondered, if he'd followed through on what she thought had been clear intent in those tempestuous eyes?

A thrill rippled through her body as her imagination took hold, and she closed her eyes, lost in the moment.

"Are you planning to nap there all day? I've got somewhere to go to, even if you haven't."

Gladys's raspy voice jarred her out of her reverie.

"I'm sorry, I'll be out of your way in a minute," Tamsyn said, lurching to her feet and stacking the chair back where she'd found it.

Accompanied by mutterings of "young people these days," she headed back out the main door and onto the street. Behind her, Gladys activated an alarm, clanged the front doors closed and methodically locked them.

"You still here?" the old woman asked as she reached the pavement.

"I was wondering if you could tell me where I can find the information center."

"That'd be me," Gladys said crustily.

"Oh, okay. Maybe you can help. My mother is from here and I'm trying to track her down."

"Hmmph. I thought you had a familiar look about you. Your mother a local, is she?"

"I…I think so. Ellen Masters, have you heard of her?"

Gladys fossicked through her voluminous crocheted handbag before extracting a lighter and applying it to the cigarette still hanging from her wrinkled lips. She sucked long and hard on the filter, an expression almost close to happiness spreading across her lined face.

"Can't say as I have. Maybe she doesn't want to be found."

The old woman's statement hung on the air between them. Tamsyn was initially at a loss for words but pressed on.

"Well, do you know where I can view an electoral roll?"

Gladys took another long pull at her cigarette, the smoke filtering out between her lips as she spoke. "Library could be your best bet. Ask for Miriam, tell her I sent you."

"Thank you. Where can I find the library?" Tamsyn answered, but she was talking to thin air.

For an old lady Gladys sure did move fast, and she was barreling down the pavement toward the local pub as if she was on a deadline. Frustrated and unsettled by the comment about her mother, Tamsyn pulled out her phone and keyed in a search request. Ah, there it was. The library should be just around the block from where she stood now. Given that the blocks were tiny, she was there in five minutes, only to find the doors closed.

She gritted her teeth as she studied the opening hours on the neatly hand-printed notice stuck on the inside of the glass door. She'd just missed them. She jotted a note on her phone with the hours and promised herself she'd be back on Wednesday before she attended her first day as the seniors' coordinator.

For now, there was nothing for it but to head back to the cottage and take out her frustration for a few hours on the weeds growing through the garden. Her car was hot from sitting in the sun and she waited a while with the windows open for it to cool down before starting the engine. She looked around the township from where she sat. The place was quaintly idyllic. Everywhere she looked people greeted one another with a cheerful smile and a wave or a toot of their horn.

So, if everyone was so darn friendly why was it proving so hard to find anyone who'd met her mother? What was it with this place? Was everything and everyone conspiring to prevent her from finding her?

Eight

The garden looked as if a whirlwind had torn through it, Finn realized as he stepped out of his car the next morning. Clumps of weeds lay in piles here and there all over the slightly overgrown lawn. He made a mental note to drag out the ride-on mower and run it around the grass sometime soon. But what Tamsyn had done with the untidy garden was nothing short of spectacular.

"Good morning!" she called, stepping out onto the veranda to welcome him.

She was a sight for sore eyes today, dressed in shorts and a tank top that already showed the efforts of her labors, stained as they were with a combination of perspiration and dirt.

"You've been busy," he said, getting out of the Cayenne.

"I started yesterday and kept going this morning. I'm not used to sitting around doing nothing, and I hate leaving a job unfinished," she said. "It's enough to drive a woman to drink."

And wasn't that exactly what had driven her mother to the bottle back in Australia? Finn thought privately. Being forced to sit around, doing nothing, just being decorative? Always at Tamsyn's father's beck and call, but only getting attention from him in dribs and drabs? Even the children, he'd heard, had been mostly raised by nannies.

He pasted a smile on his face and pushed the stories he'd heard from Lorenzo to the back of his mind.

"Would an espresso do?" Finn offered.

Tamsyn gave a heartfelt groan of appreciation. "I'd do anything for one."

Deep down, Finn's gut clenched tight. Oh, yeah, he was doing well so far. Not. Less than five minutes in her company and he was already fighting a hard-on. Willing his errant body back under control, he stepped up onto the veranda.

"I'm sure your boyfriend wouldn't like you going around making that offer," he finally answered.

"No boyfriend at the moment. I'm off men."

"Off men?" Finn reached for her left hand, his finger stroking the white line on her ring finger. "This the reason?"

Her hands, despite the grime from the garden, were soft. Tamsyn looked down at where he touched her. Finn watched as a gamut of emotions played across her expressive features.

"Yes," she said abruptly, tugging her hand free. "I need to rinse off. You know where everything is, I take it?"

Ah, so she didn't want to talk about that either. Had the Aussie princess met her match in her former fiancé? Was that why she was so intent on finding Ellen? he wondered. Was she looking for affection now that her fiancé was no longer in her life?

Finn told himself not to jump to conclusions. He needed to understand her in order to keep a lid on this situation. To control it and to guide Tamsyn away from trouble. Trouble, in this case, being finding out anything to do with Ellen whatsoever.

He went through to the kitchen and pulled out Lorenzo's favorite coffee cups and the imported Italian-branded coffee beans the older man swore by. Putting the required scoops in the grinder, Finn set the machine to work.

"My own personal barista, how did I get so lucky?" Tamsyn said a few minutes later from behind him, startling him with her arrival in the kitchen.

She'd taken a very quick shower, judging by the fresh

soapy scent of her, and changed into the jeans she'd worn yesterday, teamed this time with a pale pink T-shirt.

"Well, the luck stops here. You're doing the rest. I'm here to show you how, remember?"

She shrugged. "No problem. Let's start with how many beans you measured into the grinder."

Finn went through the steps. She was a quick learner, grasping the use of the machine easily.

"Let's take these out the front and enjoy looking at your efforts in the garden," he suggested when the cups were poured.

"It's been a while since someone has worked in it, hasn't it?" Tamsyn asked as they settled into a pair of cane-and-wicker chairs.

He just nodded, not really trusting himself to speak. The garden had always been Ellen's domain, but in recent years it had become too much for her. Lorenzo, busy overseeing the staff who tended the vines on the joint property he shared with Finn, had little love for working in the rambling cottage garden Ellen had created and had done the barest minimum to keep the weeds at bay. Finn had frequently suggested they employ someone to help out around the house, but his business partner had adamantly refused.

Considering he and Ellen were still only in their late fifties it was an emotional outburst, but Finn respected that it couldn't be easy for Lorenzo to slowly see the woman he had loved for so long slowly wither away physically and mentally. Lorenzo hadn't wanted to admit that Ellen could no longer handle the tasks she'd once loved, like gardening. The early onset of her dementia had been devastating news for them all.

Finn and Tamsyn settled into an easy silence together, broken only when she finished her coffee and placed her cup back on its saucer on the small glass-topped cane table between them.

"That was pure gold. I feel like a new woman," she declared with a happy sigh.

"Something wrong with the old one?" he queried, always ready to delve into what made Tamsyn Masters tick.

"A few things, but I'm working on them," she answered vaguely. "I got a job, by the way. Not paid work, but I'm volunteering in town at the hall."

"Seriously? Gladys is letting you help her out?" Finn's eyebrows rose in tandem with the incredulous note in his voice.

Tamsyn laughed, the sound plucking at his chest. God, he loved it when she laughed.

"Oh, no, as tempting as it is to set her office to rights, I wouldn't dare trespass on her domain. No, they needed someone to fill in for the seniors' program coordinator. She hurt herself last week, apparently, and won't be back until the new year."

"You're planning to stay here that long?"

Finn was surprised. Surely she intended returning home long before Christmas?

"I don't have any other demands on my time."

"But your family? They'll expect you back for Christmas, won't they?"

Tamsyn shrugged. "As far as my immediate family goes, it's only Ethan and me and he's recently engaged. I think it would be nice for him and Isobel to enjoy their first Christmas together without having to worry about me tagging along. The rest of my family is big enough and noisy enough not to miss me too much. Besides, I'm *needed* here now." She gave him a bright smile that didn't quite reach her eyes.

There was a note to her voice it took him a moment to place—she was feeling lost and vulnerable. He didn't doubt for a second that her family would miss her over Christmas, but she obviously felt they didn't need her. If anything, she needed the voluntary position here in the community more than they needed her.

The realization knocked his impression of her back a couple of notches. No matter which way he turned it, she was looking less and less like the spoiled little princess he'd built up in his mind. Had he been so determined to see the worst in her that he hadn't opened his eyes to the person she really was? Obviously the scars that Briana had left had gone far deeper than he'd thought if he was incapable of seeing the good in a person anymore.

After all, he thought, looking out over the garden, would someone who didn't understand hard work or dedication have worked so diligently to expose the carefully cultivated loveliness behind the weeds?

"I'm sure the old guys at the center will be thrilled to have you. You're far easier on the eyes than their usual co-ordinator."

"Oh, I'm sure the novelty will wear off soon enough," she said, brushing aside his comments even as a delicious blush spread up her chest and neck before tinting her cheeks with a delicate pink.

"Well, I had better get back to work," Finn said, rising to his feet.

"What is it you do exactly?" she asked, getting up to lean on the railing that skirted the edge of the veranda.

"This and that. At the moment I'm developing a new idea."

"Oh, hush-hush, is it? Tell, and you'd have to kill me, is that it?"

Finn chuckled. "No, nothing like that. I used to be in I.T.," he said, downplaying the company he'd established on the internet and then sold for several billion dollars a few years ago. "Nowadays I dabble in all sorts of things, including the vineyards around us. The owners here and I are partners in this lot."

He opened his arms to encompass the surrounding land.

"I'm impressed," Tamsyn answered with a smile. "I'll bet this is a lot more fun than being lashed to a computer all day."

"Different strokes. What I did was fun at the time. Leaving it was even more so as it gives me the freedom now to do what I please, although I'm more of a silent partner with the vines. We grow for supply to the local wineries and it turns over a good living."

He started to walk toward his car, Tamsyn following him.

"I enjoyed the coffee," she said, "and the lesson in how to make it. Thank you for coming over."

"No problem. Say, are you busy for dinner tonight? I was wondering if you'd like to come up the hill and eat with me. Beats eating alone."

"Are you sure I won't be any bother?"

"One steak or two on the grill, it makes no difference to me."

"Okay, then," she agreed. "I'd like that. How about I bring a salad and something for dessert?"

"I've got dessert covered, but if you'd like to bring a salad that'd be great. See you around six?"

"Sure." She nodded eagerly, her dark eyes glowing. "I'm looking forward to it already."

Nine

The afternoon dragged interminably. Tamsyn dusted and polished and vacuumed the cottage feverishly. She'd had to keep busy to keep her mind off the dinner ahead.

Over and over she'd told herself it was just a neighborly gesture, but she couldn't forget that moment yesterday when they'd almost kissed. Of course, she'd castigated herself several times over for a fool for even contemplating kissing another man. It had only been a matter of days since she'd broken her engagement. But had it been a true engagement?

She'd thought so at the time, even though their relationship had been low on intimacy and high on society events. Looking back, she realized that Trent had been grooming her to be his very public partner right from the start of their relationship—introducing her to the senior partners of the law firm where he worked at his earliest opportunity. She could see now that she'd been a smoke screen to hide the parts of himself that his conservative bosses wouldn't have liked, and now that the shock was receding, she was angry. Angry at him for using her so badly and, even more so, angry with herself for not realizing she was being used.

Perhaps if she hadn't had such a sheltered upbringing at The Masters. Perhaps if she'd traveled widely, like her soon-to-be-sister-in-law, Isobel, or been more outgoing or... well, anything—it might have saved her from making herself into the biggest fool in her family's history. Whatever, she'd grown up the way she had, made the choices and decisions that had led her to Trent and now here. She had nothing to be ashamed of.

Yet, if that was the case, why did she feel she had so

much to prove? Why was it so important to her that a man like Finn Gallagher find her attractive? She'd be stupid not to have seen the way he looked at her. She'd done a fair bit of looking herself—he was, after all, gorgeous, and he made her feel almost gorgeous herself. Maybe a fling with a man like Finn Gallagher was exactly what she needed.

She was going to dinner with an attractive man. One who'd asked for her company. One who she'd seen every day since she arrived here. That had to count for something, surely. He'd chosen to seek her out, chosen to spend time with her. The idea gave her a happy buzz and she went out to the vegetable garden with a spring in her step.

Bringing a salad for tonight's meal might not be much of a contribution, but she'd make sure it was the best salad Finn Gallagher had ever seen. After picking the salad greens and some early ripe cherry tomatoes, and pulling a couple of fresh radishes from the plot, she took everything inside to wash and drain. Afterward, she went for another brief shower and decided on what to wear tonight. Jeans just felt too casual and she'd already bundled up the skirt and blouse he'd seen her wear on Saturday for recycling—never wanting to ever wear them again. Given her limited options, that pretty much left the purple-and-blue dress she'd worn on Sunday.

Well, why not, she decided, pulling it off the hanger and slipping it on over her head. She loved it and she might as well get the use out of it. She brushed her hair out thoroughly until it crackled beneath the bristles then swept half of it up into a loose knot, leaving the lower section to tumble down her back and over her shoulders. Glancing at herself in the mirror she found herself smiling. Yeah, she liked the effect.

A quick application of the limited cosmetics she'd had in her handbag when she'd boarded the flight to New Zealand and she was ready.

Putting the salad together only took a few minutes and the colorful combination of the vegetables and tomatoes was both appetizing and attractive. A quick glance at the carriage clock on the sideboard in the dining room confirmed it was five minutes to six. Perfect. She covered the bowl with cling wrap and, grabbing her keys from the hall table, she locked up and went out to her car.

Lucy lifted her head briefly from where she lay curled up on one of the wicker chairs at the front.

"I'm off on a hot date, Lucy," Tamsyn called to her. "Don't do anything I wouldn't do while I'm gone."

Inside the car, Tamsyn closed her eyes and took a deep breath, trying to settle her nerves, with little success. Her hand shook slightly as she reached to put her key in the ignition.

This was ridiculous, she thought as she finally managed to insert the key and set the engine to life. It was dinner. That was all. Nothing more. Nothing less. If that was the case, then why did her heart beat so fast and why were her cheeks lit with a flush of anticipation?

Because she was being stupid, she told herself sternly as she guided her car up the hill toward Finn's residence.

Once again she was struck by the majesty of his home as she pulled up outside. The imposing entrance, with its cathedral style two-story ceiling, made her feel small and insignificant as she got out of her car and started toward the door, bowl in hand. She felt as if she should be bearing a gift of more significance—not merely a salad.

She lifted, then dropped, the heavy iron door knocker and waited. When the door opened, Finn literally took her breath away. Hair still wet from his shower, jeans slung low on his hips, he was still buttoning his shirt, giving her a glimpse of a hard ridged abdomen and a broad muscled chest. Words failed her.

"Sorry, I'm running a bit late, I had a phone call," he said as he finished his buttoning. "I'm not usually this disorganized. Here, come in."

"Here's the salad," Tamsyn managed to say past a throat that had been temporarily paralyzed with longing.

"Great, it looks delicious. Follow me, I'll take it through to the kitchen."

Tamsyn followed behind, noticing that Finn had bare feet that hardly made a sound on the polished wooden floors. God, even his feet were sexy, she thought as her inner muscles clenched involuntarily. She dragged her eyes upward, focusing instead on a point just between his shoulders in an attempt to drag her contrary hormones under some form of control.

"Take a seat while I check on the marinade," Finn said, gesturing to a set of solid-wood high-backed bar stools at the edge of a large granite breakfast bar.

"Thanks. Do you mind if I take my shoes off?" Tamsyn asked, feeling just a little overdressed.

"Make yourself at home." He smiled in response before applying his attention to the dish he had on the countertop and turning the meat inside it.

Tamsyn was assailed with the aromas of ginger and garlic and felt her mouth begin to water.

"That smells great," she commented.

"It's going to be," Finn said with a conspiratorial wink that did weird things to her stomach all over again. "Can I offer you a glass of wine?"

"Sure, that'd be nice."

"Red or white?"

"How about you surprise me," she answered, all capability of making any rational decisions gone in his company.

"Okay," he said. "I'll be back in a minute. Unless you'd like to see my wine cellar?"

She laughed. "Does that fall under the same category as seeing your etchings?" Heat flamed in her cheeks as she realized what she'd just said and she clapped a hand to her mouth. "Oh, I'm so sorry, I didn't mean anything by that, it just slipped out!"

Finn laughed, his eyes crinkling at the corners in genuine amusement. "It's no problem and, for the record, no, this isn't in the same category at all. The cellar is through this way," he said, reaching for her hand.

Tamsyn tried not to think about the way his warm dry hand encapsulated her own or how the sensation of his palm against hers sent her synapses into meltdown. Instead, she focused on her breathing as they walked through a door off the kitchen and down a couple of stairs before continuing along a short tiled corridor.

"The cellar is built into the side of the hill," Finn said as they went down a couple more stairs before stopping at a door. "Obviously it's easier to keep it temperature controlled this way."

He opened the door and Tamsyn couldn't stop the captivated sigh of appreciation as she saw the shelved walls open up before her.

"This is impressive," she said, stepping forward and checking the labels on some of the several hundred bottles of wine on shelves that crisscrossed the walls. "Ethan would love this."

"Ethan?" Finn asked, raising one brow.

"My brother. He's our head winemaker at The Masters."

"Maybe he'll visit sometime," he said blandly before selecting two bottles from the shelves. "Here we go. How about a pinot gris to start and then a pinot noir with dinner?"

"Sounds great," Tamsyn agreed and turned to precede him out of the cellar and back to the kitchen.

While Finn opened the white wine and poured two glasses, Tamsyn drifted over to the wall of French doors that opened out onto a wide patio.

"This is quite a house you have," she said as she accepted the glass of wine Finn brought over to her.

"It's big, yeah, but it's home," Finn said, reaching past her to open the glass door and guided her outside onto the patio. "Take a seat," he invited. "I'll just get some appetizers."

Tamsyn perched on the edge of a comfortably padded patio chair and waited for Finn to return. Her eyes widened in surprise when she saw him return with a tray laden with antipasto.

"Wow, you put all this together?"

"One of my many talents," he answered with a smile. "A…close friend of my father's taught me to appreciate life with all its flavors. These are just some of them."

"Sounds like a great friend to have."

Finn took a sip of his wine before nodding. "The best. When my dad died and my mother became unwell, he stepped up and provided me with a home. I'll always be grateful to him for that. I owe him a lot."

Tamsyn heard the subtext behind Finn's words. Whoever this man was, he'd obviously been a big influence in Finn's life.

"You were young when your father passed away?"

"Twelve. Mom got sick soon after."

"That must have been hard. I'm really sorry," Tamsyn said with her heart behind every syllable.

"It was a long time ago." Finn sat staring out at the ranges for a while before leaning forward and lifting the antipasto platter toward her. "Here, try some."

"This is really lovely," Tamsyn said, taking a piece of artichoke and lifting it to her lips. "You have an amazing setting here."

Finn nodded. "I love it. I could never imagine living anywhere else."

"I used to feel that way about The Masters…" Tamsyn let her voice trail away.

Right now she wondered if she'd ever feel it was home again. She felt so disordered, as if her life was so jumbled that she might never feel settled again.

"Used to?"

"Things change," Tamsyn said with a shrug, thinking of both the lie her father had perpetuated for most of her life—letting her and Ethan think their mother had died—and Trent's duplicity. "People frequently turn out to be someone different to what you thought."

There was more to it than that. The lies had driven her away…but with the perspective that came from distance, she realized that she hadn't been happy, even before she knew the truth. She'd always felt safe at The Masters—sheltered and protected. But she'd never felt truly, fully alive. Nothing about her job had her deeply invested; nothing in her personal life made her deeply happy. Perhaps she'd outgrown "safe and sheltered." Maybe she needed something more.

"Sounds deep. Want to talk about it?"

Tamsyn sat silent for a moment or two. Did she want to talk about it? She wasn't sure. She certainly didn't want to spoil what had started out to be a lovely evening by delving into her doubts and questions.

"Not really," she decided out loud. "I'll deal with it in my own way."

"If you ever need an ear or a shoulder—" he tapped himself on the chest "—you can apply here."

They turned their discussion to generalities about the area and Finn soon had Tamsyn in stitches over some of the stories about Gladys from the hall office from when he was a boy. Seems she'd been old even then. Mind you, Tamsyn mused, maybe some people were just born old.

Finn suggested they return inside after he'd grilled the steaks. He turned perfectly baked potatoes onto their plates together with their steaks and took them to a casual dining table just inside the French doors. He put her salad onto the table, poured them each a glass of red wine and sat down.

By the time they finished, it was growing dark. They lingered over their wine, Tamsyn mindful that she still had to negotiate the driveway and a small section of road before she reached home tonight.

"You know," she said, gesturing to the darkening vista spread before them, "where your house is reminds me a lot of Masters Rise. It was our family home before it was destroyed by bushfires nearly forty years ago. But it had an outlook like this, over the vineyards."

"It must have been a struggle for your family rebuilding after the fire."

"Yeah, it was. I think that's part of the reason our father was so distant with us as kids. He was focused on re-creating what the old days had been like for the family. Between him, his brother and my aunt, they have all had a hand in restoring the vineyards and the family business. It was pretty demanding."

So demanding that the man hadn't had time for his wife, Finn thought angrily. He'd been eight years old when Lorenzo and Ellen had arrived here and he still remembered the incredibly fragile woman Ellen had been. One thing had been constant for her, though. Her love for the children she'd been forced to leave behind. And now one of them sat here, with him. Finally making an effort to reconnect with a woman for whom it was all very possibly too late.

Finn forced his attention back to his guest.

"And your mother, where did she fit into all this?" It was hard to keep his emotions out of his voice.

"You know, I barely remember her. Sure, I have snippets of memories here and there, but I was just turning three when she left. I wonder, sometimes, what kind of woman just walks away from her children."

"There are always two sides to every story."

Finn reached for his wine and took a deep swallow. He ached to defend Ellen, but he couldn't, not without betraying Lorenzo's trust.

Tamsyn laughed. A sound that totally lacked humor, however, and bordered on the satirical.

"In our case I think there are way more than two sides. I grew up thinking my mother was dead. It was kind of a shock to find out she wasn't."

"Dead?"

Finn felt a chill seep through him. What had happened? Had John Masters been so intent on ensuring his wife walked away with nothing from their marriage that he'd even lied to their children? What kind of father did that to his kids? And what did that do to the children when they grew up and learned the truth?

Ten

"Ethan and I only found out recently, after our father died. If Ethan hadn't queried some financial statements in the estate we still wouldn't know."

"Tell me what happened," Finn urged, suddenly reminded of his own words that there were two sides to every story. So far he'd only heard Ellen's version of events through Lorenzo's protective filter.

"All I know is my mother tried to leave my father. Apparently she had Ethan and me in a car with her. She'd…she'd been drinking and lost control. Ethan and I were briefly hospitalized. Dad told our mom she could go if she wanted, but she wasn't taking us with her. He agreed to pay her a monthly sum if she'd stay away. And she did. She just left. Dad had been making payments to her all this time. She accepted money to leave us behind."

"And that's why you want to find her now? To find out why?"

Tamsyn turned her wineglass around and around in her hands and he watched her as she stared at the ruby liquid inside the crystal bowl, her face pensive.

"Yes," she said decisively, putting her wineglass down on the table with an audible clink. "I think I deserve to know why I had to grow up without a mother."

There was still a raw pain echoing in her; Finn could feel it as if it were a tangible thing in the room with them. He felt his earlier assumptions about Tamsyn Masters begin to crumble.

It can't have been easy for a little girl to grow up with a

distant father and no mother, no matter how efficient her nannies must have been and no matter what other family she had around her. Kids needed their parents, both of them. He'd been lucky, at least for the first twelve years of his life and then, subsequently, with the love and support given to him by Lorenzo and Ellen.

"Don't get me wrong, I didn't want for anything at all growing up. Ethan and I were close, he's always been so protective of me, Dad loved me in his way and I've always been tight with my cousins. I just want to know why she left us. Why we were so unimportant to her that she could just walk away."

Finn ached to tell her there was so much more to Ellen's story than that, but it wasn't his information to share.

"I hope you get to find your answers," he said softly, at a loss as to what else to say.

"Yeah, me, too." Tamsyn gave him a wobbly smile.

"So, about dessert," Finn said, injecting a lighter note into his voice. "Are you ready for some?"

"Sure, bring it on. I've already eaten way too much this evening, what're a few more calories. The seniors at the center are probably going to work it all off me tomorrow anyway."

He reached out and took her plate. From what he could tell, she'd eaten hardly enough to keep going. Still, it wasn't his place to harangue her into stuffing herself. Instead, he retrieved the container of hokey-pokey ice cream from the freezer and dished it up into two bowls. Putting them on a tray and reaching for a container of chocolate sauce, he carried them over to the table.

"Ooh, ice cream!" Tamsyn exclaimed.

"Not just any ice cream," Finn said with a mock-stern expression on his face. "New Zealand's finest."

Tamsyn lifted her spoon and scooped up the tiniest mouthful. "Oh, is that toffee inside it?"

Finn smiled at the expression of sheer delight on her face. "You haven't lived until you've tried it. It's better in a cone, but I thought we should be civilized for our first dinner together. Here," he said, extending the chocolate sauce to her. "Try this on top."

She tried the new combination, the chocolate sauce freezing to a hard crust as it drizzled over the ice cream. A deep sound of appreciation hummed from her throat, sending a jolt of lightning-hot desire straight to his groin. He'd been able to hold it together most of tonight, to keep her at arm's length. But right now he wanted to do nothing more than lay her on the table and eat dessert right off of her. He shifted uncomfortably in his seat.

"Oh, that's good," she said, taking another spoonful. "I can't believe I've lived this long and never tried it."

Finn scooped up a generous mouthful and shoved it in his mouth. Maybe the icy concoction would chill his fiery libido. Difficult to achieve success on that score, he noted, while watching Tamsyn savor every mouthful of her own. Her tongue swept out and traced her upper lip, seeking and finding a tiny trace of chocolate that had lodged there. He closed his eyes briefly, trying to rid himself of the urge to find out what that dainty tongue would feel like on his body. Jeez, he needed to get a grip here.

It wasn't until Tamsyn's spoon fell with a clatter in her bowl that he realized she'd finished. Heaving a sigh of relief, Finn reached for her plate.

"Here, let me take that for you," he said, pushing his chair back.

"Oh, I can do that," Tamsyn insisted, taking both his bowl and hers out of his reach and rising also. "You've already done so much for me this evening. Can I do the dishes before I head off?"

"That would be a definite no," Finn said, following her

into the kitchen. "Besides, that's what dishwashers are for, right?"

"If you're sure…"

"I am," he said, taking her hand and leading her away from the kitchen. "Can I offer you some coffee? My machine isn't as flash as yours, but it makes a good brew."

Tamsyn shook her head. "No, I'd better get going. I want to be fresh for tomorrow. Thank you for tonight. It was really lovely."

"You're welcome, I enjoyed it." *I enjoyed you,* his mind reiterated. He lifted her hand to his lips, pressing a kiss to her knuckles. "I'm glad you came."

"I—um, me, too," she said, suddenly flustered.

As disconcerted as she was, she made no effort to pull away, so Finn did what naturally came next. He leaned forward and kissed her. The instant their lips touched he forgot everything he'd ever thought about her—all the nastiness, all the subtle envy he hadn't even realized he'd allowed to build up over the years. In their place, he allowed himself to be lost in her softness.

Her lips felt like warm petals against his. While a clawing need deep inside him demanded he plunder their tender surface, a voice of reason warned him to hold back, to tease instead, to coax, and when her lips parted on a swift rush of warm breath, he took advantage. He gently sucked her lower lip between his, tentatively tracing his tongue along the tender inner edge.

The shudder that went through her body at his touch saw him step closer. Saw him wrap one arm around her waist, drawing her slender form against his strength, molding her against him. He deepened their kiss, his mind a fog of need and want, and yet beneath it all lay an overpowering urge to cherish.

Her arms snaked around his waist, her hands pressing

flat against his back. Finn fought back a groan of satisfaction as her lips began to move against his, as her tongue boldly followed where his led. She tasted intoxicatingly sweet and he knew, even with this one kiss, he would be addicted forever.

He was shaking when he pulled away. Aware that what they'd shared wasn't enough, would never be enough, but also aware that he didn't want to frighten her away. He could sweep her off her feet…but he'd so much rather she come to him when she was ready.

The pupils of Tamsyn's eyes all but consumed the dark velvet brown of her irises and her lips were slightly swollen from the intensity of their kiss.

"I…I need to go."

"Yeah, I know."

He took her by the hand again and led her through to the front entrance and to her car. He opened her door for her and watched as she settled herself behind the wheel. She reached out to pull the door closed and gave him a small wave before sending her car down the driveway. As Finn watched her taillights disappear down the hill, he wondered how, just a few days ago, he'd ever actually *wanted* to see her drive away.

Tamsyn could barely remember the short drive back to the cottage. Her emotions were in a crazy jumble It had been just a kiss. One normal everyday kiss between two consenting adults. So why had it left her feeling like this? How had a simple caress suddenly become so intense, so complicated, so layered with feeling?

Her entire body vibrated with sensation. When Finn had leaned forward to kiss her she'd expected it to be nice. Nice? She snorted in disgust with herself. She should have known a man like Finn didn't do *nice*. No, he did earth-shattering, mind-blowing, skin-searing fantastic. Not once, with Trent, had she ever experienced a kiss like that. With Finn, her entire body had turned molten, her brain scrambled and then reassembled with one purpose in mind.

And then he'd pulled back. It had left her feeling way off kilter, suddenly fearful that perhaps he hadn't felt the same way as she had. But she'd seen the turbulence in his eyes. Eyes that had darkened to the color of rainwashed slate. Her heart had thrilled to the knowledge that he wanted her with as much force and need as she wanted him. That knowledge, however ephemeral, was balm to her wounded soul.

It shocked Tamsyn to realize that if Finn had suggested they take their embrace further, she would have wholeheartedly thrown caution to the winds and let him take her to bed.

She pulled her car to a halt outside the garage, turned off the engine and sat in the dark, mulling over the enormity of what had happened between them. Where did they go from here? Did he want to take things further? They'd known each other only a few days and yet...

She started suddenly, a small scream erupting from her throat as a dark shape landed on the hood of her car.

"Lucy! You scared me half to death," Tamsyn scolded as she got out of the car and scooped the cat up in her arms.

Lucy merely bunted Tamsyn's chin with her head and began to purr loudly. Inside the house, Tamsyn made sure that the cat was fed and watered and went through to her bedroom. Her mind still raced and, despite all her activity in the garden this morning, she felt totally wired and ready to do something, anything, rather than go to sleep.

Anything? she thought to herself. *How about Finn Gallagher?*

She giggled, earning a quizzical look from Lucy, who, after completing her supper, had jumped up onto Tamsyn's bed and begun grooming herself.

The chirp of her phone distracted her from her thoughts. Who could be ringing at this hour?

"Hello?" she answered cautiously.

"It's me, Finn. I just wanted to check and see if you got home safely."

Warmth spread through her body in response to his rich deep voice.

"I did, and thank you again for tonight. I enjoyed it." She hesitated a moment before adding, "All of it."

She could hear the smile on his lips as he answered. "Me, too. By the way, I still have your salad bowl. Okay if I drop that around to you tomorrow?"

Her heart leaped in her chest. Okay? Of course it was okay. She couldn't wait to see him again.

"Sure, I'll be home after one."

"I'll be around shortly after, then. Good night, Tamsyn."

"Good night," she whispered, suddenly reluctant to lose the all-too-brief connection between them.

She felt like a teenager waiting for the other person to hang up first, not prepared to be the one to do it herself. She heard the beep as he disconnected the call and finally hit the end button on her phone.

Well, clearly her silly rush to leave after their embrace hadn't put him off wanting to see her again, Tamsyn thought as she brushed her teeth and readied herself for bed. Later, as she lay between her lavender-scented sheets and absently stroked Lucy, who had curled up by her waist, she played the evening back in her mind.

Relived that all-too-brief kiss. A kiss that had ignited a passion she'd feared she was incapable of igniting—both within herself and within a partner. A passion that had been unequivocally reciprocated. The realization was both empowering and terrifying in equal proportions.

She sighed in the dark, squirming a little against the mattress as her body started that slow burn all over again, aching and wanting. Tamsyn shifted position and tried to rid her thoughts of anything to do with Finn Gallagher. God, she thought as she finally began to drift off to sleep, if a single kiss could leave her this flummoxed, what would she be like if they ever made love?

Or maybe she should be asking herself, *when* they made love?

Eleven

Tamsyn made it into town early after a surprisingly deep sleep. It seemed that a delicious meal and good-night kiss from a supersexy man was enough to chase the doubt demons away. She really should do it more often, she thought with a cheeky smile at herself in the rearview mirror of her car.

She parked near the hall and then made her way to the library, determined today to find the librarian, Miriam. The library doors stood open as she approached, always a good sign, and when she entered, she saw that it was doing a brisk business. As she mounted the stairs to the entrance, several people gave her a second glance—something she was beginning to get used to around here. Perhaps they treated all newcomers that way.

An older woman, with hair an interesting shade of pale blue, was busy checking out books at the front desk. Tamsyn waited until the line receded before stepping forward.

"Excuse me, I'm looking for Miriam. Gladys sent me."

"Oh, you must be the new seniors' coordinator," the woman said brightly, her pale blue eyes sparkling through the lenses of her pink wire-framed glasses.

"Yes, temporarily at least." Tamsyn smiled. "Are you Miriam?"

"Yes, dear, I am. How can I help you? Looking for a specific title?"

The woman changed windows on the computer in front of her and looked expectantly at Tamsyn, her hands poised over the keyboard.

"I'm looking for my mother, actually. Ellen Masters. I

was wondering if I could view the electoral rolls to see if she's still a resident in the area."

"The electoral rolls? Did Gladys send you here for those?"

"Well, she did say you'd know where I could find information about people living in the area."

"Hmm." Miriam slipped her glasses off her face and chewed thoughtfully on the tip of one arm. "Well, the electoral rolls aren't kept here. They used to be at the post office, but since all the smaller ones were closed down some years ago, your best bet for that information would be in Blenheim, or even Nelson. What did you say your mother's name was?"

"Ellen Masters, have you heard of her?"

Tamsyn held her breath, hoping against hope that Miriam would smile and tell her that of course she knew her mother, but her hopes were dashed as the older woman shook her pale blue head.

"I don't know anyone of that name."

Tamsyn forced a smile to her face. "Thanks anyway."

"You're welcome, dear, and good luck for today."

"Today?"

"With the oldies," Miriam said with a conspiratorial wink.

"You think I'll need it?" Tamsyn said, this time with a genuine smile.

"Some of those old men can be a bit of a handful. Mind you, most of them always were. You'd best hurry on then. You don't want to be late on your first day."

Miriam hadn't been kidding, Tamsyn realized later on. Every man there, whether he be in a wheelchair or ambulatory, was an incorrigible flirt. By the time twelve-thirty rolled around she'd received no less than three offers of marriage and a few offers of other things she wouldn't touch with a barge pole. It was all in fun, though, and as she took the box with the door takings to Gladys she felt as if she'd been a part of something worthwhile for a change.

Her life had become so superficial, she realized as she said her goodbyes to Gladys. She'd lost touch with the simpler things, the ones that made her feel valuable and valued. At The Masters, her work had become a daily treadmill of boosting sales for their luxury accommodations and winning business for functions and weddings, together with all the various, and sometimes outrageous, requests those events demanded. Even events that should have been meaningful lost their warmth and humanity when they became that grand and elaborate. Her work had stopped being personally satisfying a long time ago.

Today had been a much-needed shot in the arm. A reminder that a little effort, a little care, went a long way. Tomorrow she would go into Blenheim again and find those blasted electoral rolls and, if she had no luck there she'd also go to Nelson.

Gladys was on the phone and just waved at Tamsyn to put the box with the takings on her desk. Tamsyn did so and then walked to her car. She wound the windows down to let out the accumulated heat and checked her phone. In her email, she saw a forwarded mail from their father's lawyer confirming the address she'd been given was the correct one.

She struck her steering wheel in frustration. It was like being caught in a continual loop, each time ending with Finn Gallagher. Surely if he knew anything about her mother at all, he would have said something by now? It just didn't make any sense. Still puzzling over the situation, she started her car and headed back to the cottage.

Tamsyn kept the car windows down on her drive, hoping the breeze whipping through would help clear her mind. As she turned up the driveway, she heard the roar of a mower.

It grew louder the closer she got to the house. Her eyes widened in appreciation as she espied the source of the noise.

Dressed in jeans and rubber boots and with a pair of earmuffs bracketing his head, Finn Gallagher rode a mower across the tangled lawn, making short work of the piles of weeds she'd left the other day as well as the overlong grass. The sweet scent of freshly cut grass hung in the heated air, but it was nowhere near as sweet as the view of raw male that presented itself to her.

Sweat gleamed across the tanned surface of his back and she watched the muscles at his shoulders bunch and shift as he turned the wheel. A deep throb built inside her body, sending heat and moisture of a different kind to pool at the juncture of her thighs. Finn executed a neat three-point-turn and began to drive the mower toward her, his hand lifting in acknowledgment as he saw her standing there.

She was grateful she didn't need to speak because right now, with him driving toward her, shirtless, she doubted she'd be able to form a single comprehensible word. Lines of sweat gathered in the ridges of Finn's taut abdomen. It seemed the more moisture collected on his body, the dryer her mouth became.

He cut the engine on the mower and braked to a stop in front of her.

"H-hello," she said hesitantly.

"Hello yourself."

The effect of his smile curled all the way to her toes.

"I finished my work early this morning and came down to return your salad bowl. I've left it at the front door," he said and gestured to the veranda. "Since I was at a loose end, I thought I'd surprise you with the lawns."

Oh, he'd surprised her, all right.

"You look…hot," she said, feeling a fair amount of that heat radiating all over her body.

"I wouldn't mind a drink of water."

"I'll get you some."

She shot away, more as a measure of self-preservation than anything else. In the kitchen she sloshed cold tap water into a jug, sliced a lemon and threw the pieces into the water together with some ice from the freezer and a sprig of mint from the plant at the back door, then put the jug and two glasses on a tray. Several deep steadying breaths later, she carried the tray out onto the veranda.

"Here," she said, pouring a glass of water for Finn and handing it to him.

"Thanks."

He took the glass and downed it in a couple of long easy swallows. Tamsyn was mesmerized by the muscles working in his throat and forced herself to look away.

"Another?" God, was that her voice? That weird strangled sound?

"You read my mind," Finn answered, handing her his glass.

Thank goodness he wasn't reading hers, she thought quietly. She swiftly poured him another glass of water and handed it to him, this time determined not to watch as he drank it. But where did that leave her to look? At the breadth of his bare shoulders? The small dark brown nipples that lay flat on his chest? Or maybe she should watch the trail of a bead of sweat as it trickled over those too-perfect abs and down past the waistband of his jeans.

She'd be needing to tip a glass of water over herself if she continued like this. Instead, she picked up her glass and drank.

"How did your first day go?" Finn asked, leaning one hip against the veranda railing.

"It was good, thanks. The women were a little wary of me to begin with, the men hopeless wannabe Romeos, which was sweet. Overall I think I held my own. Next week will probably be easier. At least, I hope so."

"They didn't scare you off?"

"It'd take more than that to put me off. When I commit to something, I like to go all the way."

The words hung in the air between them, her unintended double entendre assuming the proportions of a six-foot-high neon sign. Tamsyn wished the wooden floor could just open up and swallow her whole.

"I'm pleased to hear it," Finn said, putting his glass on the wide veranda railing and fixing her with his gaze.

A flutter started in her chest and she knew they weren't talking about the community work anymore. The fine hairs on her forearms rose in a prickle of awareness and heat flooded the lower regions of her body. Her fingers curled tight around her glass. Any minute now there'd be steam rising, she thought. If she reacted like this to just a look, how would she feel when he touched her—really touched her?

She couldn't wait to find out.

"I'd better get back to the lawns," he said, breaking the spell that bound her in its sensual haze. "I'm heading out tonight and will be away until Friday afternoon. Will you be okay until then?"

"Okay? Of course. I should be fine." Tamsyn smiled to hide the disappointment that flooded her at his words. It shocked her to realize just how easily she'd become dependent on these moments they'd shared each day. "It'll give me time to do some more research in my hunt for my mother."

Was it her imagination or did Finn's face suddenly harden? No, it had to just be the effect of the sun slipping behind a cloud, casting him into a pocket of shade, she decided.

"How's that going?" he asked, picking up his glass and bringing it over to put it on the tray beside her.

He smelled delicious. Warm and slightly sweaty, but with a freshness about him that made her wish she could press her nose against his bare flesh and inhale more deeply. If she knew him better, more intimately, she'd close that final distance between them, lay her hand on the broad plane of his chest—feel the hardness of his strength, the nub of his nipple, beneath her palm.

"Tamsyn?" he asked, jerking her from her suddenly inconvenient daydream.

"Um, not so well, actually," she said, trying to gather her scattered thoughts together. It was about as easy as hunting down the free-range eggs the chickens on the property seemed to delight in hiding all over the place. "But I'm going to go to Blenheim tomorrow to see if I can find her on the electoral roll. It'll be a start. What I don't understand is why Dad's lawyer is certain that your address is the right one for her. It's where they insist they've been sending her mail. You're not hiding her somewhere, are you?"

Tamsyn laughed but didn't miss the change in Finn's body language. He angled himself away from her and she felt a definite cooling in the air between them.

"I'm certainly not hiding anyone at my house," he said firmly.

She put a hand out, touched his forearm. His skin was moist and hot, his muscles bunching under her fingertips.

"I didn't mean to offend you, Finn."

He moved away. "You didn't. I'm going to finish the lawns and then I'm heading back up to my place. I'll put the ride-on back in the shed when I'm done."

"Thanks, and thanks for doing the lawns for me. I was getting around to it."

"No problem," he said, stepping down off the veranda and striding toward the mower.

The roar of its engine precluded any further attempt at communication. What had she said to make him so reserved all of a sudden? She played their conversation over in her mind. The only thing she could think of was her allusion to him hiding her mother. Had there been some truth to her question? No, there couldn't be. If there was, why would he have denied her mother's being there right from the start? Tamsyn couldn't quite figure it out. But one way or another, she was going to.

Twelve

Finn shoved the earmuffs back onto his head and steered the mower around the back of the property. Irritation burned inside his gut. Irritation at himself, at Tamsyn, at Lorenzo—hell, at the whole world. It was crazy having her stay here right in Lorenzo and Ellen's home. She was bound to discover the truth eventually, yet Lorenzo was still adamant that Finn do whatever he could to ensure she be kept in the dark. Lorenzo was lucky that the network of friends they had in and around town were equally as protective of Ellen's fragile peace of mind as he was. So far no one had let anything slip.

But every day she stayed here, every day she went into town, the odds increased that Tamsyn would stumble over something or someone that would lead her to her mother. And what if, for some reason, she gained access to the locked room? He knew the deadlock on the door was a good one—he'd installed it himself and had the only key on a hook in a cupboard in his office, but it still made him uneasy to think of how many secrets were separated from Tamsyn by only one door.

He executed a line and turned to come back the other way, constantly aware of Tamsyn's presence inside the cottage. She was going to be devastated when she found out the truth. And furious with him. Lorenzo had put him in an untenable position, one he planned to discuss with the older man tomorrow morning when he caught up with him in Wellington.

Finn had to meet with some business associates during his time in the capital city, but he planned to spend as much time as he could at the hospital with Ellen, too. He needed to see for himself if she'd be capable of withstanding a visit from the daughter she'd left so long ago.

He tried not to think about what had happened with his own mother. About how her mental state had been so fragile that when her medical team had finally deemed her well enough to have a visit from her only son, it had tipped her completely over the edge instead. All the twelve-year-old Finn had known at the time was that he was somehow responsible for what had happened. That seeing him, a younger version of his father, had made her elect to give up resuming her old life. That it would make her choose to opt out of life altogether.

He couldn't let that happen to Ellen. Couldn't let that happen to another mother figure in his life. But he couldn't stand the thought that choosing to protect Ellen set Tamsyn up to be hurt instead.

Finn finished the lawns and rode the mower toward the implements shed. He grabbed his T-shirt from the shelf where he'd thrown it and tugged it on. He hadn't been oblivious to Tamsyn's unmasked appreciation of his body. If he hadn't been so determined to tread softly with her he might have done something about it today, but her casually thrown out remark about him hiding her mother had hit just a little too close to the mark.

He *was* hiding Ellen from her. Maybe not physically, but he was definitely keeping the truth from her. A truth he was struggling now to justify keeping to himself. He forced himself to clear his mind. To focus instead on his visit to Wellington and the decisions he would make after he'd seen Ellen for himself. And the fight he would no doubt have with Lorenzo when he made them.

Friday rolled around all too slowly. Tamsyn had been achingly aware of the empty house up on the hill the whole time Finn had been away. It had left her unsettled, especially as they'd parted on what she thought were less than good terms. She hoped to rectify that today and had already left a message on his voice mail inviting him for dinner at the cottage tonight. Depending on how his trip had gone, she hoped he'd prefer an evening where he didn't have to fend for himself. Even so, her voice had been a little on the wobbly-nervous side when she'd left her message.

Yesterday's trip into Blenheim had been another wasted effort and today's to Nelson was no better. She was beginning to wonder if her mother had even lived in the region at all. It was hard not to just give up on it all and walk away.

She reminded herself that today marked only the seventh day since she'd arrived in New Zealand. It was still way too early to call it quits. Maybe she needed some professional help in her quest, though. Next week she might look into hiring a private investigator.

Somehow, though, she was reluctant to turn the search over to someone else. This was her journey, her need to find her mother. She wanted so much to have control over it. Her father had taken away her right to know her mother. Trent had taken away her right to expect happiness and a future through their relationship. She'd worked too hard for too long to please men who, in the end, had chosen what was best for themselves with no genuine regard for her feelings or needs.

So where did that leave her with Finn? She sank into a worn easy chair in the sitting room of the cottage and stared out the bay window. Lucy, as usual, sat in pride of place, her eyes drifting closed in the sun now her toilette was complete.

Finn hadn't made her any promises. He'd just been here. Available—except for the past two days. He hadn't pushed her when they'd kissed on Tuesday night, a kiss she still relived in all its sensation-soaked glory each night when she went to bed, leaving her sleep fractured and her body unrested and aching with unresolved tension. She'd tried physical exertion around the cottage to wear herself out each afternoon and into the early evening, but it had only served to add more aches upon the pains. Even a soak in the large tub each evening hadn't been enough to ease them away.

Tamsyn let her eyes drift closed, let her senses relax, her body sag into the chair. Outside she could hear the birds and the drone of the bumblebees that favored the flowering plants she'd revealed among the weeds. It wasn't long before she'd drifted off to sleep.

She woke with a start about an hour later. Her phone was ringing. Where the heck had she left it? She staggered to where she'd left her handbag.

"Hello?" she answered groggily.

"Did I wake you?"

Finn's voice filled her ear, warming her from the inside out.

"Caught me napping, guilty as charged," she answered, trying to keep her voice light, especially considering the awkwardness that had developed between them the last time they spoke.

"I'm jealous."

It sounded as if a faint smile played around his lips. Tamsyn hugged one arm around herself and leaned against the wall, imagining his face as he spoke.

"Don't be, I've given myself a crick in the neck."

"Maybe I can help you out with that later on," he said smoothly. "I'm told I have good hands."

A flush suffused her body. She just bet he did. Broad palms, long capable fingers. Her legs weakened just at the thought.

"I got your message," he continued, "and yes, I'd love to come for dinner tonight. What can I bring?"

"How about a nice bottle of wine from that impressive collection of yours," she suggested. "Something white. I'm doing chicken. Nothing fancy."

It was one of the few things she could cook successfully. Growing up at The Masters they'd had staff for just about everything, something she'd learned to appreciate when she'd gone to university and had had to fend for herself in the kitchen of the small flat she'd shared.

"Anything I don't have to cook and prepare myself sounds great. What time do you want me?"

Want him? Oh, about 24/7, to be totally honest. She gathered the raveled strands of her mind together and gave them a swift tug into submission.

"Sixish suit you?"

"Perfect. See you then."

He ended the call, leaving her standing there like a love-sick teenager still holding the phone to her ear. The disconnect signal beeping in her ear galvanized her into action. It was four o'clock, and she still had so much to do. She swept into the kitchen and grabbed the two chicken breasts she'd put into the fridge last night to defrost. Still a bit on the icy side, she realized, and put their plate on the countertop to finish defrosting, covering them carefully so Lucy wouldn't be tempted to check them out.

Okay, what was she going to do with the chicken? Stuff it? She mentally went over the range of ingredients she had at her disposal and decided on a carpetbag-style concoction that had been popular with her flatmates. She even had some frozen scallops in the freezer to stuff the chicken with. She put them on a separate plate to defrost, making a mental note to replace them the next time she shopped for groceries.

Boiled baby potatoes, seasoned with parsley butter, and asparagus spears would be a perfect accompaniment to the chicken. Moving swiftly, Tamsyn prepared a marinade for the meat, throwing the almost-defrosted breasts into a dish with lemon juice, tarragon, some finely chopped garlic, salt and ground black pepper and covering it again.

The baby potatoes were easy. She grabbed the box she'd bought at a grocery store on the way back from Nelson and rinsed a few under the kitchen faucet before popping them in a saucepan with water and a dash of salt and setting them on the stove to cook later. The asparagus she rinsed and snapped and put in a dish ready to steam in the microwave just before serving. She wished she'd paid more attention at home when the cook had prepared hollandaise sauce with their asparagus dishes, and contemplated looking up a recipe on the internet. In the end she decided against it. What if it didn't work? She'd rather have a practice at it first before dishing it up to Finn, who had served her such a delicious dinner, himself. She badly wanted to impress him.

She sobered for a minute, the wild excitement of planning and preparing her meal deserting her. Insecurity trickled its icy fingers into the corners of her mind. What, in all honesty, was she trying to prove? Was she so desperate for male approval that she was prepared to put herself through hoops again already?

Tamsyn stepped away from the kitchen counter and walked out the back door, sinking onto the wooden steps that led down to the vegetable garden. She pulled her knees up under her chin, growling at herself under her breath. She needed to get a grip, to stop defining herself by the men in her life.

She'd invited Finn to dinner because she enjoyed his company and, frankly, enjoyed the way he made her feel. She wanted to know if that feeling could go further, that was all. And, whether it did or it didn't, she would handle it like an adult.

They would enjoy a nice meal together, then a nice evening together. What happened next…well, she shrugged and pushed herself back up to her feet again. What*ever* happened next, just happened.

She went back into the kitchen and turned the chicken. She had the main course planned, which left her with a question. What was she going to do for dessert? She opened the refrigerator and studied its contents again. Cheese and crackers with some fresh sliced fruit? It would have to do, she decided. She was no Cordon Bleu cook by any means. Which left predinner nibbles… She hoped he liked crudités with hummus. She could slice some carrot sticks and celery as well as a red bell pepper and arrange them all on a plate.

Right, the food was sorted, which just left her. What the heck was she going to wear? She thought for a minute then decided on the gypsy-style skirt she'd bought yesterday from the boutique in town. Another item by the same designer as her purple-and-blue dress, it had cost a pretty penny, but the swirl of color, in shades of coral over a sumptuous midnight blue, and the sheer femininity of the item had filled Tamsyn with delight. She'd team it with a blue silk knit singlet and a pair of navy ballet flats that she'd picked up while in Nelson today.

Satisfied she'd done all she could for now in the kitchen, Tamsyn quickly zoomed through the sitting room, clearing away old newspapers and tidying the stack of magazines on the shelf under the coffee table. There, tidy, but not staged. She groaned. Who was she kidding? She was staging everything in anticipation of Finn being here tonight. It didn't matter how sternly she talked to herself, deep down it mattered to her what he thought.

Acknowledging that was a freedom in itself and allowed her to make a decision about another question that had been playing around the back of her mind. She went straight to the linen cupboard in the passageway and grabbed out fresh linen for her bed.

She was going to be prepared for every eventuality tonight. Come what may.

Thirteen

Finn approached the cottage slowly. His visit to Wellington had gone well, businesswise, but not so well when it came to Ellen. For the first time, she hadn't recognized him. He'd expected it, thought he'd been prepared for it, yet when it happened it hurt far more than he'd ever anticipated.

Lorenzo had been apologetic, Alexis understanding, but none of it made up for the fact that Ellen was slowly but surely slipping away from them all—and that included Tamsyn. She was running out of time to meet her mother. It put him between a rock and a hard place. Lorenzo remained adamant that Tamsyn be kept from finding Ellen.

In some ways Finn totally agreed. He knew that the woman Tamsyn would see was not the mother she had hoped to find. Ellen was far past the point of being able to answer the questions Tamsyn carried. Perhaps it would have simply been easier for everyone if Tamsyn continued to believe her mother had passed away. Rare now were the days when there was even a glimmer of understanding in Ellen's faded brown eyes.

Lorenzo was never far from her side, constantly on the alert for the opening of those precious windows in her mind—each one a gift beyond price. While Finn warred with Tamsyn's right to at least see her mother, could he honestly deny Lorenzo those moments? What if seeing Tamsyn sent Ellen hurtling away into the far reaches of her dementia? Her last days would be nothing more than hours of emptiness for those who loved and cared for her. Finn couldn't do that to another human being.

He pulled his SUV to a halt at the end of the driveway

and pulled himself together. He probably shouldn't have accepted Tamsyn's invitation tonight. He doubted he'd be good company, but when he'd heard her voice mail issuing the offer, he knew he couldn't deny himself the respite of her company.

Finn grabbed the wine carrier, with its two chilled bottles of wine nestled inside in one hand, and the bunch of tulips he'd bought at the florist's after getting Tamsyn's call in the other. The soft pink long-stemmed blooms reminded him of her—their exquisite smooth petals a perfect shield for their additional beauty when they opened to the sun. She was just like that. Guarded smooth walls of perfection on show to the rest of the world, and yet when she was given warmth and affection she flourished.

He nudged the car door shut with his hip and covered the distance to the house in long strides. Now he was here, he was eager to see her again. She opened the door before he could juggle his items and knock.

The sight of her knocked the breath clean out of his lungs. She had her hair up in some twisted knot on top of her head, exposing the slender arch of her neck and making her look divinely feminine and impossibly fragile at the same time. Every male hormone in his body rose to the occasion, making him ache to be her knight—to be that one man to protect her from all wrongdoing, from all sorrow. He swallowed hard. No woman had ever made him feel this way, so desperate to be her valiant defender. The sensation was primal and dark, yet uplifting and filled with warmth at the same time.

"Good evening, are those for me?" she asked, reaching for the tulips that he'd forgotten the instant he'd laid eyes on her.

"Yeah, I hope you like them."

"I love them, thank you so much. Come inside."

She stepped aside to let him in and as he walked past her

he caught a whiff of her fragrance. Subtle, like her, like the way she'd inveigled her way into his psyche, the blend of sweetness and spice wound around him in a sensual spell of promise.

"I'll pop these in some water right away. Can I take the wine through to the kitchen for you?"

"It's okay, I'll do that," he said, still feeling a little awe-struck.

She'd done something with her makeup that made her dark eyes look huge and warm, and the fresh pink lipstick she wore made him itch to lean forward and kiss it all off. And there was something different about her tonight—a soft confidence that radiated from her. It was there in the smile in her eyes and in the way she walked. He liked it, he decided. He liked it very much.

In the kitchen Finn automatically reached for the cham-pagne flutes on the hutch dresser and extracted a bottle of a locally made sparkling wine. The second bottle, a sauvi-gnon blanc, he put into the refrigerator.

"Are we celebrating?" Tamsyn asked, noting the label on the bottle. "Oh, I've always wanted to try that."

"It's very good. It's been made here in Marlborough since the late 1980s. They blend seventy percent pinot noir with thirty percent chardonnay. Here," he said, passing her a glass filled with the rapidly bubbling straw-colored liquid. "Try it."

"I can't do that without a toast," she said with a secretive smile. She raised her glass toward his. "To new friends."

He liked that, although right now his feelings toward Tamsyn Masters went way beyond friendly. He clinked glasses. "Indeed, to new friends."

Their eyes remained locked together as they sipped their wine. He'd never be able to drink it again without thinking of this moment—of her.

"Mmm, that is lovely," she said, flicking her tongue over

her lower lip as she set her glass down on the countertop and picked up the vase of flowers. "Can you bring my wine while I take these to the sitting room?"

Finn reached for the glass, and followed her through. She was as enticing from the rear as she'd been face on. The sway of her hips as she walked made the fabric of her skirt swing gently from side to side, caressing her thighs and the backs of her calves. He'd never been envious of a skirt before. It was a new and distinctly unfamiliar sensation.

He could not, in all honesty, say that his growing feelings for Tamsyn were normal. Not in his experience, anyway. These feelings were consuming. Invading his concentration and disturbing his usually short but fully restful sleep at night.

"Crudité?"

He looked up as Tamsyn passed him a small platter decorated with vegetable sticks and one of those dips females seemed to like so much.

"Sure," he said, helping himself to both.

It was tasty, the garlic and lemon tang in the hummus leaving a fresh aftertaste in his mouth. Maybe there was something to the dip after all.

"How was your trip away?" she asked, settling herself on the sofa and slipping her feet out of her ballet slippers to tuck them up beside her.

He took the chair opposite, not trusting himself to sit closer.

"Ah, yeah, Wellington. It's a beautiful city."

"And your business? It went well?" she continued.

"It did."

"But something's still bothering you, isn't it? You looked...I dunno, worried, when you arrived. Is everything okay?"

Damn, did it show that much? He decided sticking close

to the truth was better than fabricating a whole bunch of lies that he might struggle to remember.

"I spent some time visiting a good friend in the hospital. It was hard to see them so unwell."

"I'm really sorry to hear that," Tamsyn said softly, her voice filled with genuine sympathy.

"Thanks."

Finn took a long drink of his sparkling wine. It served as a good way to stop himself from giving her any more details about exactly who he'd been seeing. As if sensing he didn't want to talk about it further, Tamsyn shifted the conversation to what she'd been doing the past couple of days while he'd been gone. He felt a tug of relief when he heard she had gotten no further in her search for Ellen, but that tug was tempered with a powerful sense of guilt over her very evident disappointment.

She worked her way past it though and the conversation soon shifted to books they'd recently read. She had a very sharp wit and they enjoyed many of the same authors. By the time she served cheese and crackers and fruit back in the sitting room after dinner, Finn was feeling very relaxed. Due in part to the glasses of wine they'd shared, but mostly due to her company. He'd enjoyed entertaining her at his house a couple of nights ago, but he loved watching her in this environment too. She was more in control here, adapting this place to her own patch. Now, as they sat side by side on the sofa, he was looking forward to seeing more.

"You never mentioned you were such a great cook," Finn said, slicing a sliver of ripe Brie and placing it on a lightly flavored rice cracker.

"That was the sum total of my expertise. Ooh, could you pass me one of those, please?" she said with a cheeky smile, and leaned forward to accept it from him as he changed its trajectory from his lips to hers.

Her teeth bit into the cracker, her lips brushing the tips of his fingers just as he started to pull away. The butterfly-soft sensation of her skin on his set up a chain reaction through his body and he suddenly found himself craving the feel of her lips everywhere.

"More?" he asked, his eyes fixed on her face as she clearly relished the morsel he'd fed her.

"Yes, please," she answered. "More."

A tremor rippled through him. He hoped she meant what he was thinking she meant. He went through the motions again, spreading some of the ripe cheese on a cracker and taking it to her mouth. This time she lightly grasped his wrist, held his hand in front of her parted lips. When she took the cracker she lingered over the action. Her lips, this time, deliberately grazing his thumb and forefinger.

Finn's body went from semi-aroused and languidly comfortable, to rock hard and aching in a nanosecond. A crumb from the cracker fell to the top of the curve of her breast. All night he'd been treated to the enticing shadow of her décolletage, but now he had fair reason to explore further. Without wasting a moment, he bent his head and licked up the crumb. Beneath his mouth her skin contracted and a flush of color spread across its surface.

She tasted like more. Like sunshine and heat and warmth and woman. He was starving—for her. He traced his tongue on her skin again, heard her moan, felt her drop her head onto the back of the sofa, exposing the tantalizing line of her throat. He welcomed the invitation and nuzzled the point where her shoulder curved up to the side of her neck and pressed his mouth into the hollow just above her collarbone.

Her gasp of pleasure urged him on and he continued his journey up, to the fine contour of her jaw, to the corner of her lush lips. Then, finally, to capture those lips with his once more. She was no quiescent participant this time around, instead she was heat and fire all focused on that point where their bodies fused and melded.

It wasn't enough, it could never be enough. Finn raised shaking hands to her waist and began to tug at her top even as he felt her fingers working his shirt buttons. He yanked the stretchy material up, exposing the soft curves of her belly—the striations of her rib cage, the swell of the underside of her breasts fettered inside flimsy lace—to his ravening touch. Still, he wanted more.

Fourteen

Tamsyn squirmed against him, frustrated by the barriers of their clothes. She wanted to feel—him, everything—like she'd never felt before. Her fingers fumbled on his buttons and impatiently she tugged even harder, barely noticing as she ripped the remaining fastenings from the cotton of his shirt.

Finally, she could do what she'd wanted to for what felt like so long. Her hand spread upon his heated skin, sweeping across his chest, her fingers lingering to gently pinch his nipples into even tighter nubs. In answer to her actions, she felt his teeth at her neck—a gentle-enough nip, but one that made every internal muscle in her body clench on a white-hot wave of sensation. She felt as if she could melt right here on the spot.

Her singlet was bunched at the top of her breasts and she lifted herself forward, holding on to his torso as he pulled the garment up and over her head.

"God, you're so beautiful," he groaned against her skin, his mouth hot and wet against her.

She shifted, offering herself toward him in aching invitation. Finn continued to torment her, his tongue lightly tracing the contours of the lace of her bra. Why, oh why, had she worn one? The rasp of his teeth through the lace sent a jolt of electricity spiraling into her body. Her nipples pebbled into painfully taut beads, the texture of her bra near unbearable as she waited for his touch.

"There, oh please, there," she begged, threading her fingers through his short cropped hair and holding him to her. She felt his hand reach around behind her, felt the clasp of her bra fall undone and her flesh become exposed as he peeled the garment away. Hot breath tantalized, her heart now beating a frantic tattoo as she anticipated what came next. She wasn't disappointed. Closing over her peak, he drew her into his mouth, his tongue drawing her in deep, his teeth a gentle scrape against oversensitized skin.

Something pulled deep inside her, as if the two most sensitive parts of her body were joined by one glorious shimmering thread.

Finn shifted his attention to her other breast, eliciting the same penetrating response. She was panting, her mind fracturing as sensation after sensation poured through her body. He pulled away from her and she murmured in protest, her hands reaching for him.

"Let's take this to the bedroom," he said, his voice uneven.

He rose to his feet and offered her his hand to help her up. She was grateful to him for that as her legs felt like water, almost incapable of holding her up. As if he knew, he swept one arm behind her back, the other behind her knees, and lifted her into his arms. Instinctively she burrowed her face in his chest. Her lips caressing the smooth skin, her hands now clasped around his neck.

"Which one?" he asked, his breathing barely changing as he carried her.

"Second on the right," she whispered.

When they reached the door, he slid her to her feet, stabilizing her with his solid presence. She reached up, cupping his face between her hands and, going up on tiptoe, she kissed him—long and deep, leaving him in no doubt that she wanted every second of what was yet to come.

Outside it was growing dark and she pulled away to close the bedroom drapes. Even though there was no chance anyone could see them from the roadside, she wanted to close them in, to cocoon them in their own little world. He sat on the bed and toed off his loafers and shed his socks as she moved around, lighting the candles she'd placed throughout the room—just in case tonight would end this way.

"Come here," Finn said as he sat with his legs spread wide on the edge of the bed.

Tamsyn moved between them, resting her hands on his shoulders. He flicked one nipple lightly with the tip of his finger.

"A man could be forgiven for thinking he's being seduced," he said with a knowing smile.

"A man could," she agreed with a laugh, loving that even as her body wound tight as a drum, they could still find humor in their situation.

"Should I be asking what your intentions are?"

"Only if you're man enough to hear them," she teased, lifting her hands up to pull the pins from her hair, one by one, until it tumbled over her bare shoulder, tendrils teasing her breasts.

She reached behind her to unzip her skirt, let it drop in a cascade of color and softness and kicked it away from her feet. Finn's eyes roamed her body as she stood there, dressed only in a scrap of café au lait–colored lace and satin. The appreciation, the marvel on his face gave her a strength she'd never known she was capable of possessing.

Emboldened, Tamsyn skimmed her hands over her belly and up over her rib cage, until she cupped her breasts in both hands. His eyes darkened, his tongue swept out to moisten his lips and she saw a tremor rock through him as she squeezed her nipples between thumbs and forefingers. Moisture pooled, hot and slick, at the apex of her thighs—a steady throb building there as she tweaked and pulled, caught in the spotlight of his stare.

Finn's hands went to the belt of his jeans, making fast—if unsteady—work of the buckle.

"Too damn many clothes," he said through clenched teeth, his eyes never straying from her body.

In seconds he had unbuttoned his fly and shoved his jeans and boxers down over his hips. His erection sprang free, the rigid flesh jutting proudly from a nest of dark curls.

"Man enough for you?" he asked, a tiny smile playing around his lips.

She smiled in return, moving forward to straddle his thighs, her hands at his shoulders. She felt his length twitch against her.

"Oh, I think you'll do," she answered, shifting so she could reach one hand between them.

She wrapped her fingers around the thick, hot shaft and stroked him from base to tip, then shifted slightly so she could reach the small box she'd secreted under her pillow after remaking her bed today. "I think we need to move on to the next step."

"I think you're right and I see you're prepared."

She tapped herself on the chest with one finger. "Event manager, I'm always prepared."

He started to speak, but his words were lost on a hiss of air as she began to apply a condom, adroitly smoothing the thin sheath over his penis.

"I'm an event?" he asked, keeping things light even though his voice was strained.

"No," she corrected him, moving her hips so he was positioned at her entrance. "*We* are."

Banter ceased the instant she began to slide down, to accept him into her body. Tiny shocks zapped her as her muscles accommodated his size. She moaned in pleasure, unable to hold back as he filled her, stretched her, completed her. Finn's hands gripped her hips and he lifted her slowly, hesitating for what felt like an aeon before inching her down again.

She gripped his shoulders as they found their rhythm,

then increased in tempo, spiraling into a cacophony of sensation. Until they peaked together in a penetrating awareness of pleasure that swamped them in forceful waves.

Finn fell back onto the bed, pulling her on top of him. Beneath her cheek she could feel his heart hammering in his chest, feel the answering thud of her own. One of his hands traced up and down her spine, while the other held her firmly to him, anchored at the hip as if he couldn't bear to let her go. She could still feel his pulse inside her, felt the answering squeeze of her own.

"As events go, I'd say that was a resounding success," he said against the top of her head.

She chuckled, filled with a sensation of well-being. She'd never had a relationship like this, one where you could banter and have mind-blowing sex at the same time.

"I'd have to agree," she said, lifting her head and nipping at his chin.

He rolled to the side, finally allowing their bodies to disengage. "Let me get rid of this, I'll be right back."

She watched his taut buttocks and long legs appreciatively as he stepped across the hall to the bathroom and stretched languorously across the bed. She ought to move, to pull the covers down and make the bed comfortable for them both. Unless, now that they'd made love, he planned to leave?

Insecurity flooded her, making her dash across the room to where she'd slung a robe over an easy chair. She shrugged herself into it and knotted the sash, like a barrier across her body.

"What's wrong?" Finn asked as he reentered the room.

"Nothing," she insisted.

He walked straight up to her and gathered her in his arms. "You having regrets?"

"None," she answered as firmly as she could, but even so, she couldn't meet his eyes. "You?"

She tensed, waiting for his reply.

"Same, so why the frown?"

He traced twin lines between her eyebrows with his forefinger and she forced herself to relax the muscles.

"I—I guess I just don't know what happens next. It's been a while since I…since…" She shook her head in frustration, struggling to find the words she needed to say.

"Since you've been in a new relationship?"

She sagged against him. Was that what this was to him? A relationship? A tiny light of hope flared in her chest. Logically she knew it was far too soon for her to even think about embarking on a new relationship with someone. It had been a week—just one week—since she'd walked in on Trent and Zac. A week since she'd given Trent back his ring and walked away from her old life.

But why shouldn't she grasp this, whatever it was, with Finn while she could? Grasp it and hold it tight, and ride it for what it was worth. It went against her nature, went against every instinct that told her to play it safe…but last time her "safe" choice of boyfriend hadn't been enough to keep her from getting hurt. What did she have to lose by taking the risk?

"Yes," she replied. "And it's not that long since my last one."

"I figured as much. Do you want me to leave?"

"Not at all!" The vehement response was out of her mouth before she could censor it.

Finn laughed. "It's okay if I stay then?"

"Do you want to stay?" There was still that kernel of doubt niggling at the back of her thoughts.

"I do. Very much."

His big warm hands slid up her back and to the back of her head, his fingers sending tingles through her scalp and releasing the tension she had there. When he bent to kiss her it was gentle, reassuring. Not the crazy heady kiss they'd shared earlier, but one that started a mellow simmer that radiated from her core. Between them she could feel his arousal stirring, felt an answering response in her.

She slid her hands around his waist, relishing the taut muscles that played beneath her fingers, relishing the fact he was here, for her and her alone. This was right, for now at least, and, reminding herself of her earlier vow, she meant to make the most of it.

This time their coming together was slow and languid. Each touch a measured stroke, each kiss lingered. When he slid inside her she was hit with that feeling of rightness, and when his long strokes drew them both to climax she tumbled over the precipice knowing she was safe and secure in his arms.

Knowing she could trust him.

Fifteen

Finn lay awake in the predawn hours, Tamsyn sprawled across his chest, her leg across his hips. He'd never been a snuggler, but somehow this felt right. So right he hadn't wanted to lose a moment of it in sleep.

She was so vulnerable, so innocent in all this. He felt like the lowest of the low deceiving her—deliberately holding her back from what she sought. She would never forgive him when she found out, and he didn't doubt that one day she would. The district was too close-knit for Ellen's whereabouts to remain a secret forever.

But for now he had her in his arms, and maybe, just maybe, now that they'd crossed this bridge into intimacy together, he'd be able to keep a closer eye on her—find a way to keep the secret and still protect her for a bit longer.

His fingers curled around her as he thought about the truths she'd shared in the dark, about how she'd happened upon her fiancé and his lover, a man who was *her* PA no less, in bed together. How she'd been betrayed by the two men she'd had every right to trust and expect loyalty from. It made his blood curdle when he heard that her ex had brushed off his affair, still expecting her to carry on as if nothing had happened, as if she deserved no better than to be second best in their life together.

It must have been made even harder for her with the timing—finding out about her fiancé so shortly after discovering the truth behind her father's lie that her mother had died. She had come here to get away from the lies, and the expectations, and the falseness that seemed to fill every aspect of her life. She'd come to find her mother and learn the truth…and instead, she'd found him—master betrayer of them all.

His gut clenched painfully at the thought of the hurt he would inflict on her, of the guilt he carried with him. Another mantle to bear, he realized with a deep breath that filled his senses with her special scent. She stirred in his arms, a small cry erupting from her mouth as she startled awake.

"Finn?" she mumbled, sounding disoriented.

"You okay?"

"I had a bad dream. I couldn't find you."

"I'm right here," he assured her, tightening his arms around her again. "Go back to sleep. I've got you."

For now, he thought as he felt her body relax against his again. But for how much longer?

Tamsyn woke feeling extraordinarily refreshed. She couldn't quite wipe the smile off her face. She'd woken after nine, and couldn't remember the last time she'd ever slept so late. Mind you, she couldn't remember the last time she'd spent half the night making love, either. She stretched against the sheets, wondering what Finn was up to.

The scent of a rosebud perfumed the air and she turned her head toward the source. As she did so, a whisper of paper on the pillow beside her caught her attention. She lifted first the rose, then the sheet of paper, that happy smile widening as she read its contents.

Finn apologized for not being there when she woke and said that business had called him away for the day. He'd be back late that night but hoped to see her again on Sunday. While Tamsyn knew she'd miss him, at least she knew she'd be seeing him again soon. She held the rose to her face, deeply inhaling the heady fragrance, touched that he'd thought to pick it for her and leave it with his note.

Her insecurities of the night before had faded into nothing. She'd never thought she'd ever share with another person, outside her family, what had happened with Trent, but confiding in Finn during the night had been cathartic. He'd listened without judgment and, afterward, he'd made love to her again as if she was the most precious creature on the planet, wiping away any lingering doubts about her attractiveness or femininity.

He was a skilled lover and had driven her body to heights she'd never experienced before. Heights she was looking forward to experiencing again. Hopefully, tomorrow.

Over the next few days they fell into a pattern of sharing meals, and nights, together. For the first time since she'd discovered her mother still lived, Tamsyn's need to find her softened. Oh, she still knew she wanted to track her mother down, but the urgency had faded, and exploring Finn's likes and dislikes held more immediate appeal.

Maybe she was in avoidance mode, as it had occurred to her that she might not like what she discovered. Her mother had chosen not to be part of Tamsyn's life years before. Did she really want to risk the pain of an in-person rejection when she could, instead, focus her time and attention on a man who made her feel so cherished? Being part of a twosome with Finn Gallagher had brought her more happiness in the past week than she'd known in a long time and she reveled in it. Plus, this week at the hall with her community group had gone exceptionally well. Every day, she felt more comfortable and at home in this town.

All in all, life was sweet, she thought as she prepared a meal for one the following Friday night. Finn was away again. He'd been distracted the past couple of days and she had the distinct impression that something was worrying him, but when she'd pressed him, he'd said he was fine.

The wind had come up today and thick black clouds, heavy with rain, banked up in the sky. It looked like it could be a rough night. Tamsyn didn't mind a storm, it was always good for blowing away the cobwebs, but this would be the first time she'd weathered one on her own.

"Prrrp!" Okay, so not completely on her own, she smiled to herself, bending down to stroke Lucy, who wound around and around her legs.

"It's just you and me tonight, Luce," she said before straightening and looking outside.

She'd have to try to round up the chickens into their coop if the weather kept deteriorating. She didn't look forward to the experience but figured with some chicken feed she should be able to tempt them into safety.

After her meal, she did just that, finally settling the last of the birds just as the first big fat drop of rain hurtled from the sky and hit her smack in the forehead. As if it had given carte blanche to the clouds to simply open up, the drops increased until the rain was bucketing down. Tamsyn raced to the house, struggling as the back door was almost torn from her grip by a particularly vicious gust of wind.

She got inside and slammed the door closed. Locking it behind her for good measure. It had only taken seconds but she was drenched to the skin. A long soak in a warm bath with a good book was just what she needed. Lucy curled up on the bath mat beside her as she lit the last candle in the bathroom, shed her wet and now-cold clothing and tested the temperature of the water.

"Perfect." She sighed as she sank into the enveloping warmth and reached for the glass of chardonnay she'd poured to enjoy with her book.

The lights overhead flickered, then brightened.

"Uh-oh," she said to the cat, who appeared unperturbed by the glitch in the electricity. "That doesn't look promising."

The words were no sooner out of her mouth than another massive gust of wind hit the house, causing the lights to flicker again before going out, this time completely. Tamsyn sat upright in the water and waited for them to come back on, but she waited in vain. Deciding she could do nothing about it for now, she dropped her book on the floor next to the bath and sank back in the water. At least she had light, thanks to the candles she'd lit earlier. As for the blackout, well, it would be a good excuse to have an early night.

Her sleep was fractured, punctuated by the crash and boom of thunder as the storm built through the night. Even ducking under the covers and pulling them up over her head did little to block the noise. The time gap between flashes of lightning and the explosive rumbles that followed got shorter and shorter until they seemed to land one on top of the other.

What a night for Finn to pick to be away, Tamsyn thought as she fought the rising fear that clawed at her throat. Even Lucy had deserted the top of the bed and was, Tamsyn suspected, cowering under it instead. She wished there was room enough under there to join her.

Bang! Cr-a-ck! Tamsyn jumped out of her skin. That was too close for comfort, the report sounding as if it was right on top of the house. Should she find a coat and check for damage? Another flash of lightning, followed a few seconds later by an almighty clap of thunder, warned her of the stupidity of that idea. She burrowed back under the covers, pulling her pillow over her ears for good measure. Tomorrow would be soon enough.

Morning dawned, as it so often does after a storm, with a fresh new promise of a beautiful day. Thankfully, at some time during the early hours, the power had been restored. Tamsyn was bleary eyed as she drank her morning coffee and waited for the caffeine to hit her bloodstream. Once she'd finished, she'd borrow a pair of rubber boots from the laundry and inspect outside. Even here from the kitchen window she could see there was some damage from the storm. Plant debris scattered through the vegetable garden and she could see she'd have to tie up the tomatoes again.

Coffee finished, she found the boots and clumped outside. The back of the house didn't look too bad, she thought, gathering up the detritus of leaves and small branches into a wheelbarrow from the implements shed as she went. It wasn't until she was close to the front that she saw the shattered window with a broken tree branch resting half in and half out of the room.

A Venetian blind swung drunkenly in the morning breeze, attached at only one end and, from the looks of it, bent and damaged beyond repair. This had to be the locked room, she thought as she moved closer. The owners wouldn't be happy about this. She'd have to call the property manager and see if they could get someone out to repair the window and contact the owners about replacing the blind. In the meantime, she'd see if she could find something to board the broken window up.

Before she went back to the shed to see if they had any plywood and nails stored there, she moved over to the house. Thankfully, the deep eaves on the property had kept most of the rain out. Broken glass littered the windowsill and, from what Tamsyn could see by jumping repeatedly, the floor of the room inside.

She started to turn for the shed, hoping to return with a stepladder and a saw in addition to plywood and nails. As she did so, the curtain billowed out of the window. She caught a glimpse of what looked to be a framed photo on the opposite wall. Tamsyn turned over the wheelbarrow and stood on it for a better look. The woman in the photo looked familiar....

In fact, she looked very much like the face that greeted Tamsyn in the mirror each morning.

A cold trickle started at the base of her neck and ran a rivulet down her spine. She had to get into that room to make sure she wasn't imagining things. Jumping down from the wheelbarrow, she jogged to the shed and spotted the ladder she needed hanging on the wall, together with a set of leather gardening gloves nearby that would protect her hands from the broken glass.

The rubber boots were going to be too clumsy to wear going up the ladder and through the window frame so, after lugging the ladder and a saw across the lawn to the house, she dashed inside and pulled on the runners she'd bought a couple of weeks ago. Once she was level with the window, she could see the room was stacked with boxes and the walls and the dresser top appeared to be the repository for every framed photo that had probably adorned the rest of the house before the owners went away.

Tamsyn worked determinedly at the branch with the saw until one end fell down into the garden. The other rested just inside the window frame and down onto the glass-strewn floor. Swiping away the broken glass from the sill with a gloved hand, Tamsyn pulled herself up and through the window, feeling like nothing more than a burglar. She told herself not to be so stupid. She was being a fastidious tenant, ensuring that the damage inside wasn't severe, that's all. Once inside, she pushed the drapes wide open, letting light flood into the room.

Ignoring the crunch of broken glass beneath her feet, she crossed the room and lifted the photo frame off the wall. It was like looking at a picture of herself in another five or ten years' time. That chill ran down her neck again as she studied the woman in the photo more closely, mentally comparing it to the wedding photo she'd found on the internet. She and Tamsyn were a lot alike, from the shape of their face to their figures. While the photo was somewhat faded, Tamsyn could make out the color of the woman's eyes. Dark liquid brown, just like her own, except rather than being fresh and bright, the woman's were sad and slightly unfocused.

In the photo, a man with light brown hair and a sun-weathered face stood beside the woman, just slightly taller and bearing a look of pride that beamed out to all and sundry that he was well satisfied with his world. She had no idea who he was…but she was increasingly certain that she knew the woman. There had to be more photos, maybe even some papers that might confirm who the woman was.

She turned and ripped open one of the boxes and found it filled with albums all neatly dated on the spines. She ran her hand over the dates, choosing one from about three years after her mother had left. Sliding down onto a clear space on the floor, Tamsyn began to turn the pages. With each one she became more and more certain that the couple pictured were her mother and Ellen's partner, who seemed very much in love with her.

There was more. Several pictures had a young girl in them, aged about two or three years old. Honey blonde but with the same dark brown eyes as her mother, she looked to be a happy child and always had a coloring pencil in one hand and paper in the other—either that or she was dressing a doll in all manner of garments.

Tamsyn turned another page and felt a wave of shock hit her fair smack in the stomach. She blinked away the black dots that began to swim before her eyes, closing them briefly—unable to believe what she saw before her. She took a steadying breath, then another, before opening her eyes again.

The picture swam before her and she blinked once more to clear her vision. Yes, it was still the same as before. The shock of it was fading, but the image's ramifications were no less devastating. There, right in front of her, stood the woman Tamsyn believed to be her mother, with the man and an older version of the little girl…and with a young boy aged about twelve. A young boy with brown hair and gray eyes.

A young boy who looked very much like Finn Gallagher.

Sixteen

Finn Gallagher knew her mother!

He'd lied to her all this time. Confusion warred with anger inside her until, with a bubbling rising fury, anger won. How dare he? He'd known she was looking for her mother and yet he'd never given the slightest indication he knew her mother at all. In fact, he'd deliberately and calculatedly told her Ellen didn't live there. Well, didn't live up on the hill at his house, maybe, but that was splitting hairs.

Tamsyn slammed the album shut and staggered to her feet, unsure of what to do next. The sound of a car coming up the driveway gave her her answer. It could only be one person.

She turned to the door and easily unlocked the deadlock from inside—it was, after all, designed to keep people out of the room, not in it. She left the door ajar as she strode down the hallway toward the front door. Finn stood there in all his God-given glory, fresh and handsome in a pale gray suit, white shirt and tie.

"I heard about the storm, are you all right? You look—"

She jabbed him in the chest with her forefinger, taking him completely by surprise. "You knew!" she shouted, unable to contain her anger a second longer. "You knew all along and you lied to me! Why?"

For a second he almost looked as if he was about to deny her accusation, but then a cold, calm expression settled over his face, his eyes turning arctic.

"I never lied to you."

"You did," she insisted, fighting back the burning sensation that began to sting her eyes. Be damned if she was going to cry in front of him. He didn't deserve her tears after the way he'd taken her trust, her fragile heart and stomped them under his feet as if she was nothing. "You deliberately withheld the truth from me when you could have told me from day one where I could find my mother. Worse, you let me *trust* you."

"Look, I told you that Ellen didn't live at my house. That's the truth."

"But you never thought to tell me that she lived here." Tamsyn uttered a bitter laugh. "Oh, I bet you had a good old chuckle about that when I took on the lease. What a freaking joke. Tamsyn Masters living in her mother's house and not even knowing it. I suppose the whole town has been having a roaring time at my expense. Tell me, does everyone know?"

His silence told her everything.

"How could you do that to me?" she asked brokenly, the anger suddenly leaving her in a rush, leaving behind an awful hollowness.

"How did you find out?"

"Is that all you can say?"

Tamsyn stood and waited for his response, but he simply continued to stare her down. The generous lover who'd left her bed yesterday morning was a far cry from the man standing before her now.

"The storm did some damage, broke a window in the room with the locked door. I was trying to clear it up a bit from outside when I saw a picture on the wall."

"Show me."

She turned and went back up the hall, standing outside the now-open door and gesturing inside. Finn stood next to her as he surveyed the damage, the twisted blinds, the remnant of tree branch still dangling from the window frame.

"You broke into the boxes? Into their personal effects?" he asked.

"Wouldn't you?" Tamsyn defended herself and pushed past him to pick up the album that had held the damning evidence that showed his complicity. "Who is this?" she demanded, stabbing at a photo of the blonde girl.

"That's Alexis."

The name was familiar. Yes, the designer. "Alexis Fabrini?"

"She's your half sister."

Tamsyn wobbled on her feet, her legs suddenly as weak as if she'd emptied a flagon of wine straight down her throat. It was only the solid presence of the doorjamb that kept her upright. She had a sister? She looked at the photo again, this time noticing the similarities between them, the things they'd both inherited from Ellen.

"Is there anything else you're not telling me?" Her voice was weak, thready with shock. She let out a bitter laugh. "Why am I even bothering to ask? I've got no reason to believe anything you tell me anymore—or ever again."

Finn tried to ignore the clawing pain in his chest. He had known this would come to pass, that he'd hurt Tamsyn immeasurably. He'd just hoped to stave it off for longer, for Ellen's health to rally and for Lorenzo to perhaps agree to let Tamsyn visit her mother in the hospital. Then he could have told her the truth himself—broken it to her gently. He'd never wanted her to find out like this.

"Look," he said, shoving a hand through his hair, "Ellen is a much loved member of this community. If people didn't talk about her it's because they wanted the best for her— to protect her."

Pain streaked across Tamsyn's face, leaving it even paler and more drawn than it had been seconds ago.

"Protect her from me? Her own daughter? Why, Finn? Why wouldn't I be considered to be the best for my mother?"

His arms ached to reach out and comfort her. Finn closed

his eyes and wished fiercely that he could turn back time, could avoid the trip that had taken him away from Tamsyn and left her alone when she was exposed to the truth.

"I guess most people feel that you took your time trying to find her." The words sounded lame, even to his ears.

"But you know I only found out this year that she was even still alive. She walked away from us, Finn. She left her two children in the hospital—injured in an accident she caused—and never looked back. Abandoned us, for what? So she could be with her lover?" Tamsyn stabbed her finger now at a picture of Lorenzo. "I didn't know where she was, Finn, you know that and I know that. Ellen, however, knew exactly where Ethan and I were and she never tried to contact us. I want to know why. Don't I deserve to know why she left us and why she never came back? Why was she happy to be dead to us?"

Finn put out a hand to touch her but she flinched away from him. It cut him to his core to know he'd irreparably damaged the relationship they'd begun to develop. Damaged? Hell, he'd destroyed it, crushed it like a bug, pure and simple. He'd done it for Lorenzo, for Ellen—people he'd do anything for. But, God, how he wished he'd never had to do this.

"I can't tell you that, but I'll do what I can to see you find out."

She looked at him from eyes bruised with disappointment and grief. "That's it? That's all you're going to do? You're not going to tell me where she is?"

"I can't promise any more than that, Tamsyn. I'm sorry, but they're not my secrets to tell."

"So, at least you admit that you've been keeping secrets from me."

"I have, and I regret it. If I could—ah, what's the point?" He cursed under his breath. "I'll do what I can, and I'll get someone on to that window, too."

He turned and walked down the hall, painfully aware of her gaze drilling steadily into his back as he left.

Tamsyn watched him go—a stranger to her now. She'd thought Trent's betrayal had cut her deep, but this was something else. She stalked down the hall and slammed the front door shut, then slid down the wall into a heap on the floor. Shock and anger had rendered her numb for the time being, but even through the numbness she could feel waves of pain building.

She daren't open her mouth for fear of the scream she knew would come out. Instead, she clenched her teeth, wrapped her arms around her body and rocked in silent agony.

Her mother left her. Check. Her mother didn't try to stay in touch. Check. She'd been let down by her mother. Check. She'd been lied to and let down by—oh, let's see—her father, her extended family, her ex-fiancé, her personal assistant, Finn. Check, check, check, check and double check.

At the last she began to feel her tentative control break. What did it matter to her that Finn had added his name to the illustrious list? It wasn't as if they'd known each other long or as if they'd promised undying love for one another. It wasn't as if she even *should* have thought she could trust him. Hadn't there been that tiny niggle in the back of her mind for some time that he was hiding something?

Instead of listening to her instincts, she'd allowed him to play her for a fool. She'd been so pathetically desperate to be spontaneous, to be carefree, to be happy that she'd let herself be blinded to the truth. A man like Finn, he was no better than the rest. Worse, even, for having used her pathetic need for acceptance against her like that. For having inveigled his way into her day-to-day existence so that she'd come to rely upon him, need him. Love him.

No! Not that, never that. Tamsyn squashed down so hard

on the thought that her head began to throb with pain. It had been attraction. Pure and physical. Okay, very physical, she amended as she burrowed her face into her hands. She didn't love Finn, she couldn't. Her senses had been seduced by his attention, that was all it was. She'd have to have been both blind and stupid not to find his attentiveness appealing. It had been a salve to her wounded pride like nothing else could be. And look where that had left her, she thought bitterly.

Tamsyn pushed off the wall and went to the door to the previously locked room. She ought to pick up the broken glass, set the boxes back to rights, but she couldn't summon the care or the interest required to do so. Instead, she went back to her bedroom, kicked off her shoes and pulled the covers up over her. She felt as if she'd been hit by a freight train—physically and mentally. She craved oblivion, even if only for a couple of hours. Then she'd be able to cope, to figure out what she had to do next, because right now it all seemed far too hard.

The sun was low in the sky when the constant chirp of her mobile phone woke her. Tamsyn groggily reached out to the bedside table for the device.

"Hello?"

"Ms. Masters? It's Jill from the letting agency."

"Ah, yes, about the damage—"

"I've talked with the property owner, Mr. Fabrini, today and he's asked that you move out."

Move out? While a pane of glass was being replaced?

"I beg your pardon? That seems extreme." Tamsyn forced her sluggish brain to function. "It's only a pane of glass that needs to be replaced. Surely I can remain while that's done?"

"I don't think you understand me, Ms. Masters. Mr. Fabrini has requested you vacate the property permanently."

The words slowly sank in. "What? Vacate the property? But the lease—"

"Is a week-by-week agreement that can be terminated at any time by any party without notice. You will be refunded for any overpayment."

"Yes, yes, I'm aware of that." Tamsyn had thought the rental conditions to be very unusual at the time, but they'd suited her so she hadn't questioned it. Of course, she'd assumed she'd have at least a week's notice of the owners' intention to return before being asked to vacate.

"Then you'll make other arrangements?"

"Of course. I don't suppose you have any other properties on the books at the moment that might be suitable?"

"I'm sorry, no. There's a festival in the area and all our casual rentals are completely booked out. Have been for some time."

"Oh, I see. Well, if you could just give me a few days until I find something—"

"Ms. Masters, I'm sorry. Obviously I didn't make my client's wishes clear. Mr. Fabrini wants you out of the cottage today."

Seventeen

"Today?"

"He was most insistent."

She just bet he was. What was it Finn had said before he left? That he'd do what he could? Well, it appeared he'd done it, all right. He'd obviously spoken with this Mr. Fabrini and her eviction was the result. Anger slowly began to replace the hollow pain that had consumed her this morning.

"Fine, I'll be a couple of hours."

"That will have to do, I suppose."

Too damn right it would, Tamsyn thought, severing the connection without saying goodbye. She pushed up off the bed and methodically stripped the sheets, taking them through to the laundry and throwing them in the machine together with the towels from the bathroom. She had half a mind to leave them in there, wet, but her own standards wouldn't let her slide that low no matter how badly she was being treated. Or by whom.

Methodically she went through the motions of setting the house back to exactly how she'd found it—pushing the vacuum cleaner through, remaking the bed, laying fresh towels in the bathroom and clearing the perishables from the fridge. By the time she'd finished, and her case was packed, she felt completely empty inside. Not surprising, she realized, as she'd eaten nothing all day. Still, the thought of food was the furthest thing from her mind. More pressing was the need to find somewhere to stay tonight. And the next. Mr. Fabrini probably wanted her to leave New Zealand, too, but that wasn't happening. Not today. Not until she found her mother—no matter who stood in her way.

After feeding Lucy, and shooing her outside and locking up the house, she drove into town to leave the key with the letting agency. Then she stopped in a local café. Christmas decorations hung in a jaunty display of festivity in the window, and the sound of carols greeted her as she went inside. Feeling more like a modern-day Scrooge than anything approaching Christmas cheer, she ordered coffee and a slice of quiche to eat while she searched on her smartphone for local accommodations.

Starting with Penny's place, she began calling around. Half an hour later she was no nearer to finding a roof to put over her head. Everything in town, and beyond—even the local motor camp—was booked solid. At this rate she'd be sleeping in her car.

At least the rental car company hadn't canceled her contract on that, she thought cynically, using her fork to push the now-cold quiche around her plate. She knew she should eat, but her appetite had deserted her.

"There you are. I've been looking for you."

Finn towered over her table, forcing her to crick her neck to look up at him.

"What, not finished lying to me yet?" she replied, determined not to show any sign of weakness to this man who'd proven as two-faced as all the rest of them.

"I heard what Lorenzo did. I want you to know I didn't have anything to do with that."

"You really expect me to believe you? Goodness, and when you've been so honest and forthcoming with me already." The sarcasm fairly dripped from her tongue. "You'll have to excuse me. I've had my full quota of unpleasantness today."

She picked up her bag, grabbed her car keys and rose to her feet, determined to head back out to her car and put a decent amount of distance between her and Finn. She'd no sooner gotten out of her chair when a wave of dizziness hit her, sending her straight back down again. She rested her head in one hand, her elbow on the table, as she waited for the world to right itself again. Finn's hand descended on her shoulder.

"Are you all right?"

She gave a strangled laugh. "Of course, I'm fine. I have a mother who is determined to hide from me, a friend who betrayed my trust, a landlord who's evicted me and a dearth of places to stay tonight. Things couldn't be better, thank you."

"Come with me. Stay at my house."

She lifted her head and stared at him incredulously. "You have to be kidding me, right?"

His eyes bored straight back into her. "Why not? I have plenty of room. I won't touch you, if that's what you're worried about."

Of course she wasn't worried about that. There was no way she was letting Finn Gallagher touch her ever again.

"I'd rather sleep in my car."

She got up to leave again, but that same dizziness sent her reeling, making her drop her keys. Finn's hand shot out to steady her.

"You're in no condition to drive anywhere. What were you thinking of doing? Settling down for the night here on the main street?"

She shot him a malignant glare. "If I must."

"Not happening. You're coming with me. We can pick your car up tomorrow."

He swiped her keys from where they'd fallen on the table and called out to the man behind the café counter. "Hey, Bill, could you park the blue hatchback around the back for me for tonight? We'll be back tomorrow for it."

"Sure, Finn, no problem."

Finn tossed the keys to Bill then wrapped his arm around the back of Tamsyn's shoulders and pulled her into his side. She resisted for as long as she could, but then found herself sagging into him. The rough stormy night combined with the morning's revelations and the eviction had completely done her in. For now, it was easier to simply let him take charge. Tomorrow, however, would be another story altogether.

Tamsyn woke the next morning to the sound of someone coming into her room. She jolted upright in bed, clutching the covers to her.

"What do you want?" she demanded as Finn settled a cloth-covered tray on the bed beside her.

"I thought you might like breakfast." He whipped the cloth off the tray. "And we need to talk."

"Unless you're going to tell me where my mother is, I have nothing to say to you," she said.

Her mouth watered as she looked at the freshly buttered toast and preserves he'd laid out on the tray, and her nostrils twitched at the enticing coffee-scented aroma borne on gentle wafts of steam coming from a white porcelain mug.

"Then maybe you can listen." He sat down on the bed and repositioned the tray across her thighs. "Eat," he commanded.

Figuring that if her mouth was full she wouldn't have to talk to him, Tamsyn spread some orange marmalade on a slice of toast.

"I talked to Lorenzo last night."

"That was good of you," she conceded mockingly around a mouthful of toast. "And what did the illustrious Mr. Fabrini have to say? Did he rescind his eviction order?"

Finn's mouth twisted. "No, he was adamant he didn't want you staying at the house any longer."

"Tell me, what did I ever do to him to make him hate me so much?"

"It's not you, it's—look, I can't say. I gave my word I

wouldn't tell you and I'm honor-bound to hold to that. I owe Lorenzo a lot."

"I see," she said before taking a sip of her coffee. "And your honor doesn't extend to telling me anything that he doesn't want me to know—which means anything about him or my mother, is that right?"

"I'm sorry."

"That's it? You really expect me to accept that as an apology?"

Finn sighed. "No, I don't. But I can't give you what you want so, it will have to do." He stood up and started walking to the door, hesitating in the entrance a moment. "You're welcome to stay here for as long as you need to. I'll try again with Lorenzo. He's pretty angry right now."

"Well, that makes two of us."

"You'll stay?"

"I don't have much choice, do I?"

He inclined his head in acknowledgment. "I'll be in my office. If you need me, go downstairs, to the end of the gallery then turn right."

He was gone before she could think of an appropriate rejoinder.

After she'd finished eating, Tamsyn got up and showered and dressed—grudgingly grateful that Finn had removed her suitcase from her car and brought it with them when they'd returned to his home. She needed armor, and that meant feeling good in what she was wearing, so she chose the gypsy skirt and blue tank top again. Before slipping on the skirt, she studied the label. Alexis Fabrini was embroidered in silver cursive script on a dark purple satin background.

She thumbed the silky material. Her sister—her half sister to be more precise. Was it strange that her sister's talent had appealed to her so much or was it simply a connection they'd shared without knowing? Either way, it was strange to discover that out there, somewhere, was another sibling. Another connection, forged in blood. Another secret exposed. She'd have to tell Ethan, eventually, but right now that was low on her priorities.

How many more secrets would she have to uncover before she could find her mother? She had absolutely no idea and the prospect was more daunting than it had seemed a few weeks ago.

She'd always lived her life with purpose, careful and measured. Each step meticulously planned, each outcome virtually assured. Until she'd tried to surprise Trent, until she'd decided to find her mother and turned her back on every security she'd ever known and trusted. And look where those decisions had led her. Straight down the barrel of heartbreak and disappointment. One thing she knew for sure—unexpected and spontaneous decisions weren't for her. Not anymore. Not ever again.

From now on, she vowed, she'd go back to her old ways. To being careful, considered and safe. She should have taken Ethan up on his suggestion to use an investigator to do the hard work first instead of racing off with no obvious plan other than to just show up. She hadn't been thinking clearly, not since she'd been told that her mother still lived. But now everything was crystal clear. Her mother didn't want to see her. And Tamsyn wasn't going to go back to Australia until she did. Once she'd cleared away all the lies, all the secrets, all the evasions…then and only then would she go home.

She finished dressing, collected the tray from the bed and took it through to the kitchen. Still slightly hungry, she grabbed an apple from the fruit bowl and went to find Finn. She wanted her car and she needed him to help her go and pick it up. She hoped the café was open on a Sunday because she'd be annoyed if she had to wait, at Finn's and the café owner's convenience, a day more than necessary for her link to independence.

The interior gallery shared a stone wall with a court-yard outside. Even so, long windows shed ample light to showcase the works Finn had spread along the wall. Local scenes mostly, by the look of them, although one in particular made her breath catch in her throat. Painted from the bottom of a valley, with its outlook stretching up a hill, it featured a looming ruin—a dark brooding stain on a clear blue sky. She knew that ruin, had viewed it virtually every single day in living memory.

Masters Rise, the original home of her family, destroyed by bushfires. Too expensive to rebuild and refurbish, the ruin remained on the ridge of the hills overlooking The Masters, her family's vineyard estate and business, a con-stant reminder of how far they'd fallen and how far they'd come to fight back to where the family flourished today.

But what was the painting doing here? She peered at the artist's signature, surprised to see the letters E and F inter-twined in the corner. Ellen…Fabrini? No wonder she hadn't been able to find her if she'd changed her name.

This was her mother's work? Tamsyn studied the picture again, in particular how her mother had captured the old ruin. It looked menacing, forbidding even. Was that how it had felt to Ellen living there at the base of the hill? As if she was being watched and perhaps found wanting?

Tamsyn could only speculate. Without access to her mother, she certainly wasn't going to hear it from Ellen's point of view, was she? Maybe she was imbuing too much into Ellen's interpretation of her home, there on the wall. Yet she couldn't keep from feeling that the painting was help-ing her understand a little better why her mother had cho-sen to leave. Tamsyn had known from an early age that the presence of the ruins was what motivated her father every day. He'd told her that it reminded him that he wouldn't be beaten by the elements, that he would prevail and ensure his family prevailed along with him.

Everything he'd done, every decision he'd made, had all been with the one purpose of ensuring the Masters family remained great. Granted, it had meant he was entirely driven, focused more on his work and its output than on his growing children. Had Ellen struggled with that? Was that why she'd sought a lover? Left her home, her family, her children?

Tamsyn groaned in frustration. The questions were simple, the answers probably equally so. But when would she have the chance to hear them, to judge for herself or, alternatively, to heal and forgive her mother for what had happened?

She turned away from the work on the wall, determined not to let it mess with her head a second longer.

Directly ahead of her was a door, and she opened it without thinking, surprised to find a very-well-set-up home gym inside. So, that explained Finn's impressive physique. A lick of heat started, but she quelled the sensation before it could take hold. He might be physical perfection, he might be the best lover she'd ever enjoyed sex with, but he was just another liar, she resolutely warned herself.

She left the room, closing the door behind her with a snap and turned down the hallway toward what she hoped was Finn's office. A door was open just ahead of her and she could hear Finn's voice. Her steps slowed as she made out what he was saying. She paused where she was, unashamedly eavesdropping and thankful that the soft soles of her ballet flats hadn't announced her coming. He sounded very worked up. Was he…could he be talking to her mother?

Eighteen

"Yes, of course she's staying with me. I couldn't very well let her sleep in a roadside layby, now, could I?"

He sounded frustrated. Tamsyn wished she could hear the words on the other end of the line.

"What were you thinking kicking her out of the cottage like that?" Another pause. "Yes, yes, I know she went into the room, but she was merely checking the damage, not outright snooping. Look, I really think you should talk to her yourself."

Tamsyn's stomach coiled into a knot and the bite of apple she'd taken as she walked down the hall stuck in her throat.

"Lorenzo, calm down. I know how you feel about the whole Masters family, but Tamsyn was just a little girl when it happened. She and her brother were told Ellen was dead. She only found out the truth this year, after her father died."

Her whole body tensed, poised for what she hoped would come next. Clearly, Lorenzo Fabrini was her mother's gate-keeper. If she could only get past him.

Finn's sigh echoed down the hall.

"Yeah, yeah, I know. You only want what's best for Ellen, and I agree it could be upsetting for her to see Tamsyn." Tamsyn's stomach sank. She should have expected it…but it still hurt to hear that no one, not even the man who'd been her lover just a few nights ago, was willing to put her feelings first.

"While you think about it," Finn continued, "hopefully Tamsyn will stay here. I've left it open to her to stay as long as she needs, but she's not my prisoner. It would have been easier for her to remain at the cottage and keep herself busy there… Okay, okay, enough already. Call me tonight."

A sharp expletive rent the air as Finn ended the call. Tamsyn rocked back on her heels and thought about what she'd just heard. She still didn't understand why everyone seemed to think it would be bad for her mother to see her. And she certainly didn't understand why it had been necessary to lie to her all along. But she had to admit, Finn had seemed truly interested in helping her, as much as Lorenzo would let him. She wasn't ready to trust him or even forgive him yet, but it did take the edge off her anger.

She waited a minute before continuing the short distance to his office. He wheeled around to face her as she gently knocked on the door and entered the room.

"Hi," she said awkwardly. "Any chance we can pick up my car this morning?"

"After lunchtime will be best, the café will be busy with a crowd after the morning church services in town."

She nodded, accepting that she could do nothing without his assistance. She ached to ask him about the phone call, but that would mean admitting she'd overheard part of his side of the conversation. Tamsyn very much doubted he'd be happy about that. She finished her apple, tossed the core into a small trash bin and then wandered over to the window. In front of it was a large table with a three-dimensional plan of a set of buildings next to a painted lake.

"You're into development?" she asked, studying the layout of the buildings carefully. They looked similar in design to Finn's house, making the most of the natural contours and features of the molded land.

"For this, yes."

He came and stood beside her. Even though he was a good few inches away, she was acutely aware of the heat of his body, of the answering heat of her own. On the pretext of examining the board from a different angle, she moved away.

"What will it be?"

"Well, if I ever get decent road access to the property, it will be a respite center for families with a loved one suffering from mental illness."

"Why a respite center?"

"Personal reasons." He swung away from the model and went back to his desk.

"More secrets or is this actually something you can tell me?" Tamsyn pressed. They had time to kill before going to collect her car—he may as well fill it for her since he'd put her in this position.

"I've seen from personal experience, the strain it puts on a family to care for another family member undergoing mental health treatment—it's especially tough on kids. I think it's important for them to have a safe place to go, to chill out, where the people around them really do understand what it's like. I'm hoping to build family chalets, as you can see. Each one would be private from the others but still near enough for a sense of community for people. Also, I'd like to see children's camps run there too—in those buildings on the other side of the complex. Have camp counselors, trained in dealing with the issues that arise for kids with parents or siblings under care, that sort of thing."

Tamsyn came and sat down opposite Finn's desk. "It's an ambitious project. What was that you said about needing road access?"

He pointed to a gray ribbon of road that came down from the hill. "I can create it by rebuilding my driveway as a two-lane road and then going down here from the top of the hill, where the house is. As you can see, to make a decent and safe road, it would have to cut into the contour of the land considerably and would have quite a few twists and turns to it. If I can get access here—" he gestured to a level tract of land that butted up to the lake and then stretched back to the main road "—I can put in a straighter road that will make it easier for everyone—suppliers, contractors, visitors and staff."

"So what's holding you back?"

"This piece of land is owned by a trust and, while I've tracked the trustee company to a firm of lawyers in Auckland, I haven't been able to get a response out of them with respect to a partial sale of the land. It would just be an easement, right on the boundary of our two pieces of land and I'm prepared to build the road so they'd have access from every point along here if they so desired. But so far, I've heard nothing."

"Frustrating," Tamsyn commented. "What will you do if you don't get the easement?"

"I'll still go ahead, but it will mean a bigger investment into the road construction and less into the complex itself. We'd have to do the complex in stages. Perhaps start with the children's camp and move on in a few years to building the chalets, or vice versa. I'm still hoping we won't have to make that decision."

"You mentioned personal experience…your family?" she probed carefully.

"My mother. She was—" He broke off and his lips firmed into a straight line, his eyes becoming unfocused for a moment. "Fragile, I guess you could say. She probably should never have been a farmer's wife, but she loved my father with a passion that knew no bounds. She lived for the very moment when he'd walk through the door each evening and she died a little every time he went back out again in the morning. Dad was shifting stock one day, his last herd. It wasn't long after he and Lorenzo had formed a partnership, converting part of Dad's farmland into a vineyard and amalgamating it with the Fabrini land where Lorenzo had already begun growing. Dad's quad bike rolled, and he was crushed beneath it. Lorenzo and I found him late that night, guided by one of his farm dogs barking. The dog had stayed with him the whole time. But by the time we found him, there was nothing anyone could do."

His succinct telling of the story didn't diminish the flash of pain in his eyes. A rush of sympathy filled her. Hard enough to lose a parent, but to be one of the people who discovered him? Grim didn't even begin to describe it.

"Finn, I'm sorry. That must have been awful. How old were you?"

"Twelve. Mum was devastated. At first she coped, barely, but I ended up having to take on more and more of the duties around the house—on top of school, on top of doing Dad's chores around the farm. Eventually it got to be too much and it showed. I got into some trouble at school when some kids started teasing me about falling asleep in class. My teacher came over to talk to Mum one day—they'd known each other when they were younger. When she saw how bad the situation had gotten, she called the authorities."

Finn rubbed his eyes and got up from his chair. He opened a nearby cupboard, which turned out to be an integrated bar-fridge door. "You want water or a can of soda?"

"Water, thanks." Tamsyn accepted the bottle he passed her and screwed off the cap. "What happened then? Did you get help around the farm?"

He ripped the tab off the soda he'd pulled from the fridge and took a long swallow before answering. "We were both put into care. Me into a foster home in town, Mum into a secure facility outside of Christchurch. I didn't know it then but she'd begun self-harming. I couldn't see her for a long time. Lorenzo and Ellen approached social services about providing a permanent home for me and eventually I moved in with them. With Lorenzo's help, the farm was slowly converted to what you see today—one of the most prolific and high-yield vineyards in the district. While we've never produced our own wines, we get a certain satisfaction when the wineries we supply produce another gold medal winner."

She could see now why the bond between Lorenzo Fabrini and Finn was so strong. The older man had been a father figure to him, a mentor, a savior. But it still didn't explain his not telling her where Ellen was. If Ellen didn't want to see her, why not simply tell her that and spare her the wild-goose chase? And for that matter, were they being honest with Ellen either? Did she even know that Tamsyn was looking for her, or had her menfolk simply circled the wagons and kept her in a state of oblivion? She couldn't bring herself to ask.

"So, you want to establish the respite center in your mother's memory?"

"She's part of the reason," he agreed. "The other part is I have a whole lot of money sitting around doing nothing and I feel the region has a need that I can fulfill. I want to give back. If it's successful, I'd like to develop centers all around the country."

Tamsyn sat back in her chair and deliberately took another sip of her water. She had no words to say. Finn's philanthropic nature appeared in total contrast to the way he'd treated her. Which man was the real Finn Gallagher? She was inclined to believe that it was Finn the philanthropist. The one the entire township knew and obviously had a very high regard for. The one who'd been helpful and solicitous even while hiding her mother's whereabouts from her at the same time. So why had he done it? What secret was he still holding back that would explain the rest of the puzzle?

"After we've collected your car, would you be interested in visiting the site?" Finn surprised her out of her reverie.

"Visiting the site? You have access now?"

"It's a rough track, still, but we can do it on the quad bike." At her look of concern he hastened to add. "I'll take it easy. We'll be quite safe."

She took only a moment to make up her mind. "Okay, that sounds like a great idea. I'd like to see it. I guess jeans and runners would be more in order than this," she said, gesturing to her skirt.

"Definitely." He flicked a glance at his watch. "How about you get changed now, and we can head into town and get your car. On the way back I'll check on Lucy and the chickens and then meet you back here."

A twist of anger flared in her chest as he mentioned Lucy and the chickens. If Lorenzo wasn't being so unreasonable she'd be there now, tending to her responsibilities. She nodded to Finn in answer and rose from her seat.

"Give me five minutes," she said.

"Sure, I'll be out front in the car."

Finn rubbed his hand over his face again as Tamsyn left the room. That had been close. The call from Lorenzo hadn't gone as he'd hoped. When it came to protecting Ellen from what he saw as the terribleness of the Masters family, he was almost rabid. It didn't seem to matter what Finn said, Lorenzo's mind was made up.

Added to his overprotective nature was his fear, because no matter what the doctors did, no matter how hard Lorenzo fought to hold Ellen here, she continued to deteriorate. He was desperate to safeguard what he saw as his last weeks with her.

Finn understood why Lorenzo was so scared. Talking about his mother, remembering how it felt, day in and day out, trying to hold everything together around the farm, trying to support his mom through her grief while virtually having to ignore his own, had left deep scars.

There'd been days when he'd resented her deeply, had wished she'd been more like other mothers—loving and capable, present in the moment instead of locked inside some awful living tomb. Then, of course, he'd be assailed with guilt and shame. She missed his father—they both did—

and without his father's booming, happy presence, it was up to Finn to fill the gaps.

But he'd failed. He'd failed her then, and he'd failed her later by insisting on going to see her before she was ready to see him again. By forcing her to face him, he'd forced her to face her own failures as a parent, and that had been enough to make her withdraw from reality completely. She refused to eat, refused to leave her bed—eventually dying in her sleep. Lost in her anguish. Alone.

He'd been responsible for his mother choosing death over life and, all guilt over keeping Tamsyn from seeing her mother aside, he'd be damned if he visited that responsibility onto Tamsyn as well.

Nineteen

Riding the rutted track on the quad bike, with Tamsyn's arms reluctantly secured around his waist, was bittersweet. With every bump in the road he felt her press against him— the softness of her breasts, the involuntary thrust of her hips. She'd started the journey determinedly holding on to the back of the seat, but as the track had grown rougher she'd been forced to relinquish her hold and cling to him like a limpet.

He released a breath he hadn't realized he was holding when they reached the flat and she didn't let go. The going was easier but still she held on, her slender arms like a band around his waist. He allowed himself to enjoy it while he could, certain it wouldn't last long.

She'd barely said a word to him since he'd returned to the house after their jaunt into town. She was still mad about the cottage, he knew. Mad about the secrets he was still keeping, mad about the whole situation. He didn't blame her, but there was nothing he could do. Nothing but to try and distract her in the meantime.

Fire lit his groin at the thought of various sensual ways he could distract her but he fought himself back under control. For now he needed to earn her trust back. He'd wounded her, he knew that, and it hurt with an almost physical pain to admit it.

He opened the throttle some more and swiftly covered the remaining few hundred meters to the lake's edge where he'd optimistically begun to peg out the buildings a couple of weeks ago. The sooner they dismounted the quad bike the sooner he'd be able to rid himself of the sensation of her fastened against him, and of how right it felt.

"This is a beautiful spot," Tamsyn commented as she got off the bike and walked over to the lake's edge. "You didn't want to build down here for yourself?"

"My parents' house used to be over there." He pointed to a stand of trees where a crumbling chimney and fireplace were all that remained of his former home. "A wiring failure one night led to it burning down after I went into foster care. I always said I'd rebuild there, but as I grew older I began to appreciate that it was probably better to make a new start. Besides, I love the outlook from my home now."

"King of the castle and master of all you survey?" Tamsyn said dryly.

"Hardly," he answered with a small frown.

Was that how she saw him? Autocratic and wanting to control everything?

"I think it's the freedom of the space that appealed to me most up there. The sensation of not being boxed in. Plus, it was symbolic of a new start for me after I sold my business. Fresh horizons and all that."

She nodded and started to walk along the waterline, her hands shoved in her pockets. He followed her a few steps behind.

"I thought this trip to New Zealand would be a new horizon for me," she said softly.

He could feel the pain in her voice.

"You know, I think I would have been better off not knowing that my mother is still alive. Alive and, from the looks of things, not wanting to see me." She huffed a humorless laugh. "Not wanting me, period."

Finn reached out and grabbed her arm, spinning her around to face him. He had to tell her something, give her *something* she could hold on to.

"Your mother has loved you all your life. I've known

her for much of mine and she never stopped thinking about you or your brother. *Never.* Believe me or not, but it's true."

He pushed as much honesty into his words as he could. She had to believe him. He knew he'd failed when he saw Tamsyn's expression cloud over, saw anger make her eyes turn hard.

"Well, if she has, she sure has a funny way of showing it. I've been here, searching for her, for weeks with not a word from anyone to tell me where to find her. They kicked me out of their house. There's no way they're ever going to want to see me, is there?"

He couldn't lie. "That's something you might just have to come to terms with, Tamsyn. As hard as it is, as awful as it is, it's out of both our hands."

He let his hand slide down her arm, his fingers tangling with hers. She didn't resist and he couldn't help but feel a surge of triumph that she didn't pull away.

"C'mon, let me show you where I've pegged out the chalets and main buildings. It's not far from the jetty over there." He pointed with his free arm. "My dad and I built it and it's still solid. We used to have so much fun here at the lake. That's what I want to give the families that come here. A chance to play together again. To create good memories." He wanted desperately to give *her* good memories of her time in New Zealand—something to take away the sting of the situation with Ellen. But would she let him?

The sun beat down on them as they walked the perimeter of the proposed respite center and Tamsyn felt a trickle of perspiration run down her spine. Jeans had obviously been the practical choice for the quad bike ride and walking in the long grass but, oh boy, did they make a person hot. She lifted her hair off the back of her neck, allowing the breeze to cool her ever so slightly. The lake looked cool and inviting.

"Thirsty?" Finn asked, as if he could read her mind.

"Yeah, although I wouldn't say no to a swim either. Shame we didn't bring bathing suits."

"We don't need suits."

She snapped her head around to look at him.

He gave her a nonchalant look in return. "It's totally private here. I can't even see this edge of the lake from my house, so if you want to take a dip, go for it."

"But…"

Whatever she was going to say flew from her mind as he tugged his T-shirt loose from his jeans and yanked it up over his head. Her eyes were drawn like magnets to his naked torso, to the play of muscles across his chest and lower. He reached down to undo his trainers and slid them and his socks off before his hands went to the waistband of his jeans.

"What are you waiting for?" he asked, a cheeky gleam in his eyes. "Last one in is a rotten egg."

The band of his boxer briefs was already showing. Not one to be left behind, Tamsyn slid her tank top off and toed off her runners while rapidly undoing her jeans. Jeans and socks came off in a smooth movement and she shoulder-barged him as she went past, putting him completely off balance and sending him to the ground in a tangle of jeans and limbs.

"Cheat!" he called after her.

He was only seconds behind on the wooden planks of the jetty and she squealed as she heard his rapid footsteps gaining. She was about a meter from the end when she felt his arms close around her waist, felt him lift her in the air, take another long step and twist to fall back backward into the lake.

Freezing cold, the water closed over her head and shocked the air out of her, but she didn't panic, didn't squirm. Instinctively, despite everything, she knew she was safe. Finn's arms were locked around her like a band and she felt his strong legs kick them back toward the surface. And that wasn't all she felt. His body was responding to hers and he wasn't trying to hide it.

Their heads broke the water and he released her.

"Man, that feels good," he said with a grin that went ear to ear.

She couldn't help but agree. The sweltering heat that had made her so uncomfortable before had been driven out of her body. But rather than chilling her to the bone, the water felt like silk stroking against her skin—making her aware of each of her nerve endings as they responded to the sensation, and to the nearness of the almost-naked man treading water beside her.

"Sometimes during the school holidays, when Dad would come back to the house at lunchtime, we'd race each other off the jetty. I lived for those moments. Mum would bring a picnic lunch for us and we'd all sit together afterward until he had to get back to work."

"It sounds like you guys had a great relationship," Tamsyn said, adopting a lazy breaststroke to swim in circles around him.

"We did. I'm lucky. Even though he died, I still have so many great memories. You missed out on that, didn't you? Doesn't seem from what you've told me that your father took time out with you kids."

"No, he didn't, but we didn't miss out altogether. We grew up with our cousins, Judd, Raif, Cade and Cathleen. We were always off on one adventure or another, when we weren't working on the estate somewhere."

Although she'd quietly envied her cousins their mothers while she was growing up, she'd still had a pretty carefree childhood. Ethan had seen to that. Protective, inclusive—he'd been her rock, and still was in so many ways. And her dad had been there, too, in his own gruff workaholic way, along with her uncle and aunts. But there had still been that vital component missing for her.

The water began to feel chilly again and she gave a little shiver.

"Let's get out," Finn suggested, obviously noticing her discomfort. "We can dry in the sun and have something to eat."

"You brought food?"

"And wine," he admitted. "Or you can have juice or water if you prefer."

"Wine would be nice," she said, striking out for the ladder on the side of the jetty.

She was acutely aware of Finn's presence behind her as she started up the ladder. It kept her from concentrating as she should on the slippery rungs. Her foot shot off the bar and she started to fall, only to be halted by warm hands at her hips steadying her. The feel of Finn's hands on her body had her senses reeling and heat flashed through her.

"You okay?" he asked from slightly below her.

"Y-yes, I'm fine," she said through gritted teeth.

Slowly and determinedly she made her way up the ladder, out of his reach—but only for a moment as a hunk of wet, dripping male came up the ladder right behind her.

He'd have had a good eyeful of her backside, she thought as she finally put her feet onto the wooden jetty and began to walk to where they'd tossed their clothes. She picked up her things and held them in front of her like a shield as he drew closer, suddenly feeling vulnerable in her dripping, clingy underthings.

Finn's gaze swept over her like a blast of hot air and she clutched her garments closer to her wet chest.

"Here," he said, grabbing his T-shirt up off the ground. "Wear this if you'd be more comfortable."

"But I'll make it wet," she protested, even as she accepted it from him.

He shrugged. "It'll dry, it's only lake water." He picked up his jeans and shook them out. "You want to turn your back a second?"

Color rushing to her cheeks, Tamsyn did just that and heard the wet plop of his briefs hitting the ground followed by the sound of him easing denim up long damp legs.

"It's safe to look now," he said, and she turned slowly.

Safe? He had to be kidding. With his hair all wet and spiky, his skin gleaming and his jeans slung low on his hips he was anything but safe.

"Um, perhaps you'd like to do the same for me?" she asked, her voice betrayingly husky.

"Sure. In fact, I'll set up our meal by the old fireplace. Join me when you're ready."

He shoved his socks inside his shoes and, tying the laces into a knot together, he hooked them with a finger and began to head back toward the bike. She watched as he increased the distance between them. Something pulled deep in her belly, as if there was an invisible thread that lay between them. A thread that tightened a notch at a time as he took each step away.

She shook her head. This was ridiculous. She was still angry with him, he'd lied to her. But he'd also made sure she had a roof over her head and food in her belly. And, from what she'd overhead in his conversation with Lorenzo Fabrini earlier today, he was trying to get the older man to agree to her seeing Ellen.

The sun slipped behind a cloud and a breeze off the lake caressed her skin, reminding her that she was standing here chilled, almost naked. Tamsyn lifted Finn's shirt up to her face, checked to ensure he still wasn't looking and inhaled. His scent filled her, consumed her almost. Spice and wood and quintessential Finn. It made her whole body ache for him.

He'd reached the quad bike and was lifting a large box off

the back. With his back still toward her, he headed toward the ruins of his old home. Secure in her privacy, Tamsyn quickly unsnapped her wet bra and pulled his T-shirt over her head before shimmying out of her wet panties. Instantly she felt warmth begin to seep through her, as if she'd been enveloped by the man himself. How did he do that? How did he make her feel so secure and yet so vulnerable at the same time? It wasn't fair.

Her hair still dripped down her back and she twisted its length to one side, wringing out as much excess water as she could before lifting it and, in lieu of having a band to tie it with, twisting it in a damp knot at the top of her head. A small twig, about the length of a chopstick, shoved through the knot held it from slipping in wet coils down her back. Satisfied she was more comfortable, Tamsyn followed in Finn's wake.

He'd spread a blanket on the grass and was taking out some pots of food as well as a pair of wineglasses.

"Better?" he asked as she drew closer.

"Thanks, yes." She spread her bra and panties in the sun on the bricks of the old fireplace and sank to her knees on the blanket.

"You must be hungry. It's ages since I brought you breakfast."

"I am a bit," she admitted, realizing now that she was ravenous.

"Help yourself while I pour the wine."

Tamsyn eyed the spread he'd laid out—smoked chicken, coleslaw, fresh bread rolls as well as olives, baby gherkins and sundried tomatoes. Her mouth watered. "It looks great," she commented, filling the plate he handed her. "I suppose you just threw this together?"

"Ha! I wish I could take the credit. No, I asked Bill at the café to put this together for us." He looked at her, his features softening. "You remind me a lot of her—Ellen."

"I do?"

"Yeah. You look like her, of course, but it's also the way you move, the way you sit. It reminds me of when she used to declare dinner a picnic, even in the middle of winter, and we'd sit around on the floor—Ellen, Lorenzo, Alexis and me—eating with our fingers off the plates. She'd laugh, how she'd laugh."

At first his words hurt, opened wider the gap between what she'd had and what she'd lost when her mother had left her. But then she felt a different sensation, almost tenderness, as a similar picture flooded her mind. Of her mother and Ethan and herself as a small girl, sitting in front of the fireplace at The Masters, rain pelting against the side of the house and yet they were cozy, together—enjoying a meal as if it was the simplest and most fun thing in the world. And she could hear her mother's laugh echoing through her memories; sense the touch of her mother's fingers on her face as she brushed away a clinging scrap of food from a cheek.

Tamsyn swallowed against the rise of emotion that clogged her throat.

"Damn, Tamsyn, I didn't mean to upset you. I just thought—"

"No, you haven't upset me," she choked out, "not at all."

"Then why are you looking so sad?"

"I just had a similar memory. Just a snippet, but I know it was real." She reached across the short distance between them. "Thank you," she said in all sincerity.

"For what?" He curled his hand over hers.

"For sharing her with me. Even just that little bit."

He lifted her hand to his lips and pressed them against her knuckles. "I wish I could do so much more for you, Tamsyn."

"I know," she answered, and she did. It still stung a little that she was being prioritized last, but she understood why his loyalty to Lorenzo went deep. And really, he was doing everything he could for her that didn't directly challenge that loyalty. That had to mean something.

He took her empty plate with his free hand and stacked it with his. Tamsyn's heart rate skipped a beat as he turned his gaze back to her. He still held one hand in his, and with the fingers of the other he traced the contours of her face—his touch so gentle, almost reverent.

"I want to make love to you again," he said, his voice a soft growl. "Will you allow me that honor?"

Twenty

Tamsyn felt the shiver of desire run from the base of her spine and all the way up into her clouded brain. She could refuse him, pull her hand free and withdraw from his request. He'd respect her decision, she was certain. For all that he'd withheld truths from her, she understood he was an honorable man. But her body had its own demands and try as she might to hold on to her anger with him, she couldn't resist him.

"Yes," she answered, her voice a whisper taken on the breeze that nuzzled and eased around their bodies.

His irises widened and she heard his breath hitch just that little bit. Enough for her to know he'd been anticipating a no from her. Enough to know what it meant to him that she'd said yes.

"Thank you," he said, pulling her toward him and meeting her lips with his own.

His kiss was tender at first, a soft play of his lips against hers—sucking, teasing kisses that enticed and tempted. Her nipples tightened beneath the cotton of his shirt, pressing against the fabric with an ache that spread all the way down to her core. A soft moan fled her mouth as he traced her jawline with his mouth, sucking softly at the sensitive skin of her throat.

Tamsyn hitched herself against him, her legs falling on either side of his, her rapidly dampening center pressing against the ridge that told of his body's own silent entreaty. Finn's hands were at her waist, pushing up the fabric of his shirt, tracing her ribs and slowly, oh so tormentingly slowly, moving higher to cup the fullness of her breasts.

His thumbs grazed against the tight nubs that peaked at their tips and she shuddered, pressing harder against him. He squeezed and rolled the taut beads between thumb and fingertip and in response she arched her back, flexed her hips against him, against his straining erection. Finn's mouth traced a blazing trail of wet heat to the fullness of her breasts until he took first one, then the other nipple in his mouth, rolling them with his tongue, suckling and grazing them with his teeth.

Her hands gripped his shoulders, her nails embedding in his skin as with each pull of his mouth he sent a spear of sensation to her aching core. She needed him—inside her, outside her, everywhere…all the time. Acknowledging that fact was a pleasure-pain that drilled into the back of her mind. This was no fling for her, not anymore. Somehow they'd crossed the invisible boundary of simply being lovers. Somewhere on this journey, she'd fallen irrevocably in love.

A sharp pang resonated through her as the truth hit home. Was she forever destined to fall in love with men who'd put others' needs before her own?

Now wasn't the time to reach for the answer to that question. Now was a time to take, to share, to give in return. And she did. They shed their clothes until they lay on the blanket, bare in the glorious sunshine, dappled by the shadows of the tree on the outer perimeter of the ruins. How symbolic, she thought, that their coming together like this, right now, should be within the confines of a home, a life, ruined by fire. Hadn't it been so with her own family? Hadn't they then risen from the ashes, stronger and better than before?

She could only hope that what she shared with Finn would be the same. That it could withstand the elements that battered against it. That they could rise together in the aftermath. A unit rather than two individuals. And so she gave herself over to the rhythm of their lovemaking, and when he slid his length inside her, she cried out in welcome, closing around him, holding him there as if she wished she need never let go of him again.

Afterward they lay together, legs entangled, his body half across hers. Their heartbeats hammering crazily in their chests as perspiration dried on their skin. Ripples of pleasure still ran through her body, each one gentling in its turn as her breathing slowly returned to normal. A deep lassitude spread through her body. If only they could stay here, like this, forever. No worries about the outside world, about the people within it or the decisions they made.

The sun slid behind a cloud, sending a change through the air. Nature's reminder that nothing remained in a state of suspension forever. She thought about Finn's earlier words, about coming to terms with the fact that she might not see Ellen, ever. Could she settle for that? Could she let go of the need to ask the questions that only her mother could answer and still be happy, still move forward with her life?

Only time would tell.

Back at the house, Finn asked Tamsyn to move into his room and heaved a sigh of relief when she agreed. He might not be able to offer her what it was she wanted most, but he could openly give himself as much and as often as she'd have him.

Over the next two weeks, they settled into a pattern together, one interrupted only by her volunteer work in town. For the rest of the time, he'd invited her to help him with the early planning stages of the respite center.

Her experience at The Masters proved surprisingly useful as they discussed the construction and outfitting of the family chalets. Her work in restoring and converting the old laborers cottages on their family property into luxury accommodation gave her insights and ideas that he found integral moving forward.

They made a terrific team. So terrific that he could barely

sleep at night, wondering when it was all going to fall apart. What would Tamsyn do when she found out the last se-cret—that Ellen had not chosen to bar Tamsyn's access to her after all but was, instead, dying…and that he'd known it all along? Would she ever forgive him when the truth came out? Was there any way he could keep from losing her?

Christmas loomed in just ten days' time. He'd half ex-pected Tamsyn to at least want to head home for the holi-day but she'd shown no inclination to want to be with her family. Instead, she'd teased him into buying a tall tree and festooned it with lights and decorations, some of which were ones his mother had carefully collected, spared in the house fire since they'd been stored in the detached garage.

He'd forgotten he had them, to be honest, until she'd started in about the tree. Decorating it with her had brought happier memories back to the surface in his heart. Memo-ries of times with his parents when they looked forward to the festive season and made a huge fuss over him. Memo-ries of Lorenzo, Ellen, Alexis and him sharing Christmas meals and the spirit of giving.

Each night he and Tamsyn had begun their own ritual, turning on the tree lights as soon as they finished their work, even though dark didn't come until closer to eight-thirty in the evening. Before they prepared their evening meal to-gether, they'd share a glass of wine and share stories as they sat by the tree, his peppered with vignettes of life with Ellen and Lorenzo, as well.

Tonight, though, she'd become quiet before eventually asking him to stop talking about Ellen.

"I'll never find my peace with the fact she doesn't want to know me if I'm constantly wishing for what I never had—for what she gave to you."

Her words had cut him to the bone, scourging him anew with guilt. He wondered whether the gift he'd chosen for her for Christmas, the one he had yet to place under their tree, was still the right thing. A self-portrait, Ellen had done the painting about ten years ago. It was one of his favorite pictures of her and he'd believed Tamsyn would appreciate having it. Now, he wasn't so sure. Would it just reinforce the loss she felt all over again?

He had quietly cursed Lorenzo's dictates and his own promise to the man who'd raised him from adolescence into adulthood. But he'd held his tongue, and would keep his word to both Tamsyn and Lorenzo inasmuch as he was able.

One thing he knew above all others now, though. He loved Tamsyn. She'd inveigled her way into his life, but he'd welcomed her into his heart and his home, and now he never wanted her to leave. How they could work that out going into the weeks and months ahead was a problem.

Finn drifted to sleep no closer to finding an answer today than he'd been in all the days and nights before.

The subtle buzz of his mobile phone on the bedside table roused him from sleep a few hours later. Carefully, so as not to disturb Tamsyn, he slid out of bed and left the room, answering the call only when he'd closed the bedroom door securely behind him.

"Finn?"

Lorenzo's voice was different. More strained than usual.

"Lorenzo, are you okay? Is Ellen—?"

"She dying, Finn. She's letting go. Each hour, each minute, a little more. The doctors…they say it won't be long now."

The older man's voice broke and tears burned at the back of Finn's eyes, a massive lump fixed in his throat. All along, Lorenzo had been strong for Ellen, strong for Alexis, too, when she'd returned home from Italy. Now he was crumbling and he needed someone else to lean on as he faced the biggest loss of his entire life.

"I'll be there as soon as I can," Finn promised, blinking

back the tears and biting back the fear that he might be too late to be of any help to anyone.

"Whenever you arrive, my boy, it cannot be too soon," Lorenzo said, confirming Finn's worst fears.

"If I have to charter someone to take me there, Lorenzo, I'll be there. I promise."

He ended the call and made his way to his office, settling in the chair and, waking up his sleeping computer, he punched the appropriate keys to bring up flights and availability from Blenheim to Wellington. The first flight out was at 7:05. He flicked a glance at his watch: 5:00 a.m. Allowing for the half an hour preboarding check-in and the half hour or so to get to the airport, he'd need to leave soon. He booked himself on the flight, printed his ticket and boarding pass and headed back upstairs toward his bedroom so he could gather some things together.

Tamsyn.

The thought of her stopped him in his tracks. All he wanted to do was protect her from the inevitable pain ahead. What should he tell her? What *could* he tell her?

The answer came in a resounding echo in his head. Nothing. He could tell her absolutely nothing.

Twenty-One

Tamsyn sleepily rolled over, her arm reaching out beside her. The sheets were cold. Instantly awake now, she sat up and listened. Finn wasn't in the en suite bathroom. A glance at the clock confirmed it was still early, only a quarter to seven. So where was he?

She slipped from the bed and draped her robe around her. In the kitchen there was still no sign of him. The coffeepot was cold and no breakfast dishes lurked in the sink. Even his office was empty. She racked her brain to remember if he'd said something last night about having to go away, but nothing came to mind.

Her phone, which she'd left on the kitchen counter, buzzed to life and she snatched it up, recognizing Finn's number on the caller I.D.

"Finn? Is everything okay?"

In the background she could hear engine noise and the sound of lots of people.

"I'm sorry, but I got called away again. I'm not sure how long I'll be gone. Look, they're doing the last call for my flight. I have to go. Take care, okay?"

"What about Lucy?" she thought suddenly.

It still grated that Finn went daily to the cottage to feed the cat and spread feed for the chickens. If she'd been allowed to stay there… She shook her head. It didn't pay to dwell on the issue.

Finn uttered a short expletive. "I forgot about that. Are you okay doing it?"

"Yes, of course I am," she answered. She knew where he kept the key, so that wasn't going to be a problem. "I'll take care of it. You had better go. I'll see you when you get back. I'll miss you."

"I'll miss you too," he said. "We'll talk when I get back. I've been thinking…about the future. *Our* future."

"Our future?" Tamsyn's heart fluttered in her chest.

Her love for Finn grew stronger every day. To hear him mention a word like *future* was a light in the darkness. A shred of hope that things would come right.

"I—hell, I didn't want to say this the first time over the phone, but I need to. I love you, Tamsyn. I'll be back soon."

He cut the link between them before she could answer but it didn't stop her continuing to press the phone to her ear as if doing so could extend their contact a few moments longer. Eventually she put the phone down and wrapped her arms around herself as joy built from deep inside. She danced a little jig around the kitchen island, hugging herself tight until she threw her arms out with a squeal of happiness. Everything was going to be all right. She just knew it.

It was a week before Christmas and the crowd for the end-of-year Christmas potluck meal at the seniors' center was swollen with extras Tamsyn had never met before. Given the greetings that flew back and forth, several had been away or unwell and unable to attend, but all had made a monumental effort to attend this last get-together for the year. The tables groaned with the bring-a-plate offerings and the Secret Santa gifts under the artificial tree Tamsyn had erected and decorated quickly this morning were plentiful.

This was going to be a great day, she thought as she watched everyone's happy faces. She moved through the crowd, ensuring all the guests had what they needed. As she did so, she picked up snippets of conversations that made her smile. Grandparent rivalry was thick in the air, from all accounts. One conversation, though, made her pause as a name hung in the air.

"Did you hear how Ellen is doing?" one of the new faces asked one of the regulars.

"Still in hospital from what I heard," the regular responded with a dour look on her face. "And it's not looking good."

"Oh, dear, that poor woman. Poor Lorenzo."

Her mother was in hospital? Was that why Lorenzo was being so protective? All the air drove out of Tamsyn's lungs.

The new woman continued. "So is she still local? Can we visit?"

"No," came the reply. "She's in Wellington. They airlifted her there weeks ago. Heart, kidneys, liver—all failing. Tragic, just tragic."

The other woman nodded in understanding. "So sad."

Tamsyn wheeled away from the group, desperate for a quiet place where she could think for a moment—process what she'd just heard. She'd hoped, eventually, for a snippet of information to come her way and lead her to her mother, but she'd never anticipated it being anything like this.

A gnarled hand on her arm, accompanied by the reek of stale cigarettes, made her flinch.

"You heard that, didn't you?" Gladys rasped. "Are you all right, lovey?"

Tamsyn could only shake her head.

"'spected as much. It was only a matter of time before someone let something slip."

"I have to go," Tamsyn finally managed to say through numb lips.

"I'll take care of things," Gladys said with a look of understanding in her rheumy eyes that was just about Tamsyn's undoing. "For what it's worth, we're all very sorry about your mum."

Afterward she didn't remember actually driving from town back to Finn's house. All she remembered was sitting in his office, the office of the man who'd known all along that her mother was in a hospital in Wellington, dying, and who had kept that information from her. Honor? Promises? Love? They could all be damned. This situation went beyond a vow, beyond loyalty to another man.

Anger kept her from falling apart as she methodically checked every hospital in the book until she struck pay dirt. Her glow of success was short-lived, hitting a wall when the patient-inquiries staff wouldn't give her the status of her mother's health, insisting she was not on the authorized list of family members.

More research turned up a flight to Wellington that would take a half hour. She sank back in the chair. All this time her mother had been just across Cook Strait, a short hop in a plane. Determination saw her book the last seat on the next flight out, and kept her sane as she drove to Blenheim airport.

"I'm sorry, miss, but we cannot disclose the patient's details." The young woman behind the patient-inquiries window was sympathetic but adamant.

"Can you at least tell me if she's still alive?" Tamsyn pleaded.

"Please, I will be forced to call security if you don't leave. I've told you all I can."

"But you've told me nothing! She's my mother and she's dying. I just want to know if I'm too late to even see her one last time. Is that too much to ask?"

Tamsyn's voice bordered on the hysterical and the clerk reached for her phone, her hand hovering over one quick-dial button in particular.

"Miss, I understand this is distressing for you, but my instructions are quite clear."

Tamsyn tore herself away from the window, utter dejection dragging down every cell in her body. She looked toward the elevator bank and weighed the prospect of visiting every floor in the hospital, trailing through each ward searching for the room that had her mother's name on the door. She'd begun to move toward the elevators when the doors of one car opened and her heart jumped in her chest.

Finn. All the breath in her lungs disappeared on a *whoosh*. There was an older man with him, she noticed, and a woman perhaps a little younger than herself. Lorenzo Fabrini and his daughter, Alexis. Chills ran through Tamsyn's body as she recognized them both from the photos at the house, as she laid eyes on her sister in person for the very first time.

Alexis lifted a tissue to her eyes with one hand, wiping fiercely; the other was tucked firmly into the crook of her father's arm. From here, Tamsyn couldn't be sure who was supporting whom. Suddenly the ramifications of what she viewed struck home. The older man's eyes were red-rimmed, as were Finn's, and Alexis still wept. It was still visiting hours—they wouldn't have left Ellen entirely alone unless…unless…

Was she too late? Had she come this far only to fail? The awful possibility hit her in the chest with the weight of a well-aimed sledgehammer and she staggered, the movement attracting attention from the self-contained group that approached.

Lorenzo's dark eyes bored straight through her for a moment before he turned to Finn, anger suffusing his haggard features.

"I thought you were keeping her away," he said, the words sharp and clear on the air.

"Papa!" Alexis remonstrated, tugging at his arm.

But the words were said. Damning words that confirmed that Finn had not just been withholding information from her, he'd actively ensured she didn't find her mother's location. Hurt piled upon hurt.

"I'm my own person," Tamsyn said shakily, stepping up

to the small group. "You can't keep on pushing me away, hoping I'll just disappear. I want to see my mother."

"You're too late," Alexis said softly. "Our mother passed away two hours ago. I'm sorry. If I'd known you were here—"

"If you'd known, nothing!" Lorenzo spat. "She's a Masters. You know what they did to your mother, how they broke her spirit."

"Enough!" Finn said firmly, stepping between Tamsyn and Lorenzo. "Now isn't the time for recriminations. Alexis, take your father back to the hotel. I'll look after Tamsyn."

Tamsyn stood there, numb and disbelieving. Her mother was dead? Every opportunity she'd had over the past four and a half weeks was irrevocably lost. Every question she'd ever want answered, every story she'd ever want told— gone. Forever.

She couldn't even summon a reaction as Finn took her arm and led her out toward the taxi rank. The journey to his hotel was swift and, before she knew it, she was in his room, a slug of brandy in a short tumbler thrust into her hands.

"Drink, you've had a shock," he insisted, cupping his hands over hers and lifting the glass to her lips.

Automatically she obeyed, automatically she swallowed the burning liquid, felt its trail from her lips to her tongue and down to her stomach where it hit and spread, infusing her frozen senses with some sense of warmth.

"Why?" she asked, her voice cold and empty. "Why did you keep me from her? I wouldn't have hurt her. I just wanted my mother!"

Her last words rose to a pained peak and tears brimmed in her eyes before they began to roll, one swiftly after the other, down her face.

"It wouldn't have made any difference, Tamsyn. Whatever you wanted from her, you wouldn't have been able to get. I'm sorry, she was too sick."

"How can you say that? You never even gave me a chance."

Finn sighed and sat in the chair opposite her, his forearms resting on his knees, his head dropping between his shoulders for a minute before he lifted it and faced her.

"For the last ten years Ellen has been battling early-onset dementia. It progressed dramatically in the past year. Coupled with that, she had underlying health problems created and subsequently exacerbated by her alcoholism. Her life has been a battle for a very long time. One she fought bravely." He shoved a hand through his hair, making the ends spike in disarray. "Ellen wouldn't have known you, Tamsyn. She didn't even know Lorenzo or Alexis these past few weeks. She disappeared into a part of her mind where she could hide until she had to face the end."

"And you knew this all along?" Pain edged every word she uttered.

"Yes." The single word made her shudder. He started to reach for her, but his hand stopped halfway, clearly sensing his touch would not be welcome. "It wasn't my choice to keep you in the dark. Not once I got to know you, once I understood that you hadn't been deliberately staying away."

"Deliberately? What are you talking about?"

"We always thought you knew she was still alive."

"But I told you the truth ages ago."

"I know that, and from that time forward I begged Lorenzo to let you see her—maybe not visit her, but at least see her—but he was adamant." Finn dropped his head again.

"Why not let me visit her?"

"You have to understand, Tamsyn. After my father died, my mother couldn't cope with what she saw as her failure to be a good farm wife, to be a good mother. I wasn't allowed to see her for months, but when I did I was a reminder of all that she'd failed at. After my visit, she was so ashamed of herself that she stopped eating, stopped getting out of bed—until eventually she stopped living.

"*I* did that to her. I know what it feels like to be the catalyst for something so awful it was beyond my comprehension at the time. Seeing you? Well, if Ellen *had* recognized you, given how traumatic her departure from Australia was—leaving you and Ethan behind—and how it's colored her entire life since, who knows what would have happened? If she had recognized you it might have only caused her more pain, more guilt, more regret. It could have driven her to her death sooner.

"I didn't want you to go through what I went through. I didn't want you to feel the same guilt, to have to live with that all your life."

Tamsyn pushed up from the chair and moved over to the bottle of brandy on the bureau against the opposite wall. She sloshed another generous measure into the glass and sipped it slowly before responding.

"So that's why you didn't want her to see me. But you never told me that, never explained. You just kept me from being able to see her. That wasn't your decision to make."

"No, it wasn't. The decision to keep you away from Ellen was Lorenzo's. Mine was in agreeing with him for, I believed, all the right reasons. Believe me, Tamsyn, you wouldn't have wanted to remember Ellen the way she was before she died. *She* wouldn't have wanted you to see her like that."

"I'll never know now, will I? And you'll have to forgive me," she said, sarcasm beginning to color her voice an unpleasant shade, "if I find it difficult to believe you when you say you did any of this for me. From day one you lied to me. Tell me, was our affair a deliberate choice on your part? Did you set out to seduce me to distract me from finding her? Was everything we did together, everything we shared, all based on a lie?"

Finn locked gazes with her and she saw the damning truth reflected back at her.

"In the beginning, yes. But not later, Tamsyn. Definitely not later."

It didn't matter to her now. His intent from the outset was clear. The lies aside, the hurt aside, he'd just confirmed to her that she was worth nothing—just as her father had done, just as Trent had done. Without another word, she carefully placed her glass back on the bureau, picked up her handbag and walked out.

Twenty-Two

"You love her, don't you?"

Finn shot a look of surprise at Alexis, pausing in his task of handling the details to bring Ellen's body home to rest. He couldn't lie to her, not this girl who'd grown into a beautiful young woman—one he regarded as a sister.

"Yes," he answered simply, then folded the papers they'd completed and pushed them back into an envelope before handing the envelope to her to return to the undertaker.

"Then what are you still doing here?"

"What?"

"Go after her. I can cope with this, Finn. We've been expecting it a long time. I know Papa is beside himself with grief—despite the evidence in front of him he couldn't let her go, couldn't believe that one day she wouldn't get well again. I did my grieving for the mother we both remember a long time ago. I'm sad now, but I know she's finally at rest. It's been a long time coming. Too long."

Finn's throat choked up. She was right, on all counts. She didn't need his help for this. And he had to get back to Tamsyn. He hadn't had the heart to try to stop her when she'd left him today. He knew he'd done a number on her—had betrayed the fragile trust he'd painstakingly rebuilt on the backbone of a very shaky start. But he owed it to her to go after her. To apologize, to convince her—

His gut twisted. Could he convince her that his love was real? That he'd believed he was acting in her best interests as well? He wanted to believe the answer was yes…and feared that it was no. That's why he was stalling, as if he could convince himself that she was back home waiting for him, loving him, as long as he wasn't there to watch her pack her bags and leave. But sooner or later, he'd have to go home and see for himself.

"I'll head to the airport right now," he said, throwing his meager supply of things into an overnight bag and heading for the door.

He stopped briefly to give Alexis a kiss on the cheek.

"Thank you," he said simply.

"It's what I'm here for. To remind you sometimes that you're not always right."

He gave a strangled laugh. Nothing changed between them. Even though she knew he'd been a complete ass with Tamsyn, and she'd soundly told him that not five minutes ago, they still had a connection that not even their eight-year age difference could sever. Friends, family. The lines had always been blurred, but one thing was certain. They were always there for one another and were always one hundred percent up front.

"You're growing cobwebs," she said with a cocked eyebrow.

"I'm gone. Wish me luck."

"You're going to need more than that, but I'll wish it for you anyway. Now, shoo!"

He was gone.

A last-minute ticket came at a premium, but Finn didn't care. Money wasn't the issue, he'd have paid whatever it took if the ticket could guarantee he'd be able to stop Tamsyn from leaving him. He was flooded with relief as he saw her rental car parked outside the front door to his home. The trunk was open. Clearly he was just in time.

Her keys hung in the ignition and he pocketed them for safekeeping. If she still chose to leave after what he had to say, then he would have to watch her go, but in the meantime he wanted her to have to listen to him.

He found her in their bedroom shoving the last of her

things into her case. Her face was pale, her eyes holding a world of hurt as she looked up and saw him. She turned her attention back to her case, wrestling with the tab on the zipper and uttering a string of curses before the thing came off in her hand entirely. Defeated, she slumped onto the floor beside the case.

"Need a hand?" he asked, stepping closer.

"Go away," she replied, her voice tearful, shaky.

He had the distinct impression that if he reached out and touched her she'd shatter into a thousand pieces where she sat. She was clearly operating on her last reserve.

"Don't go, Tamsyn. Please?"

"There's nothing left for me here now. Do you hear me?" She turned her face to him, her beautiful lush mouth twisting as she repeated herself. *"Nothing!"*

She'd meant the words to hurt him, and they had.

"I'm sorry, so sorry."

"Empty words," she said, forcing her attention to trying to clip the zipper tab back on her case. "I don't want to stay here anymore, I don't want to see you anymore."

"I understand, you have every right to feel this way, but please stay. At least for Ellen's funeral."

She uttered a sound, a bitter ringing laugh. "Your precious Lorenzo wouldn't let me see her alive, what makes you think he'll let me be around now she's dead?"

"He was only trying to protect the love of his life, the way I was trying to protect mine."

"Don't give me that," she said, her voice cracking under the strain of holding on to her anger, of holding back the tide of her grief. He knew how it felt. He was doing exactly the same thing himself. "The choices you made right from the beginning had nothing to do with what was best for me. You were his willing puppet all along. He must have commended you on going above and beyond the call of duty. You're quite a guy."

"You deserved to see Ellen—we were both wrong to stop you. I saw that earlier on but I couldn't convince him of that. I couldn't go against him, not when I knew how much he loved her. He'd never have forgiven me if I let any harm come to her—just like I'll never forgive myself for what I did to you."

"I don't believe you. Why would you begin telling me the truth now?" She gave a small sound of satisfaction as she got the tab onto the zipper and managed to successfully close her case.

"Because I love you and because I want you to stay."

She shook her head. "Good try, but not working."

Tamsyn rose fluidly to her feet and extended the handle of her bag. Finn rose to block her way.

"Stay, at least for Alexis's sake. She wants to meet you properly."

About to step around him, he was relieved to see that his words had temporarily stopped her in her tracks.

"Alexis? She wants to talk to me?"

"More than that, she really does want to get to know you," he assured her.

Tamsyn visibly sagged. All the bravado, all the fight leeching out of her before his eyes.

"All right. For her, I'll stay, but not in here. If I didn't know for a fact that the whole town is booked solid, I'd get a hotel room. Instead, I'll use the room I had before."

"Thank you."

She lifted her head, her eyes hollow and filled with sorrow. "I'm not doing it for you."

No, of course she wasn't. He understood that as he'd understood nothing else before. But it was a small victory. She was here, still under his roof. As she walked from the room and down the hallway he closed his eyes and thanked his lucky stars he still had this much. And, he hoped, time enough to convince Tamsyn to stay for good.

* * *

Tamsyn hung on the outskirts of the throng of mourners attending Ellen's wake at Finn's house. She'd never felt more utterly alone in her life. Ethan and Isobel had tried to come but, this close to Christmas, they'd been unable to secure flights to get them here in time. As it was, with Christmas only three days away, she'd been lucky to get a flight out of Blenheim to Auckland for later this evening.

The local townspeople had done Ellen proud. The hall was used for her funeral and it had been filled to the seams—with more chairs, speakers and screens outside—with those who'd come to pay their respects. Several people came up to Tamsyn, to offer their condolences, many with apologies for their own guilt at keeping the truth from her reflected in their eyes.

Throughout the activity of the day, Tamsyn was constantly reminded that no matter how well everyone had known and loved her mother, nobody here could answer her questions. No one could explain why Ellen had abandoned her children and left them to grow up thinking she was dead. The last remaining person who could have done that was being laid to rest in the small graveyard beside the church.

She'd sat between Finn and Alexis for the service—dry eyed, stoic—and learned for the first time how others had seen her mother. Yes, she'd been flawed and, yes, she'd struggled with alcohol abuse, but in her stronger moments she had been the kind of woman that Tamsyn knew she would have wanted to know. Ellen's contributions to the district had varied and she was fondly remembered for the art classes she'd taught in the community. It reminded Tamsyn of the paintings she'd seen at Finn's house in the gallery, signed with her mother's initials. She ached to possess something of her mother's. The closest thing she had was the new sister in her life.

Alexis had been a surprise. Sunny-natured with not an

unpleasant bone in her body, her half sister was easy to be
with and even, Tamsyn knew, to begin to love. That Alexis
held Finn in a state of near hero worship reminded Tamsyn
very much of her relationship with her own brother growing
up. And, like Tamsyn with Ethan, Alexis was clear-eyed
about her foster brother's flaws.

Under Alexis's less than subtle onslaught of friendship
over the past five days, Tamsyn had begun to rationalize,
again, Finn's reasons for keeping the truth from her, but that
did nothing to ease the pain and emptiness that echoed inside her every day. And, rationalization aside, she was still
angry with him. However valid he'd made his reasons seem,
she'd deserved the opportunity to make the final judgment
about trying to see her mother herself. Just one last glimpse,
one final opportunity to hold her hand, to feel the connection that had been missing for most of her life. Her right to
choose what to do had been stolen from her and she struggled to forgive that.

Distance and space to think in was what she needed most
right now. She was waitlisted on several flights out of Auckland, hoping to be home in time for the twenty-fifth, where
she could lick her emotional wounds among her own people.

"Miss Masters?"

Tamsyn wheeled around at the accented sound of Lorenzo's voice. He'd avoided her completely since his return
to the cottage at the bottom of the hill and she couldn't
mask her surprise at having him approach her now. Her eyes
roamed his face. He was still a handsome man, although
grief clouded his eyes and aged him.

"I would speak with you. Will you walk with me a moment?" he asked, offering her his elbow with old-fashioned
courtesy.

Every instinct within her wanted to refuse the man who'd
deliberately thwarted her attempts to find her mother and
she opened her mouth to do exactly that.

"Please, Tamsyn, in your mother's memory, I beg this of you," he asked, his voice solemn.

They strolled away from the house in silence, to the edge of the manicured lawns where the vineyard started, and then they strolled along one long row after another. Tamsyn began to feel uncomfortable, to wonder what it was that Lorenzo wanted to talk to her about.

"I am sorry for what I did to you," he said heavily as they reached the end of a row and stopped. "I was wrong, I see that now. I was acting from a point of fear, when I should have been acting from a point of compassion. Worse, I made Finn keep his word to me even when I knew it was destroying him inside. I was a desperate, foolish old man and I hope that one day, in time, you can find it in your heart to forgive me, to forgive Finn, for what we both did. Once he got to know you, he was not a willing partner in our deception, believe me."

"I...I don't know if I can forgive, Mr. Fabrini. I really don't."

"I understand," he said, closing his eyes and bowing his head. "I have something for you. I wanted to be sure you had this before you go home to The Masters again."

He reached in his pocket and withdrew a fat bundle of envelopes tied with a length of faded ribbon. Lorenzo's thumb played along the narrow band of light purple-colored satin for a moment before he drew in a deep breath and passed the packet to her.

"These are your mother's. More correctly, they are from her to you and your brother. She wrote the letters inside over many years but never posted them. She'd promised your father she would never make contact with anyone at The Masters again, but it didn't stop her from writing what she needed to say. Here."

Tamsyn's hand shook as she took the envelopes, as she saw her mother's handwriting for the first time, scrawled in lilac-colored ink across the fine linen stationery. Tamsyn smiled a watery smile. Her childhood room had been decorated in shades of purple—that obviously had been her mother's hand at work. Knowing that now brought a flicker of warmth to her heart that had been missing for days.

"Thank you," she whispered.

"You're welcome. I hope her words can bring you some peace, show you the kind of woman she was before she became ill."

"I'll treasure them."

He nodded, his eyes filling anew with tears. He sniffed loudly and turned his head, too proud to let her see his tears fall. "I'll go sit over there in the sun. I am in no hurry to go back to that crowd up there. When you are finished, I will answer anything I can for you if you still have any questions. Take your time, eh?"

"I will," she promised. She watched as he settled himself on a wooden bench seat that gave a view over the vineyards and down to where his and Ellen's cottage nestled against the bottom of the hill.

She lowered herself to the ground and put the letters in her lap before carefully undoing the ribbon and lifting the first envelope to her face. She closed her eyes and inhaled deeply, trying to catch the scent of her mother, to see if there was anything that still remained of who she'd been.

There it was, ever so faintly. A fragrance that reminded her of childish giggles, of summer sunshine, of the warmth of a woman's embrace. Her mother's embrace.

Tamsyn lowered the envelope, slid a nail under the flap and began to read.

Twenty-Three

She cried many tears over her mother's words, words threaded with guilt that she'd failed to protect her children from her own weakness. She'd been running away from The Masters—from her marriage and the failures she'd struggled to live with—to Lorenzo, who waited for her at the airport with tickets for all of them to travel to New Zealand, when she'd crashed her car.

John, her husband, had arrived, distraught to find his children injured and furiously angry to find his wife under the influence of alcohol and sobbing on the side of the road. He'd used the weight of the Masters name to see the police suppress their evidence against her, and eventually drop all charges, on her promise that she'd leave, without her children, and never return. Plus, he'd arranged to pay her a stipend to ensure she stayed away, out of all their lives forever.

Ellen had battled with her guilt, and her drinking, for years after that, but had continued to accept the money from John Masters month after month, year after year. Lorenzo hadn't wanted Masters money to touch the life they'd rebuilt for themselves in New Zealand, so she'd saved it in a separate account, eventually using it to buy some land, which was being held in trust for Ethan and Tamsyn. While her biggest regret in life had been not fighting harder to maintain a relationship with her children, she'd at least ensured she had something to give them, something definite and valuable to remember her by.

She closed the last letter with the name of the legal firm in Auckland that oversaw her and Ethan's inheritance.

Tamsyn struggled to her feet, easing the stiffness out of her muscles as she walked toward Lorenzo, who rose to greet her.

"We don't need the land, Lorenzo," she said after explaining what Ellen had done. "It should be yours. We already have far more than we need at home, you especially should know that."

"I do know that. I worked for your family for many years and I know what your family land means to you all. This is why you should know what this meant to Ellen to give you something that is purely yours, from her. You and your brother may do with it whatever you want, but remember, it was her only way of leaving you something of her. Think on it, and make your decision once you have talked to your brother, yes?"

Tamsyn nodded. "Okay."

Back at the house, after everyone had gone, she gathered her things together for her flight away from here. Away from the pain, away from the memories, both good and bad. Finn waited at the door as she approached, a wrapped rectangle in his hands. She'd done her level best to avoid being alone with him since Ellen's death and with her spending so much time with Alexis, it hadn't been difficult. Finn, too, had been out of the house a lot—helping to coordinate the funeral as well as being a constant support for Lorenzo. Tamsyn had told herself she was relieved he hadn't had the opportunity to wear down her shaky resolve to leave, but right now she felt so raw it was as if she was bleeding inside.

"Before you go, I'd like you to have this," he said, handing her the parcel.

She looked at the bright Christmas wrappings and shook her head. "No, Finn. Please. Not a Christmas gift. We're not...I can't..."

"It's yours, you have to take it."

"Fine then," she said, grabbing it from him and shoving it under her arm as she pushed past and carried on to her car.

She wouldn't open the gift, she decided as she got into her car and, without a backward glance, drove down the hill toward the road that would take her to the airport.

Once she reached Auckland, she could have stayed with either of her cousins. Judd Wilson, who had grown up with her and Ethan at The Masters, lived in the city with his wife, Anna. So did Judd's sister Nicole, who'd grown up in her father's custody in New Zealand and who Tamsyn had only gotten to know in the past year, with her new husband, Nate. But the prospect of having to explain what she'd been through this past month or so was more than she could bear. The anonymity of a hotel was just what she needed and she'd been fortunate when a last-minute cancellation had secured her a room in one of Auckland's most prestigious hotels.

The next morning Tamsyn checked with the airlines several times. Nothing was available, not even taking a more circuitous route through Sydney or Melbourne. It seemed everyone wanted to go to Australia for Christmas. To take her mind off the unsettled feeling that she'd left something vital behind in Marlborough, she phoned the lawyers her mother had mentioned in her letter. To her surprise, she was able to get an appointment immediately.

Later, sitting in a café on the waterfront, Tamsyn sipped a latte and let the news she'd just received sink in. She needed to talk to Ethan and dialed him up immediately.

"Have you got a flight yet?" he asked as he answered his phone. "We're looking forward to having you back where you belong."

Did she really belong there, back at The Masters? Sure, it was where she'd been brought up, but she had been restless, unsettled, for a long time. That feeling had begun to lift while she'd been in Marlborough, while she'd been with Finn. She stubbornly pushed that last thought aside before answering her brother.

"No luck with flights yet but I'm on the lists. Just keep your fingers crossed, okay? In the meantime, there's something I need to talk to you about."

"What's that?"

"Our mother. She left us property here in New Zealand. Apparently she had been putting the money Dad sent her into some land close to where she was living. Once she'd paid it off, the balance went into an account that's been held in trust in both our names."

"Seriously? She did that?"

"There's more. She wrote us letters, lots of them. They explain everything."

Tamsyn gave him the full rundown on the letters' contents. There was a long pause before Ethan answered.

"And do you feel better about everything, about her, now?"

Did she? Had reading the letters brought her any closer to understanding, to making peace with the myriad of answers she'd sought?

"I think I understand her a little more. She was miserable inside, before. She made some stupid, totally wrong, decisions and she paid for them dearly. I still wish we'd had a chance to know her, but I can't pin the rest of my life on something I can never have or change. So, yeah, I do feel better, stronger even."

"Should I be scared?" he teased and she smiled in response. The first genuine smile to stretch her face in almost a week.

"Funny, Ethan, very funny. Now, about this land. Obviously I don't expect you to make a decision right now—but we'll need to think carefully about what we want to do."

"I don't think we need it, Tam. Do you?"

"I agree. I said as much to Lorenzo, but he was insistent that Mom wanted us to have it, to do with it whatever we wanted."

"Hmm. Then how would you feel about selling the land? Maybe donating the money toward a charity or something in her name, something that might help other people going through what she went through."

Tamsyn felt herself nodding. "That's a good idea. I'll put some thoughts together and we can discuss it when I get home, okay?"

They said their goodbyes and Tamsyn decided to walk back to the hotel as a vague feeling of disquiet still niggled at her. Saying "home" hadn't felt quite right. For some reason, it felt as though the vast tract of land encompassing The Masters, including the imposing ruins of Masters Rise on the hilltop, belonged to another Tamsyn, another time, another world apart from what she'd begun to think of as home now. Did she even belong there at all? Did she belong anywhere?

From her harbor-facing hotel room window she watched as seagulls lazily circled in the air. She felt displaced, and wasn't that what had led her to try to find her mother in the first place? The only time she'd felt as though she truly belonged anywhere was when she'd been in Finn's arms. The past couple of weeks, working with him, just simply *being* with him, had felt so very right.

Her chest ached with a definite physical pain. She missed him already, even though he'd hurt her, even though he'd lied. As Alexis had stressed, Finn had acted with the very best intentions—not just toward Lorenzo, but toward her, as well. Perhaps not immediately, but certainly within the first week of knowing why she was there.

On the table beside her, her phone chimed with a new

text message. Idly, she picked it up, surprised to see it was from Alexis and contained a link to a clip in a national current affairs show.

Hi sis. Hopefully ur still in NZ. U HAVE to see this! Luv Ax.

Tamsyn swiftly texted back asking what it was about but only received a watch it! in response.

She thumbed the link, hoping it wouldn't be a total waste of her data allowance, and watched as the show advertising scrolled across the screen. The presenter's words immediately made her sit up and take notice.

"Tonight we have well known philanthropist Finn Gallagher with us, to tell us about his exciting new project. Finn, what led you to this project in particular?"

Tamsyn watched, enthralled, as Finn filled the screen of her smartphone, as his measured voice came from the tiny speakers. She recognized the suit he was wearing as one he'd had on when he'd returned from a day trip to Wellington last week, so the interview itself was very recent.

During the interview he spoke eloquently about the respite center and about the families and children he hoped it would serve, and why. It seemed to take a toll on Finn, putting such a public face on one of his very personal projects, which fit in with what Alexis had told her about him and how much he supported those less fortunate in the community.

It hurt to watch him, yet it filled Tamsyn with a deep sense of calm as well. He was, essentially, a good man with a heart that beat for those he loved. He'd told her she was one of those people, but with everything that had happened afterward, she'd been too angry, too wounded and too scared of making herself vulnerable again to believe him.

Thinking back now, she remember how he'd sounded

when he'd said the words before he went to be with Ellen as she died. He'd obviously been distraught at the knowledge that the mother figure, who'd been there for him while he was growing up, was leaving them all for good, yet he'd taken the time to call Tamsyn. To give her that piece of himself.

The current affairs piece was wrapping up and Tamsyn forced her attention back to the screen.

"And do you have a name for the center?" the presenter asked.

"Yes, I do. I'm naming it for a very special woman. To honor her strength and my love and admiration for her, I'm calling it, Tamsyn's Place."

Tamsyn didn't hear whatever it was the presenter said next. All she could hear were Finn's words repeating in her head as she tried to comprehend the enormity of his action in wanting to name the center after her. She didn't deserve the accolade. She would have thought, after all they'd been through, the last thing he'd have wanted would be the constant reminder of her in his life. But it seemed she was very wrong. And if she was wrong about that, maybe she'd been wrong about other things as well.

She looked at the documents poking out from her handbag lying on the hotel bed—the copy of legal title to the land her mother had left her, and realized why looking at it caused that niggling sense of familiarity. It was the land Finn had tried to get for the easement—the one he needed for the road to Tamsyn's Place. And as she stared at the papers, she knew what she needed to do.

More, she now knew exactly where her place was. And maybe in going to claim it, she could stand to be spontaneous just one more time after all....

Twenty-Four

The persistent hammering at the front door woke Finn from his slumber on the couch where he'd collapsed last night. The racket matched the hammering in his head.

Last night, all his duties to everyone else behind him for a while, he'd done some serious damage to a bottle of whiskey and now he was paying the price. Still, it had been worth it for the brief oblivion it had given him. He mourned Ellen, but he was dying inside for what he'd done to Tamsyn and for how his choices had lost her from his life for good.

He caught sight of himself in a wall mirror and made a sound of disgust. He looked terrible. Hair unkempt, clothing slept in, face unshaven. Maybe he could just scare away whoever was at the door without having to speak—something he was sure would make his head ache even more.

Finn swung the front door open with a growled greeting and felt the world tilt at his feet when he saw Tamsyn standing there. He rubbed his eyes—clichéd, he knew, but he couldn't quite believe what he saw.

"You look like hell," she said, walking past him and into the house before he could say anything. "We need to talk."

"By all means, come in," he said, closing the door behind her and following her down the hall to the kitchen.

He stood there, saying nothing, just drinking her in as she moved around the kitchen preparing a fresh carafe of coffee. She was a sight for sore eyes and he was glad those sore eyes didn't deceive him, but what the hell was she doing here?

Once the coffee was brewed, she poured them each a mug and handed one to him.

"Drink," she ordered then went to sit at the casual dining table in front of the French doors.

He joined her and took a long draw of the life-sustaining brew. She'd made it strong. Good, he had the feeling he'd really need his wits about him for whatever came next.

"I have a proposition for you," she said, pulling a sheaf of papers from her voluminous handbag and setting them on the table.

"A proposition?"

It certainly wasn't what he'd expected to hear from her lips. He sat up a little straighter. She was a far cry from the desperately unhappy and wounded woman who'd driven away from him two days ago. Something had happened to change her, but what? Whatever it was, he was grateful it had brought her back here, to him, even if only for a short time. Grateful enough to give his full attention to whatever proposition she wanted to make, no matter how badly his head hurt.

"A business proposition, actually. I don't know if Lorenzo told you—"

"I haven't spoken to him since the funeral on Monday," he interrupted.

Tamsyn nodded. "Okay, well, it seems that my brother and I are the proud owners of this."

She pushed a copy of a title plan toward him, and her finger pointed at the acreage adjoining his own. The very acreage he needed a slice of to complete his dream for the respite center. His headache grew to new proportions. How on earth had she and Ethan gotten possession of the land? And why was she telling him this? Was it so she could have the satisfaction of rubbing his face in it, in telling him that for what he'd done to her he could wait until hell froze over before he could have that easement?

"I don't understand. I've been approaching the trustees for months with no satisfaction. How did you get hold of it?"

"Ellen gave it to us."

She lifted her eyes and stared at him, gauging his reaction, no doubt, and he didn't disappoint. The shock that hit him now was second only to the shock that had shaken him when he'd opened his front door to her just a few minutes ago.

"Ellen?"

She nodded. "It seems she bought it many years ago with money she'd saved from what my father had sent her. He paid her a lot to stay away and Lorenzo wouldn't let her use it for their new life together. I think that's why my father's solicitors had your address for mailing—did she maybe have her mail redirected to your address?"

Realization dawned. Lorenzo and his parents had shared a letter box on the road and when Finn had built up here on the hill he hadn't seen any point in changing what had worked for a couple of decades or more. He quickly explained it to Tamsyn.

"So that's why my mother's checks were coming here, except you wouldn't have known that, would you?"

He shook his head. "We just leave each other's mail in the box for whoever it was addressed to, to pick up. It's always been as simple as that."

"Ellen was determined to leave something for Ethan and me, something that had meaning to her and that she hoped would have meaning to us, as well. Ethan and I have only talked about this briefly, but we're one hundred percent on the same page about it. We both feel it's very important to honor her memory and in that vein, we want to gift the land to the respite center."

"Are you sure? I mean, you know what getting that easement is going to mean to the overall development, but—"

"Finn, you misunderstand me. We're not offering you the easement."

Confusion muddled his already aching head. He sup-

posed he deserved it if she wanted to deny him the easement, but then what had she been talking about?

"What do you mean, exactly?"

"We're offering you everything, the entire acreage."

His fingers tightened around the coffee mug. "Seriously?
The whole thing? What's the catch?"

"Just the one—well, two actually."

He wasn't entirely surprised. He sighed. "Okay, let's get
it over with. Give me your terms."

"One, I want naming rights to the retreat."

"No way. It already has a name and I'm not changing it."

She leaned back in her chair and he watched as her face
lit up, a smile pulling her lips into a gentle curve. "Oh-kay, I
can live with that, but the other condition is nonnegotiable."

"And it is?"

"That you'll let me continue to work with you on the
development."

"Are you serious? You want to stay?"

"With you, if you'll have me."

He was on his feet and pulling her from her chair before
his brain even fully assimilated what he was doing.

"*If* I'll have you? You have to be kidding me. I thought
I'd never see you again, that I'd destroyed every last chance
I could have to keep you in my life."

She lifted her hands and bracketed his face. "Finn, I
know how hard it was for you, how torn you must have
been toward the end. I've been so focused on just one thing,
finding *my* mother, for so many months now and you were
the person standing in the way. I thought that you couldn't
possibly love me because you didn't simply hand over what
I wanted. I never stopped to think, until just recently, what
that was doing to you. How it pulled at your honor, at your
heart. You didn't just lose one mother, you've lost two, and
I forgot all about that because all I wanted was mine. I
couldn't see all the ways you showed me you loved me since

I was so focused on the one thing you wouldn't do. I was single-minded and selfish and I'm sorry."

"No," he protested. "What Lorenzo and I did was wrong. I'm the one who's sorry, Tamsyn, you'll never know how sorry."

"Shh," she said, laying a finger across his lips. "We have to let it go now. Put it in the past where it belongs. We need to honor the women who brought us here, who brought us to this, to each other."

"You can forgive me?"

"I already have, Finn. Sure, I wish things could have been different, but no one can change the past. The only thing we can do is move forward."

She lifted her face to his, her lips a tender entreaty, one he accepted with every beat of his heart.

When they broke apart he shook his head. "I can't believe I was so wrong about you right from the start. I've been a total idiot."

"What do you mean?"

"From when I was about fifteen I started keeping tabs on you and your brother, on your family's lifestyle. It used to make me mad to see you guys had so much, that your life was so easy, when Ellen had so little and worked so hard. You all seemed so happy without her. I allowed those impressions, formed when I was too young to fully understand, to color how I treated you when you arrived here."

"You were pretty cold, but you've thawed out nicely," Tamsyn said with a forgiving smile he really didn't deserve.

"You thawed me out. You made me see the real you, the beautiful woman inside that perfect exterior. It's why I want to hold on to naming rights for the center."

"You really want to call it Tamsyn's Place?"

"You know about that?"

"Alexis sent me a link to the clip on TV."

He smiled. Of course she had. "Are you okay with that?"

"Well, I would have preferred to see it named after Ellen, but maybe we can do that with the next one."

"I like the sound of that. Tamsyn, I want our future to be together, planning everything together, no secrets, no lies."

"Me, too," she answered softly.

"Then, will you marry me? Will you have a family and grow old with me?"

"Oh, Finn, yes! I will."

Much later, after they'd sealed their reunion with a wealth of physical promises and lay, replete, in one another's arms, Tamsyn reflected on how she finally felt as though she'd come home. Tomorrow would be Christmas Day and while she would miss her family she knew she was exactly where she was meant to be. With this man, for the rest of her life.

Thinking of Christmas reminded her of the gift Finn had thrust at her after the funeral when she'd left for Auckland. She hadn't gotten around to unwrapping it, yet hadn't quite been able to bring herself to discard it, either.

"Finn? What was the parcel you gave me the other day?"

"You didn't open it?"

"Not yet."

"Then why don't you?" he suggested.

She slipped from the bed and pulled on his T-shirt and went outside to her latest rental and dragged her case from the trunk. Bringing it upstairs to the bedroom, she unzipped it and burrowed through her clothes to where she'd stashed the package, cushioned in the center.

Sitting cross-legged on the bed beside him, she ripped away the paper, her eyes filling with tears as she saw the image of her mother looking back at her.

"Oh, Finn. She was so beautiful."

"Inside and out, just like you," he replied, dropping a kiss on her shoulder.

"But this picture, it must have been special to you. Why did you give it to me?"

"Because you deserved to have something of her. Something you could keep forever to remember her by and something that I know she, too, was proud of."

Tamsyn carefully placed the picture on the bedside cabinet and turned to the man beside her. If she'd had any doubts whatsoever they were all banished now. She'd made the right choice in coming back to Finn, in coming home. Finally she could be secure in the knowledge that, for the first time in her life, she was finally where she truly belonged.

In his arms, in his life, and ahead of all others in his heart. Always.

* * * * *

"Connor."

Maggie jabbed her finger in his chest for emphasis. "Just so we're clear. I'm not going to have sex with you."

He looked down at her finger, then up to meet her gaze. "Still negotiating, huh?"

She whipped her hand away and immediately missed the sizzle of heat she'd gotten from touching his chest.

"I'm serious, Connor," she said, hating that her voice sounded so breathless. "I'll share your room with you, but that's it."

"It's a suite," he corrected, and slowly leaned over and kissed her neck.

Dear lord, what was he doing? She knew she should slap him, push him away, but instead she shivered at the exquisite feel of his lips on her skin.

"Say it with me," he murmured. "Suite."

"Suite," she murmured, arching into him when he gently nipped her earlobe. This had to stop. Any minute now.

"Sweet," he whispered, then pulled her into his arms and kissed her.

* * *

Second-Chance Seduction
is part of the MacLaren's Pride trilogy:

From Scotland to California, three brothers are ready to claim their legacy—and love!

SECOND-CHANCE
SEDUCTION

BY
KATE CARLISLE

Published in Great Britain 2013
by Mills & Boon, an imprint of Harlequin (UK) Limited,
Eton House, 18-24 Paradise Road, Richmond, Surrey TW9 1SR

© Kathleen Beaver 2013

ISBN: 978 0 263 90495 6

51-1213

Harlequin (UK) policy is to use papers that are natural, renewable and recyclable products and made from wood grown in sustainable forests. The logging and manufacturing processes conform to the legal environmental regulations of the country of origin.

Printed and bound in Spain
by Blackprint CPI, Barcelona

New York Times bestselling author **Kate Carlisle** was born and raised by the beach in Southern California. After more than twenty years in television production, Kate turned to writing the types of mysteries and romance novels she always loved to read. She still lives by the beach in Southern California with her husband, and when they're not taking long walks in the sand or cooking or reading or painting or taking bookbinding classes or trying to learn a new language, they're traveling the world, visiting family and friends in the strangest places. Kate loves to hear from readers. Visit her website, www.katecarlisle.com.

One

"You need a woman."

Connor MacLaren stopped reading the business agreement he was working on and glanced up. His older brother Ian stood blocking his office doorway.

"What'd you say?" Connor asked. He couldn't have heard him correctly.

"A woman," Ian repeated slowly. "You need one."

"Well, sure," Connor said agreeably. "Who doesn't? But—"

"And you're going to have to buy a new suit, maybe two," his brother Jake said as he strolled into his office.

Ian followed Jake across the wide space and they took the two visitors' chairs facing Connor.

Connor's gaze shifted from one brother to the other. "What are you two? The social police?"

Ian shook his head in disgust. "We just got off the phone with Jonas Wellstone's son, Paul. We set up a meeting with us and the old man during the festival."

Connor frowned at the two of them. "And for this you expect me to buy a new suit? You've got to be kidding."

"We're not kidding," Ian said, then stood as if that was the end of the discussion.

"Wait a minute," Connor insisted. "Let's get serious. The festival is all about beer. Drinking beer, making beer, beer-battered everything. This is not a ballet recital we're going to."

"That's not the point," Ian began.

"You're right," Connor persisted. "The point is that I've never worn a suit and tie to a beer festival and I'm not about to start now. Hell, nobody would even recognize me in a suit."

That much was true. Connor was far more identifiable in his signature look of faded jeans, ancient fisherman's sweater and rugged hiking boots than in one of those five-thousand-dollar power suits his two brothers were inclined to wear on a daily basis.

Frankly, this was why he preferred to work at MacLaren Brewery, located in the rugged back hills of Marin County, thirty miles north and a million virtual light years away from MacLaren Corporation in the heart of San Francisco's financial district. The brothers had grown up running wild through those hills. That's where they had built their first home brewery, in the barn behind their mom's house.

Over the past ten years, the company had grown into a multinational corporation with offices in ten countries. But the heart and soul of MacLaren Brewery still thrived in those hills, and Connor was in charge of it all: not just the brewery, but also the surrounding farmland, the dairy, the fishery, the vineyards and the brew pub in town.

And he wasn't about to wear a freaking business suit while he did it.

Meanwhile his older brothers, Jake, the CEO, and Ian, the marketing guru, took care of wheeling and dealing at their corporate headquarters in San Francisco. They both lived in the city and loved the fast pace. Connor, on the other hand, avoided the frantic pace of the city whenever possible. He only ventured into headquarters on days like this one because his brothers demanded his presence at the company's board meetings once a month. Even then, he wore his standard outfit of jeans, work shirt and boots. He'd be damned if he'd put on a monkey suit just to discuss stock options and expansion deals with his brothers.

Connor glanced at the two men, who were closer to him than any two people on the planet. "What made you think I would ever dress up for the Autumn Brew Festival? I'd be laughed off the convention floor."

True, the festival had become a very important venue for the fast-growing, multibillion-dollar beer production industry. In the past few years it had expanded to become the largest gathering of its type in the world. The powers that be had even changed the name of the event to reflect its importance. It was now called the International Brewery Convention, but Connor and his brothers still called it the festival because more than anything else, people showed up to have a good time.

It was a point of pride that the festival was held annually in their hometown at the Point Cairn Convention Center next to the picturesque marina and harbor. It was one of the biggest draws of the year, and the MacLaren men had done their best to ensure that it continued to be a not-to-be-missed event on the calendars of beer makers and breweries around the world.

But that still didn't mean Connor would dress up for it. What part of "good time" did his brothers not understand? The words did not equate with "suit and tie" in anybody's dictionary.

Jake gazed at him with a look of infinite patience. As the oldest of the three, he had perfected the look. "Wellstone's scheduled a dinner meeting with all of us and his entire family. And the old man likes his people to dress for dinner."

"Oh, come on," Connor said, nudging his chair back from the desk. "We're buying out their company. They're dying to get their hands on our money so the old man can retire to his walnut farm and enjoy his last days in peace and quiet, surrounded by nuts. Why would he care one way or another how we dress for dinner?"

"Because he just does," Jake explained helpfully. "His son, Paul, warned us that if Jonas doesn't get a warm and cozy, old-fashioned family feeling from the three of us at dinner, there's a good chance he could back out of the deal."

"That's a dumb way to do business."

"I agree," Jake said. "But if it means snagging this deal, I'll wear a freaking pink tuxedo."

Connor frowned. "Do you honestly think Jonas would back out of the deal over something so minor?"

Ian leaned forward and lowered his voice. "It happened to Terry Schmidt."

"Schmidt tried to buy Wellstone?" Connor peered at Jake. "Why didn't we know that?"

"Because Wellstone insists on complete confidentiality among his people," Jake said.

"I can appreciate that."

"And Paul wants it to stay that way," Jake continued, "so keep that news under your hat. He only brought up the Schmidt situation because he doesn't want another deal to fail. He wants our offer to go through, but it all depends on us putting on a good show for Jonas. Apparently the old man's a stickler."

Ian added, "Terry blew the deal by wearing khakis and a sweater to dinner with the old man."

"Khakis?" Shocked, Connor fell back in his chair. "Why, that sociopath. No wonder they kicked him to the curb."

Ian snickered, but just as quickly turned sober. "Jonas Wellstone is definitely old school. He's very conservative and very anxious that the people who take over his company have the same family values that he has always stood for."

"He should've gone into the milk shake business," Connor muttered.

"Yeah, maybe," Jake said. "But look, he's not about to

change, so let's play the game his way and get the old man firmly on our side. I want this deal to go through."

Connor's eyes narrowed in reflection. "Believe me, I want that, too." Wellstone Corporation was a perfect fit for MacLaren, he mused. Jonas Wellstone had started his brewery fifty years ago, decades before the MacLarens came along. He had been at the front of the line when lucrative markets in Asia and Micronesia first began to open up. Yes, the MacLarens had done incredibly well for themselves, but they had to admit they were still playing catch-up to the older, more established companies. Last year, the brothers had set a goal of acquiring a strong foothold in those emerging territories. And here they were, less than a year later, being presented with the opportunity to purchase Wellstone.

So if all it took to attain their objective were some spiffy new clothes, the decision was an easy one. Connor would go shopping this afternoon.

"Okay, you guys win." He held up his hands in mock surrender. "I'll buy a damn suit."

"I'll go with you," Jake said, adjusting the cuffs on his tailor-made shirt. "I don't trust your taste."

The hand gesture Connor flipped his brother was crude but to the point. "This is the reason I hate coming into the big city. I get nothing but grief from you two wheeler-dealers."

Ian stood to leave. "Spare us the country bumpkin act. You're more of a cutthroat than we are."

Connor laughed and stretched his legs out. "My rustic charm conceals my rapier-sharp business skills."

Ian snorted. "Good one."

Jake ignored them both as he checked his wristwatch. "I'll have Lucinda clear my schedule for this afternoon."

"Fine," Connor said. "Let's get this over with."

Jake nodded. "I'll swing by here around three and we'll

head over to Union Square. We've only got a week to buy you a suit and get it tailored. You'll need shoes, too. And a couple of dress shirts."

"Cuff links, too," Ian added. "And a new belt. And a haircut. You look like one of Angus Campbell's goats."

"Get outta here," Connor said, fed up with the whole conversation. But as his brothers headed for the door, Connor suddenly remembered something. "Wait. What was that you said about needing a woman?"

Ian turned back around but didn't make eye contact. "You need to bring a date to dinner. Jonas likes to see his partners in happy relationships."

"And you didn't tell him that's a deal breaker?"

Ian scowled and walked out as Jake and Connor exchanged glances.

"Just find a date," Jake said finally. "And don't piss her off."

Definitely a deal breaker, Connor thought.

Abandon hope, all ye who enter here.

There should've been a sign announcing that sentiment, Maggie Jameson thought as she stared at the massive double doors that led to the offices of MacLaren International Corporation. But Maggie wasn't about to give up hope. She was on a mission, so rather than whimper and crawl away, she summoned every last bit of courage she could muster and pushed through the doors to announce herself to the pleasant, well-dressed receptionist named Susan at the front desk.

"He's expecting you, Ms. James," Susan said with a genuine smile. "Please follow me."

James? You had to give them a fake name to even get near him, the voice inside her head said, jeering. *Walk away before they toss you out on your ear.*

"Shush," Maggie whispered to herself.

But the sarcastic little voice in her head wouldn't stay silent as Maggie followed the charming receptionist down the wide, plushly carpeted halls. And as if to amplify the mental taunts, everywhere she looked there were signs that the MacLaren brothers had succeeded beyond anyone's wildest dreams. Huge posters of the latest MacLaren products hung on the corridor walls as she passed. Lush plants grew in profusion. Glassed-in office spaces boasted state-of-the-art furnishings and technology.

Maggie was even treated to the occasional stunning view, through wide windows, of the gleaming San Francisco Bay in the distance. Just in case she forgot that this was the penthouse suite of the office building owned by the MacLaren Brothers of Point Cairn, California. As if she could.

Despite her best efforts, Maggie felt a tingle of pleasure that Connor MacLaren had done so well for himself.

Yeah, maybe he'll give you a nice, shiny medal for doing him such a big favor.

Maggie sighed and glanced around. The receptionist was many yards ahead of her down the hall, and Maggie had to double her speed to keep up. How long was this darn hallway anyway? Where was Connor's office? In the next county? She should've left a trail of bread crumbs. If she had to leave in a hurry, she'd never find her way out. Heck, she could wander these corridors for years. It was starting to feel as if she was stuck on some kind of never-ending death march.

Stop whining. Just turn around and walk away before it's too late.

If she had a choice, she would take her own subliminal advice and hightail it out of there. She'd taken a big risk coming here and now she was regretting it with every step she took. Hadn't she spent half of her life avoiding risks? So why in the world was she here?

Because she didn't have a choice. She was desperate. Truly, completely desperate. Connor MacLaren was her last hope.

But he hates you, and for good reason. Walk away. Walk away.

"Oh, shut up!"

Susan stopped and turned. "Is something wrong, Ms. James?"

Yes, something's wrong! That's not my real name! Maggie wanted to shout, but instead she flashed a bright smile. "No, absolutely nothing."

As soon as the woman continued walking, Maggie rolled her eyes. Not only was she talking to herself, but now she was arguing with herself, too. Out loud. This couldn't be a good sign.

Her life truly had descended to the lowest rung of the pits of hell, not to be overly dramatic about it.

Even the cheery receptionist had caught on to the desperation vibe that hung on Maggie like a bad suit. She had taken one look at Maggie's faded blue jeans and ancient suede jacket, and smiled at her with so much sympathy in her eyes that Maggie wouldn't be surprised to have the woman slip her a ten-dollar bill on her way out.

Treat yourself to a hot meal, sweetie, Maggie imagined the woman whispering kindly.

Unquestionably, Maggie had been hiding out in the remote hills of Marin for way too long. Glancing down at her serviceable old jacket and jeans, she realized that she'd lost the ability to dress for success. Her boots were ancient. She hadn't been to a beauty spa in more than three years. True, she hadn't exactly turned into a cave dweller, but she certainly wasn't on top of her fashion game, either. And while that wasn't a bad thing as far as Maggie was concerned, it was probably a mistake not to have factored it in when she was about to go face-to-face with one of Northern California's top power brokers.

The man whose heart everyone believed she'd broken ten years ago.

Someday she would find out why Connor had allowed everyone in town to believe it was her fault they'd broken up all those years ago. It wasn't true, of course. They'd had what could charitably be called a mutual parting of the ways. She could remember their last conversation as if had happened yesterday because Maggie was the one who'd ended up with a broken heart. Her life had changed drastically after that, and not in a good way.

Why had her old friends turned their backs on her and blamed her for hurting Connor so badly? Had he lied about it after she left town? It didn't seem like something Connor would have done, but she had been away such a long time. Maybe he had changed.

Maggie shook her head. She would never understand men and she wasn't even sure she wanted to. But someday she would ask him why he did it. Not today, though, when she had so many bigger problems to deal with. She didn't dare take the risk.

Turn around. Walk away.

"Here we are," Susan the receptionist said cheerfully as she came to a stop in front of another set of intimidating double doors. "Please go right in, Ms. James. He's expecting you."

No, he isn't! He's not expecting a liar!

Maggie smiled stiffly. "Thank you, Susan."

The woman walked away and Maggie faced the closed doors. She could feel her heart pounding against her ribs. The urge to walk—no, *run*—away was visceral. But she'd come this far on sheer nerves, so there was no way she would walk away now. Besides, even if she did try to leave, she'd never find her way out of this office maze.

"Just get it over with," she muttered, and praying for strength, she pushed on the door. It opened silently, gliding across the thick carpeting.

At her first glimpse of Connor, Maggie's throat tightened. She tried to swallow, but it was no use. She would just have to live with this tender, emotional lump in her throat forever.

He sat with complete ease behind an enormous cherry wood desk, unaware that he was being watched as he read over some sort of document.

She was glad now that she'd made the appointment to see him here in his San Francisco office instead of facing him down back home. Not only would she avoid the gossip that would've invariably erupted when people found out she'd been spotted at the MacLaren Brewery, but she also would've missed seeing him backlit by the gorgeous skyline of San Francisco. Somehow he fit in here as well as he did back home.

For a long moment, she simply reveled at the sight of him. He had always been the most handsome boy she'd ever known, so how was it possible that he was even more gorgeous now than she remembered? He was a man now, tall, with wide shoulders and long legs. His dark, wavy hair was an inch or two longer than was currently fashionable, especially for a power broker like him. She had always loved his remarkable dark blue eyes, his strong jawline, his dazzling smile. His face was lightly tanned from working outside, and his well-shaped hands and long fingers were magical…

A wave of longing swept through her at the thought of Connor's hands and what he was capable of doing with them.

Maggie sighed inwardly. Lovemaking was one aspect of their relationship that had always been perfect. Yes, Connor had taken too many foolish risks with his extreme sports, and yes, Maggie's fears for his safety had driven her crazy sometimes and had ultimately led to their breakup. But when it came to romance, theirs had been a match made in heaven.

Maggie remembered her grandpa Angus saying that the MacLaren brothers had done well for themselves. Now, observing Connor in this luxury penthouse office, she could see that Grandpa's comment had been a gross understatement. She probably had no right to feel this much pride in the brothers' accomplishments, but she felt it anyway.

At the thought of her grandfather, Maggie dragged her wandering mind back to the task at hand. Grandpa Angus was the main reason she was daring to show her face here today.

Connor hadn't noticed her yet, and for one more fleeting moment, she thought about turning and running away. He would never have to know she had been here and she would never have to experience the look of anger and maybe pain in his eyes. And he would never know to what extent she'd been willing to risk humiliating herself. But it was too late for all that. She had been running from her mistakes ever since she first left Connor, and it was time to stop.

"Hello, Connor," she said at long last, hoping he couldn't hear the nerves jangling in her voice.

He looked up and stared at her for a long moment. Had she changed so much that he didn't even recognize her? But then one of his eyebrows quirked up, and not in a "happy to see you" kind of way.

He pushed his chair away from the desk and folded his arms across his muscular chest. After another lengthy, highly charged moment, during which he never broke eye contact with her, he finally drawled, "Hello, Mary Margaret."

The sound of his deep voice made the hairs on her arms stand at attention. Amazingly, he still retained a hint of a

Scottish accent, even though he'd lived in Northern California since he was in grade school.

Anxious, but determined not to show it, she took a few steps forward. "How are you?" Her voice cracked again and she wanted to sink into the carpet, but she powered forward with a determined smile.

"I'm busy." He made a show of checking his watch, then stood. "I'm about to go into a meeting, so I'm afraid I don't have time to talk right now. But thanks for stopping by, Maggie."

She deserved that, deserved to have him blow her off, but it hurt anyway. She took slow, even breaths in an effort to maintain her dignity, for she had no intention of leaving. "Your meeting is with me, Connor."

He smiled patiently, as though she were a recalcitrant five-year-old. "No, it's not. Believe me, I would never have agreed to meet with you."

She said nothing as she watched him study her for several long seconds until she saw the moment when realization struck.

"Ah, I get it," he said evenly. "So you're Taylor James. Inventive name."

"Thank you," Maggie murmured, even though she could tell by his tone that he wasn't the least bit impressed by her cleverness. She'd managed to use part of her real last name and had come up with a first name that could be male or female. She tugged her jacket closer. Had the temperature dropped in here? Probably not, but she felt a chill right down to her bones.

"Why the subterfuge, Maggie?"

She kept her tone as casual as she could manage. "I wanted to see if I could make it in the business without leaning on my family name." It was the same lie she'd been telling herself for the past three years she'd been back in Point Cairn. The truth was too embarrassing to admit.

"How intrepid of you," he said dryly.

She watched for a smile or even a scowl, but Connor revealed nothing but indifference. No real emotion at all. She had anticipated something more from him. Hurt. Anger. Rage, even. She could've accepted that. But Connor didn't appear to be fazed one way or the other by anything she said or did.

That's where the chill came from. She shivered again.

But honestly, what did she expect? Happy hugs? Not likely since she'd found out that he'd considered her departure such a betrayal. But if his current mood was any indication, he had obviously moved on long ago.

And so did you, she reminded herself.

He circled his desk and leaned his hip against the smooth wood edge. "I heard you've been back in town for a while now. Funny how we've never run into each other."

"I keep a low profile," she said, smiling briefly. The fact was, she'd spotted him a number of times on the streets of their small hometown of Point Cairn. Each time, she'd taken off running in the opposite direction. It was self-protection, plain and simple, as well as her usual risk aversion.

She'd returned to Point Cairn three years ago in a low state, her heart and her self-confidence battered and bruised. There was no way she would've been strong enough to confront Connor on his home turf. Not back then. She was barely able to do so right this minute. In fact, she could feel her thin facade beginning to crack and wondered how much longer she could be in his presence without melting down.

"How's your grandfather?" he asked, changing the subject. "I haven't seen him in a few weeks."

She smiled appreciatively. He and his brothers had always had a soft spot for Angus Campbell, and the feeling was mutual. "Grandpa is…well, he's part of the reason I've come to see you today."

He straightened. "What's wrong? Is he ill?"

Maggie hesitated. "Well, let's just say he's not getting any younger."

Connor chuckled. "He'll outlive us all."

"I hope so."

He folded his arms again, as if to erect an extra barrier between them. "What is it you want, Maggie?"

She reached into her bag and pulled out a thick folder. "I want to discuss your offer."

He reached for the folder, opened it and riffled through the stack of papers. They were all letters and copies of emails sent to someone named Taylor James. Many had been signed by Connor, himself, but there were offers from others in there, too. He looked at Maggie. "These were sent to Taylor James."

"And that's me."

"But I was unaware of that fact when I made those offers. If I'd known Taylor James was you, Maggie, I never would've tried to make contact." He closed the folder and handed it back to her. "My offer is rescinded."

"No." She took a hasty step backward, as though the folder were on fire. "You can't do that."

For the first time, his smile reached his eyes. In fact, they fairly twinkled with perverse glee as he took a step closer. "Yes, I can. I just did."

"No, Connor. No. I need you to—"

In a heartbeat, his gaze turned to frost. "I'm not interested in what you need, Maggie. It's too late for that."

"But—"

"Meeting's over. It's time for you to go."

For the briefest second, her shoulders slumped. But just as quickly, she reminded herself that she was stronger now and giving up was not an option. She used her old trick of mentally counting from one to five as she made one last effort to draw from that sturdy well of self-confidence she'd fought so hard to reconstruct.

Defiantly she lifted her chin and stared him in the eyes. "I'm not leaving this office until you hear what I have to say."

Two

He had to admire her persistence.

Still, there was no way Connor would play this game with her. At this point in his life, he wanted less than nothing to do with Mary Margaret Jameson. Yes, they'd been high school sweethearts and college lovers. At age twenty-two, he'd been crazy in love with her and had planned to live with her for the rest of his life. But then she'd left him with barely a word of warning, moved to the East Coast and married some rich guy, shattering Connor's foolish heart into a zillion pieces. That was ten years ago. At the time, he vowed never to be made a fool of again by any woman, especially Maggie Jameson.

Except it now looked as if she'd succeeded in fooling him again. All it took was a convenient lie. But then, he'd found out long ago just how good Maggie was at lying.

The last time they'd spoken to each other was on the phone. How screwed up was it that Connor could still remember their final conversation? He'd been about to go on some camping thing with his brothers and she'd mentioned that she wouldn't be there when he got home. How could he have known she meant that she *really* wouldn't be there? Like, gone. Out of his life. Forever.

Well, until today. Now here she was, claiming to be the very person he'd been trying to track down for months.

Odd how this mystery had played itself out, Connor thought. Eighteen months ago, a fledgling beer maker began to appear on the scene and was soon sweeping medals and gold ribbons at every beer competition in the western states. The extraordinary young brewmeister's name was Taylor James, but that was all anyone knew about "him." He never showed up in person to present his latest formulation or to claim his prize, sending a representative instead.

Taylor James's reputation gained ground as the quality of his formulas grew. He won more and more major prize categories while attracting more and more attention within the industry.

And yet no one had ever seen him.

Connor had been determined to find Taylor James and, with any luck, buy him out. Or hire him. But he hadn't been able to locate him. Who was this person making these great new beers and ales while continuing to hide himself away from his adoring public? For the past year, Taylor James had continued to beat out every other rival. Including, for the first time ever, MacLaren's Pride, the pale ale that had put the MacLaren brothers on the map and helped them make their first million. Losing that contest had been a slap in the face and had made the MacLarens even more determined to find the mysterious beer maker.

Through one of the competitions, Connor was able to obtain Taylor James's email address and immediately started writing the guy. He received no answer. From another competition, Connor unearthed a post office box number. He began sending letters, asking if the elusive brewer would be interested in meeting to discuss an investment opportunity. He never heard a word back—until this moment.

Now as he stared at the woman claiming to be the reclusive new genius of beer making, Connor was tempted to toss the fraudulent Ms. James out on her ear. It would be even more fun to call security and have her ignominiously escorted out to the sidewalk. The shameful exit might give her a minuscule taste of the pain and humiliation he'd endured when she walked out of his life all those years ago.

But that would send the wrong signal, Connor reasoned. Maggie would take it as a sign that he actually cared one way or the other about her. And he didn't. The purely physical reaction to her presence meant nothing. He was a guy, after all. And he had to admit he was curious as to why she'd hidden herself away and worked under an assumed name. She was a talented brewer, damn it. Her latest series of beers and ales were spectacular. And why wouldn't they be? She came from a long line of clever Scottish brewers, including her grandfather Angus, who had retired from the business years ago.

So he'd give her a few minutes to tell her story. And then he'd kick her excellent behind right out of his office.

With a generous sweep of his hand, he offered her one of the visitors' chairs. Once she was seated, he sat and faced her. "You've got five minutes to say whatever you came to tell me, Maggie."

"Fine." She sat and cleared her throat, then smoothed her jacket down a few times. She seemed nervous, but Connor knew better. She was playing the delicate angel, a role she had always performed to perfection.

He scowled, remembering that he used to call her his Red-Haired Angel. She still had gorgeous thick red hair that tumbled down her back, and her skin was still that perfect peaches and cream he'd always loved to touch. God, she was as beautiful as she was the day he met her. But she was no angel. Connor had learned that the hard way.

"My formulas have won every eligible competition for the past eighteen months," she began slowly, picking up speed and confidence as she spoke. "I've singlehandedly transformed the pale ale category overnight. That's a quote from the leading reviewer in the industry, by the way. And it's well deserved. I'm the best new beer maker to come along in years."

"I know all that." Connor sat back in his chair. "It's one of the reasons why I've been trying to hunt down Taylor James all these months. For some reason, *he* didn't feel compelled to respond."

"*He* wasn't ready," she murmured, staring at her hands.

Connor was certain that those were the first truthful words she'd uttered since walking into his office.

She pursed her lips as if weighing her next sentence, but all Connor could think was that those heaven-sent lips were still so desirable that one pout from her could twist his guts into knots.

His fists tightened. He was about to put an end to this nonsense when she finally continued to talk.

"Here's my offer," she said, leaning forward in her chair. "I'll sell you all of those prizewinning formulas and I'll also create something unique and new for MacLaren. It'll be perfect as a Christmas ale and you'll sell every last bottle, I guarantee it."

"At what price, Maggie?"

She hesitated, then named a figure that would keep a small country afloat for a year or two. The amount was so far out in left field, Connor began to laugh. "That's absurd. It's not worth it."

"Yes, it is," she insisted. "And you know it, Connor. You said it yourself. The Taylor James brand is golden. You'll be able to use the name on all your packaging and advertising and you'll make your money back a thousand times over."

She was right, but he wasn't going to admit that just yet. He stared at her for a minute, wondering what her real motivation was. Why had she come to him? There had to be other companies that wanted to do business with her. Or rather, with *Taylor James*.

"Why now, Maggie?" he asked quietly. "Why do you want to sell those formulas? And why sell to me?"

"Why?" She bit her luscious bottom lip and Connor had to fight back a groan. Irritated with himself as much as he was with her, he pushed himself out of his chair and scowled down at her. "Answer me, Maggie. Tell me the truth or get the hell out of here. I don't have time for this crap."

"You want the truth?" She jumped up from her chair and glared right back at him. "Fine. I need the money. Are you happy? Does it fill your heart with joy to hear me say it? I'm desperate. I've been turned down by every bank in town. I would go to other beer companies, but I don't have the time to sift through bids and counteroffers. I need money now. That's why I came to you. I've run out of choices. It's you or…"

She exhaled heavily and slid down onto the arm of the chair. It seemed that she'd run out of steam. "There. That's it. Are you happy now?"

"At least I'm hearing the truth for once."

She looked up and made a face at him. He almost laughed, but couldn't. She'd expended all her energy trying to finagle a deal with him and she just didn't have it in her. She might well be the worst negotiator he'd ever dealt with. And for some damn reason, he found it endearing.

For his own self-preservation, he'd have to get over that feeling fast.

"Where did all your money go?" he asked. "You must've gotten a hefty settlement from your rich husband." He gave her a slow up-and-down look, taking in her faded jeans and worn jacket. "It's obvious you didn't spend it all on shoes."

"Very funny," she muttered, and followed his gaze down to her ratty old boots. After a long moment, she looked up at him. "I know what you must think of me personally, but

I'm too close to the edge to care. I just need a loan. Can you help me or not?"

"What's the money for?" he asked.

She pressed her lips together in a stubborn line, then sighed. "I need to expand my business."

"If you're selling me all your formulas, you won't have a business left."

"I can always come up with new recipes. My Taylor James brand is going strong, growing more profitable every day. And my new Redhead line is popular, too."

"Then what's the money for?" he asked again, slowly, deliberately.

"I need to upgrade my equipment. I need to hire some help. I need to develop a sales force." She sighed and stared at her hands. "I need to make enough money to take care of my grandfather."

He frowned. "You mentioned Angus earlier. Is something wrong with him?"

It was as if all the air fled from her lungs. Her shoulders slumped and God help him, he thought he saw a glimmer of tears in her beautiful brown eyes.

"He's been to the hospital twice now. It's his heart. I'm so worried about him. He runs out of breath so easily these days, but he refuses to give up his goats. Or his scotch."

"Some things are sacred to a man."

"Goats and scotch." She rolled her eyes. "He insists that he's hale and hearty, but I know it's not true. I'm scared, Connor." She ran one hand through her hair, pushing it back from her face. "He needs medication. They have a new drug that would be perfect for someone in his condition, but we found out it's considered experimental. The insurance won't cover it and it's too expensive for me to pay for it."

Connor frowned. This wasn't good news. Angus Campbell was one of the sweetest old guys he'd ever known. Connor and his brothers were first inspired to make their own beer while watching Angus at work in the Campbell family pub. That brew pub had been on Main Street in Point Cairn for as long as Connor could remember. Growing up, he and his brothers had all worked there during the summer months.

Then five years ago, Angus lost his beloved wife, Doreen. That's when Maggie's mom sold the pub to the MacLaren brothers. Angus insisted that she move to Florida to live with her sister, something she'd been talking about for years. But that left Angus alone with his goat farm, though he got occasional help from the neighborhood boys. This had all happened during the time Maggie was living back east with her rich husband.

Now Maggie was back home and the only family she had left in Point Cairn was her grandpa Angus.

Connor made a decision. "I'll pay for that medication."

"We don't need charity, Connor."

Her words annoyed him at the same time as he admired her for saying them. "I'm not talking about charity, Maggie. Call it payback. Angus was always good to us."

"I know," she said softly. "But he's almost eighty years old. There'll be lots more medication in the future, along with a hundred other unexpected expenses. I need cash going forward to get my brewery up and running. That way, I'll be able to generate enough funds of my own to pay for Grandpa's health care needs." She started walking, pacing the confines of his office as if she couldn't bear to stand still any longer. "I'll also be able to hire some workers for both me and Grandpa and maybe make a few improvements to the farm. I'm looking to arrange a business deal, Connor. A fair trade, not a handout. And I need to do it right away."

"What happened at the bank?"

"I expected them to come through, but they turned me down. They explained that with the economy and all…" She gave a dispirited shrug.

Connor had been watching her carefully. He had a feeling there was something she wasn't telling him. Why wouldn't the bank loan her the money? Even though she was divorced, she must have received a hefty settlement. Her beers and ales were kicking ass all over the state, so she had to be considered a good risk. Was she hoarding the settlement money away for some reason?

And another thing. She and her grandfather owned at least a hundred acres of prime Marin farmland that would make excellent collateral for any bank loan.

She might not be lying to him at the moment, but she was holding back some information. Connor would pry it out of her eventually, but in the meantime, a plan had been forming in his mind as they talked. If he wasn't mistaken, and he rarely was, it would be the answer to all their problems. She would get her money and he would get something he wanted.

Call it restitution.

"I'll give you the money," he said.

She blinked. "You will?"

"Yeah." He hadn't realized until Maggie showed up today that he still harbored so many ambivalent feelings for her. Part of him wanted to kick her to the curb, while another more rowdy part of him wanted to shove everything off his desk and have his way with her right then and there.

He thought she had a lot of nerve showing up here asking for money. And yet he also thought she showed guts. It was driving him nuts just listening to her breathe, so why shouldn't he pull her chain a little? Just to settle the score.

"What's the catch?" she said warily.

He chuckled. Once again, she'd thrown him off base. She should've been doing cartwheels, knowing she'd get the money, but instead she continued to peer suspiciously at him.

"The catch," he explained, "is that it won't be a loan. I want something in return."

"Of course," she said, brightening. "I've already promised you the Taylor James formulas."

"Yeah, I'll take those formulas," he said, "but there's something else I want from you."

Her eyes wide, she took a small step backward. "I don't think so."

"Take it or leave it, Maggie," Connor snapped.

"Take or leave what?" she said in a huff. "I don't even know what you're talking about."

He shoved his hands in his pockets. "It seems I need a date."

"A date?" she scoffed. "You must know a hundred women who would—"

"Let me put it this way. I need a woman who knows a little something about beer. You more than meet that requirement, so I intend to use your services for a week."

"My...*services?* What are you talking about?"

"I'm talking about taking you up on your deal. I'll pay you the entire amount of money you asked for in exchange for your formulas, plus this one other condition."

"That I'm at your *service* for a week? This is ridiculous." Agitated, she began to pace the floor of his office even faster.

"It's only for a week," he said reasonably. "Seven days and nights."

"Nights?" she repeated, her eyes narrowing.

He shrugged lightly, knowing exactly what she was thinking. Sex. "That's entirely up to you."

"This is blackmail," she muttered.

"No, it's not. I'm about to give you a lot of money and I want something in return."

"My services," she said sarcastically.

"That's right. Look, the Autumn Brew Festival is next week."

"I know that," she grumbled.

"I need a date, and you're the perfect choice. So you will agree to be my date the entire week and go to all the competition events with me. I'll also want you to attend a number of meetings and social events with me, including the Friday night gala dinner dance."

That suspicious look was back. "Are you kidding?"

"What? You don't like to dance?"

She looked stricken by his words but quickly recovered. "No, I don't, as a matter of fact."

That was weird. Maggie had always loved dancing. "Doesn't matter," he said. "You're going to the gala."

"We'll see about that." Her eyes focused in on him. "And that's it? We pal around for a week at the festival and I get the money?"

"That's it. And I'll expect you to stay with me in my hotel suite."

She stopped and stared at him. "Oh, please."

"You want the money or not?"

"You know I do, but I can drive in and meet you each morning."

"That won't work. I expect us to keep late hours and I have a number of early morning breakfast meetings scheduled. I don't want to take any chances on you missing something important."

"But—"

"Look, Maggie. Let me make it clear so there's no misunderstanding. I don't expect you to sleep with me. I just expect you to stay at the hotel with me. It'll be more convenient."

She frowned. "But I can't leave Grandpa for that long a time."

"My mother will look in on him," he said, silently patting himself on the back for his split-second problem-solving abilities. Deidre MacLaren had known Angus for years, so Connor knew she wouldn't mind doing it.

"And at the end of the week," he continued calmly, "I'll give you the money you asked for in full."

"And all I have to do is stay with you for a week?"

"And be my date."

"In your hotel room."

"It's a suite."

"I'll sleep on the couch."

"You'll be more comfortable in a bed."

"And you'll sleep on the couch?"

"No."

Her eyes widened. "Stop kidding around."

His lips twitched. "Am I?"

"Wait," she said suddenly. "I'll get my own room."

"The hotel is sold out."

A line marred her forehead as she considered that for a moment, and then she brightened. "We can switch off between the couch and—"

"Take the deal or leave it, Maggie."

She flashed him a dark look. "Give me a minute to think."

"No problem."

She took to pacing the floor again, probably to work out the many creative ways she would say *no* to his outlandish offer. But she would definitely say no, wouldn't she?

Hell, what in the world was he thinking? God forbid she agreed to his conditions. What would he do in a hotel suite with Maggie for a week? Well, hell, he knew what he *wanted* to do with her. She was a beautiful woman and he still remembered every enticing inch of her body. He'd never forgotten all the ways he'd brought her pleasure. Those thoughts had plagued him for years, so living with her for a week would be a dangerous temptation. It would be for the best if she refused the offer.

And once she turned him down, Connor would go ahead and pay for Angus's medication, even if he had to sneak behind her back to do it. And as for Maggie getting a loan to grow her business, he figured that would happen eventually. She'd either find a bank that would agree to it or she'd tap one of the other brewery owners.

That thought didn't sit well with him, though. He didn't want anyone else getting their hands on her beer formulas. Or her, either, if he was being honest.

And in case he'd forgotten, he still needed a date for the Wellstone dinner meeting. As much as he hated to admit it, Maggie would be perfect as his date. Jonas Wellstone would fall in love with her.

So maybe he'd gone too far. If she turned him down— hell, *when* she turned him down, he would simply renegotiate to get those formulas and to convince her to be his date at the Wellstone dinner. That's all he really wanted.

Meanwhile, he had to chuckle as he watched her stomp and grumble to herself. A part of him wanted to take her in his arms and comfort her—in more ways than one. But once again, that wayward part of him was doomed to disappointment, because other than the obvious outward attraction to her, Maggie meant nothing to him now, thank goodness. He counted himself lucky that he'd gotten over her duplicity years ago. This offer of his was just sweet payback, pure and simple. It felt damn good to push some of her buttons the way she'd pushed his in the past, saying one thing but meaning something else. Keeping him in a constant state of confusion. Now it was his turn to shake her up a little.

"So what's your answer, Maggie?" he asked finally.

On the opposite side of the room, Maggie halted in her pacing and turned to face him. A big mistake. She could feel his magnetic pull from all the way over there. Why did he still have to be so gorgeous and tall and rugged after all these years? It wasn't fair. She could feel her hormones yipping and snapping and begging her to take him up on his offer to spend a week together in that hotel suite of his.

What was wrong with her? Unless she'd missed the clues, he was clearly out for revenge, pure and simple. Imagine him insisting that she provide him *services* for a week. Even though he'd assured her that she wasn't expected to sleep with him, she had a feeling he wasn't talking about a plain old dinner date here and there.

Services, indeed!

At that, her stomach nerves began to twitch and buzz with excitement. *Services!*

Oh, this wasn't good.

"Maggie?"

"Yes, damn it. Yes, I'll do it," she said, waving her hands in submission.

He hesitated, then took what looked like a fortifying breath. "Good."

"But I won't sleep with you." She pointed her finger at him for emphasis.

He tilted his head to study her. "I told you I don't expect you to."

"But...the hotel suite." She let go of the breath she didn't know she'd been holding. "Okay. But...never mind. Good. Fine. That's fine." She stopped talking as she felt heat rise up her neck and spread to her cheeks. She tended to turn bright pink when she was embarrassed, so Connor probably noticed it, too. Even though he'd made it clear he didn't want to sleep with her, she'd assumed...well. That's what she got for assuming anything. Apparently he just wanted to keep tabs on her.

If she'd thought about it for a second or two, she would've realized that he could have any woman he wanted. They probably waited in line outside his door and threw themselves at him wherever he went. Why would he want to sleep with Maggie, especially after he'd spent all these years thinking she had betrayed him? All he wanted was a date, someone who knew something about the brewery business. And that description fit her perfectly.

"I misunderstood," she admitted.

"Yeah, you did," he said, his tone lowering seductively as he approached her. "Because if you and I were to do what your mind is imagining, Maggie, there wouldn't be much sleeping going on."

Staggered, Maggie felt her mouth drop open. "Oh."

"So it's settled," he said, breezily changing tempo again as he tugged her arm through his and walked her to the door. "I'll pick you up Sunday morning and we'll drive together. Be sure to pack something special for the gala and a few cocktail dresses. We'll be dining with a number of important business associates, and I want them to walk away impressed."

She refused to mention that she only owned two simple cocktail dresses and nothing formal, having given away most of her extensive wardrobe to the local consignment shop three years ago. Instead she turned and jabbed her finger in his chest for emphasis. "Just so we're clear, Connor. I'm not going to have sex with you."

He looked down at her finger, then up to meet her gaze. "Still negotiating, huh?"

She whipped her hand away and immediately missed the sizzle of heat she'd gotten from touching his chest. She told herself it meant nothing. It had just been a while since she'd touched a man. Like, years. No wonder she was getting a contact high.

"I'm serious, Connor," she said, hating that her voice sounded so breathless. "I'll share your room with you, but that's it."

"It's a suite," he corrected, and slowly leaned over and kissed her neck.

Dear Lord, what was he doing? She knew she should slap him, push him away, but instead she shivered at the exquisite feel of his lips on her skin.

"Say it with me," he murmured. "Suite."

"Suite," she murmured, arching into him when he gently nipped her earlobe. This had to stop. Any minute now.

"Sweet," he whispered, then pulled her into his arms and kissed her.

Three

The heat was instantaneous. Maggie felt as if she were on fire and she reveled in the warmth of his touch. She couldn't remember feeling this immediate need, not even years ago when she and Connor first made love. And certainly not in all her years with Alan Cosgrove, her less than affectionate ex-husband.

Good grief, why was she thinking about a cold fish like Alan when Connor's hot, sexy mouth was currently devouring her own?

She gripped his shirt, knowing she ought to put an end to this and leave right now. Talk about taking a risk! This was madness. She had to stop. But oh, please, no, not yet. For just another moment, she wanted to savor his lips against hers, his touch, his strength, his need. It had been much too long since any man had needed her like this.

Connor had always been a clever, considerate lover, but now he was masterful as he maneuvered her lips apart and slid his tongue inside to tangle with her own, further melting her resistance. His arms encircled her, his hands swept up and down her back with a clear sensual awareness of her body as his mouth continued to plunder hers.

And just at the point where she was ready to give him anything he wanted, Connor ended the kiss. She wobbled, completely off balance for a moment. She wanted to protest and whine for him to kiss her again. But she managed to control herself, taking time to adjust the shoulder strap of her bag and straighten her jacket.

Then she glanced up and caught his self-satisfied smile. He looked as if he'd just won a bet with someone, maybe himself.

She remembered that smile, remembered loving it, loving him. Times changed, though, and just because they'd shared an amazing kiss didn't mean she had any intention of sleeping with him. Still, at least she knew what she was up against now. Was she crazy to have such strong feelings for him after so many years? No, it would only be crazy if she acted on those feelings. She needed to remind herself of the only thing that mattered: getting the loan, by almost any means necessary. Which meant that she would walk through fire to get it. And Connor MacLaren was fire personified.

She took a deep breath and struggled to maintain a carefree tone. "I guess I'll see you Sunday, then."

"Yes, you will." And with a friendly stroke of her hair, Connor opened the office door. "Drive home safely."

"I will. Goodbye, Connor."

She strolled from his office in a passion-soaked haze. But despite her earlier concerns, she somehow found her way out of the large office maze and down to the parking garage. And before she knew it, she was driving toward the Golden Gate Bridge and heading for home.

The kiss meant nothing, Connor assured himself as he closed his office door. He'd just been trying to teach her a lesson. Testing her. Keeping her on her toes. He'd wanted to prove she was lying when she claimed she wouldn't dream of having sex with him. And, he told himself, he'd done a hell of a job. She had practically ripped his shirt off right there and then. Hell, if he hadn't put an end to the kiss when he did, they would be going at it naked on his office couch by now.

And didn't that paint a provocative picture? Damn. The

image of her writhing in naked splendor on the soft leather couch was stunning in its clarity, causing him to grow rock hard instantly. In his mind's eye, he could almost touch the gentle slope of her curvaceous breasts, could almost taste her silky skin.

"Idiot," he muttered, straining to adjust himself before settling back to work. "Explain again why you stopped kissing her?"

At the time, it had made sense to stop, he argued silently. But now, as he hungered for more…he shook his head. Maggie had always had the ability to tie him into knots and now she was doing it again. Damn it, he was a different man than he was ten years ago. Stronger. Smarter. He wasn't about to let her call the shots again. He would be the one in control of the situation while they were together next week.

But the voice inside his head began to laugh. *Control. Good luck with that.*

He ruthlessly stifled that mocking voice. So maybe he hadn't always had a firm grip on things when he was with Maggie before. Things were different now. He still didn't trust her as far as he could throw her, which was pretty far, seeing as how she'd lost some weight since he'd last seen her. She was just as beautiful, though. Maybe more so. When he first looked up and saw her standing in his office doorway, she had taken his breath away. She'd always had that power over him, but he was older and wiser now and not about to fall for her charms again.

He wouldn't mind kissing her again, though, and was momentarily distracted by the searing memory of his mouth on hers. And it went without saying that he would do whatever it took to get her into bed with him. He was a red-blooded man, after all. Didn't mean he cared about her or anything. It was just something he'd be willing to do if the occasion presented itself—and he had every intention of making sure that the occasion presented itself.

Absently, Connor checked the time. Damn, he only had twenty minutes before Jake would show up to drag his ass out to shop for a new suit. He figured he'd better get some real work done in the meantime so he'd be ready to go when Jake got here. His brother had already warned him that he'd be on the phone with the Scottish lawyers this afternoon, and that always put Jake in a foul mood.

The lawyers from Edinburgh had been trying to convince one of the MacLaren brothers to fly to Scotland to take care of the details of their uncle Hugh's estate. Whoever made the trip would be stuck there for weeks. But that wasn't the real reason none of them wanted to go there. No, it was because Uncle Hugh had been a hateful man. Jake, Ian and Connor couldn't care less about the terms of Hugh's last will and testament, despite the fact that they were his beneficiaries, in a manner of speaking.

Even though Connor and his brothers had grown up around Point Cairn in Northern California, they'd been born in the Highlands of Scotland. They were the sons of Liam MacLaren and heirs to Castle MacLaren. But when Connor was a baby, their uncle Hugh, an evil bastard if ever there was one, swindled their father out of his inheritance.

Their dad never recovered from the betrayal and died a few years later, leaving their mother, Deidre, a widow with three young boys to raise. Unwilling to live in the same area as her despised brother-in-law, she moved with her boys to Northern California to be near her sister. Connor had no memory of any other home except the rugged hills that overlooked the wild, rocky coast of Marin County.

Connor stared out the office window at the stunning view of the Golden Gate Bridge and the Marin shoreline beyond. Maybe in some small way, their uncle had done them all a favor because Connor couldn't imagine living anywhere else in the world. Hell, he never would have met Maggie Jameson otherwise, he thought, and then wondered if that was a good thing or a bad thing. He wasn't ready to decide on that one, but he couldn't help smiling in anticipation of spending the following week in a hotel suite with the gorgeous woman.

By the time she arrived home, Maggie felt relatively normal again. Her heart had finally stopped hammering in her chest, and her head had ceased its incessant buzzing. All that remained from Connor's onslaught was a mild tingling of her lips from his devastating kiss.

Mild? That was putting it, well, mildly. But never mind his kiss. What about his demands? For someone so risk-averse, Maggie still couldn't believe she'd entered the lion's den and put herself in such a perilous position. After all the lectures she'd given herself and all the positive affirmations she'd memorized, she had taken one look at Connor and practically rolled over, allowing him to take hold of the situation and make choices for her.

She pulled her car into the garage next to the barn and walked across the circular drive to the large ranch-style home she shared with her grandfather. The afternoon sun barely managed to hold its own against the autumn chill that had her tugging the collar of her old suede jacket closer to her neck. She still took a moment to appreciate the land that rolled and dipped its way down to the sheer bluffs that overlooked the rough waves of the Pacific Ocean. Despite some sorry choices in her past, she had to marvel at her own good luck. She was home now, living in a beautiful house in a magical location. Her darling grandfather, despite some tricky health issues, was still kicking, as he liked to put it. She was proud of herself, proud of how she'd finally arrived here, both emotionally and physically.

Connor MacLaren had no idea how much it had cost

her to show up at his office door with her hat in her hand, and Maggie had no intention of ever revealing that to him. She'd fought too hard to get to where she was today, and she wasn't about to gamble it all away on some *tingling* feeling she'd received from a simple kiss.

She jogged up the porch stairs and into the house, where she checked the time on the mantel clock. Her grandfather would be out in the barn milking his goats. Dropping her bag on the living room chair, she went to her bedroom to make a phone call. She was determined to avoid sharing a hotel room with Connor—even if it *was* a luxurious penthouse suite, as he had emphasized more than once.

But when she called the convention hotel to make a reservation, she was told that they were sold out, just as Connor had warned. And when she called the next closest hotel, she was quoted a price that was so far out of her range she almost laughed out loud at the reservationist.

She merely thanked her instead and hung up the phone. Then she spent a few minutes at her computer, searching for information. Finally, with nervous fingers, she dialed Connor's number.

"MacLaren," he answered.

"It's Maggie and I've been thinking, Connor," she began. "It's probably best if I commute to the festival from home after all. Grandpa isn't well and I'd rather be home each night to see him."

"I've already talked it over with my mother, Maggie," Connor replied dryly. "She plans to stop by your place twice a day and spend the night there, too. I know Angus won't put up with two women fussing at him day and night, so you'll be doing him a favor by staying away for the week."

"I'm not sure if—"

"And besides," he continued in steamroller fashion, "you've already agreed to be my date for the week, remember? In exchange for which I'm going to give you a lot of money. I think that's a pretty good deal for you."

"Pretty good deal," she echoed darkly.

"Maggie, I explained all this to you and I thought you had agreed. I'm going to need you to accompany me every day, starting with breakfast meetings and going into the late evenings with all the social events I've got to attend."

She frowned into the phone. "You never liked all that social stuff before."

"That was true ten years ago," he said smoothly. "Now I figure it's a small price to pay to get what I want."

"The price of doing business?"

"Exactly. And it won't hurt you to be seen with me, Maggie. It'll be good for your business to meet the people I know, too."

She knew he was right about that. But still. "Okay, but I'm not going to the dance."

"You're going with me, Maggie."

"You don't know what you're asking."

There was a moment of silence, and then Connor said, "Are you saying this is a deal breaker?"

Her shoulders slumped as she recognized that hard-nosed tone of his. She wasn't about to break their deal, but she still had no intention of attending the stupid dance. Especially because it wasn't just a dance. Maggie had looked it up on the festival website. The dinner dance was actually a formal affair, a gala event, meant to celebrate the culmination of the festival year and probably as snooty as any high-society ball she had ever attended in Boston. But since she didn't want to argue anymore, she left it alone for now. After a minute more of conversation, she disconnected the call.

She couldn't tell him that she didn't mind being his date for all the events during the week. That wouldn't be any problem at all. But the thought of having to share his hotel suite with him? It made her want to run through the house screaming. She didn't know how she would manage it, but unless another hotel room opened up in the next few days, she would soon find out.

But even another hotel room wouldn't fix the somewhat smaller dilemma of her not attending the dance. Maggie groaned and pushed that little problem away. If they managed to make it through the week together, Connor would just have to understand.

None of this would've been necessary if the banks hadn't turned down her loan. But the money was critical now. Even though Grandpa insisted that he was still hale and hearty and fit as a fiddle, Maggie was so afraid that one of these days he would need more care than she could afford to give him. She had gone through most of her meager settlement money fixing the roof of the house and then she'd bought a number of replacement items for the brewery.

She had been hoping to use the remaining funds as collateral, but now that Angus needed expensive medication and possibly even surgery someday, she'd reached the point of desperation. Her business was on the verge of expanding into a wider market, and that would bring in more money eventually, but before that happened, she needed to raise some capital to keep things going. And that was where Connor came into the picture. Negotiating and trading her beer formulas for cash was better than going to the bank. This way, she wouldn't have to pay back a loan.

She suddenly felt so tired and gazed at her comfortable bed longingly. How nice it would be to climb under the covers and take a long nap, but first she wanted to help Grandpa feed the goats.

As she stripped out of her "nice" jeans and pulled on her old faded pair, she had to laugh at herself. A few years ago, she wouldn't have dreamed of wearing jeans to a meeting in the city. Not even her "nice" jeans. But happily, jeans and work shirts had gradually replaced most of the clothing she'd worn during her marriage.

Alan, her ex-husband, had expected her to dress up every day, usually in smart skirts and twin sweater sets with pearls. It didn't matter what she was planning to do that day.

"You must always be seen wearing fashionable yet sensible clothing," her ex-mother-in-law, Sybil, was forever reminding her, usually in a scolding tone of voice.

Three years ago, when Maggie first arrived back in Point Cairn after her divorce, she'd had no idea what an emotional mess she was. She just knew that her marriage had gone disastrously wrong and she was determined to get past the whole experience and move forward. She wanted to catch up with old friends and explore the town she'd missed so dearly. So one day, shortly after she'd returned, she drove into Point Cairn to do the grocery shopping.

While at the store, she ran into some of her old high school friends she hadn't seen in years. She was thrilled to reconnect, but they quickly put her in her place, telling her they wanted nothing to do with her. They were still resentful that she had turned her back on the town. More important, they were livid that she'd hurt Connor so badly all those years before. Her friends had made it clear that while Connor was still universally loved and admired by one and all, Maggie was most assuredly *not*. One friend put it more succinctly: Maggie could go stuff it as far as they were concerned.

It was another blow to Maggie's already fragile self-esteem and she had limped home to cry in private. For a full month afterward, she lived in her pajamas, wandering in a daze from her bed to the couch to watch television and then back to bed again. The thought that she might've hurt Connor was devastating to her, but the notion that Connor had lied to her old friends about their mutual breakup was just as bad. Why would he do that?

She remembered tossing and turning at night, unable to sleep for all the pain she might have caused—without even meaning to do so!

Then one day, her grandfather told her he could really use her help with the goats.

Maggie's spirits had lifted. Grandpa needed her! She had a reason to get dressed and she did so carefully, choosing one of her many pastel skirts and a pale pink twinset with a tasteful gold necklace and her Etienne Aigner pumps.

When she walked into the barn, Grandpa took one look at her and asked if she thought they were going to have a tea party with the goats. He chuckled mightily at his little joke, but Maggie jolted as if she'd been rudely awakened from a bad dream. She stared down in dismay at her outfit, then ran from the barn and stumbled back to the house in tears. Poor Grandpa was bewildered by her behavior and blamed himself for upsetting her.

But Maggie knew where to place the blame. It was her own damn fault for being so weak, so blind and so stupid. She'd been well programmed by her manipulative ex-husband and could still hear his sneering voice in her head, telling her what to do, how to behave, what to wear and what she'd done wrong. As soon as their wedding vows were exchanged, Alan's disapproval began and never let up. It had come as such a rude shock and she realized later that she'd been in a terribly vulnerable state after leaving Connor. Otherwise, she might have recognized the signs of cruelty behind Alan's bland exterior.

During her marriage, she'd occasionally wondered why she ever thought Connor's love of extreme sports was too risky for her when compared to the verbal assaults she received constantly from her husband and his mother.

Maggie still couldn't get the sound of their menacing intonations out of her head.

She had thought that by moving three thousand miles

away from her ex-husband and his interfering mother, she would be rid of their ruthless control over her. But the miles didn't matter. Alan and Sybil were still free to invade Maggie's peace of mind with their disparaging comments.

That moment in the barn with Grandpa provided Maggie with a sharp blast of reality that quickly led to her complete meltdown. For days, she couldn't stop crying. Grandpa finally insisted on taking her to the local health clinic to talk to a psychologist. But how could she make sense of something so nonsensical? All she knew was that everything inside her was broken.

Gradually, though, Maggie came to realize that she was not to blame for succumbing to Alan's masterful manipulations. Through the outpatient clinic, she met other women who'd survived similar relationships. And she discovered, quite simply, that if she stayed busy with chores and projects, she didn't have time to worry and fret about the past. Oddly enough, it was Grandpa's quirky flock of goats that helped her get through the worst of it.

Lydia and Vincent Van Goat, the mom and dad goats, didn't care what Maggie was wearing or whether she was depressed or flipping out. They just wanted food, and Lydia and the other girls needed to be milked. The milk had to be weighed and recorded, then taken to the local cheesemongers to be turned into goat cheese and yogurt. The goats demanded fresh water to drink and clean straw to sleep on. Their hooves needed trimming. The newest goat babies needed special care and eventually, weaning.

They couldn't do any of it by themselves; they needed Maggie to help them survive. Maggie soon realized that she was dependent on them for her survival, too. The goats gave her a reason to get out of bed every morning. She had priorities now, in the form of a flock of friendly, curious goats.

For the next six months, much of Maggie's energy was spent tending the goats. She filled out her days by preparing meals for Grandpa and taking long walks along the cliffs and down on the rough, sandy beach. She grew a bit healthier and happier every day.

Eventually she was able to acknowledge that Grandpa was perfectly able to do most of the work with the goats himself. Thanks to Grandpa, Maggie was nearly back to being her old self, which meant that it was time for her to find a real job and make some money. Sadly, the idea of working in town where she could run into her former friends was just too daunting. That's when Grandpa suggested that while she was figuring things out, she might enjoy dabbling in her father's old family beer-making business.

The microbrewery equipment lay dormant in the long, narrow storage room next to the barn. Her father had called the room his brew house, and it was where he used to test some of the beers they served at their brewpub in town. The storage room had been locked up for years, ever since her dad died.

Maggie had fond memories of following her father around while he experimented with flavors and formulas to make different types of beers, so the idea of reviving his brew house appealed to her. Within a week, she was hosing down and sanitizing the vats, replacing a few rusted spigots and cleaning and testing the old manual bottling and kegging equipment her father had used. She spent another few weeks driving all over the county to shop for the proper ingredients and tools before she finally started her first batch of beer. And it wasn't half bad.

That was three years ago. Now Maggie could smile as she tapped one of the kegs to judge the results of her latest pale ale experiment. She had entered this one in the festival and fully expected, or *hoped,* anyway, to win a medal next week.

Once her glass was filled, she made a note of the liquid's

light golden brown appearance, then checked its aroma. Next, she tasted it, trying to be objective as she tested its flavor and balance.

"Perfect," she murmured. It just might be her best formula yet. Finished for the day, she closed off the valve and cleaned up the counter area, then took her small glass of ale out to the wide veranda that circled the house. There she relaxed and finished her drink as she watched the sun sink below the cliffs.

At this time of the afternoon, it wasn't unusual to spot a family of black-tailed deer or the occasional tule elk foraging its way past live oak trees, arroyo willows and elderberry shrubs. Maggie spied a brush rabbit scurrying across the trail, seeking cover from a red-tailed hawk that glided in the sky.

Maggie loved the wild beauty of these hills, loved the scent of sea salt in the air. She never got tired of staring at the windblown, impossibly gnarled cypress trees that lined the bluffs at the edge of the property. When she was young, she'd been certain that elves lived in those trees. Everything was magical back then.

The magic seemed to disappear after her father died. His death had marked the beginning of too many bad choices on Maggie's part. In the past few years, though, she had managed to turn things around and was now determined to bring some of that old magic back. That was one reason why the revival of her father's beer-making legacy was so important to her.

The upcoming Autumn Brew Festival would be the culmination of all her struggles to establish herself as a key player in the industry her father had loved. Maggie had come a long way and was proud to be the owner and operator of "possibly the best new small brewery in Northern California," as one critic had called her burgeoning enterprise.

But her smile faded as she was reminded again of the deal she'd struck with the devil, aka Connor MacLaren. If Maggie's old high school friends had anything to say about it, Connor should feel entirely justified in seeking his revenge next week. The slightest negative word from Connor would be enough to destroy Maggie's standing among her industry peers.

If Maggie was being honest, though, she would have to admit that it wasn't Connor's style to be vindictive or mean. On the other hand, he had blamed her for the breakup and might be willing to do something to get even with her over the next week.

But while the possibility of dirty tricks and sabotage alarmed her, Maggie's real concern was Connor himself and his dangerous proximity. How was she expected to survive a full week in the same hotel suite with him? For goodness' sake, the man had only improved with age to become the sexiest creature she'd ever seen. Maggie knew full well that he had every intention of luring her into bed with him. Could she possibly resist his sensual onslaught? Did she even want to?

She left that question unanswered, but she was adamant that whatever occurred, it would be by her own decision. She would never again allow herself to be coerced by a man. She was no longer a weak-kneed, passive girl but a confident, successful woman in control of her own destiny. And she would decide if that destiny included a sexy roll in the hay with Connor MacLaren.

The strong, confident woman giggled at that image as she went inside to start dinner.

Later, as they dined on meat loaf, mashed potatoes and freshly harvested green beans, she and her grandfather talked about the festival. "I'm afraid I'll be gone all week, Grandpa."

"I'm glad you're getting out and having some fun," he

said jovially. "And don't you worry about me. I'll be fine while you're gone."

"I won't worry," Maggie said, "because Mrs. MacLaren has already promised to stop by for a visit every day."

"That wasn't necessary," Grandpa muttered, but Maggie could tell his grumbling was just for show. He and Deidre MacLaren, Connor's mother, were lifelong friends and would have a great time visiting. More important, Mrs. MacLaren was a retired nurse so she would be able to tell in an instant if anything was wrong with Grandpa.

Maggie thought the rest of the week would drag on forever, but almost before she knew it, Sunday morning arrived and so did Connor MacLaren. She met him outside as he pulled up to the house in a shiny black pickup truck. Ignoring the sudden rush of heat she felt as she watched him approach, she carried her overstuffed suitcase awkwardly down the porch steps. He met her halfway, took the bag and easily lifted it into the back of his truck.

"I hope you have room for my kegs," Maggie said.

"That's why I brought the truck," he said, and followed her to the beer house. They made several trips back and forth, carrying the heavy kegs and securing them in the truck bed.

"Just one more thing," Maggie said, running back to the beer house. She emerged a minute later with a dolly loaded with three cases of bottled beer for the official judging.

"I guess I don't have to ask if you've entered the competition yourself," he said dryly.

"I honestly wasn't sure I would until the last minute," she admitted. "But the festival is so important I had to give it a try. But don't worry, I'm only entered in the small brewery category so I won't be competing with MacLaren."

"Good," he muttered. "You beat our asses off last time."

"I did, didn't I?" She smiled broadly.

As he loaded the cases, he noticed the markings on the box tops. "You've entered under your real name?"

"Yes." She sighed. "I decided it was time to come out of the shadows."

"Good. People should know who they're dealing with."

Was he talking about himself being deceived by her false name? Maggie kept silent, figuring the less said about that, the better.

He opened the passenger door and held her arm as she climbed up into the cab. Maggie almost groaned as her arm warmed to his touch.

"Should be an interesting contest," Connor said lightly, and slammed her door shut.

Something about his tone aroused Maggie's suspicions and they grew as she watched him circle the truck and jump into the driver's seat.

"Let me guess," she said, her heart beginning to sink. "You're one of the judges."

It was his turn to smile as he slipped the key into the ignition and started up the truck. "Yeah. Problem?"

"Oh no," she said glumly. "What could possibly go wrong?"

"No need to worry, Maggie. It's a blind tasting."

"Then why are you wearing such an evil grin?"

As Connor chuckled, she settled in for the ride.

Four

As soon as they arrived at the convention center hotel, they stowed their belongings with the bellhop, who would hold everything until their room was ready. One of the festival handlers took her kegs and assured her that they would be delivered to the beer garden, where many of the brewers served their latest beers to the festival goers all week long. Maggie took personal custody of the dolly that held the three cases she'd designated for the competition. Then Maggie and Connor went their separate ways.

Maggie could finally breathe again. The tension in the truck had been palpable and she wondered for the umpteenth time how she would survive a week in a hotel room with him. After only twenty minutes in the close quarters of his truck, she'd been *this* close to begging him to pull off to the side of the road so she could have her wicked way with him.

She could still feel the shivery vibes coiling in her spine as she recalled him coming to a stoplight, then turning to stare at her.

I want you.

He didn't have to say the words out loud. She simply knew it—and felt it. His eyes practically burned with intensity.

Goose bumps tickled her arms, heat filled her chest and—she still blushed to think about it—a tingling warmth grew between her thighs as she became aware of what he was thinking.

God help her, but she wanted him, too.

Slowly Connor had begun to grin, as if he could read her mind, damn him.

Then the signal changed to green. He'd turned away from her and stepped on the gas. And the moment was gone.

But he hadn't stopped grinning like a lunatic.

Maggie's first impulse had been to jump out of that truck and run as fast and as far as she could go. But she'd talked herself out of that plan, shook off her feelings and pulled herself together. She could handle this!

They had spent the rest of the ride making small talk, chatting about his mom, her grandfather, the goats, anything she could think of to keep herself from dwelling on Connor's sexy mouth, his dark unfathomable eyes, his impressive shoulders.

And she still thought she could avoid him for a whole week in the intimate confines of a hotel suite? Was she out of her mind? Maybe. But she'd already called the hotel twice to check on available rooms. There was nothing. In fact, there were no rooms anywhere in the area. She was stuck.

But on the other hand, maybe the hotel would have a few cancellations today.

During the ride, she had confessed to Connor, "Once we get to the hotel, I'm going to try one more time to see if there's another room available."

"Not ready to give up yet?"

"No," she said, and felt a twinge of pride. Why should she give up trying to stand on her own two feet?

He glanced at her sideways. "Fine. But you're doomed for disappointment. I have every intention of sharing the suite with you."

"But why?"

He shrugged. "I want to keep an eye on you. It's a big hotel. Anything could happen."

"What's that supposed to mean?" she demanded. "I'm perfectly capable of taking care of myself, Connor."

"I know," he said patiently, as if she might've mentioned it once or twice before. Well, maybe she had, but it bore repeating.

She continued. "I just think it's wrong for us to be…"

"Sharing a bed?" he said, finishing her sentence. "Living in such close proximity? Breathing the same air? What's the matter, Maggie? Don't think you can handle it?"

"I can handle it," she protested.

"Can you? Aren't you afraid I'll melt your resistance and have you begging for my body tonight?" He flashed her that cocky grin. "I don't blame you for being worried. Let's face it, I'm awesome. I'm smart, I'm wealthy, I'm hot, I'm, like, the perfect guy. It'll be a real challenge for you."

She burst out laughing. "Right. You wish."

Smiling agreeably, he took hold of her hand in what should've been a casual gesture, but it sent electric shock waves zipping up her arm and had her stomach muscles trembling with need.

"Look," he said. "We can check the room availability if you insist, but even if they do have something, I'd rather we stayed together. In case you forgot, you're my date for the week. You agreed to that, remember?"

"I remember." How could she forget when he kept reminding her? And she *had* agreed to abide by his terms of the deal. Not that she'd had a choice, but it was too late to whine about it now. She sighed inwardly. He was just doing this to get back at her for leaving him ten years ago. He wanted to teach her a lesson. Fine. She could handle his little power trip. If staying with him meant that she would obtain the loan money, she was willing to do whatever it took.

That money was vital to her future.

As she crossed the hotel lobby, it was clear to Maggie that as long as she kept looking for a way out of their deal, Connor would fight her at every step. And she wouldn't put it past him to fight dirty, either. So was it worth her time and energy to keep trying to pitch a flag on this hill? Probably not.

But that still didn't mean she would sleep with him, no matter what he might be planning.

After confirming with the reservationist at the front desk that there were definitely no rooms available, Maggie needed coffee. She was in luck; there was a coffee kiosk right in the lobby. After slugging down a medium café latte, she again felt capable of adult conversation.

She spent the rest of the morning on the lower level of the conference center, checking in with the judging officials. It took a long time to go through all the necessary paperwork and get her cases of beer unloaded and marked. She didn't mind the rules and procedures. The officials wanted to make sure that the so-called blind tastings were carried out in a forthright and aboveboard manner.

It was common knowledge that anyone who won a festival award was practically guaranteed thousands of additional orders along with a tremendous amount of free advertising and marketing. So to ensure that each entrant's beverages received a fair review, the festival operators went to great lengths to set up numerous firewalls and protective measures.

Maggie had no idea security would be so elaborate. Because of her need to remain anonymous, she'd managed to personally avoid the contest circuit for the past three years, so she almost laughed when she was instructed to step behind a thick red drape in order to shield herself from the curious eyes of other contestants in line.

Once behind the privacy curtain, she was greeted by a tall, beefy fellow in a tight black T-shirt who wore a name tag that read Johnny. He looked like a bouncer. "Got your copy of the entry form?"

Maggie handed him the multipage form and waited while he checked off boxes on a sheet of paper clipped to an official-looking clipboard.

"You're with Redhead Brewery?" he asked in a low voice to avoid being overheard.

"Yes," she whispered. The paranoia was contagious.

"I've never heard of Redhead Brewery and I've never seen you around here."

"It's a division of Taylor James," she said defensively, and was proud of herself for thinking fast to invoke the false name she'd used recently.

"Yeah?" Johnny looked impressed. "I love his stuff." He turned to the table next to him and sifted through one of many storage boxes filled with thick, sealed envelopes. He finally found the one he wanted and pulled it out. "Okay, I gotcha."

"Good," Maggie murmured, relieved.

Johnny glanced at her, took in her long red hair tied back in a ponytail and nodded. "Redhead Brewery. Now I get it. So what're you? Chief Executive Redhead?"

"That's right," Maggie said with a smile.

Johnny grinned as he leaned forward. "Okay, Red, here's the deal. You got three beers entered in the Small Brewery category. Tell me if these are the right names." He read off the quirky names of her pale ale, amber and lager.

"Yes, those are mine," Maggie said.

"Good." He opened the envelope and pulled out three index cards with printing on one side. "These are the official numbers the judges will use to review your entries. No names. Just numbers."

She watched him take a thick marker and write the corresponding numbers on each of her cases of beer.

Then he handed the index cards to her. "Don't let anybody see those cards, got it? We wouldn't want anything to compromise the outcome."

"Got it."

"I'm Johnny," the guy said, tapping his name tag as if she hadn't seen it before. "You got problems, you come see me."

She picked up her tote bag and purse. "Okay, thanks."

"Hold on, Red," he said, grabbing her arm. "I want to see you put those cards away where nobody else can see them." He wiggled his eyebrows at her, adding, "We don't want someone voting for you just because you're pretty."

"What? No." She whirled around to see if anyone had overheard him, then felt a chill skitter up her spine as she realized what she was doing. She was looking for her ex-husband! Alan used to freak out whenever anyone complimented her. He would accuse her of flirting and tell her she was turning into a whore. It wasn't fun. But good grief, she'd been away from him for three years. Enough already.

Would she ever be a normal person again? The thought depressed her, but she took in a few deep breaths and managed to work up a warm smile for Johnny as she slipped the cards into her purse. "Thanks, Johnny. I appreciate your help."

"You bet," he said, then jerked his head in the direction of the exit. "Now get outta here. And have a nice day."

Three hours later, Maggie sat on the sunny lobby level near the coffee kiosk. She had no idea where Connor was or when he would text their room number to her. But she figured she had enough time to enjoy her vanilla latte before she had to face the real challenge of the week: Connor MacLaren.

She'd had a busy day already. After signing in with Johnny at the judges' hall, she'd spent over an hour touring the huge convention floor, watching dozens of volunteers at work setting up booths, arranging kegs and glasses and signage. There was a band stage and a dance floor set up at one end of the room. The spacious beer garden overlooked the stage. The energy and excitement were infectious and she thought about volunteering next year.

After a while, she'd found an empty conference room, where she sat and studied the judges' guidelines again. Then she pored over the official program, highlighting the seminars she hoped to attend during the week. As she got up to leave, four brewpub owners walked in and she ended up having a spirited conversation with them about the industry and everything that was good and bad about it. Maggie had walked out in a cheery mood, feeling as though she was on her way to becoming part of a warm, friendly community.

As she had approached the escalator, another man joined her, grinning as they both stepped on the moving stairway at the same time.

"Enjoying yourself?" he asked.

"Yes, I am," Maggie said as she studied him briefly. He was nice looking in a passive, nonthreatening way. "I'm Maggie Jameson."

"Nice to meet you, Maggie." He gave her hand a hearty handshake. "I'm Ted Blake. I haven't seen you around the festival before. Are you in the business or just visiting?"

"This is my first time at the festival. I run my own microbrewery and I've entered some of my beers in the competition."

"How many workers do you have?"

She was a little taken aback by the direct question, but then figured he was just making friendly conversation. After all, they were all here to share information and grow the industry. "I'm it, for now."

"That's got to be hard."

"I enjoy it."

"What about your sales force?"

She frowned a little. "It's just me."

"Huh." He handed her a business card. "When you get tired of doing all the heavy lifting by yourself, give me a call."

She stared at his card, then looked up as they reached the main floor and stepped off the escalator. At that moment, Maggie noticed a pretty brunette staring fiercely at her from a booth a few yards away. The woman looked vaguely familiar—and she continued to glare directly at Maggie. Maggie was so surprised by the angry frown directed at her that she couldn't look away. After another long moment, the brunette tossed her hair back and turned away.

What in the world was that all about?

Nonplussed, Maggie glanced at her momentary companion. "It was nice meeting you, Ted."

"Hey, don't rush off," he cajoled.

But Maggie was desperate to spend a few minutes alone. "Sorry, but I'm meeting someone."

Now, as she sipped her vanilla latte by the wide plate-glass window, she tried to shake off the irritation she still felt from that woman's odd reaction to her.

Beyond the patio terrace and swimming pool area, the picturesque Point Cairn Marina bustled with activity. The small port had started life as a fishing village, and fishing was still a staple of the region. Fishing boats chugged their way back into the marina after a long day, pulling up to the docks to unload their catch of the day. Sailboats motored past on their way out to the ocean, where they would unfurl their sails and battle the strong winds and waves. In this part of Northern California, sailing was a sport for adrenaline junkies.

One sleek, teak-hulled yawl brought back memories of her father and his first sailboat. Maggie was ten years old when she and her mom and dad first started sailing together. It had been thrilling to skim across the water and feel the breeze ruffle her hair. That first summer on his new sailboat had been so much fun, with her father barking out orders and Maggie and her mom saluting and laughing as they trimmed the sails and adjusted the rigging according to his commands. They would sail to a small inlet where the waters were calm and the winds light. There they would drop anchor and have a picnic lunch. Once they even spent the night out on the water. It was magical.

But after that first season, her dad began to seek out rougher waters and more turbulent weather conditions. Maggie was ashamed to admit it, but she was too afraid to go with him after that. Her mother stopped going, too, and more than once, she tried to explain to Maggie why her father needed to seek bigger, more challenging adventures. White-water rapids, rock climbing, hiking the tallest mountains, parasailing. Her father tried it all and kept searching for wilder and more dangerous tests of will.

Maggie never did understand why being with her and her mother hadn't been enough for him.

Shaking off the melancholy, Maggie turned away from the marina view and glanced around the bustling lobby. The hotel was beginning to fill up with festival visitors and she wondered if she might recognize a friendly face or two. But she didn't see anyone she knew. Not yet, anyway. One of her goals for the week was to talk to and get to know as many people as she could manage.

Of course, she was also hoping to avoid any locals who might be less than happy to see her.

"Because I need something else to worry about," she muttered, shaking her head at the different directions her thoughts were taking her.

Since she wouldn't have much spare time later, Maggie pulled her schedule out of her purse and studied it one more time. Then she checked her judging number cards to make sure she hadn't lost them. They were still tucked inside her purse and she smiled as she pictured Johnny's stern look as he pretended to threaten her if she showed them to anyone. He might've been big and intimidating, but she knew he wouldn't hurt a flea. Johnny was the classic tough guy with a heart of gold.

She frowned as she recalled her own reaction to his offhanded remark about her being pretty. It annoyed her to know that she could still cringe at comments like that, a holdover from her years with Alan. Back then, if a man had complimented her, Alan would accuse her of having an affair with the guy. Once at a party, she and two other women had been joking about something. Later that night, Alan had wondered if the three of them might be forming a prostitution ring. She was so shocked she laughed at him. That had been a mistake. She learned quickly to avoid being friendly with other women and became an expert at discouraging attention from other men.

"Pitiful," she said, shaking her head. Even after three years back home, she was still living her life in the shadows, still trying so hard to be invisible that it came as a complete shock when a man noticed her, let alone complimented her.

But she refused to be depressed about it. She was so different from the woman she'd been even a year ago. She was happy to be at the festival and she was staying there with a gorgeous man, even though he had sort of blackmailed her into it. She had no intention of doing anything with him except sleep, preferably in a separate bed or on the couch. Still, it was exciting to be here.

Her phone beeped and she knew what that meant. Connor had sent her a text. Taking a deep breath, she read the message. Room 1292. Luggage is here and so am I. See you soon.

Suddenly she felt light-headed and wondered if it was caused by the caffeine or by Connor's message.

Did she really have to ask? It was Connor. Definitely.

Grabbing her tote bag and purse, she stood and tossed her empty coffee cup in the trash and headed for the elevator banks. Once in the elevator, she checked her purse again to make sure the number cards were still inside the zippered pocket.

Johnny would be happy to know how paranoid he'd made her.

Still, she was grateful for all the protective measures the festival had taken to ensure complete anonymity in the judging. Connor would never be able to figure out which entries were hers.

She frowned. She wasn't truly worried that he would try to sabotage her, was she? That wasn't his style, was it?

She brushed her concerns aside, but they creeped back in. How could she not worry just a little? Even though he'd been a perfect gentleman so far, they were still on shaky ground. Who knew what he really had in mind? Maybe he harbored a secret plan to humiliate her in front of the entire industry. Maybe he was going to all this trouble, only to destroy her fledgling reputation. Who could blame him? From his point of view, she'd apparently betrayed him all those years ago, left him behind with nothing but a broken heart.

It wasn't true, of course. He had been perfectly happy to break up with her. So why had he taken it so hard? At the time, Maggie had thought he was relieved to be rid of her. After all, he'd been the one to urge her to take that trip back east.

But she had obviously been wrong about his feelings. If her former high school friends were to be believed, Connor hadn't taken her departure well at all. So now she had to figure he might want to take her down a notch if the opportunity arose.

Would he stoop to searching out her secret judging numbers? Maybe he didn't even need to know them. Connor had worked for years in this business, tasting and testing and reformulating. And he'd been taking part in contests for all those years, too. He could probably decipher most of the different nuances of every brand and style of beer on the market.

Had he studied her particular formulas and techniques? He'd been following her progress for months—even though he'd thought he was following Taylor James, not Maggie. But didn't it stand to reason that after paying such intense attention to her techniques, Connor might be able to discern which beers were hers? And if he could, then why wouldn't he think about pushing her out of the running?

He certainly had strong motivation to sabotage her— and not just because she was his competition. No, Maggie figured that even after all this time, he might see this as a chance to get back at her for leaving him.

Revenge, after all, was a dish best served cold.

"Just stop," she muttered. She would drive herself crazy if she kept up that line of thinking. It would help if she could keep reminding herself that she had been with a good guy and a bad guy, and Connor was definitely one of the good guys. Besides, she had a bigger problem to deal with than the beer competition. Specifically, how to get through a whole week with Connor living in the same suite as her.

The elevator came to a quiet stop at the twelfth floor, otherwise known as the penthouse level. Maggie stepped out into the elegant hall and paused, taking in the parquet marble floor, the crystal chandeliers, the Louis XVI rococo furnishings. For a guy who preferred denim work shirts and blue jeans to an Armani suit, Connor MacLaren certainly liked to live in style. Maggie didn't know whether to be impressed or amused.

"Let the games begin," she muttered, and strolled toward the suite, once again wondering what in the world she'd gotten herself into.

* * *

Connor heard the water in the shower turn off and esti-mated that Maggie wouldn't be much longer. He reminded himself once again that he had shown excellent character earlier when he'd resisted the urge to follow her into the bathroom and join her in the shower like he'd wanted to.

While he waited, he glanced around the sitting room of the hotel suite. Earlier that day, in the hope that adding some romantic touches would somehow convince Maggie to fall into his bed, he'd arranged with the hotel florist and catering staff to bring bouquets of fragrant flowers and some champagne on ice to the room. Now soft jazz was playing in the background and a delectable dinner had been ordered. The kitchen staff was standing by to prepare and deliver it as soon as he placed the call.

This wasn't the first seduction scene Connor had ar-ranged. If memory served, he'd done something similar the first time he'd made love with Maggie all those years ago. He could still remember the day as if it were yester-day. The lavish picnic on a deserted beach at sunset, ach-ing desire, sweet hesitancy, shy touches, her giggles, his need, their bliss. For a while, anyway.

Connor ruthlessly shut off those flashes of memory and concentrated on his plans for right now. This time, he thought as he glanced around the room, at least he would know what he was doing.

As he double-checked that the champagne was prop-erly chilled, he accepted that there would be no pretense of "making love" this time around. No, this time when he and Maggie got around to doing the deed, it would be good old-fashioned, sweaty, hard-driving sex—and plenty of it. That was the plan, anyway, despite Maggie's words of pro-test. The way she kissed him in his office told a different story. At least he hoped so.

And what about that searing hot gaze she'd cast his way

that morning in the truck? If that was any indication of her feelings, he figured it wouldn't be too hard to bring his plan to fruition. So to speak.

They both seemed to be on the same wavelength. And why not? After all, he mused, as he carried a large vase of stunning red roses over to the mantel, this wasn't their first rodeo together. They'd done this before. So why not do it again, for old times' sake? They were two consenting adults, right?

And in case she didn't see it that way, Connor figured the flowers and champagne would go a long way toward softening her attitude.

He didn't mind putting on a romantic show for a woman when the situation called for it, as long as it worked out in his favor. And yeah, by that he meant sex. He wasn't ashamed to admit that that was the bottom line.

Connor stared out the window at the sun setting over the ocean view and frowned. Was he starting to sound callous or deceptive? Because he wasn't that guy. He didn't expect Maggie to say yes simply because he was loaning her some money. He grimaced at the very thought. He would never make sex a condition for the loan, for Pete's sake. He didn't have to, he thought with a grin. His charm and persuasive abilities would take care of any qualms she might have.

Although why she would have qualms, he didn't know. She wanted him as badly as he wanted her, that much Connor knew. Maggie's expressions were still easy for him to read, so he figured he wouldn't have to work too hard to make it happen.

"This is a beautiful room."

He whirled around. Maggie stood near the doorway to the bedroom, using a towel to fluff her still-damp hair. She was dressed casually in a cropped T-shirt and a pair of those sexy yoga pants some women wore that fit like a second skin. Connor gave a brief prayer of thanks for that current fashion choice.

"I was in such a rush earlier," she murmured, and took her time meandering about, touching a knitted throw rug hanging off the sofa, studying the artwork, smelling the roses. "Oh, the flowers are gorgeous, aren't they?"

Connor couldn't help staring at her as she moved with supple ease around the room. Her feet were bare, her petite shoulders straight. Her hair, thick and healthy, became lighter and more lustrous as it dried. He could see the outline of her breasts as they rose and fell with each breath she took.

His groin tightened.

How had he forgotten how sexy her toes were? How perfect her skin was? To give himself some credit, he'd never forgotten her breasts.

As beautiful as she was, Maggie seemed more fragile now than when she was younger. She was quieter, too. Or maybe it just seemed that way because they were getting to know each other all over again. He would have to wait a few days to decide if that was true or not.

Only one thing marred the perfection of her face, and that was her eyes, where he caught the slightest hint of sadness that didn't seem to fade, even when she smiled.

He glanced down at her feet again, then rubbed his hand across his jaw when he realized what a complete fool he was. Damn it, he wanted her as he'd never wanted anyone before—except her, of course, all those years ago. At the same time, he wanted to lash out at her and demand to know why she'd left him, why she'd betrayed him, why she'd broken his heart ten years before.

But he would never say those words aloud. She didn't need to know how ridiculously vulnerable he was in her presence. Hell, she'd been driving him crazy ever since she walked into his office last week. He'd thought about her all week, at every hour, no matter where he was or what he was doing. She didn't have to be in the same room with him or, hell, the same city. He couldn't get her out of his mind. But he would. Once they'd slept together again, Connor would be able to rid himself of these lingering feelings and get on with his life.

Maggie had circled the room and was now standing in front of the ice bucket holding the bottle of expensive champagne. She turned to him. "What's this for?"

"Us," he said, crossing the room to open the bottle. "Champagne. I thought we'd celebrate."

She blinked in surprise. "Celebrate what?"

He thought quickly. "This is the first time you've attended the festival, right?"

"Right."

"So we're celebrating."

"Okay. Let me get rid of this first." She took the damp towel back to the bathroom and returned in seconds. "So, what's the plan tonight?"

"I thought we could dine here in the room." Connor pulled the chilled bottle out of the ice and wrapped it in a cloth. "Do you mind?"

"I don't mind at all. It sounds perfect."

"Good." He removed the metal cover and wire cage, then carefully twisted the cork until it popped. After filling two glasses with the sparkling liquid, he handed one to Maggie.

"Cheers, Mary Margaret."

"Cheers," she murmured, and took her first sip. "Mm, nice."

"I hope you still like steak," he said.

"I love steak."

"Good, because I've taken care of ordering dinner for us."

She swallowed too fast and began to cough. Setting

her glass down, she breathed in and out a few times and coughed to clear her throat.

"You okay?" he asked, ready to pound on her back if necessary.

"I'm fine." She folded her arms tightly across her chest and pinned him with an angry look. "You had no right to do that, Connor. I can order my own food and pay for it, too."

He shrugged. "I guess you could, but I already took care of it."

She stomped her foot. "How dare you?"

"Dial it back a notch, will you?" he said, his annoyance growing. "It's just dinner. Besides, how did you plan to pay for it? You came to me for money, remember?"

Her eyes widened as she clenched her teeth together. She looked about ready to scream, but seemed to swallow the urge and just stood there staring at him.

"What's the problem here, Maggie?"

Instead of answering him, she whirled around and paced, muttering under her breath. Connor could only hear every third word, but it didn't sound flattering to him. Abruptly she stopped in her tracks, inhaled and exhaled once, then again, and continued her pacing.

What in the world had just happened to her?

On her third pass, he grabbed her arm to stop her. "What the hell's wrong with you? I didn't order you gruel, for God's sake. Besides, you can order anything you want, you know that."

"Do I?" she asked.

Incredulous, he instantly replied, "Of course you do." Surprised by his own anger, he took a long, slow breath, then continued quietly. "But why should you? I ordered all your favorite foods. Steak, medium rare, baked potato with butter *and* sour cream, lightly grilled asparagus. Chocolate mousse for dessert. I thought you'd be happy. You used to love all that stuff."

She gaped at him for so long it was almost as if she was seeing him for the first time. Then she sucked in a big gulp of air as if she'd been underwater for too long. As she exhaled slowly, her anger seemed to deflate at the same time.

"You okay?" he asked, searching her face.

"Yes." She shook her head, clearly dismayed. "Yes. I'm fine. And I'm sorry, Connor. That was really stupid."

"No, just confusing," he said, flashing her a tentative smile.

Still breathing deeply as though she was centering herself, she ran her hands through her hair and then shook her head. Her eyes were clear now and she smiled. "Dinner, um, sounds great. You have a good memory. Those foods are still my favorites."

"Glad to hear it," he said cautiously, and handed her the glass of champagne she'd forgotten about. "But there's something I did that set you off. Tell me what it was so I don't do it again."

She took a healthy sip of champagne. "It's nothing you did. It's just something that I... Never mind." She walked to the window, then turned. "Just...thank you for ordering dinner. I know it'll be delicious."

"Oh, come on, Maggie," he said, losing patience. "After all this time, we can at least be honest with each other. Tell me what I did so I don't make the same damn mistake again."

She chewed her lower lip and Connor wondered if she might start crying. *Crap.* "Maggie, please don't cry. I'm sorry for...whatever I did."

"For goodness' sake, Connor, I'm not going to cry. And you didn't do anything. I just get a little carried away sometimes."

"If you say so."

"I do."

He watched her for another moment, then said lightly,

"Okay, I'm glad it's nothing I did. But I want you to know you've got the green light to yell or cry if you feel the need to."

"A green light? To cry?" She nodded, biting back a smile. "I appreciate that, but I have no intention of crying."

"You never know." He gave a worldly shrug. "Happens all the time."

She laughed. "Somehow I don't picture women bursting into tears around you."

"Not so much," he admitted, adding to himself, *Not ever.* The sophisticated women he'd dated over the past ten years would never dream of revealing their true emotions, let alone break down in tears. If for no other reason than it would ruin their expertly applied makeup.

And that was fine with him. Emotions could get messy and out of hand, and he wasn't interested in that. That's why, despite being a fairly casual guy with a laid-back style, he preferred to go out with worldly women who knew the score, who knew they could count on him for a great evening of dining and dancing, always followed by great sex, and that was it. What more could he ask for? No mess, no fuss.

"Tell you what." He took her arm and led her over to the sofa. "Come sit and relax. Enjoy your drink. There's no pressure here."

She did as he suggested and sipped her champagne. He sat down at the opposite end of the couch and she turned to him. "You must think I'm a fool."

He stared at her for a moment. It would be a mistake to get lost in those big brown eyes and that perfectly shaped mouth, but he wanted to. He really wanted to. Maybe later. For now, he wanted some answers. "I don't know what to think, Maggie, because you won't tell me."

She gazed at the bubbles in her glass, and Connor could tell her mind had gone a thousand miles away. Fine. She wouldn't reveal anything to him. And why should she? They weren't exactly friends anymore. She was only here because she needed the money. So what did that make them? Business partners? Hardly. Jailor and prisoner? Absolutely not, although she might look at things differently.

After another minute of silence, he figured he might as well send for dinner and reached for the telephone.

"My ex-husband," she began quietly, "also used to choose my meals for me. Among other things."

"Ah." Connor still wasn't clear about the problem, but he was glad she was finally talking. "Did he force you to eat liver or something?"

She laughed. A good sign. "No, he ordered what he thought I should eat. He didn't think I was capable of making my own decisions."

"Was he some kind of a health nut?"

"No. He was just convinced that he knew better than I did what I should be eating. And drinking. And wearing."

"Huh," he said, frowning. "Sounds like a control freak."

"Oh, *control freak* doesn't begin to describe him," she said, struggling to keep a light tone. "He made all my decisions for me. So when you said you ordered my dinner for me, I guess I flashed back to a different time and place and…well, sort of lost it."

"Sort of."

She reached over and touched his arm, gave it a light squeeze. "I'm sorry."

"Stop apologizing. I just wanted to know where that reaction came from. Now I know where I stand and we can move on. And I promise I won't make any more decisions for you."

She laughed for real this time and her eyes twinkled with humor. "Oh yes, you will."

He grinned. "You're probably right. But you can always punch me in the stomach if you don't agree."

"Thank you. You have no idea how much that means to me."

"Hmm." He rubbed his stomach. "I'm afraid to find out."

With a lighthearted chuckle, she held her glass out to his. "Cheers."

"Cheers," he said, clinking his glass against hers and then taking a drink. He was relieved to see her relaxed and smiling again and he wanted her to stay that way. So as much as his curiosity was gnawing at him, there was no way he would bring up the subject of her ex-husband again tonight. Besides being an obvious buzz kill, the guy sounded like a real jackass.

Okay, so the evening hadn't started out exactly as he'd planned, but that didn't mean it couldn't end up exactly where he wanted it to.

With Maggie in his bed.

Five

The dinner was fabulous, as Connor knew it would be. The steak was cooked to perfection, the chocolate mousse was drool-worthy and their conversation was relaxed with plenty of laughs and easy smiles. Connor had kept the champagne flowing and had consciously avoided any talk of ex-husbands and old betrayals.

Sated, he sat back in his chair and watched Maggie as she savored the last luscious spoonful of chocolate mousse. He'd enjoyed the dinner, too, but had found himself getting much more pleasure from observing her delight than from his own meal. Maybe too much pleasure, if the relentless surge of physical need that had grabbed hold of him was any measure to go by.

But what could he do about it? He was mesmerized by her luxuriant tumble of reddish-brown hair that floated over her shoulders and down her back. And her face, so delicately shaped and porcelain smooth, begged to be touched. Her lips were soft, full and voluptuous, and Connor's fervent desire to taste them again was driving him dangerously close to the edge.

He cursed inwardly. His famous self-control was slipping. He had to find a way to pull the reins in on his rampant libido. But how could he look away while Maggie still licked and nibbled at her spoon, lost in her own little world of chocolate mousse goodness, for God's sake?

She was killing him. He wouldn't survive another meal. Not until he'd had her in his bed.

Soon, he promised himself. Very soon. For now, he forced himself to stop watching her pink tongue darting and nipping at the spoon. Instead he glanced up and tried to appreciate the elegant and somber artwork on the wall while he shifted unobtrusively in his chair, carefully adjusting himself so she wouldn't notice the rather prominent bulge in his pants.

When he finally could speak in coherent syllables, he said, "So, I take it you enjoyed dinner?"

"Oh yes," Maggie murmured as she set down her spoon. "Delicious. Thank you, Connor."

"My pleasure." Connor was just glad she'd put down that damn spoon. One more lick and he would've been a dead man.

She lifted her teacup and took a sip, then set it down and smiled at him. "This has been so nice."

Nice? he thought. He was barely grasping hold of the edge of madness and she was having a tea party.

He needed to get a grip.

"Why don't we move over to the sofa?" he suggested, standing and reaching for her chair. "We can talk some more and you can finish your tea."

She hesitated a moment, then nodded. "Yes, all right."

They settled at their respective ends of the comfortable sofa. Maggie seemed a bit shy again, now that she didn't have the safe barrier of plates and food between them. But Connor kept the conversation light and she eased back into it.

Every time Connor thought about what Maggie had told him about her ex-husband, he felt more and more bemused. She hadn't been living the high life as he'd always assumed, and now he didn't know what to think. Really, though, how bad could it have been? The guy was worth millions. Should Connor feel badly for Maggie because the guy she ended up marrying turned out to be kind of a jerk?

After twenty minutes of safe conversation centered mostly on goats, beer, Angus and Deidre, Connor's mom, Maggie yawned. "It's been a long day and tomorrow will be a busy one. I think I'd better go to bed."

She stood and reached her arms up in a stretch that caused her shirt to tighten dangerously across her perfect breasts. Connor had to look away or beg for mercy.

After a minute, she relaxed, picked up her teacup and took it over to the dining table. Connor followed her, but before he could say anything or make a move, Maggie turned and stopped him with a firm hand against his chest.

"You got your way, Connor," she said. "I'm staying in the suite with you. Dinner was lovely, thank you, but I'm not going to sleep with you, so don't bother trying to make me."

"*Make* you?"

"That's right, don't try to talk me into anything." She folded her arms under her chest in a stubborn move that only accented her luscious breasts. "I'm not going to change my mind."

He held up both hands innocently. "I never expected you to."

"Yes, you did."

"No, Maggie. You're the one who keeps bringing it up."

"What? Me? No, I—"

"And frankly, I don't think it's a good idea."

Her eyes narrowed in suspicion. "You...don't think *what's* a good idea?"

"Sex," he said easily, though he was cringing on the inside. "Look, we had a nice evening, but as you said, tomorrow's going to be another long day, so I think we should call it a night."

She frowned. "You do."

"Yes, I do." He nodded calmly, mentally patting himself on the back for putting on this show of levelheadedness. "Look, you said it would be wrong and I'm agreeing with you."

"You're...agreeing with me. Okay. Good." It took her a moment, but finally she gave him a tentative smile. "Well, then, good night. Thank you again for a lovely evening."

He glanced down at her hand still pressed against his chest. "Good night, Mary Margaret."

"Oh." She whipped her hand away. "Okay, good night."

"Wait." With an innocent smile, he reached out and took hold of her arms. "I'll sleep better if I can have a good-night kiss. Just one. For old times' sake."

She gave him a look. "Oh, all right." Then she seemed to brace herself as she puckered up for a chaste kiss.

But instead of kissing her mouth, Connor bent his head and kissed her shoulder. Then he moved an inch and kissed the small patch of skin at the base of her neck.

She was gasping by the time he reached her jaw line. "What are you doing to me?"

He nibbled and kissed her ear, then whispered, "We're not sleeping together, no matter how much you beg me."

"Beg you?" She stretched her neck to give him more access to the pale smoothness of her skin. "This is crazy."

"I know," he murmured. "I wish you'd stop it."

"I'm not..."

But she couldn't seem to finish as he began licking each inviting corner of her mouth. When she moaned aloud, he pressed his lips to hers in an openmouthed kiss more erotic than anything he'd ever experienced. She was sweeter than chocolate and more intoxicating than the cognac they'd shared earlier.

He realized his mistake immediately, tried to keep the kiss light, but it was no use. He wanted her with the intensity of a red-hot sun, wanted to pull her down on the couch and touch her everywhere, from the tips of her sexy pink toenails to the top of her gorgeous red mane. And each place in between, too. He could do it, he knew. She was willing and wanted the same thing he did. And damn, he needed her now, needed to be inside her, to spread her shapely legs and press into her, sheathing himself in her dusky depths.

Damn it. He'd set up this whole evening to be a romantic interlude leading directly to sex. But despite her body pressed tightly against his, he knew she needed time to get used to being with him again. So why didn't he stop? He knew with every kiss that he was making things worse for himself. He'd go insane before much longer if he didn't put an end to this right now.

But then she moaned and he reconsidered, and somehow his hand moved to cup the soft swell of her breast. And a part of him felt as though he'd come home after being away a long time. He recognized the sweet roundness and wanted nothing more than to get lost in her, nothing more than to touch his tongue to her beaded nipples and hear the familiar sound of her little gasps and whispers of bliss.

And if he didn't stop now, he never would. With unearthly strength of will, he forced himself to end the kiss and pull away from her soft curves. And immediately missed the warmth.

He ran his hands up and down her toned arms, then squeezed them lightly, before taking another step back. The only reward for his good behavior was her look of dazed wonder. He wasn't sure it was worth his sacrifice, but it was too late to change his mind.

"Time for bed, Mary Margaret." He wrapped his arm lightly around her shoulder and led her into the bedroom, where he gathered up a blanket and pillow.

She dropped onto the bed and watched him.

He smiled tightly and held up his hand in a sign of farewell, as though he were a soldier heading for battle. "Good night. Sweet dreams."

"G-good night, Connor. Thank you."

He walked out of the room and closed the door behind him.

So much for tactical retreats, Connor thought the next morning, after he tried to roll over in bed and slid off the couch onto the floor instead.

"Damn it," he grumbled, rubbing his elbow where it smacked against the coffee table. "Where the hell...oh yeah."

After a minute, he managed to pull himself up off the floor and sat on the couch with his elbows on his knees, head resting in his hands. As his brain slowly emerged from the fog of sleep, he played back the events of last night that had ultimately led to him sleeping on the couch.

At the time, it had appeared to be a brilliantly strategic move. After several long, hot kisses, he had no doubt Maggie had been tempted to give in to her desires and join him in bed. But no, Connor had decided that rather than moving in for the kill, he would leave her wanting more. His theory, which clearly needed work, was that with any luck, tonight she would be seducing him instead of the other way around.

It had seemed like such a smart idea at the time.

"Idiot," he muttered, scratching his head. "How's that strategy working out for you?" Cursing under his breath, he gathered up the blanket and pillow off the couch.

He entered the bedroom and found Maggie sound asleep. So she was still enjoying a restful night's sleep while he was wide awake and whining in misery. Glaring at her, all peaceful and snug in their comfortable bed, Connor vowed that it wouldn't happen again. There was no way he was sleeping anywhere else tonight but in this bed—with Maggie tucked in right next to him.

He quietly rummaged around in one of the drawers until

he found his gym shorts and sneakers and slipped them on, then took off for a bracing run along the boardwalk.

Halfway through the run, despite his determination to take in the crisp ocean breezes and enjoy the clear blue sky, he caught himself grumbling again. Uttering a succinct oath, he forced himself to shove the surly thoughts away and look on the bright side. So maybe last night hadn't gone exactly according to plan. It didn't matter. He was a patient man and he knew he would have Maggie in his bed soon. He'd stoked not only his fire, but hers, as well. She might've slept soundly but he was willing to bet he'd been a major player in her dreams.

Tonight, it was going to be different. He had all day to convince her that she wanted him as much as he wanted her. Maybe more.

Grinning now, he thought about Maggie and how she'd nearly succumbed to her own needs last night. It wouldn't take much to bring her to that point again. Hell, he loved a good challenge and she was nothing if not challenging.

He would prevail, of that he had no doubt. And with that happy thought in mind, he jogged back to the hotel to take a shower and get ready for the long day ahead.

Maggie heard the suite door close and checked the bedside clock. Connor had mentioned the night before that he might go running this morning, so Maggie figured she had at least a half hour to get ready for the day. She jumped out of bed and took a quick shower, then dried her hair and dressed in black pants and a deep burgundy sweater. She slipped her feet into a comfortable but attractive pair of flats because she had no intention of walking around the convention floor all day in heels. If Connor insisted that she dress up for dinner, she would come upstairs and change into her killer pumps. Otherwise, she was going for comfort.

Last week he'd made it clear that their week would be

more business-oriented than fun-filled, so she shouldn't be bothered to pack any blue jeans or work boots to wear this week. She mused that it should've bugged the heck out of her that Connor had dared to tell her what to wear, but after he'd explained what they'd be doing, it made sense.

But she'd still slipped one old pair of jeans and sneakers into her suitcase, on the off chance that she'd have some time by herself during the week.

The good news was that Connor would be forced to suffer in his business attire as much as she would, since, based on everything she knew about him, he lived in denim work shirts and blue jeans every day, too.

Maggie wrote a note for Connor telling him she would be waiting somewhere near the coffee kiosk downstairs. Then she grabbed her lightweight blazer and left the suite.

Forty-five minutes later, her heart stuttered in her chest at the sight of the smiling, handsome man walking right toward her. She could get used to that sight, she thought wistfully, but just as quickly, she banished the thought away. Getting used to having Connor around would be a major league mistake and she'd be smart to remember that. They were only spending this week together because she was desperate for money and he seemed to want to teach her a lesson.

Still, it couldn't hurt to look her fill.

He was so…formidable, despite his clean-cut outfit of khakis worn with a navy V-neck sweater over a white T-shirt. He should've come across more like the boy next door. Instead he looked dangerous, powerful, intense as he prowled confidently across the room like a sexy panther stalking his mate. Maggie noticed other women giving him sly looks as he passed, and part of her wanted to stand up and shout, "He's mine!"

But he wasn't *hers,* Maggie reminded herself, and he never would be again. The thought depressed her, but she pushed it aside instantly. She could be sad and whiny about that later. For now, for this week, she vowed to enjoy every minute of her time with him.

After convincing Connor to have a quick breakfast of coffee and a muffin, Maggie and he walked across the hotel to the convention entrance. She was surprised to see the convention floor packed with people, even though the festival was not yet open to the general public.

These first few days were mainly devoted to programs and workshops designed to appeal to those industry professionals in attendance. Maggie was looking forward to attending several of them and had them highlighted in her program booklet.

But already, hundreds of booths were doing a brisk business serving tastes of every type of beer and ale imaginable and selling all sorts of souvenirs. It was a clear sign that the beer-making community enjoyed partaking of its own products.

As they strolled through the crowd, Connor would occasionally take her hand in his to prevent them from being split up. Maggie tried to remember it didn't mean anything, but his touch was potent and unsettling. Each time, he seemed to set off electrical currents inside her that zinged through her system and left her dizzy and distracted.

It didn't help that every few minutes, Connor would run into someone he knew. He would stop and talk and introduce Maggie, assuring his friends that she was destined to be the next superstar in their industry.

Maggie wasn't quite sure what to think of Connor's kind words and she had absolutely no idea what to do with all the positive energy being directed at her from his friends and business associates. She smiled and chatted and appreciated it all, of course. Who wouldn't? These people could open important doors for her that had been closed and locked until now.

But it was confusing. Was this Connor's way of teaching her a lesson? Of getting back at her for breaking his heart ten years ago? If so, it was diabolical. He was killing her with kindness, the beast!

To divert herself, she concentrated on the swarm of festival attendees and the cheerful babble of twenty different conversations going on around her. She warned herself that if she thought it was crowded now, just wait until the weekend. The place would be packed wall to wall with people, and the noise level would be overwhelming with rock bands playing and even more demonstrations and activities going on. Maggie couldn't believe she was actually looking forward to the crush of humanity.

Connor continued to run into friends and associates every few seconds. It was amazing to see how many people he knew. But of course, he'd always been outgoing and charming. His mom used to say that Connor had never met a stranger, and it was true. Everyone he met became a friend.

He persisted in pulling Maggie over to introduce her to each new person, and she began to relax and enjoy herself, grateful that he would think to include her in both his business and his personal conversations with people. She hadn't expected it. Frankly, she was still trying to convince herself that she knew him, knew he was not the type to resort to sabotage. But was that true? May not be, but it didn't seem to be on his agenda today. At least, not yet.

And the fact that he was being so generous and inclusive and kind to her made it all the more difficult to cling to her determination not to sleep with him.

Not that she would have sex with him simply because he'd given her a few good business contacts. No way. Her gratitude didn't extend *that* far. But it was getting more and more difficult to ignore the fact that Connor MacLaren was simply a thoughtful, honorable man, a good person, just as he'd been when she knew him ten years ago. He hadn't changed.

It was Maggie who had changed. Who would have guessed that when she and Connor broke up, she was simply trading one set of risks for another worse set? The result was that now, after ten years, she was more guarded, more tentative, more jumpy. All those years with Alan and his mother had not been good for her.

But those years were over. It was all in the past and she was moving forward, living in the present and planning for the future. She was doing okay.

The fact that she'd stepped out of her comfort zone, taken the risk and faced down Connor MacLaren in his own office a week ago was something to be proud of. And, she thought as she gazed around at the festival crowd, she was actually out having fun. It was such a dramatic change from the way she'd been three years ago that she wanted to jump up and give a little cheer. Go, Maggie, go!

She smiled to herself. Good thing nobody was monitoring her goofy thoughts.

"Maggie," Connor said, interrupting her meanderings. "Come meet Bill Storm, one of the top-selling beer makers in the country."

"Aw, hell, boy," the older man drawled. "I'd be the *very* top if it wasn't for y'all and your MacLaren's Pride."

Maggie smiled at the man, who had what was quite likely the world's largest mustache and a personality to go with it.

She shook his hand. "Hello, Mr. Storm."

"Call me Bill," he said jovially. "Mr. Storm is my old man."

"Thanks, Bill."

"Now, Connor here tells me that some of the pale ales

you've been producing might just be the hottest beers to hit the market in years." Bill scratched his head in thought. "Don't mind me being a little skeptical, but I can see with my own eyes what your actual appeal to him might be."

Suddenly wary, she glanced at Connor, who merely smiled at his friend's good-natured teasing. Maggie decided that the old guy meant no offense and turned back to Bill with her business card in her hand. "I'll be glad to give you a personal tasting of my latest beers and ales tomorrow."

"And I'll be glad to take you up on that, Maggie." He handed her his business card, too, and Maggie slipped it into the pocket of her tote bag. Then Bill drew Connor into a more personal conversation about a mutual competitor and after a minute, Maggie decided to wander around a bit.

She stopped at several booths to check out the competition and met so many friendly beer makers and brewpub operators that she was reminded of something her father had once told her. The beer-making community was famously close-knit and friendly and helpful toward one another. Yes, there was plenty of competition, but they generally cheered their rivals on and supported each other.

At the fourth booth she came to, she stopped and stared and then began to laugh.

"That's the reaction I get most of the time," the guy said cheerfully.

His three featured beers had been given the silliest names she'd seen in a long time.

Maggie had learned early on that one of the joys of running a small craft brewery was coming up with a colorful name for the final product. Some brewers went for shock value, others enjoyed grunge and still others tried for humor.

The names of Maggie's beers were rather tame compared to some. This year she'd chosen the names of famous redheads to call attention to her Redhead brand. Her three competition entries were Rita Hayworth, Maureen O'Hara and Lucy Ricardo.

The barrel-chested, sandy-haired man running the booth turned out to be the brewery owner, who introduced himself as Pete. "Would you like a glass of something?"

"It's a little early for me to be tasting," she said with a smile. "But I was wondering who came up with these names of yours."

Pete beamed with pride. "My three sons come up with most of our names."

"Must be nice to have sons," she said. "Do they help you out with the brewing?"

"No way," Pete said, laughing. "Not yet, anyway. They're all under the age of seven. They're the creative arm of the company."

"Ah, that makes sense," she said, nodding, and picked up one of the bottles. "I was wondering what inspired you to name this one Poodle's Butt."

"That came from the warped mind of my five-year-old, Austin. But don't be fooled. Poodle's Butt is a fantastic, full-bodied beer with a hint of citrus and spice that I think you'll find unique and flavorful—if you can get past the name."

She chuckled. "I love the name. I'll try and come back for a taste later today." She pointed to another bottle. "Now, what about Snotty Bobby Pale Ale?"

"Bobby's my oldest. He came up with that idea last year when he had a cold. Laughed himself silly over his idea," Pete said, then added sheepishly, "I did, too. Guess they got their sense of humor from me."

Maggie patted his arm. "You should be very proud."

"I really am."

"Hey, Maggie."

She turned and came face to face with the quirky man she'd met the first day. "Oh, hello, Ted."

He flashed her a crooked grin. "I hope you thought about what I told you the other day."

"I really don't think I—"

"There you are," a voice said from close behind her.

Maggie whirled around and found Connor standing inches away. Her stomach did a pleasant little flip. "Hi."

But Connor wasn't looking at her. He was staring over her shoulder at Ted.

"Have you met Ted?" Maggie asked. "He's…" She turned, but Ted was gone. She spied him halfway across the room, jogging through the crowd.

"That was weird," she murmured.

"How well do you know that guy?" Connor asked bluntly.

"Not well at all."

"You might want to keep it that way."

Someone cleared his throat behind her. "Oh, Pete! Connor, have you met Pete? He owns Stink Bug Brewery."

Connor and Pete shook hands and talked for a minute or two, and then Connor grabbed her hand. "We should go. I want to check the judging schedule downstairs."

Maggie promised Pete she'd return later; then she and Connor left to find the escalators. Once they were descending to the lower level, Connor let go of her hand and glanced around. "This place is going to be packed by Friday."

"Isn't it fabulous?"

"Fabulous?" He gave her a curious smile. "Most people would be annoyed with all the crowding. But not you."

"This is my first festival, after all."

"Right. No wonder you're so excited." They stepped off the escalator and walked the long corridor toward the judges' hall. "So all this time you were entering competitions under your Taylor James name, you never actually showed up for any of the awards?"

She shook her head. "Not once."

"Why not?"

She really didn't want to have this conversation, but she owed him an answer, even if it was lame. "I'm shy."

He snorted a laugh. "You've never been shy a day in your life. What's the real story?"

Back when he knew her, no, she hadn't been shy. But over the years with Alan, she had learned to become invisible. She couldn't say that, though, so she tried to keep it simple. "Things change. I'd been away for so many years, and by the time I got back home, I didn't really know anyone anymore. Some old friends had left town. New people had taken their place. You know how it is. So I wasn't as sure of myself as I used to be. Especially when it came to competing in this business."

"But your father ran a brewpub. I remember he was always winning medals. You must know you'd be welcomed wherever went."

"If only that were true." She smiled reflectively.

"Okay, even if nobody knew you, you've got this business in your blood. You had to know that your product was excellent. Seems like you'd want to show up in person and get the accolades."

"You're right, I should've," she admitted, "but I didn't. My confidence was pretty low, especially after a few run-ins with people in town. It made me realize I wasn't ready to take on the general public, so my cousin Jane and her boyfriend agreed to attend the competitions on my behalf."

"What run-ins?"

Maggie cringed inwardly. Leave it to Connor to hone in on that key detail. She hadn't meant to blurt it out like that and she was wondering how to explain herself when they were interrupted.

"Hey, Red, is that you?"

Maggie turned and saw Johnny, the muscleman she'd met at yesterday's check-in.

"Hi, Johnny," she said, smiling. "Do you know Connor MacLaren?"

"Aw, hell," Johnny said with a grin. "Of course I do. How you doing, man?"

"Hey, Johnny." The two men shook hands. Then Connor looked at Maggie. "I'm going to head inside the hall for a minute to check the schedule."

"I'll wait out here."

"I won't be long."

He took off and Maggie chatted with Johnny for another minute until he had to get back to his line of people. Then she began to browse the long tables that had been set up to display the hundreds of promotional gadgets and give-aways. There were flyers, as well, and booklets that described the latest seminars and vendor products that might be useful to the industry professionals attending the festival.

She picked up a few clever gadgets and grabbed some flyers that looked interesting. Five minutes later, she glanced up and saw Connor waving at her as he exited the door at the far end of the judges' room.

Just as Maggie started walking down the corridor to meet him, three attractive women approached Connor from the opposite direction. There was a loud, feminine shriek and all three began to flutter and buzz around him. "Connor MacLaren! I thought it was you!"

"Ooh, it is Connor!" the blonde said. "Hey, you! You're looking good."

Maggie recognized the blonde as Sarah Myers, one of her best friends from high school. Sarah was also the first person to turn on Maggie when she returned home.

"Hi, Connor," the second woman said, and wound her arm around his. "I was hoping we'd see you here this week."

"Hi, Connor," the brown-haired woman said. She seemed more shy than the other two and as she got closer, Maggie recognized her. She was the angry woman who had stared at her the first day of the festival. The one who had glowered and glared and frowned, then flipped her hair and walked away.

And now she was staring at Maggie again. Maggie had an urge to rub her arms to ward off the chill.

Connor nodded at the brunette. "Hey, Lucinda. Are you working today?"

"No." Ignoring Maggie now, she grinned up at Connor. "Jake gave me the day off and we decided to check out the festival before it gets too crowded."

Did she work for MacLaren? Maggie wondered. If so, it was no wonder she wasn't quite as forward with Connor as her two friends were.

Sarah looked up at the Judges Only sign over the doorway. "Oh, hey, are you one of the judges? That's so cool!"

Maggie's stomach did a sharp nosedive. She felt ridiculous just standing there thirty or forty feet away from them, but she had no intention of joining the group and watching Connor be devoured by drooling groupies. There was no reason to be so annoyed. She had no claim on him, but that didn't seem to matter to her topsy-turvy emotions. She whipped around and took off in the opposite direction, praying that Connor hadn't seen her rapid retreat.

Maggie walked quickly, skirting the crowd until she reached Johnny's check-in line. She had resigned herself to the fact that she would eventually run into some familiar faces from town, but she didn't think it would happen until the weekend when the festival was opened to the public. Just her luck that Sarah and her posse had decided to show up early.

She slipped between the short queue of people waiting for Johnny and made her way farther down the hall to the ladies' room.

It was blessedly empty. Maggie stepped inside one of the stalls and locked the door. She leaned her forehead against the cold steel door and wondered how long she would have to stay in here. She felt like a desperate escapee trapped in here, but at least she was safe.

Safe?

"For goodness' sake, lighten up," she scolded herself aloud. Those silly women out there couldn't hurt her.

But they *could* hurt her, that was the problem. And she knew they would be more than happy to attack her again, only this time they would have an audience. Namely, Connor.

"They can only hurt you if you *let* them," she whispered. That was what the clinic counselor had told her a few years ago. Maggie knew those words were true, but knowing the truth hadn't made it any easier to ignore the taunts.

Maggie pounded her fist against the stall door. Damn it, wasn't ten years enough time to suffer for the presumed sins she'd committed against her high school boyfriend? Couldn't they behave like adults?

Even as she thought it, she had to laugh, since hiding in the bathroom wasn't exactly a grown-up move. She had to face this. Port Cairn was her home again and she couldn't spend all of her time running from people she'd once been friends with. Maggie had to find a way to convince Sarah to call a truce.

She would get to work on that right away, she thought with a soft laugh, as soon as she stopped shivering like a scared pup in this cold tiled bathroom. She wasn't exactly dealing from a place of strength at the moment.

She hated this feeling of shame. After three years of hard work and trial and error, she had accomplished so much and built an excellent reputation for herself. She should've been able to face her detractors with poise and confidence. But none of her achievements meant anything, as long as she was hiding in a bathroom stall like a sniveling coward.

"Not a pretty picture," she muttered, and with a defiant shake of her head, she straightened her shoulders. All it took was a little guts and determination to walk out of here with her head held high. And she would. Any minute now. It wasn't as if she was procrastinating or anything. But with the restroom still empty, this would be the perfect time to call and check in with her grandfather.

Pulling her phone out, she pushed Speed Dial and seconds later, Grandpa answered.

"Hi, Grandpa, it's Maggie."

"There's my sweet lass," he said, his Scottish brogue sounding stronger than she remembered. "Are ye having a bang-up time of it?"

"Best time ever," she lied. "Connor knows so many people and I've already made a lot of new contacts. Everyone is so nice and there's so much to see and do."

"Ah, that's lovely to hear, now."

"I miss you, Grandpa."

"Now, there's no need," he said. "I'm right here as always, tending to me darlings."

"Have you seen Deidre?" Maggie asked, anxious to make sure that Connor's mom had been stopping by.

"She interrupts me on an hourly basis," he grumbled.

"Good," Maggie said firmly. "I'm glad she's taking care of you."

"She's a good cook," he muttered. "I'll give her that much."

"She's a great friend."

"Yes, yes," he said impatiently, clearly not pleased that he'd been assigned a *babysitter*. "Now, Deidre mentioned that Connor's taking you to a fancy dance party. When is that?"

"It's Friday night, but I'm not going, Grandpa. You know I hate to dance. I didn't even bring a formal dress to wear."

"Ah, lass. You used to love to dance."

"Not so much anymore."

"You go to the dance," Grandpa insisted. "Connor deserves to dance with his beautiful girl."

"He'll have to live with the disappointment," she muttered, and quickly changed the subject. "How are Lydia and Vincent doing?"

"Och, they're randy as two goats."

She chuckled. "Grandpa, they *are* goats."

But he was already laughing so hard at his little joke that he began to cough.

"Grandpa, drink some water. You're going to choke."

"I'm fine," he said, but his voice was scratchy and he coughed another time or two. "Och, I haven't laughed like that in years. You're a tonic for me, Maggie."

She smiled. "I really do miss you, Grandpa."

"You'll be home soon enough, lass, soon enough," he said. "I'm pleased that you're getting out and about. You take some time and have fun with your Connor. And drink plenty of beer. It's good for you."

"I know, Grandpa. I love you."

"You're a good lass," he said softly, and Maggie understood it was his version of *I love you.*

They ended the call and Maggie sat and stared at the phone for a few seconds before she realized her eyes were damp. She wiped them dry; then with more resolve than courage, she left the stall, exited the bathroom and stepped out into the corridor.

"Maggie!"

She glanced around and spotted Connor waving at her from halfway down the football-field-length hallway. She didn't see any of the women with him, thankfully, so she waved and walked toward him. He met her midway.

"Where the hell have you been?" he asked.

"You looked busy a few minutes ago, so I went to use the bathroom and then called my grandfather."

"How's he doing?"

"He sounded fine. Your mom's already been there a bunch of times, so I know he's well looked after."

"Good." He slipped his arm around her shoulder, out of habit or companionship or something more significant, Maggie couldn't tell. But it felt so good to be this close to him. She breathed in the hint of citrus-and-spice after-shave, reveled in the protective warmth, loved that they fit together so perfectly, even if it was just for this brief moment. For so many years, she'd been unwilling to admit to herself that she had missed him, missed these moments of closeness with him. Life with her ex-husband had never been warm or cozy. Just cold. She shivered at the memory.

"Hey, Connor, over here."

They both turned and spotted Connor's two brothers coming their way with Lucinda, the same woman Maggie had seen with Sarah and her friend a few minutes ago. The same woman who couldn't seem to keep from frowning at her. Now she was holding a notebook and pen and didn't look happy about it. Had the brothers corralled her into doing some work? Probably so. That would explain her sour expression. Or maybe it was Maggie's own presence, she mused, but briskly brushed that thought away.

Connor quickly slid his arm away and Maggie felt foolishly bereft without his touch.

"Hey, guys," Connor said.

"You go ahead and talk to them," Maggie urged Connor. "I'm going up to the convention floor to look around some more."

"Stick around. You know my brothers." Connor grabbed her hand to keep her close by.

Maggie had a bad feeling about this little reunion, but she stayed with him and tried to think good thoughts.

"Is that Maggie Jameson?" Ian said as they got closer.

"Sure is," Connor said cheerfully.

"Hello, Maggie," the woman said tonelessly.

Maggie tried to smile. "Hi. It's Lucinda, right? You're Sarah's cousin. I remember you from high school. It's nice to see you."

Lucinda's lips twisted wryly, as though she didn't quite believe Maggie's words. "It's been a long time."

"Yes, it has," Maggie said, recalling more about the woman as they spoke. Lucinda had been a few years younger than Sarah, but she used to hang around with the group once in a while.

"I work for MacLaren now," she said, her tone proudly confrontational.

Maggie blinked. Lucinda made it sound like a challenge. As if she really meant to say, *These are my men. You keep your hands off.* Frankly, Maggie couldn't blame her. If Lucinda believed her cousin Sarah, she probably accepted the story that Maggie had destroyed Connor. Now she wasn't about to allow this witch to get near his brothers.

Jake and Ian exchanged glances and Maggie suddenly had a whole new reason for running again. They looked even less happy to see her than Lucinda did.

Naturally, Connor's brothers were aware that she'd left town all those years ago and probably assumed, as Lucinda and Sarah and everyone else in town seemed to, that she'd left him with a crushed and broken heart. If the accusations of Sarah and her other high school pals were the common wisdom around Point Cairn, namely, that Maggie had betrayed Connor with another man, then Jake and Ian most likely hated her as much as her old friends did.

So this would be fun.

"Hi, Ian. Hi, Jake," she said, trying to be upbeat. "It's good to see you both."

"Yeah, good to see you, too, Maggie," Ian said carefully. "How are you enjoying the festival?"

"I'm having a great time."

"Oh yeah? Did you enter something in the competition?"

"Yes, I've got three entries."

As she spoke to Ian, Jake leaned in to say something to Connor. Connor laughed, but Jake did nothing but stare stone-faced at Maggie.

She tried to block Jake from her line of sight as she attempted to continue the casual conversation with Ian, but it was impossible. She realized she could no longer stomach this level of judgmental scrutiny. Even Ian, who was at least willing to talk to her, was emitting the same reproachful vibes as Jake.

She reached out and touched Connor's arm to get his attention. "I—I've just remembered something I have to do upstairs. You can text me when you're finished down here and tell me where you want to meet."

"Wait," he said. "I'll only be a—"

But she couldn't wait. She had to go. She turned and walked away as fast as she could move, leaving the MacLaren brothers and their silent but palpable condemnation behind.

Six

Baffled, Connor watched Maggie dash off the convention floor. The urge to follow her was strong, but first he turned on Jake. "What just happened here?"

Jake shrugged. "Guess she didn't want to hang around."

"Don't pull that crap with me. You were freaking her out with your, whatever you call it, *evil eye* thing. And I don't appreciate it."

"You're awfully defensive," Jake said, standing his ground. "I thought you were never going to speak to her again. What changed your mind?"

"I grew up." Fuming, Connor glanced down the hallway. "That was over ten years ago, for God's sake. Let it go. And besides, you're the one who told me to bring a date this week."

"I was hoping you might bring someone who everyone could get along with."

"You could've asked me, Connor," Lucinda said.

Connor ignored her and frowned in frustration at his brother. "I thought you always liked Maggie."

"Well, sure, I liked her, until she screwed you over so badly that you could barely drag your ass out of bed for, like, a year."

"That's not true."

"Truer than you'd like to believe. Maybe that time was fun for you, but it wasn't for me. Or Ian, or Mom. Maggie ripped your heart out, man. We didn't think you'd ever recover. And I don't want to see it happen again."

Even if Jake's recollection was skewed, Connor could at least try to be grateful for his concern.

He suddenly realized that Lucinda was listening avidly to things he'd rather not share with anyone outside his family. With a tight smile, he said, "Hey, Lucinda, I thought Jake gave you the day off. Why don't you go catch up with your friends and have some fun?"

"That's okay, Connor," she said cheerfully. "I don't mind staying if you guys need some help."

"No, Connor's right, Luce," Jake said. "Thanks for taking those notes for us, but that's all we needed. You should go have some fun while you have the chance."

Lucinda smiled. "Okay, I'm off, then. See you guys around."

Connor watched her walk away, then turned back to Jake. "Look, I appreciate what you're saying, I really do, but there's no way Maggie will get to me like she did before. And I'm definitely not back together with her, if that's why you're so bent out of shape. This is just business."

"Business?" Jake said skeptically. "Didn't look like you were conducting business just now."

"I have to agree," Ian chimed in. "You two looked pretty friendly to me."

"Look, she's here with me because we made a deal. She's my date for the week and in exchange, I get her beer formulas."

Connor had informed his brothers last week that Maggie was the brains behind the Taylor James beers, so they knew how important those beer formulas were.

Jake pondered Connor's words for a moment. "Sounds like a pretty lopsided deal. What's she getting out of it?"

"The pleasure of my company."

Ian snorted. "Right. What's she really getting?"

"She needs to borrow some cash," Connor admitted.

"You're giving her money." Jake's eyes narrowed in on

him. "So basically, you're paying her to spend time with you. Do you know how sleazy that sounds?"

Connor rolled his eyes. "You're such a jerk. She needs the money for Angus."

"What?" Ian's eyes widened. "Why? Is he sick?"

"He's got something wrong with his heart."

"Damn it." Jake leaned his hip against the long conference table. "I hate to hear that."

Connor nodded. "Yeah, me, too. There's some new experimental drug that's perfect for him, but it's incredibly expensive and the insurance won't cover it."

"Then we should just give him the money," Ian said.

"Maggie's too proud to take the money without giving something in return. So she's giving up her recipes."

Jake was reluctantly impressed. "I guess that sounds reasonable."

"It is. So back off, because I've got this covered."

"Now you're scaring me again."

Connor ignored that. "And next time you see Maggie, be nice. Pretend Mom's watching."

"Aw, hell," Jake muttered.

"Yeah, and no more Vulcan death stare," Ian added, scowling at Jake. "You were even scaring *me* with that look."

Connor turned to leave. "I'll see you guys later. I've got to go find Maggie."

"Hey, wait," Jake said before Connor could get away. "Are you really sure she needs the money? I heard she was rolling in dough from her rich ex-husband."

"Where'd you hear that?"

"I don't know," he said, frowning as he tried to think about it. "One of her friends, I guess."

"What friends?" Ian scoffed. "I heard from Sarah Myers that all of Maggie's friends had turned on her."

"That's her own fault," Jake grumbled.

The fact was, Connor didn't really know much about what had happened, either, but that didn't mean he would put up with Jake's attitude. Connor smacked his brother's arm. "Whatever happened between Maggie and me is ancient history and none of your business, so stop being such a jerk about this."

"All right, all right," Jake said, holding his hands up. "I'll be nice."

"You bet your ass you will," Connor said ominously.

"But here's an idea," Jake said, his tone turning derisive. "Maybe you can fill us in on the *ancient history* one of these days." He used sarcastic air quotes for *ancient history,* as if he wasn't buying Connor's claim at all.

The sarcasm pissed Connor off to a whole new level and he made a move toward Jake. Ian quickly stepped between his two brothers, ever the peacemaker.

"Easy, there," Ian said, holding up his hands. "Both of you take a step back."

"Jackass," Connor muttered.

"Lamebrain," Jake countered.

"Don't sweat it, Connor," Ian said, then turned and gave Jake a fulminating glare. "We'll all behave ourselves like gentlemen."

"You're damn straight you will." Connor jabbed his finger at Jake. "And here's fair warning. I'm bringing Maggie to the Wellstone dinner tomorrow night, so you'd better treat her like a freaking goddess or you'll be watching the whole deal fall apart like a house of cards."

Connor decided to give Maggie some time to herself and, after wandering around the lobby for ten minutes, he stepped outside for some air. Crossing the terrace, he walked down to the boardwalk and headed south.

The sun was still bright, but the wind had come up and

turned blustery. Connor didn't mind the chill after so many hours spent inside the convention center.

He still wasn't sure why he had defended Maggie so stridently to his brothers, especially since most of what Jake had complained about was exactly how Connor had felt at one time. Didn't trust her, didn't understand her, didn't want to see her again.

But that was before Maggie had walked into his office a week ago. Since then, some of his opinions had shifted a little. And wasn't that perfectly natural? Especially after he'd found out that she hadn't exactly lived a charmed life all those years she'd been away. Still, he wasn't quite willing to cut her too much slack. At least, not until he found out exactly why she left him in the first place

He wouldn't mention it to his brothers, but he could admit to himself that he liked hanging out with her. Now and then, he caught glimpses of the old Maggie he'd known and loved, and okay, the fact that she was sexier than ever was a major point in her favor. So what was wrong with enjoying himself for a few days?

That didn't mean he trusted her, of course. There was no way she could ever restore the trust he'd once had in her. Nevertheless, when he heard his brothers talking smack about her, he didn't like it. Truth be told, their sniping had riled him up so much that he'd been tempted to punch out both of them. Not that Ian deserved it as much as Jake, but hey, Ian could always use a punch in the stomach, too, just on general principle.

The thought made him chuckle as he brushed his windblown hair back from his forehead. He loved his brothers, but sometimes they could be pains in the butt. Jake in particular had always been a hard-ass, especially when it came to trusting people. He was famous for saying that he hated liars, and once his trust was broken, he never looked back.

Connor didn't blame Jake for feeling that way. He knew

exactly where the distrust had come from. It was all thanks to their deceitful uncle Hugh and his damnable will. Hugh's relentless rivalry with their own father had extended beyond the grave, as the three brothers found out last year when it came time to read Uncle Hugh's last will and testament. A miserable man even on a good day, Hugh had attempted to pit Connor and his brothers against one another in an all-out fight for their inheritance.

So far, the brothers had outmaneuvered their uncle's Scottish lawyers and the ludicrous terms of the will. But all of that was irrelevant at the moment. Right now Connor just wanted Jake to lighten up around Maggie.

He did appreciate that Jake was worried about Maggie worming her way back into Connor's heart and maybe twisting it into a pretzel and leaving him for dead all over again. But Connor was a lot smarter and stronger now and he wasn't about to let that happen. So Jake had nothing to worry about on that front.

And besides, Connor reasoned, it wasn't as if Maggie had ever lied to Jake. Hell, Connor couldn't even swear that she'd ever lied to himself, either. She'd just left him. That was all. There had been no lies. No tears. No pretending. Maggie had simply walked out of his life one day and had never looked back.

Connor rubbed at a twinge in his chest and then swore crudely. This had to be heartburn or something. It couldn't possibly be the lingering memory of Maggie's desertion that was causing this stab of pain.

He sloughed off the ache and concentrated instead on the sight of a tarnished old fishing boat as it puttered into the harbor with its catch of the day. The crusty captain had a pipe shoved in his mouth and a bottle of beer in a handy cup holder next to the wheel.

Damn it. As much as it bugged Connor to admit it, Jake might have been right to question Connor's feelings for

Maggie. Especially since, like it or not, he still seemed to have a bit of a soft spot when it came to her. Which was a little ironic since he invariably turned hard as stone whenever she was around.

But that didn't mean he suddenly trusted her. He didn't, and wasn't sure he ever would again. And because of that, it wouldn't hurt to take a page out of Jake's book and be even more watchful around Maggie than he'd been before. That redheaded beauty was more than capable of slipping under his guard if he didn't remain on full alert from now on.

Connor walked back inside and immediately spotted her exiting an elevator and heading for the lobby. As he approached, she caught sight of him and stopped in her tracks.

"I was just going to go for a walk."

He took hold of her arm. "I just came in from a walk, but I'll go back out with you."

"That's not necessary."

"Yes, it is. You're my date, remember?"

"Oh, come on. You don't need me with you every minute of the day, do you?"

"Yes, I do." When her eyes widened, he quickly added, "Because we have a deal, in case you forgot."

"Right," she said, and sighed. "We have a deal. But that shouldn't mean I don't get a break once in a while. Especially after being the target of your brother's evil stink-eye stare."

He almost laughed but managed to check himself. He didn't blame her for ragging on Jake, but he wasn't about to tell her so. "I didn't notice."

"Oh, please! He was scowling at me the whole time I was standing there. He's about as subtle as a rhinoceros."

He shrugged. "Jake scowls so often I never think much about it. But admit it, it's not just my brothers that you have a problem with."

"What do you mean?"

"You think I didn't notice you racing in the opposite direction as soon as Sarah and her friends showed up? You left me to defend myself against them. That was cruel. They're your friends, not mine."

"They are not my friends," she said flatly, then began to chuckle. "And honestly? You're complaining about having three women drool all over you? Hang on to your every word? You didn't appear to be suffering, Connor."

He chuckled, then changed the subject. "Let's go upstairs and get jackets. It's chilly outside."

The elevator arrived and she stepped inside. Connor joined her and the elevator quickly filled up, so they kept their conversation mundane. A few minutes later, they stepped out on the twelfth floor and walked to the door of their suite.

As Connor keyed open the door, Maggie said, "I don't care what you had planned for dinner tonight. I'm going to the Crab Shack and I'm having a glass of wine."

Connor grinned. The Crab Shack was one of his favorite dive restaurants and it was only a half block away. "I'm up for that."

"You are?"

He opened the door for Maggie, then followed her inside. But before she could go any farther, he grabbed her arm. "Look, Maggie. I know Jake can be a jerk, but that's not really why you ran off, is it?"

"Of course not," Maggie said, not quite meeting his gaze. "I had things to do."

"Right."

"Fine." She draped her blazer on the back of the dining room chair. "Of course I ran off. Anyone would've if they'd seen the look he was giving me. If they'd felt the chill."

"The chill?"

"Yes, the deadly chill emanating from your brother that was aimed in my direction. Forget it." She shook her head in dismissal and walked into the bathroom to brush her hair. Connor followed her and leaned against the doorjamb to watch in the mirror while she brushed her hair.

"Okay," he conceded. "I might've noticed him staring at you, but he hasn't seen you in a long time. Maybe he was mesmerized by your beauty."

"You're funny."

"Not trying to be." Connor sat on the marble ledge next to the luxurious spa bathtub and made himself comfortable while she applied a fresh coat of lipstick. Her movements were so simple while being quite possibly the most sensual thing he'd seen in forever. It took every ounce of willpower he possessed to keep from grabbing hold of her and licking the color off her mouth, then covering every inch of her body in hot kisses.

Sadly, Maggie didn't look as though she'd be open to that plan at the moment, but he had all afternoon to convince her otherwise.

The thought had him growing hard again and he subtly adjusted himself while forcing himself to concentrate on business. "Here's the thing, Maggie. Tomorrow night, you and I and my brothers will be having dinner with some very important business associates. MacLaren Corporation is involved in a very sensitive and confidential transaction with this other group, and the last thing we need them to see is friction between you and Jake."

"If your meeting is so sensitive and confidential, why do you want me to be there? I know you don't trust me."

He stared at her for a long moment. She was stating exactly what he'd been thinking earlier, that he didn't trust her and never would. And yet…he did trust her. Maybe not as far as his heart was concerned, but this was different. "In this case, I do trust you. I know you wouldn't do anything to jeopardize our business."

She blinked in surprise. "Thank you. I appreciate that.

And you're right, I would never deliberately put your business at risk."

"So you'll play nicely with Jake."

"I'm happy to get along with everyone, Connor, but your problem lies with Jake. You need to talk to him." She waved a little wand thing as she spoke, then wiped the tip of it along her lips, causing them to grow even glossier and lusciously edible than before.

"I've…um." He gulped. It was getting more difficult to follow the conversation. "I've already given Jake an earful."

"Good, because the last thing I need in my life is more friction." She met his gaze in the mirror as understanding dawned. "So you *did* notice he was scowling at me."

"Of course I noticed. But like I said, that's his normal expression. I've learned to ignore it."

"It's pretty hard to ignore when you're the target."

Connor was forced to agree with her since he had also been the target of Jake's wrath within the past half hour. "I apologize for his idiocy. I hope you can overlook it and get along with him tomorrow night."

She zipped up her cosmetic bag and turned to gaze directly at him. "We'll be fine, Connor. I'm sure your brother wouldn't do anything to jeopardize an important business transaction."

"No, he wouldn't."

"And neither would I. So it's settled. Let's go to lunch."

"Wait." He gripped her shoulders lightly. "I want to make this official in case you didn't hear me a minute ago. I sincerely apologize for my brothers hurting your feelings. You didn't deserve it and it won't happen again. And if it does, one of them will have to die."

She beamed. "Thank you, Connor. I appreciate that." She was gazing up at him as if he were some kind of heroic Knight of the Round Table, which was so far from the truth it was laughable.

"I'm not sure you should thank me," he said. "I didn't punch his lights out or anything. I should've, but I didn't."

"Thank you anyway." She continued to stare at him, the soft trace of a smile on her lips, and he no longer had a choice. He kissed her.

He fought to take it slow and easy with her, even though he was consumed with a stark need for more. But the knowledge that Maggie might still be reeling from Jake's censure forced Connor to keep the contact light. And that was one more reason why he planned to knock his brother on his ass the next time he had the chance.

Knowing she hadn't expected his kiss and wasn't ready to take it further, Connor was nonetheless tempted to break down her barriers and fulfill his deepest need to take her. Right now. In every way possible. He wanted her clothes stripped off, her breasts in his hands, his mouth on her skin, her body slick with his sweat, her core filled with his shaft.

The image made his heart pound so hard and loud his eyes almost crossed.

Connor had never been the kind of man who required instant gratification. Stretching out the anticipation made the fulfillment of his goal so much sweeter, so much more worth the wait. But now the scent of her filled his head, intoxicating him, making it difficult to remember why he'd thought it better to wait. He burned for her, wanted her more than he'd ever wanted anything before. Now. He didn't want to wait another second.

He shifted and changed the angle of their kiss and covered her lips completely. She had the most incredibly sensual mouth he'd ever seen on a woman, and he couldn't get enough of it.

Ever since the night before when he'd been stupid enough to postpone their lovemaking, he'd been craving the touch of her lips again. Waiting and wondering when the right moment would come and he could take her in his arms and fulfill his most ardent fantasies.

A soft sigh fluttered in her throat, and Connor took it as a sign of her desire for more. He eased her lips apart with his tongue and plunged inside her warmth, where her tongue tangled with his in a pleasurable whirl of desire.

As they kissed, a distant part of Connor's mind flashed to the past when he and Maggie had been joined at the lip. They'd shared hundreds, maybe thousands of kisses back then, so why did her kiss today feel so completely different and brand-new? As though they'd never kissed before this moment.

They weren't the same people, he thought. They were older, definitely. Smarter, too, he hoped. Back then, Connor had worshiped the ground Maggie walked upon. He'd treated her like spun silk, a rare treasure, something to be cherished above all else. Maybe that was why she'd left him. Maybe he'd been too wrapped up in her to notice she wasn't happy. He still didn't know.

But the Maggie in his arms today was a flesh-and-blood woman. Complicated. Beautiful. Normal. He no longer had any expectations that she was anything other than that. And that made everything different.

Better, he thought again.

When she moaned, he ended the kiss and gazed at her. "In case you couldn't guess, I want you, Maggie."

She studied him for a long moment; then she sighed. "Does this mean I'm going to miss my dinner?"

He laughed and ran his hands up and down her arms. "Only if you say so. It might kill me, but I'm following your lead—for right now."

Tonight, though, he would be the one in charge. And there was no doubt in his mind as to how they would be spending the evening.

"So, what do you want, Maggie?"

"I want… I…" She closed her eyes and leaned her forehead against his chest.

"You want…" he prompted, using his finger to lift her chin so he could meet her gaze.

"Damn it, Connor, just kiss me again."

His smile grew and he pulled her closer. "Be happy to oblige."

His mouth took hers in a white-hot kiss and Maggie met him with the same level of passion, mixed with a new level of confidence and enthusiasm. It seemed to Connor that now that she'd made the choice, Maggie could relax and go with her instincts. Maybe it came from being the one to make the decision, or maybe she just needed to hear him say how much he wanted her. Not that she couldn't have figured it out on her own by looking at a strategic part of his anatomy, but it probably also helped that he'd voiced how ridiculously desperate he was to taste her and touch her.

He refused to question her change of heart. He was just pitifully grateful that she wanted the same thing he did.

She parted her lips to allow him entrance and met each stroke of his tongue with her own. As his hands swept over her back and dipped down to lightly grasp her gorgeous butt, she let out another soft groan and arched into him.

Connor gave a mental shout-out to whatever gods were in charge of the really important things—like Maggie's body. Her well-sculpted arms. The smooth line of her stomach. The shapely curve of her thighs. Not to mention her delectable mouth. She was temptation personified and he couldn't resist any part of her. Never could.

That was probably why it had taken him so long to get her out of his system. But he *had* gotten over her.

This time, things would be different, he thought, as he slid his hand up and cupped her breast.

This time it was all about physical pleasure, pure and

simple. No hearts, no emotions, no pain. No more thinking about the past. From here on, there was only pleasure.

"Connor, I want…"

"So do I, baby," he whispered, and swooped her up into his arms.

"Oh, you never did that before," she blurted, then laughed playfully and wrapped her arms around his neck.

"I must've been crazy," he muttered, and carried her into the bedroom, were he laid her down gently on the comforter.

He followed her down and pulled her into his arms, where they gave and took in equal measure as they rolled together, exploring, begging, melting into each other as they each demanded more and more.

Connor moved up onto his knees and straddled her thighs. "You're wearing too many clothes," he said, sliding his hands under her top. "I do like this sweater."

She smiled dreamily. "Thank you."

In a blur, he whipped it up and over her head and tossed it aside.

She laughed in surprise, then sighed as he ran his hands along her bare shoulders, down her sides and across her stomach.

"I like this better," he said.

"Me, too."

He cupped her breasts and leaned over to kiss the soft roundness. Swiftly unhooking her bra, he tossed it, as well. "Better and better."

"Connor," she whispered, and moaned when he used his thumbs to tease her nipples to peak. He moved in with his mouth, taking first one breast, then the other, sucking and licking, nibbling and tasting until she was writhing under him.

He moved lower, kissing her stomach and nuzzling her belly button as he slid lower still. He slowly unzipped her pants, planting more kisses as he exposed more skin. Pulling them off, he rose to gaze at her body. "God, you're beautiful."

"Connor," she said on a sigh.

"I'm right here." He gazed at her, saw that her eyes were bright with desire. Her thick red hair was spread out in waves across the pillow like an aura. Her lips were plump and wet from the touch of his own. All she wore now was a pair of skimpy pink lace panties, the stuff of male dreams. He slid two fingers under the edge to tease her, but only succeeded in straining his already shaky control. His body was hard and aching and he couldn't wait another minute to do the one and only thing he wanted to do. Bury himself inside her.

He jumped off the bed and undressed in a heartbeat, then found one of the many condoms he'd been smart enough to pack. He quickly tore it open and sheathed himself, then returned to the bed, where she was watching him with a hunger that matched his own.

"All dressed up and ready to go?" she said saucily.

"That's right." He slid closer and planted a kiss on her smooth shoulder. "Now, where was I? Let's see."

He moved lower again, kissing and licking his way down her body. He stopped to taste her breasts once again, filling his senses, then moving along the soft contours of her stomach and hips. She was breathless by the time he reached the apex of her sleek thighs.

"Ah yes," he murmured as he reached beneath her panties with his fingers to find her hot, moist core. "I was right here."

She trembled and moaned her need as his fingers began

to stroke her inner heat, taking her to the edge and back again, driving her to the brink of release, then pulling her back once more. Her soft pleas became groans of need and Connor was certain he'd never known such all-consuming desire before. Not even ten years ago when all he'd wanted was Maggie. This was more. This was bigger. He craved her with every fiber of his being.

He hooked his thumbs around the band of her panties and tugged them off slowly, killing himself with pleasure as he watched them slide over her curvy hips and down her shapely legs. When he reached her ankles, she nudged him away with one foot while she used the other to fling the panties across the room.

He laughed and glanced up at her. Her full lips were curved in a sexy smile and her brandy-hued eyes gleamed with feminine power and pleasure. She'd never looked more beautiful to him and he decided, in that moment, that he needed honesty between them.

"I've wanted you in my bed since I saw you last week," he said, moving closer and positioning himself. In one swift motion, he entered her and crushed his mouth against hers. She gripped his shoulders as their bodies rocked together in a sensual, synchronous rhythm that seemed to arise from within them and overtake them effortlessly.

He felt her heart beating in time to his, kissed the smooth surface of her neck and shoulders. He'd never felt more alive as he strained to bring her the ultimate pleasure possible while holding out on the same for himself for as long as humanly possible. But as her body strained against his, as her sumptuous breasts pressed into his chest, as her stunning legs wrapped more tightly around his waist, he felt a stab of need stronger than any he'd experienced before. He pressed more deeply, filling her completely, building up the hunger within them both until they were clinging to the edge of sheer passion.

She fell first, crying out his name and shuddering in his arms, leaving Connor overwhelmed by a bone-deep sense of fulfillment. With one last driving thrust, he echoed her cry with his own and a dark, wild rapture hurtled him over the edge.

Seven

What did you do?

She'd had sex with Connor, she reminded herself, with a mental cuff to the head. Wasn't it obvious? The man himself was still warm, sexy, naked and snuggled beside her in their big comfy bed.

Sex with Connor. It had been even better than she remembered. More than wonderful, it was spectacular. Better than fireworks. Or rainbows. It was awesome. The best sex she'd experienced in…forever? Hard to believe, but Connor was a better lover than he used to be, and he'd been pretty darned good back in the day.

Connor had always been wonderful, thoughtful and giving. But now he was so much more than that. He was powerful and agile and…oh, mercy. Did she already mention *awesome?*

But that wasn't the point, was it? The point was, she had done something horribly wrong and stupid. How many times had she reminded herself in the past week that Connor MacLaren was out for revenge, pure and simple? How many ways had she practiced saying *No!* to him?

And with one kiss, her stratagem had crumbled. Granted, it had been a very, very *good* kiss, but now what? She'd let go of every last qualm she'd brandished as a first line of defense and now she was left with, well, nothing. If she were smart, she would get dressed and go back home to her grandfather and the goats.

More than anything else, this proved what a hypocrite

she was. After all, she'd spent years trying to avoid risks, ridding her life of any little thing that might bring her pain, and here she was again, risking it all for a chance to…to what? Find a love to last a lifetime? Yeah, right. With the guy everyone—including him—thought she'd unceremoniously dumped ten years ago? Get real.

Maggie squeezed her eyes shut even tighter.

She wished she could blame Connor for coercing her, but he'd made a point of insisting that it was her decision to continue. Awfully clever of him.

Well, Maggie would just have to chalk this up as one more bad decision in a lifetime full of them.

Alan would say—

Stop!

Maggie cringed. She had a long-standing rule never to start a sentence with her ex-husband's name.

Connor stretched, then turned and leaned up on his elbow to gaze down at her. "You're thinking too much. I can hear your brain ticking away."

"Sorry. Sometimes my inner thoughts can get pretty loud."

Smiling, he brushed a strand of hair off her forehead, then slowly sobered. That couldn't be a good sign. "Maggie, that was…"

A mistake?

A horrible error in judgment?

Was he waiting for her to finish the sentence? Was there a multiple-choice response?

"Phenomenal," he murmured, and bent his head to kiss the tender skin beneath her chin. "Incredible. Mind-bending."

"Awesome?" she suggested lightly.

"Beyond awesome." He nudged the blanket down so he could kiss and nibble her neck and her ear and her jaw and, oh, sweet mother, Maggie's synapses were starting to sizzle. She wanted him all over again.

Phenomenal, he'd said. Would this be a good time to jump up and do a little happy dance? Maybe not. And really, even though the sex was good—or rather, damn good, phenomenal, awesome—it didn't change the bigger picture, the one in which Maggie knew she'd screwed up royally. So right now she needed to stop fooling around and think about her next move. She should leave. But what if he changed his mind about their deal? What if he changed the terms? Was it awful of her to wonder about that at a time like this? Yes, but…oh dear, should she pack her bags? Should she eat something first? She ought to think about—

"You are so beautiful, Maggie," he said, trailing kisses along her breastbone. Then he reached for her. "Come here."

She stared at his tousled dark hair, ran her hands along the strong muscles of his shoulders and back and pondered whether she was making another mistake again. Oh, hell, was there any doubt?

He lifted his head and met her gaze. "Trust me, Maggie?"

Biting her lip, she stared into his dark eyes and wondered if she'd ever had a choice. He smiled then, and so did she. Because of course, she'd always had a choice.

"Yes," Maggie whispered, and didn't have to think anymore.

As the sun was setting over the ocean, Maggie and Connor slipped on jeans, sweatshirts and sneakers and walked down the boardwalk to the Crab Shack.

With peanut shells on the floor and a monstrous grinning crab crawling on the roof, it shouldn't have been romantic, but Maggie loved it. They grabbed an empty table next to the full-length plate-glass window and ordered wine. The last arc of the sun shot coral and pink cloud trails across the sky until the sun finally sank beneath the horizon. Once it was gone completely, streetlamps began to twinkle to life along the boardwalk. Their server brought their wine along with a votive candle to shed some light on the menus.

"I don't suppose you want lobster," Connor asked after a minute of perusing the specials.

"I love lobster. I haven't had it in years." She closed her menu and took a sip of wine. "Yes, that's what I'm having."

"I figured you might've gotten tired of it after all that time you spent in Boston."

"Oh no, no," she said, chuckling. "Lobster was not allowed."

"Allowed?" He frowned at her. "Is this about your ex? Because I've got to tell you, Maggie, the guy sounds like a real jackass."

She smiled. "What a lovely description. It suits him perfectly."

Their waiter was back with bread and butter and took their orders.

After the waiter walked away, Connor leaned forward. "I've got to ask you something. If the guy was such an ass, why did you ever…" He flopped back in his chair and held up his hand to her. "Wait. Never mind. Don't answer that."

"No, it's okay," she said, sighing as she buttered a slice of sourdough bread. "Go ahead and ask whatever it is you're wondering about. You deserve answers."

He pulled off a hunk of bread and popped a small chunk of it into his mouth. Did he really want to hear all the reasons why she'd stopped loving him? Hell, no. But she was right. After all this time, not to mention the past four hours they'd spent in bed together, it would be smart to get some answers. "Okay, I'll ask. Why'd you leave me for him?"

She stopped chewing abruptly and tilted her head in confusion. "Connor, I didn't leave you for him. You and I had already broken up a month earlier."

He was taken aback. "No, we didn't."

"Yes, we did," she said softly. "We broke up the day you announced that you and your brothers were going to spend a week at some skydiving camp."

He wanted to ask her what alternative universe she was living in, but he kept it civil. "Maggie, that's just not true."

"Yes, it is. I remember it as if it were yesterday because I was devastated." She tapped her fingers nervously against the base of her wineglass. "I was so proud of myself because I'd managed to keep breathing when you went on that white-water rafting trip to the most dangerous river in the country. But then you went off with your brothers to climb El Capitan in Yosemite and I was breathing into a paper bag the whole time. When you told me about the skydiving, it was the last straw for me. I told you that if you went away, I wouldn't be here for you when you got back." She waved her hand in disgust. "Such a stupid, girlish threat, but I meant it at the time."

He frowned, remembering her words in that last conversation, but not realizing their full implication at the time.

She continued. "So after I said that, you said, 'That's too bad, babe. I guess we both have things we've gotta do.' And that was it. We said goodbye and you hung up the phone. Believe me, Connor. I remember that conversation. I remember staring at the phone and then bursting into tears. My mother probably remembers, too. I drove her crazy that summer."

Apparently everyone had grasped her meaning but him. "I thought you were telling me that you were going away for a while, like, on vacation. I figured, I'd be gone a week, come home and then you'd be gone a few weeks. So we'd miss each other's company for maybe a month, but we'd get back together at the end of summer."

Her face had turned pale. "No. I meant that I wouldn't be with you anymore."

He felt his chest constrict as he considered her words. "So you were already over me."

"Oh no! No, I loved you so much, but you scared me to death. Connor, don't you remember how I used to tell you that you deserved a woman who enjoyed taking risks? Someone just like you?"

He swirled his wineglass absently. "Yeah, you said it a lot. I thought it was a little joke, because I always thought we were perfect together."

Her eyes glittered with tears as she shook her head. "No, it wasn't a joke. I wish it was, but I couldn't stand it when you took chances with your life."

"My life?"

"You and your brothers were always going off to hike up some sheer cliff, or ski over some avalanche, or ride horses down a treacherous canyon path."

He gave a lopsided grin. "The Grand Canyon trip. Hell, Maggie, we used to do that kind of stuff all the time. Not so much anymore. But I don't see why it was such a big deal to you."

"Believe me, it was a big deal. I would sit at home holding my breath, waiting for the phone call from the morgue."

And that's when Connor suddenly remembered that Maggie's father had died in a hiking accident in Alaska. He'd always known about it, but had never connected the dots. Damn, no wonder all of his wild sporting activities used to freak her out. He sat back in the chair feeling wretched, his appetite gone. "I'm so sorry, Maggie."

"So am I." She smiled sadly. "When you said you were going skydiving for a week? Oh, my God, I almost fainted. I couldn't take it anymore. Most of my life, I've been afraid to take those kinds of risks. I was ultracautious, don't you remember? I didn't even try out for cheerleading because I thought I might get hurt. It was all because of the way my dad died. He was just like you and your brothers, always looking for the next big adrenaline rush. His death was so devastating to me and my mom, there was no way I was going to put myself through that kind of pain again with you."

"Damn, Maggie." He realized now that he must've scared the hell out of her on a daily basis. As the youngest brother, he'd always been the one to take on any stupid challenge or death-defying dare. He really was lucky to be alive. "I guess that was the last straw you were talking about."

"It was." She reached across the table for his hand. "I'm sorry I didn't explain things more clearly, but I guess at the time, I just panicked."

"I'm sorry, too." He squeezed her hand in his. "If we'd taken the time to talk it out, we might've…well, who knows what could've happened?"

She gazed at him and her smile faded. "It seemed too selfish to ask you to change your lifestyle for me."

He shook his head and stared out at the darkening vista. The ocean was rougher now and the choppy whitecaps gleamed like shards of ice in the reflected light. "I would've done anything for you, Maggie."

"I know," she whispered, and blinked away tears. "But it wouldn't have been fair."

The waiter arrived with two huge platters, each with a full-size lobster, drawn butter and baked potatoes with everything on them. He poured more wine for each of them, wished them *bon appétit* and left them alone.

Connor chuckled somberly. "Are you even hungry after all this depressing talk?"

Maggie sniffled as she looked down at her lobster and then over at him. "You bet I am."

He laughed. "That's my girl." And they both started eating, their appetites and humor instantly restored.

They spent the next few minutes in silence as they wolfed down the perfectly prepared food. Finally Connor took a break and sat back in his chair. He reached for his wine and took a sip, then said, "Mind if I ask you something that might put me in a happier mood?"

"But not me?" She laughed shortly. "Sure, go ahead."

"Why'd you marry this joker?" Then, even though he knew the answer, he asked, "And what's his name again? Albert? Arthur?"

"It's Alan. Alan Cosgrove, and that's the last time I'll use his actual name out loud. I'm afraid of summoning the devil."

He chuckled. "Like *Beetlejuice?*"

"Exactly!"

It had been one of their all-time favorite movies back in the day.

Maggie drank down a hearty gulp of wine and seemed to brace herself before answering. It was one more way Connor could tell that the guy had been a real piece of work.

"After you and I broke up," she began, "I cried myself silly for weeks."

"Good to hear."

She laughed. "My mother finally sent me off to visit my cousin Jane in Boston. Jane had a summer day job, so I spent my mornings wallowing in grief and my afternoons walking for miles around Boston. There were so many charming neighborhoods and I think I saw them all. One day I walked into a fancy art gallery in the Back Bay and that's where I met him."

"Ashcroft," he said helpfully.

"Yes." She giggled. "*Ashcroft* was wealthy, nice looking, seemed stable enough. He enjoyed quiet walks, art galleries and foreign films."

"Much like myself."

She gave a ladylike snort. "Right." She went on to explain that the guy she met had seemed safe and sane and unlikely to do anything that would worry her excessively.

"Unlike myself."

"Sadly," she murmured. "At the time, I thought it was important that he wasn't a risk taker. I was so stupid."

"We were both young," he said, giving her a break.

"I suppose," Maggie continued, "but despite how good Ashcroft might've looked on paper, in reality, he was a jerk and probably a sociopath."

There was no *probably* about it, Connor thought, but didn't say it aloud.

"It turned out that he was being forced into marriage by his iron-fisted mother, who had decreed that it was time for him to find a wife. Sybil—that's his mother's name," Maggie explained. "Sybil had suggested that he find someone pretty enough, who was malleable, penniless and had very few ties to Boston. It would be easier to control her that way, she said."

"Let me get this straight. His *mother* was telling him this?"

Maggie nodded. "Yes. She definitely knew her boy."

"This is creeping me out," Connor said. "But don't stop. I want to hear it all."

She grinned. "I'm not sure I can stop now that I'm on a roll." She took a quick bite of her baked potato, then continued. "A month after we were married, Sybil called me into her sitting room to let me know how well I'd met the criteria to be her daughter-in-law. Then she proceeded to tell me everything that was wrong with me."

"She doesn't exactly sound like Mom-of-the-Year."

"She was peachy," Maggie said, and shivered. "But the good news was that I had also fulfilled Ashcroft's requirements for a suitable wife."

"Can't wait to hear his list." He held up his hand. "He obviously wanted someone beautiful, right?"

"Thank you," she said with a grateful smile. "But you really need to hear the prerequisites he gave his mother."

"Oh, I get it," Connor said. "She was the one who was going to find him a wife."

"That was the plan."

"But then he met you."

"Yes, but I had to pass muster with his mother first."

Connor shook his head. "What a guy."

"You have no idea," she murmured, her lips curving into a frown.

Connor didn't want her going too far down memory lane over this jerk, so he shot her a quick grin. "Come on, let's hear it. What did Weird Al want in a wife?"

She chuckled. "That's a perfect nickname for him. Okay, he specifically wanted someone who wasn't fat, didn't speak with a pronounced drawl, didn't snore and didn't chew with her mouth open."

Connor stared at her for a few long seconds. "Come on. You're kidding."

"If only," she said, smothering a laugh. "Sybil told me that Ashcroft was very sensitive about bodily sounds and emissions."

Connor snorted. "Yeah, most obsessive-compulsive anal-retentive types tend to be that way."

"If only I'd known this before the wedding," Maggie said. "But Ashcroft knew how to put on a good act. He swept me off my feet, promised me the moon and convinced me to marry him. What an idiot I was."

Connor didn't respond to that one, since he wholeheartedly agreed. "So, once you were married, what happened?"

"If you want to hear the gory details, I'm going to need more wine first," she said, grinning ruefully.

Connor chuckled and reached for the wine bottle. "Yeah, I think I might need a little more, too."

"Okay, the day we got married, we moved into his mother's mansion in Boston's Beacon Hill."

"You lived with his mom the whole time?"

"Yeah," she said. "They were close."

Connor almost spit his wine out. "They were demented."

"That, too." She speared a chunk of lobster and popped it into her mouth. "Oh, and none of my family were invited to the wedding, did I mention that? And within a few days of the ceremony, he was insisting that I cut off all ties with them."

"The better to isolate and control you."

"Yeah." She gazed at Connor. "I wasn't really smart about any of this. I think I was still traumatized about breaking up with you and I just kind of went along with things. It wasn't easy, because his mother was really cold and unbending. And he got worse as time went on. I just couldn't do anything to please either one of them."

"I wish you'd called me."

"I do, too, Connor." She reached across the table and touched his hand. "But I was adrift. After our last conversation, I didn't think you were all that interested in hearing from me. I wasn't sure of myself anymore. They did a good job of whittling away at my confidence."

"They sound like experts."

"Oh, they were." Her eyes hazed a bit as she remembered more. "After seven long years, I finally grew some gumption and decided it was time to divorce them both. And the very day I made an appointment to see a lawyer, Sybil died of a massive heart attack."

"Whoa."

"She left all her money to Ashcroft. And on the day of her funeral, he informed me that he was divorcing *me*."

Connor let out a string of expletives. "He did you a favor. You know that, right?"

"Oh, I know it," she said fiercely. "But even on the occasion of his mother's death, he couldn't leave it alone. No, he had to go on and on, explaining how unsuitable I was for him. How I had been nothing more than a convenience to him."

"He should be glad he's still breathing," he muttered.

"A *convenience*," Maggie repeated slowly, her hands tightening into fists. "That son of a bitch."

"Literally," Connor muttered.

She waved her anger away. "The divorce was a gift, frankly, because it meant I was blessedly free of him. He tried so hard to break my spirit, but he never broke my heart, thank God. And I'm so glad he saved me the trouble of trying to divorce him."

"Because he would've fought you to the bitter end."

"That's right." She chuckled. "Irony was always lost on Ashcroft."

"No sense of humor, that guy."

She laughed. "So I took my miniscule divorce settlement, swallowed my pride and came back home to Point Cairn. And here we are."

But Connor knew that wasn't the end of the story. His eyes narrowed on her. "Did he hurt you?"

"Physically?" She hesitated. "Not really." Then she added, "To be honest, he didn't care much for anything physical. He preferred to demoralize me mentally and emotionally."

Connor leaned forward. "We can change the subject, Maggie."

"No," she insisted, waving her fork back and forth. "I want to talk about it, because I never got to. Except to a therapist and that wasn't very satisfying. I thought when I came home, I would have my old girlfriends around to help me hash things out and get rid of those old feelings. But the girls weren't exactly happy to see me show up again."

Understanding dawned. In the years after Maggie left town, all of their friends had rallied around him and turned Maggie into the bad guy. Connor had never tried to change their opinions of Maggie because that's what he had thought, too. "That's why you ran in the other direction when you saw Sarah and the others."

She smiled tightly. "Pretty much."

"Jeez, Maggie, you've had a rough time of it."

"Oh, please, it's nothing I can't handle." She airily brushed away his concern but then began to laugh at herself. "Okay, yeah. It was really bad there for a while. Grandpa's goats became my best friends."

Connor chuckled as he poured the last of the wine into their glasses. "So you didn't have your girlfriends to hash things out with, but you've got me. I'm here. I'll help you get through it all. Tell me everything you went through with this clown Ashcroft."

She beamed a hopeful smile at him. "Really?"

"Come on." He gestured with his hand. "Come on, tell me the rest of it."

"Where shall I start?" She inhaled deeply, then said in a rush, "Okay. Well, he bought all my clothes for me."

"Hmm." Connor frowned. "I guess that's…nice?"

Her lips twisted sardonically. "Believe me, he didn't do it to be nice."

"Oh, right. That jerk." He took a sip of wine before advancing on the topic. "So…what kind of stuff did he make you wear?"

She laughed. "Probably not what you're thinking. No spandex or anything. He wanted me to be seen in expensive classics, knits and wools, sweater sets, a lot of plaids, skirts, shirtdresses, sensible shoes, pearls. Nothing garish or low class, like blue jeans or boots."

"Idiot."

"Thank you! You make a really good girlfriend."

They both laughed, and then Connor said, "Did you work during your marriage?" He struggled to get that last word out.

"Work?" Her laugh was a soft trill. "No. I couldn't work."

He nodded. "No jobs available?"

"Oh, I suppose there were jobs, but I had no skills."

He frowned. "Yes, you do."

She stared out the window for a moment, then gazed over at Connor. "But even if I could get a job, how would I get from my house to my workplace?"

"By car?"

"Oh no. I couldn't have a car because I might get lost or crash it."

"He told you that?" He squinted at her, puzzled. "But you were always a good driver."

"I know," she said with a sigh, and dunked a small piece of lobster in warm butter.

Connor took one last bite of his baked potato and it tasted like sand. He couldn't even imagine how his Maggie had lived through all this degradation and come out so healthy and normal. And what kind of vicious creep was Ashcroft to have a great girl like Maggie and treat her so badly?

"On the other hand," Connor hedged, "he had money, so you probably didn't need to work."

"True, I didn't need any extra money," she said breezily. "I would've just squandered it on frivolous things."

He studied her as he sipped his wine. "You never seemed like a frivolous person to me."

"I'm not. But he didn't agree. He thought I needed more discipline. His mother agreed with him that I was helpless in so many ways. Once we were married, he began to criticize minor things. Just here and there, you know? But after a few years, he was taking daily jabs at my appearance, my weight, my personality, my lack of social skills. You name it."

"God, what an idiot," he muttered, shaking his head in bemusement.

"That's putting it nicely. And as bad as he was, his mother could be downright evil sometimes."

"I wish I'd known. I would've rescued you."

"My hero."

The waiter placed a basket of fresh bread and butter on the table. Connor held the basket out for her, then took a piece of bread for himself. He took a bite, then waved at her to continue. "Come on, girlfriend, tell me more. Get it all out."

Maggie chuckled. "You're enjoying this too much."

"Believe me, I'm not." In fact, he was imagining finding this guy just to plant a fist in his arrogant face. "But it seems like the more you talk about how awful they were, the more relaxed you get. And I like to see that. So, anything else you want to tell me?"

"I'm afraid if I get started, I won't be able to stop." She took a quick sip of her wine. "I think what I hated most was that my opinions never mattered. They considered me either too naive or just plain stupid, depending on the situation. He always liked to tell me how sad it was that I was so intellectually challenged."

"That's it." Connor shoved his chair back from the table. He was only half kidding when he muttered, "I'm really going to kill him."

She laughed and clapped her hands. "Thank you. You're officially my best friend."

"Yeah, I am," he said, easing back into his chair, though it cost him to give her a smile. "And don't forget it."

The following afternoon, Connor stared out the bay window of the Marin Club, taking in the view of clear blue skies and tumultuous waves crashing against the sandy shore. Though he was here to meet with his brothers, all he could think about was Maggie, and not just because of the incredible sex they'd had that morning. No, she was on his mind because he couldn't forget the horror story she'd related at dinner the night before. He just wished he'd had an inkling of what she'd been going through. Damn it, he'd been so clueless back then he hadn't even realized they'd broken up. If he'd known how Maggie really felt, he would have canceled that stupid skydiving trip in a heartbeat. And he might have prevented her from running off and falling into the trap of that creep husband and his twisted mother. One phone call from Maggie and Connor would've jumped on a plane and rescued her from that hell house she'd been living in.

His thoughts were interrupted when the waitress came over and took their drink orders. Jake had called this impromptu meeting with his brothers to talk over some important family business. They'd decided to meet here instead of the festival hotel in order to avoid any big ears that might be tempted to listen in on their conversation.

The Marin Club wasn't actually a club at all, but a bar and grill the brothers had been coming to for years. The service was good, the drinks were cold and the food was great.

The waitress set their drinks on the table. "Here you go, boys. Scotch for you, Ian. Pint of IPA for Connor and your martini, Jake. Extra dry, lemon twist."

"Perfect," Connor said, taking the pint glass from her.

"You boys are so dressed up in your suits and ties this afternoon. Is there some big party I should know about?"

Jake grinned. "We've got a business dinner to go to after this."

"Ah," she said. "Not quite as exciting as I imagined, but I hope you have fun."

"Thanks, Sherry," Jake said. "You're the best."

She winked at him, slid the black plastic bill case onto the table and strolled away humming. She was an old friend of their mother's and could always count on the MacLaren boys for a large tip.

"Cheers," Ian said, holding up his glass. They all clinked their drinks together, then sipped.

"Okay, what's up?" Connor said after taking a satisfying taste of his drink, a well-crafted English pale ale that he'd been ordering for years.

Jake gave each of them his patented scowl. "I heard from the Scottish lawyers again."

"What's their problem?" Connor asked. "We've still got a few months before the terms of the will have to be met."

"They're getting antsy."

"No, they're getting pushy," Connor said.

"What do you expect?" Ian said. "They're lawyers."

"Yeah," Connor agreed. "But they're just going to have to wait until one of us can take some time off."

"It's not that I care what they think," Jake said, "but I do believe we're reaching the point where one of us will have to fly over there and survey the property, just to see what's involved."

"It's basically some land and a big old house," Ian said, shrugging. "We've all done real estate deals. What's the big mystery?"

Jake stared into his cocktail and frowned. "The lawyer mentioned something about crofters."

"We've got crofters?" Connor said.

Ian looked puzzled. "You mean, like squatters?"

"No," Jake said. "These are tenants who live and work the land around the castle. We pay them."

"We do?"

"Yeah, so whoever buys the land has to buy the crofters, too. They're a package deal."

Disgruntled, Ian said, "What if we don't want crofters? And it's kind of weird to be selling people, don't you think?"

"I doubt we're actually selling the people," Connor said dryly.

Jake shook his head in frustration. "This is why some-body has to go over there."

"One of you should go," Connor said immediately.

"Why not you?" Ian said.

"Because I've got boots-on-the-ground responsibilities up here. I've got twenty-seven new products ready to hit the market, we have three new farmers who want to join the artisanal league and we're training a replacement man-ager at the brewpub."

Ian looked askance. "Oh, so you're saying our meager office jobs are expendable, is that it?"

Connor grinned back at him. It was a long-standing rivalry among the brothers, with each of them claiming to work harder than the others. But in Connor's case, it was true. Maybe he didn't handle the corporate stuff, like finances or marketing or hiring, thank God. But he did have sole responsibility for the day-to-day production of eight different facilities, including the brewery itself and the brewpub in town, both of which had put their company on the map in the first place.

"You're the natural choice to go," Connor said to Ian. "You could check things out with the castle, then take a detour south and visit Gordon. Make sure he's still willing to grow our hops."

Ian flashed Connor a dirty look. "Everything's fine with the damn hops. The next batch will arrive on time, right after the drying season. So back off."

"Touchy," Connor muttered, exchanging glances with Jake. It always irritated Ian when they brought up the sub-ject of his recent breakup with his gorgeous wife, Saman-tha. Her eccentric father, Gordon McGregor, lived in an ashram west of Kilmarnock where he grew the hops and many of the bitter herbs used exclusively in MacLaren beers. The trade winds that warmed the west coast of Scot-land provided the perfect climate for Gordon's hops and they were among the finest the MacLarens had ever used for their beers. While Connor cared very much for his sister-in-law Sam and was sorry she and Ian had split, he knew that if they lost their main source for those rare Scottish hops, it could be disastrous.

"I can't go right now, either," Jake realized.

Ian rolled his eyes. "Why not?"

"I'm in the middle of planning the senior staff retreat," he explained. "I won't be able to go for at least three months."

"Look, we don't have to make up excuses for the lawyers," Ian reasoned. "As soon as one of us gets a break, whoever it is will go to Scotland, meet with the lawyers, check out the castle and list it for sale."

"Sounds good to me," Connor said. "I can't wait to get rid of it."

"And Uncle Hugh's bad juju along with it," Jake muttered.

Ian nodded. "Mom will be glad, too."

"She's been wanting the whole problem to disappear from day one."

"Yeah," Jake said. "Uncle Hugh pretty much ruined her life."

"But she rallied just fine," Connor said with a hint of pride. "She made a good life for all of us once she got over here."

At that, the three men spontaneously clinked their glasses together and drank in silence.

Despite acquiring the castle and all the land for miles around it after their father died, Uncle Hugh continued to be a bitter man to the very end. Since he'd never had children and hated his own brother, he fashioned his last will and testament to deliberately create an irreparable rift among his nephews, forcing them to compete against each other for their inheritance.

His will provided that all the MacLaren money, land

and power would go to whichever brother had acquired the most wealth by the twenty-fifth anniversary of their father's death. As the date grew closer, Jake was contacted by the Scottish lawyers, who required the brothers to send financial reports in order to determine which of them would eventually inherit.

That final date was coming up fast.

Connor, Ian and Jake had no intention of complying with their uncle's wishes. They had vowed at a young age not to fight against each other for the sake of a plot of land and a big old house, especially if it fulfilled their horrible uncle's wishes. Frankly, none of them could even picture the castle in their minds since Uncle Hugh had taken possession of it when they were all too young to remember it. Their mother called it "a cold, crumbling pile of Scottish stone" and cursed it on a daily basis.

The plain fact was, their home was Northern California now. They didn't want the castle or the land. So no matter which brother "won" Uncle Hugh's blood money, the three of them planned to sell the Scottish land and the castle and split the proceeds three ways.

Jake savored his cocktail. "I'll call the lawyers back and let them know that one of us will get over there within the next three months."

"Sounds good," Ian said, and glanced at his wristwatch. "So, everyone ready for this dinner with the Wellstones?"

"Yeah," Jake said, reaching for his wallet. "I'll be meeting my date at the restaurant a few minutes ahead of time."

"Sounds good." Connor stood and tossed a ten-dollar bill on the table. "I've got to get back and pick up Maggie. I'll see you guys there."

Maggie paced back and forth in front of the living room window of the suite, occasionally glancing up to check the time. Connor would arrive any minute now to take her to the important dinner with Mr. Wellstone and his sons. They planned to close a major deal tonight, and Maggie had to be on her best behavior.

So it might not be appropriate to stumble and fall on her butt.

That's why she was walking around, trying to get used to high heels again. It had been three long years since she'd been forced to wear anything like these killer stilettos. Not since the days when Alan—er, Ashcroft—required her to dress up for the fancy society balls and dinner parties they were constantly attending.

Along with her ex-husband and his crabby mother, Maggie didn't miss high heels at all.

The dress she wore was one of the few she'd salvaged from her marriage, a little black dress, short and beautifully beaded around the edges, with flattering cap sleeves and a sweetheart neckline that showed the barest hint of cleavage. She didn't mind wearing it now because Ashcroft and his mother had hated it.

Maggie was surprised at how much relief she felt after talking to Connor about her crazy marriage. There had been a few moments at dinner last night when she'd almost burst into tears, but it hadn't been because of the bad memories. It had been because Connor was so sweet to listen, so quick to take her side, so heroic in his defense of her. And the amazing sex afterward had helped, too.

One thing Connor had never asked, though, was why she'd stayed with the man for so many years. Why didn't she leave Ashcroft in the very beginning when he first started picking on her?

Maggie was so glad Connor hadn't asked because she would've found it difficult to answer him. Not because she didn't know the answer, but because part of the reason for staying was so nonsensical.

How could she explain that she'd stayed because a part of her thought she *deserved* to be punished? After all, she had broken up with Connor because she was worried that he would die someday, and she would be left alone. It sounded so selfish now, but back then, the possibility of her being devastated by his death had been too great a risk for her to take. So basically, she had ended her relationship with Connor because she was a coward.

And how ironic was it that she'd ended up marrying Ashcroft, who had seemed like such a safe, risk-free alternative? Big mistake. Because he hadn't just tried to hurt her. He had tried to *destroy* her, psychologically, bit by bit. There had been moments during her marriage when she didn't know if she would survive another day. After living with that, skydiving and rock climbing didn't look so bad.

"So much for risk aversion," she murmured. From now on, she was going to take the riskiest choice available, every time.

Her cell phone rang and she rushed to grab it, noticed the call number and said, "Grandpa, is everything okay?"

"Just lovely, Maggie. Any day I see sunshine and blue skies is a delightful day. And yourself? How's your day, Maggie, me love?"

Maggie bit back a smile. "Grandpa, did you enjoy a wee dram before you called me?"

"Before I called ye? Ha! Before, during and after's more like it." He laughed so hard he dropped the phone.

"Oh boy," Maggie murmured. It didn't take many wee drams to get Grandpa tanked up and raring to go these days. She was just glad Deidre would be by to make sure he made it to bed and didn't sleep on the couch all night.

The phone was jostled, and then a woman came on the line. "It's Deidre here, Maggie. Angus is doing just fine, not to worry. He's had a wee spot of the angel's tears, but that never hurt a flea."

Maggie chuckled. It sounded as if Deidre might be a bit tipsy, too. They were a pair sometimes. They had probably already changed into their jammies before pouring the first of what sounded like several nightcaps.

"I'm not worried, Deidre," she said. "I know you're taking good care of him."

"Aye, we're coming along just fine." She covered the phone to say something to Grandpa, then came back on the line. "How's my boy treating you?"

"He's a perfect gentleman," Maggie assured her, but her mind instantly raced to a vision of Connor and her, making sweet love last night. She decided she wouldn't be sharing that anecdote with Connor's mother.

Maggie would always be grateful to Deidre for welcoming her back to Point Cairn instead of shutting her out. She had a wonderful open heart and Maggie loved her for it.

"Now you've got the big dance coming up," Deidre continued. "And I know Connor is so looking forward to dancing with you. I hope you two have a beautiful time together."

Maggie frowned. Maybe it was the wee dram speaking, but Deidre sounded almost weepy with happiness. Maggie hated to burst her bubble, but nothing would come of this week with Connor. Other than business, they had no future together. Even though their long talk the night before had answered some questions, Maggie could still catch glimpses of suspicion in Connor's eyes. He'd spent ten long years feeling betrayed and angry with her, so while these past few days together had been lovely, Maggie didn't see how they could possibly erase the painful past.

Maggie heard her grandfather talking in the background, and Deidre said to him, "Well, of course she's going to the dance. Every girl loves to dance."

Grandpa said something and Deidre laughed. "Oh, pish

tosh, Angus. Children can make such a mountain out of a molehill, can't they?"

Angus's laugh was hearty and Deidre joined him. After a few seconds, she must've realized she was still on the phone. "Maggie? Hello? Are you there?"

"Still here," Maggie said.

"All righty, then. Goodbye, dear."

And she disconnected the call, leaving Maggie staring at the phone in befuddlement.

"All righty, then," she muttered, shaking her head as she slipped the phone into her small bag.

The door opened and Connor walked in, then stopped. "Wow. You look...incredible."

She turned and smiled, ridiculously pleased by the compliment. She kept the mood light, twirling around to show off her pretty dress. "So this will do?"

"Absolutely. I'm a lucky man." With a grin, he walked over and kissed her softly on the cheek. "If I were Jonas Wellstone and saw you walk into the room, I would give you anything you wanted."

She gazed up at him solemnly. "And all I would ask for is that he sign over everything to you."

Connor laughed as he helped her with her jacket. "I believe you just might be our secret weapon."

Eight

She hadn't embarrassed herself yet, Maggie thought, smiling inwardly, but the night was still young.

Other than her self-deprecating attitude, everything was lovely tonight. For the private dinner meeting, Mr. Wellstone had chosen a small but beautiful room that had once been an old wine cellar, with arched brick walls and stained glass windows. Candles enhanced the wrought-iron light fixtures, creating a warm, romantic feel, the perfect setting for an intimate dinner for two.

Unfortunately, there were eleven of them at the table and this meal was strictly business.

And the same could be said for her relationship with Connor. It was strictly business, too, in case she'd forgotten. No matter how wonderful their late nights together had been, they shared too much history, too many past mistakes, to risk calling this short time together anything more than business.

To be fair, though, he'd been wonderfully attentive all evening, so she couldn't complain. She just wished things could be different between them somehow. If only she had made some better choices along the way.

But that was ancient history. It was time to stop whining and apologizing about the past. She wanted to enjoy the evening and the rest of the festival. She wanted to savor every minute spent with Connor. And then she would go home and get on with her life.

"How do you like the wine?" Connor whispered next to her.

"It's wonderful," she murmured, reaching for her glass. "Everything is so nice. What do you think? Is it going well?"

Maggie followed his gaze around the table. Other than his brothers and their dates, the rest of the guests were Wellstone family members. Jonas, his son, Paul, and Paul's wife, Dana, and his daughter, Christy, and her husband, Steve. There were several small conversations occurring at once along with plenty of munching and savoring of the delicious stuffed pastry appetizers. Jake and Paul were debating the results of a recent football game.

Connor grinned at Maggie. "I think Jonas looks pretty happy, don't you?"

Maggie glanced over at the man holding court at the head of the table. "He's a kick, isn't he?"

"He's a great guy," he said quietly. "I wasn't sure I would like him because of all these hoops he was making us jump through, but I'm glad we did this tonight. I think everyone's having a good time."

So far, business had only been discussed on a general level. The state of the industry, the latest gossip, who was making waves, who had burned out. There hadn't been a mention of anything specific about the buyout.

Of course, Maggie hadn't expected any real business to be conducted tonight. The purpose of this get-together was to see if everyone got along and to make sure Jonas Wellstone approved of the MacLaren men well enough to sell them his multimillion-dollar brewery business.

The whole scene should've made Maggie unbearably nervous, but it didn't. After spending so many years faking the social niceties with Ashcroft and his snooty high-society crowd, tonight Maggie was dining with real people who laughed and drank wine and enjoyed food and each other's company. It was such a refreshing change. No wonder she felt so happy.

It dawned on her that this was the first time she'd actually been out with a group of people, *any* people, in over three years. She didn't know whether to laugh or cry at that odd little fact.

"Are you okay?" Connor asked. "You looked a little dazed there for a minute."

"I'm perfect," she said, smiling up at him. "I'm happy to be here. Thank you for including me."

"I'm glad you're here with me," he said simply.

As Maggie took another look around the table, Jonas's daughter, Christy, caught her gaze. "I've met a few successful female brewers, Maggie, but it's still pretty rare, isn't it? How did you get started in this business?"

"My mom and dad owned a brewpub for many years in Point Cairn. The same one the MacLarens own now, by the way."

"Hey, we couldn't let it close down," Connor said in defense of his brothers.

"Absolutely not," she said, chuckling. "Anyway, to supplement the brewpub, my father built a home brewery in our barn and I used to follow him around like a puppy, begging to help him. He would give me odd jobs every day, like sorting bottle caps or sweeping the room. At some point, I wound up doing every job there was to do."

"That's the best way to learn," Jonas declared.

"I agree. So a few years ago, I decided to refurbish the brewery equipment in the barn and try my hand at some of my own formulas. And I think I'm starting to make some pretty good beers."

"She's being modest," Jake said, winking at her. "She's been kicking our asses lately at every contest she enters."

Maggie was stunned, no, *flabbergasted* by Jake's compliment. She didn't know if it meant that he'd changed his opinion of her, or if he was just playing nice for Jonas's sake. She decided to take it as a true compliment and bask in the sweetness of the moment.

Under the table, Connor's hand found hers and squeezed gently, sending shivers up her arm and down her back. She glanced up at him and he flashed her a wicked grin.

She wondered if her desire for him was written all over her face. Did she dare to hope he felt the same way about her? Could she risk losing her heart only to find out he wasn't willing to trust her again? She wanted to believe herself ready to take a big risk, but this one might leave her devastated.

Jonas chuckled, interrupting her fantasy. "Competition is good for all of us. I always say a rising tide lifts all boats."

"True enough," Ian said, nodding in agreement.

"What's your father's name, young lady?" Jonas asked.

"His name was Eli Jameson," she said. "He died when I was thirteen."

"Eli?" Jonas's eyes widened. "You're Eli Jameson's little girl?"

Maggie blinked. "Did you know him?"

"Know him?" He chuckled. "Hell, yes. We were great friends back in the day. We first met at a gathering similar to this one, only not nearly as large or as boisterous. Back then, we were a fairly sedate crowd."

"Dad's always talking about the good old days," Christy said, patting her father's arm fondly.

"I loved those days, too," Maggie said. "I always felt so close to my dad when we were working to accomplish something together."

"Your dad and I were competitors," Jonas said, "but it never seemed to matter which one of us won a medal or a ribbon. We hit it off the first time we met and we stayed friends like that until he died."

"That's so nice," Dana murmured.

Jonas grabbed a bread stick and bit off a small chunk. "Your father was a fine man, Maggie. Quite an athlete, too. I went sailing with him a few times, but I couldn't keep up with him. I don't mind saying he scared the hell out of me a few times. I paid him back by dragging him out to the golf course once or twice, but that wasn't his thing. Too slow moving for him. He was what you might call an adventurer. Always looking for the next big challenge. I was sorry to hear about his death."

"Thank you, Jonas," Maggie said, smiling softly at the older man. "Your words brought him back to life for a few minutes."

"It was my pleasure," he said with a firm nod. "They're good memories."

Maggie gazed up at the wrought-iron light fixture and blinked back tears. "You know, I've always thought of my father as a larger-than-life character. But then I would wonder if that was just my own skewed perspective of a little girl in love with her great big father."

"No, he was that kind of man," Jonas assured her. "You should be very proud of him and the legacy he left behind."

"I am," Maggie said. "Thank you so much."

No one spoke for a moment, until Christy patted her father's strong, weathered hand. "That was a very sweet tribute, Dad."

He squeezed her hand but said nothing.

Maggie broke the silence, anxious to move on from the somber topic of her deceased father. "Paul, Connor tells me that you've started growing grapevines and plan to make wine. How is that coming along?"

"Yes, I've turned traitor to my heritage," he said, and his wife and father both laughed. "I'm having a great time with it. It's similar to brewing in that it's a tricky blend of science and art. But the real bonus for me is that picking grapes is so much more fun than picking hops."

"Not quite as many thorns," his wife added.

Everyone at the table chuckled at that.

"Have you bottled anything yet?" Maggie asked.

"We've scheduled our first official bottling next month at the winery. You know, we're just over the hill in Glen Ellen. You should all come join us for the celebration."

She glanced around at Connor and his brothers, who were grinning, no doubt pleased with Paul's offer.

"We'd love to join you," Connor said, speaking for everyone. "Thanks for the invitation."

Paul's wife Dana spoke up. "We've hired a chef for the winery who serves these fabulous little snacks with the tastings. I'm telling you, it's the most fun we've had in years."

"Sounds like you've got quite a setup," Jake said. "I'm looking forward to our visit."

Maggie suddenly wasn't sure if she was included in that group invitation, even though Paul had been responding to her question. It shouldn't matter. She could drive out to their winery any time she wanted to, but it would be so much nicer to go with this group of people she was starting to consider friends.

"Wineries." Jonas sighed. "Another reason why I'm selling the brewery, boys. My own son is deserting the company."

"Aw, come on Dad," Paul said guiltily.

He grinned. "I'm just teasing you, boy. I'm glad you've found something you enjoy as much as I love my brewing." His gaze slid from Jake to Ian to Connor. "Gentlemen, that's why I insist that whoever buys my company should love this business as much as I do. I don't want some buttoned-down pencil pusher running my plant and pissing off the loyal employees who've worked there all these years. I want someone who walks in every morning and takes a deep breath of that hoppy smell and actually gets excited at the possibilities."

Maggie smiled, knowing exactly what the old man meant.

"Who knows what can happen when you blend all those bitter herbs and malts together?" Jonas's eyes sparkled as he spoke. "Why, throw in a slice of lemon peel or some odd bit of vegetation and you could come up with something completely new that might dominate the industry for the next five years. I'm telling you, if you can't appreciate the scent, the shades, the taste, the…" He paused, then chuckled. "Hell, I sound like I'm talking about a woman."

Everybody laughed, but Jonas laughed the hardest. "I'm talking about beer, gentlemen. And ladies, of course. I love this damn business."

"Right there with you, Jonas," Connor said, raising his glass in a sentimental toast.

"It really is the best thing in the world, isn't it?" Maggie said dreamily. "At the end of the day, when you've hosed down the brewing station and steam-cleaned the pipes and you've tapped off your latest keg and you're hot and sweaty and you can finally sit down on the porch and taste the day's batch while you relax and watch the sun go down? I don't think there's a better moment that captures the essence of beer making than that one."

"Dang, Maggie May." Jonas grinned and she could see a sparkle in his eyes. He held up his half-empty wineglass for another toast. "That's pure poetry."

She laughed at her new nickname and held up her glass to meet his. "Here's to special moments."

"I'll drink to that," he said jovially, and chugged down what was left of his wine.

"I was right," Connor said later that night after they'd made love.

"About what?"

"You turned out to be our secret weapon," he said, reminding her of his comment earlier that night.

She gave him a puzzled look. She was stretched out on her back, her head propped on a pillow. He lay on his side, facing her, his hand resting on her smooth stomach.

"I don't know about that," she said as she absently ran her fingers along his shoulder and down his arm. "But it was fun to hear Jonas talk about my dad."

"Everyone enjoyed hearing about him," he said, earning a smile from her. "It was a good evening."

"Did you get an inkling of Jonas's decision yet?"

"Jake talked to Paul briefly while we were walking back to the hotel. "He thinks we've got a lock on the deal."

"That's wonderful."

"Yeah. I won't count any chickens yet, but I think there's a strong possibility that he'll sell to us. There's plenty of work to do in the meantime, but it would be a real coup to take over Wellstone."

"I'll say."

It struck Connor that this was an odd sort of "pillow talk" conversation to be having with a woman, but it was one more indication of how comfortable he was around Maggie.

And that wasn't necessarily a good thing, he thought suddenly, unable to keep his old suspicions from cropping back up. Yes, Maggie had given him a simple explanation for why she'd left him all those years ago. Connor completely believed that she had feared for his safety back then.

But had she truly explained the fact that, before he could even grasp that she was truly gone, he'd received the news that she had married another man? Okay, maybe she was telling the truth when she said she'd been awash in grief and made a really bad decision. But he had to wonder how "in love" with Connor she'd really been to turn around and do something like that.

It didn't matter. What was he doing, thinking about this stuff when he had a warm, beautiful woman in his bed? He should be celebrating the fact that his plan to get her into bed had succeeded. Now he could relax and enjoy the moment.

It wasn't as if they had mentioned anything about getting back together. This was a one-time deal. When the week was over, he would hand her a check and go back to his life.

He ignored the wave of melancholy that that thought brought on.

Hell, there was a simple explanation for all this angst he was feeling. He hadn't been with another woman in…gads, had it been six months? No wonder he was reeling from all these unwanted emotions. But it was about time to snap out of it, he thought. A beautiful woman was pressing her lush body against him and he had the unrelenting urge to bury himself inside her. Again. And again.

And why not? Shouldn't he be making up for lost time? And while he was on the subject, why shouldn't he and Maggie keep on doing it, as long as the sex was good? And it was definitely good. Hell, it was world class. So why should they go their separate ways once the festival ended? Connor wondered. They lived in the same town, so why not continue to enjoy each other's company? It didn't have to be a big deal. Nothing special or permanent. Or complicated. Why couldn't it just be for fun? They could be friends with benefits. Nothing wrong with that.

For now, he tugged her onto her side facing him, then rolled back until she was on top of him, straddling his solid length.

"Oh, how did I get here?" she said, teasing him.

"Magic," he whispered, and lifted her up until he could slide into her.

She sank onto him, moaning in pleasure. And there was no more pillow talk for the rest of the night.

* * *

At breakfast Friday morning, Maggie watched Connor scan his email as he finished his coffee. He was dressed more formally than usual in a black suit, white shirt and rich burgundy power tie. He looked so good Maggie wanted to rip off his clothes and have her way with him.

He set his empty coffee cup on the dining table and stood. "I've got two meetings back to back this afternoon and the second one will probably run late, so I'll meet you at the gala by eight o'clock."

Maggie stood, too, and adjusted his tie. "Connor, I already told you I'm not going to the gala."

"Let's not go through this again, Maggie," he said. "You'll be there. It's required."

She made a face. "No, it's not. I told you I didn't want to go. The truth is, I don't like these sorts of events. I didn't even bring the right kind of dress to wear."

"So what?" he said, snapping his phone into its case and shoving it into his suit pocket. "You can wear any one of the dresses you've already worn this week."

"No, I can't. The gala is formal. Nothing I have is suitable."

"I'm not dressing formally," he said, glancing down at his suit.

"Oh, please." Maggie's laugh sounded slightly desperate. "That suit's got to be worth five thousand dollars. I think you can get away with wearing it. But I'll be expected to wear a gown and I don't have one."

"You should've thought of that before now," he said as he walked to the door. "I don't care what you wear, but I expect to see you there."

"But—" She ran after him to the door. "Connor, please. I can't—"

He grabbed the doorknob, then stopped and turned.

"This was always part of our deal. It's not optional. It's business."

"But I don't dance."

"I don't care," he said heatedly.

"Why are you making such a big deal about it?"

"Because I can." He yanked her close and crushed her lips with his. She moaned and he softened the kiss, sweeping his tongue over hers. When he finally let her go, her knees wobbled from the pleasure of his kiss. "Please, Maggie," he said, touching his forehead to hers. "Please, I want you there with me."

"Big bully," she muttered, and touched her fingers to her lips to make sure that kiss hadn't been a dream.

"Coward," he whispered, then kissed her again, briefly and softly this time, and walked out, letting the door close behind him.

She absorbed the silence for a moment, then flopped onto the couch. "Now what?"

She wandered the convention floor all morning, listening to other speakers and catching up with some of the new acquaintances she'd made this week. She had lunch alone overlooking the marina, but instead of enjoying the view, she agonized over the gala. Connor simply didn't understand. Why would he? It was no big deal. Except it was, to Maggie.

Staring out at the sparkling blue water, she sighed. The thought of attending the gala should've filled her with excitement, but Maggie was filled with dread instead. It sounded ridiculously melodramatic to say she might not survive the evening, but that was exactly what she was afraid of.

The last gala event she had attended was the Hospital Society's Black & White Ball, back in Boston. Her ex-husband had been the chairman of the event and it was a huge success. He should have been flushed with happiness, but that was so *not* Alan. Maggie still wasn't exactly sure what she had done to set him off. Had she been too effusive in congratulating him? Had she danced too close to one of his lackeys? Had she spilled something on her ball gown?

Whatever small offense she'd shown, Alan was apparently intent on making sure it didn't go unnoticed, even if it meant exposing their unhappy relationship to the world.

Leaving her in the middle of the dance floor, Alan had approached the bandleader and ordered him to stop the music. He had an important announcement to make.

"My wife is a whore," he had announced to the crème de la crème of Boston society. He didn't stop there, but Maggie refused to play back the entire tawdry speech in her mind. And later that night in the foyer of their home, he struck her physically for the first time, smacking her face so hard that she fell and hit her head against the hard surface of a marble statue, and passed out.

Two days later, after her headache had subsided and she'd regained some strength, Maggie snuck out to a pay phone and called a lawyer to begin divorce proceedings. She knew it would be a vicious battle and she prayed she would survive it. Her prayers were answered when her surly mother-in-law died a few days later and Alan divorced her instead.

Maggie had never told another soul about Alan's physical attack. How could she, when she could touch her cheek and still feel the physical blow he'd delivered? And if she closed her eyes, she could still experience the rush of utter mortification she'd felt on that dance floor as her husband destroyed her in front of everyone she knew.

She would never allow herself to be so humiliated again. Even if it meant she would never stand on another dance floor again.

"Would you like anything else?" the waiter asked.

Maggie flinched. She'd been so buried in the past she'd forgotten where she was. She quickly recovered and smiled. "No, just the check, thank you."

She returned to the convention floor, but after stirring up all those unhappy memories, she was unable to enjoy herself. She went back up to the suite to take a nap, but she couldn't sleep. She was awash in misery and clueless as to why she couldn't just flick away the past, shape up, straighten her shoulders and power through this dilemma.

After fixing herself a cup of tea, she sat by the window and stared out at the calming view of ocean water and windswept sky.

The fact was, she wanted to be with Connor, even though she dreaded attending the gala. So brushing aside the dread, she focused on her present predicament. She didn't have a dress!

She mentally sifted through the practical issues before her, as if they were written on a list she could check off. First, she didn't have a proper gown or even an ultrafancy cocktail dress to wear because she'd given away all of her dress-up clothes when she left Ashcroft. For good reason. They all reminded her of horrible, embarrassing times spent with her ex-husband.

Second, now that she'd given everything away, she couldn't afford to run out and buy something new, especially something so fancy. Not to mention the shoes and jewelry to wear with it.

Third, when she first made the deal with Connor, she honestly hadn't thought it would matter whether she showed up for the gala or not. But they had grown so close during the past week, she didn't want to disappoint him.

But that brought her to issue number four. The real problem. She hated going to formal events. Hated dancing. Feared what would happen if she did the wrong thing. Over time, the fear and hate had grown into a phobia. She'd spent way too many years attending monthly charity balls and society dances with Ashcroft, trying to impress his mother and all their rich, snooty friends, knowing that no matter what she did, it was always going to be the wrong thing.

Besides the big ugly result of the final event with Ashcroft, there had been plenty of other nasty repercussions that had occurred after she'd made some miniscule faux pas at a society dance. Maggie cringed and rubbed her arms to calm the shivers she felt. She refused to dwell on the various creative, nonphysical ways her ex-husband had made her pay for her innocent social foibles.

"This is ridiculous," she whispered. She was obviously still suffering from Post-Ashcroft Distress Syndrome, which probably wasn't a real disease, but it should've been.

She really needed to snap out of it.

But she couldn't. Because of issue number five. This gala tonight was actually important to her career. There would be people at tonight's event who were vital industry contacts, business professionals, the very people she wanted to impress so badly. But how could she? She had nothing to wear. Which brought her right back to issue number one.

It was a vicious circle and Maggie's head was spinning out of control.

She yawned, exhausted from worrying so much. Sitting down on the couch, she leaned back against one of the soft pillows and tried again to close her eyes for a few minutes.

The doorbell rang, waking her up. Disoriented, she had to stare at the clock for ten seconds before it registered that she'd slept for almost two hours. So much for worrying that she wouldn't be able to fall asleep.

She ran to the door and pulled it open.

"Delivery for Ms. Jameson," the bellman said, and handed her a large white box.

What was this? She was almost afraid to take it from him, but she did.

"Thank you," she murmured, and quickly searched for a few dollars to give as a tip. Then she closed the door and set the box on the coffee table. It carried the logo of a well-known, expensive women's store. She stared at it for several minutes, unsure what to do. Was it really for her? Maybe it was something Connor had ordered for one of his judging seminars.

"You're being silly." She double-checked the box and saw her name on a label on the side, just as the bellman had said.

Finally she settled down on the couch and slowly pulled off the top and saw…a blanket of tissue covering the contents. Okay, that wasn't too intimidating. She waded through the paper and finally found the real contents of the box.

"Oh my." It was pink. That was the first surprise. It was also soft. And beautiful. She lifted the dress out of the box and held it up to her, then ran over and stared at herself in the mirror. It was strapless, with beading all over the bodice, to the waist. From there, layers of soft pink chiffon flowed in a soft column to the floor. It was formal, but sexy. And sweet. And perfect. She'd never seen a more beautiful dress.

It complemented her skin tone and her hair. It was simply ideal. Almost as if it had been made for her.

There were shoes in the box, as well. She slipped her foot into one of them and was amazed that it fit her. At the bottom of the box, she found a small pouch that held diamond earrings and a necklace.

She didn't have to guess where all of this had come from.

"Connor," she whispered, and felt a spurt of happiness that he would do something so thoughtful.

"Wait a minute," she said, as reality sank in. Why would

he ever dare to buy her a dress after she'd spent most of their dinner the other night complaining about Ashcroft doing the same thing?

So who could've bought her this beautiful dress? Connor was the only person who knew that she—

Her cell phone rang and she ran to answer it.

"Maggie love."

"Grandpa. Is everything all right?"

"Fine and dandy," he said. "And are you having a good time?"

"I am, Grandpa. Are you feeling well today?"

"Fit as a fiddle," he said, and she could hear him patting his belly.

It was an old joke. He was tall and thin and barely had a belly to pat.

Someone giggled in the background.

"Grandpa, who's there with you?"

"It's our Deidre, making dinner."

"That's nice. And how are the goats?"

"They're a delight as always," he said "But how are you, Maggie love? We wanted to call and check. Is everything hunky-dory?"

"Everything's fine," Maggie said, touched that he was so concerned. It was unusual for her grandfather to use the telephone unless he was forced to, so maybe this was Deidre's influence.

"And how will you spend your evening, lass?" he asked. "Any special plans?"

"Grandpa, don't you remember I told you…" She paused. Something was wrong. Every time she'd talked to her grandfather during the past week, he had asked her about the dance. So why was he…? Her eyes narrowed in on the pink dress. "Grandpa, did you send me something today?"

"Och, aye, lass!" he shouted excitedly. "So it arrived?"

"She got it, then?" Deidre said, clear enough for Maggie to hear. "And does it fit?"

Maggie plopped down on the couch, speechless.

"Are you there, lass?"

"Did she hang up?"

"I'm here," she whispered. "Grandpa, why? You know I don't dance anymore."

"That's just something you tell yourself, lass," he said softly. "For protection."

She blinked at his words, but before she could respond, Deidre grabbed the phone. "Now, don't blame your grandpa for speaking out of school, but I've heard a thing or two about a thing or two."

Maggie smiled indulgently as Deidre made her point. "I'll tell you a secret, Maggie. I still have the picture of you and Connor at your high school prom. Such a pretty pair, you were. You danced all night and I know you loved it. You love to dance, Maggie. I don't know why or how you decided to stop loving it, but maybe you should decide to start again."

"Is it that simple?" Maggie wondered aloud.

"Most things are," Deidre said philosophically. "And as long as I'm giving out free advice, I think it's high time you closed the door on the past and started living in the *now*. Live for yourself. Choose for yourself, Maggie. Now here's your grandpa."

Choose for herself? Maggie stared at the telephone and began to pace back and forth across the room. Choose for herself? But every time she'd made choices, she'd made mistakes.

But so what? she argued. Was she never supposed to do anything fun or risky, ever again? She might as well live in a glass bubble!

But making choices was the same as taking risks, and taking risks meant that she might get hurt. Or worse.

But if she didn't take the risk, if she didn't go to the dance, she knew she would hurt much worse. And Connor would be hurt, as well.

So it seemed she had no choice.

Oh, good grief! Of course she had a choice. She could choose to go to the dance and have fun with Connor.

Exhausted from arguing with herself, Maggie slid down onto the couch.

Angus came back on the line. "No more guff now, lass. Tell me, do you like the dress?"

"It's beautiful, Grandpa, but you can't afford to—"

"Och, there'll be none o' that," he argued. "I've a little something tucked away for a rainy day, and Deidre chipped in a bit."

"I'll pay you both back."

"You'll not pay us back," Grandpa grumbled.

Deidre grabbed the phone. "You'll pay us back by dancing your little toes off with my son. Now, you have a fancy dance to prepare for. Go. Get off the phone and go."

"Yes, ma'am," Maggie said, and laughed as she disconnected the call.

The elevator moved slowly on the trip down to the lobby, giving Maggie more time to worry about every little thing that could go wrong. She caught a glimpse of her reflection in the elevator's mirrored wall, and it helped remind herself that there were plenty of things that were going to go just right.

She had made a pact with herself that from now on, the past would stay in the past. It was time to forgive herself for the mistakes she'd made back then. She was ready to move forward, not backward.

And tonight she was going to dance. With Connor, of course, and with anyone else who asked. Deidre was right. Maggie refused to sit in a corner anymore, worrying whether she might make a mistake or do the wrong thing. It was a risk, but she was ready to take it.

Two hours ago, she had refused to even try on the pink dress because the very thought of walking into the dance to-night made her queasy. Would she have flashbacks? Would someone criticize her for laughing too much? Would people sneer at the way she danced? Would they think her dress was too sexy? Too sparkly? Too pink?

There would be hors d'oeuvres and desserts served at the dance, too. What if she spilled something? What if she used the wrong fork? Because Ashcroft had once punished her for using the wrong fork.

"Good grief," she muttered. The wrong fork? Seriously? Who the hell cared?

She began to laugh at herself, so hard that tears came to her eyes. Then she tried to picture Connor sniveling about the wrong fork, and she laughed even harder.

It was ludicrous. And worse, it was tearing her apart in-side and destroying her hard-won self-confidence. So really, wasn't it about time she drop-kicked her asinine ex-husband and his bony old mother out of her memory banks? Yes!

"And take your wrong fork with you!" she said in a loud voice, shaking her fist in the air.

Recalling her minitirade, Maggie giggled again. It was a good thing she was alone in the elevator. Otherwise, she might've received more than a few strange looks from her fellow passengers.

Nine

"Where's your date?"

Connor glanced at his brother while he casually sipped a beer, refusing to reveal how concerned he was over the subject of Jake's question. "She'll be here."

"You sure?"

"Yes," he said with a nonchalance he didn't feel.

"Good," Jake said, and grinned. "Think she'll dance with me?"

He scowled at his brother. "No."

Jake looked affronted. "Why the hell not?"

"Because you were a jerk to her."

"That's ancient history," he said, brushing away Connor's comment. "I thought we got along really swell at dinner the other night."

"Swell, huh?" Connor looked at him sideways. "That's because I warned you to be nice to her."

"That's not why," Jake insisted. "She was great. Talkative, interesting, fun. She loves the business, so she's got some smarts. Besides, if you can forgive her, who am I to judge? And Jonas loved her, so that counts for something."

"Yeah, it does." Connor refused to mention the twinge of affection he felt at hearing his brother's kind words. Instead he kept scanning the room for the exasperating woman he wanted to have standing by his side at that moment.

The place was filled with old friends and business acquaintances, wealthy competitors and a few enemies, all decked out in their fanciest attire. The men were in tuxedos or black suits and most of the women wore gowns. And they were all working the crowd. This was business, after all.

There were occasional flashes of light as the local paparazzi caught people on camera out in the wide-open foyer. The photos would eventually appear in the various industry magazines and websites, so everyone took it in good-natured fun.

But still there was no Maggie. Damn it, was she seriously planning to stand him up? But wait, could he blame her? She honestly didn't want to come tonight and he had done everything to bully her into it. And that was after she'd been so honest with him, telling him about her vicious ex-husband's behavior.

"You're a moron," he muttered miserably.

"Just so you know," Jake continued blithely, "I'm okay with you and her getting together."

Connor's eyebrow quirked. "And what's that supposed to mean?"

"It means, you know, if you wanted to actually date her, I'd be okay with it."

Connor placed his hand over his heart. "That means everything to me."

Jake laughed out loud. "Yeah, right. I know it matters, so I'm just saying, Maggie's A-okay in my book."

"You're wrong," Connor said, grinning. "It doesn't matter to me."

"Of course it matters," Jake persisted, only half kidding. "I'm the head of the family, so it's a very special occasion when I bestow my blessing upon you."

Ian overheard him as he walked up to join them. "Head *jackass* of the family, maybe."

Connor chuckled. "Good one."

"So, what were you two blathering about?" Ian asked as he sipped from a glass of red wine.

Jake pointed to Connor. "I was just telling him I'm okay with him and Maggie hooking up."

Ian smirked at Connor. "I'm sure you appreciated those heartfelt words."

"Oh, you bet," Connor said. "You know how much I look up to Jake and hang on his every word."

"Go ahead and give me grief," Jake said loftily. "But I'm not too big a person to admit when I'm wrong. I take back what I said about Maggie. She's a lovely woman and she's obviously still in love with you, so I wish you two many years of happiness together."

"Whoa," Connor said, carefully swallowing the gulp of beer he'd almost choked on. "Slow down, dude. Who said anything about, you know, whatever the hell you're talking about?"

Ian ignored Connor's protest. "As much as I hate to utter the words, I have to agree with Jake. You and Maggie have a really nice vibe together. So don't screw it up."

"Yeah," Jake chimed in. "Just make sure she sticks around this time."

"It wasn't my fault she left," he groused under his breath. But it was a halfhearted protest. He was no longer opposed to the idea of being with Maggie, even as he pretended to be so in front of his brothers. He'd been doing a lot of thinking over the past few days and he'd come to the realization that maybe he did have some culpability, after all. It was hard to admit it because he'd spent so many years blaming things all on Maggie. But after the other night when they'd talked it out, he could see that he'd done plenty to drive her crazy back then.

With the arrogance of youth, he'd carelessly ignored the warning signs she'd been giving him all along. Now he could kick himself for not paying closer attention. And while he was kicking himself, he would gladly give himself the boot for not going after her in the first place. But his pride had gotten in the way and he'd ended up wasting all those years without her.

So now that he couldn't wait to see her, where the hell was she? Not only did he miss her, but he also had some important news to give her. He wasn't sure she would appreciate him sticking his nose into her business, but that was too damn bad. She would want to hear this.

Earlier that day, Connor and his brothers had spent an hour with their longtime local banker, Dave, to discuss some hometown investments. After the meeting had wrapped up, Connor had pulled Dave aside to ask if he knew the reason why his bank had turned down Maggie's loan application.

At first Dave had been reluctant to say anything. There were privacy issues involved, naturally.

"Come on, Dave," Connor had cajoled. "We've known each other since grammar school. You can be sure that anything you tell me won't leave this room."

"Hell, Connor." He scraped his fingers across his thinning scalp.

"Look," Connor said, trying another tack, "the truth is, I'm floating her a loan, so I'd like to know if she's good for paying it back."

"Of course she is," Dave insisted. "But you know how things are these days. Her credit report came back with one black mark on it and with all our red tape, the loan wasn't allowed to go through."

"A black mark? From where?"

"Some company back East."

"Remember the name?" Connor knew that their local bank was small enough that even as executive vice president, Dave would still go over each of the loans himself.

Dave thought for a moment. "Cargrove? Casgrow?"

"Cosgrove?" Connor said.

"That's it," Dave exclaimed. "Apparently she ran up

quite a debt with them, although I've got to admit I've never even heard of them. Must be some regional store or something."

"Or something," Connor muttered.

"I felt really bad, turning her down," Dave continued. "And Maggie was devastated. She walked out of my office without even asking for her credit information."

Connor wasn't surprised, but it broke his heart to hear it. Maggie's self-esteem had taken such a beating, it figured she would simply blame herself for her inability to get a bank loan, not even suspecting that her lousy ex-husband, Alan Cosgrove, had gone and screwed up her credit rating, just to twist the knife in one more time for good measure.

Connor really wanted to meet this psychopathic dirtbag and smash his face in. He had every intention of doing it, but that happy moment would have to wait.

The Big Band orchestra had been playing softly for the past half hour as people streamed into the ballroom, but now the conductor tapped his baton and the music burst into high gear. Couples began to fill the dance floor. The lines at all four bars were growing and the crowd in front of the appetizers and dessert tables were now three deep.

So where the hell was Maggie?

"I'll be back," Connor told his brothers, but he hadn't taken ten steps before he ran into Lucinda.

"Hi, Connor," she said breathlessly, taking hold of his arm. "Don't you look dashing tonight. Oh, but you're not leaving, are you?"

"Hey, Lucinda. I've gotta run out for a minute, but I'll be back."

"Oh, good." She smiled shyly. "I expect to dance with you at least once tonight."

"Sure thing," he said in a rush, then stopped abruptly. "Sorry. Don't know where my manners went. You look really nice, too, Lucinda."

"Thank you, Connor," she said, beaming at him. "That's sweet of you."

"I'll be back."

"Okay," she said, but he was already halfway across the room.

But before he could escape, he was flagged down by Bob Milburn, the mayor of Point Cairn, who wanted to discuss the amount the MacLarens planned to contribute to the annual Christmas parade and party the town held every year. Connor had to endure five long minutes of mindless chatter before Jake and Ian finally rescued him.

"Sorry to interrupt you two, Ian said briskly. "But we need to pull Connor away to discuss some family business."

"Sure thing," Bob said amiably. "See you boys around."

As soon as the mayor was out of hearing range, Connor let out the breath he'd been holding. "Damn, I thought he would never stop talking."

"We saw you floundering," Ian said.

Jake grinned. "You looked pretty desperate."

"I was." He glanced around the room again, then checked his wristwatch. "Listen, I've really got to go find Maggie."

Jake grabbed Connor's arm to keep him from dashing off. "That won't be necessary."

"Whoa," Ian whispered.

"Guess you were right, bro," Jake murmured. "She did show up."

Connor turned and spotted Maggie standing on the threshold of the farthest doorway from where they stood.

"Wow," Jake said reverently.

"About time she showed up," Connor muttered, then couldn't say another word, just continued to stare as she walked into the room. She was a vision in pale pink, so sexy and gorgeous he wasn't sure if she was real or just a hallucination of his addled mind.

Her strapless gown clung to her stunning breasts in

a gravity-defying miracle of sparkling pink and crystal beads. At her waist, the beads disappeared and the dress flowed in a wispy column to the floor. Her gorgeous hair was held up by some pins with a few tendrils allowed to hang loose and curl around her shoulders

She looked like a sexy angel, and never more beautiful than at this moment. And that was saying a lot, Connor thought, because she always looked beautiful to him.

Connor continued to watch her as he sauntered across the ballroom to meet her. As he got closer, his insides constricted at the memory of her moaning in pleasure as he filled her completely last night. His jaw tightened as he tried to estimate exactly how long he would have to endure this party before he could take her back to their bed, where he would soon have her naked and whimpering with need.

"Glad you could make it," he said when he finally reached her.

"I'm sorry I'm late," she said, tiptoeing up to kiss his cheek. "Forgive me?"

The orchestra began to play a jazz standard, and without another word, Connor took her hand and led her out to the dance floor, where he pulled her into his arms and began to sway to the music. When Maggie rested her head on his shoulder, he was certain that nothing had ever felt more right.

After a full minute, he leaned his head back and gazed down at her. "It was worth the wait, Maggie."

An hour later, Connor felt trapped by his own success. Maggie hadn't stopped dancing, not once. It seemed that every man Connor had introduced her to during the week now wanted to dance with her. First it was Jonas, then his son, Paul, then big Johnny from the judges' room. Hell, even Pete from Stink Bug Brewery had claimed a dance.

Connor had danced, as well, with Lucinda and Paul

Wellstone's wife, Dana, and two women he barely knew who were friends of Jake's.

He was so ready to blow this party off, grab Maggie and go back upstairs. But it was not to be. No, instead he got caught up in some off-the-wall conversation with Jonas about fruit-flavored ales. The old man was waxing on about boysenberries and ten minutes had passed before Connor noticed that Maggie was standing on the sidelines talking to someone. He couldn't see the man's face, so he shifted his stance until he could get a look at the guy. And he didn't like what he saw.

"Damn it," he muttered. "What's that about?" Maggie was talking to Ted Blake. It couldn't be a good thing.

"Something's wrong," Jonas declared. "You suddenly look like you just ate a bad-tasting bug."

"I'm sorry, Jonas," he said, "but I think I'd better go rescue Maggie."

Jonas's eyes scanned the room and then narrowed in on Maggie and Ted. He nodded slowly. "Good idea, son. That boy's nothing but trouble."

Connor's stomach tightened all over again as he watched her laughing and joking with the guy who had tried to destroy MacLaren. When Ted leaned in and whispered something in her ear, Connor's vision blurred in anger.

He thought he'd warned her about Ted Blake after he saw her talking to him the other day on the convention floor. But now he realized that he'd simply glossed over it at the time. And after that one time, he hadn't seen the guy all week. It was another reason why he'd had such a good time at the festival this week. No Ted Blake to deal with.

"Maggie."

She whirled around. "Oh, Connor, there you are. You've probably met Ted before, but we were just—"

"Yeah, we've met," Connor said curtly, and grabbed her hand. "Come on, babe, time to go."

"But…okay. Nice to see you again, Ted."

"Sure thing, Maggie," Ted drawled. "Maybe we'll talk again when you're not in such a hurry."

"Don't count on it," Connor muttered as he pulled Maggie closer and walked faster.

"Connor, please, can we walk a little slower? My feet are starting to whimper from all the dancing."

"Sorry, baby," he said, slowing down. "I just wanted to get you away from him. The faster the better."

"But why?" She glanced over her shoulder to get a last look at Ted. "He seems like a nice enough guy. A little bit quirky, but—"

"He's the furthest thing from a nice guy you'll meet here." Frowning, he added, "I can't tell you who to talk to or who to do business with, Maggie. But I would highly recommend that you stay as far away from Ted Blake as possible."

She studied his face for a moment, then nodded. "All right. I've never seen you react so negatively to anyone before."

"He tried to ruin us when we were first starting out," Connor said flatly. "Lucky for us, his reputation preceded him and a few of the people he talked to in his crusade to smear us didn't believe him. But a few of them did, and we had some shaky moments there."

"What a rat!" Maggie said, and suddenly wondered if Ted had known she was attending the festival with Connor when he first approached her. Did he think he could damage her business, as well? She remembered some of the odd questions he'd asked her that first time they met. Her shoulders slumped. "You'd think I'd recognize the species after living with one for so many years."

"The thing about rats is, they're really good at pretending they're something other than a rat."

"Too true," she murmured, shaking her head in dismay.

He pulled her closer, wrapping his arm around her as they walked. "Don't worry about it. There's a lot more to the story of Ted, but I'll save it for another time. Not tonight."

"Okay." She paused, then added, "But I feel like such a fool for buying in to his act. I thought he was sort of an odd bird, but he seemed harmless enough. Is there any chance he might've changed over the years?"

"No," he said flatly. "He's always been a lying snake, and the fact that he struck up a conversation with you is a sure sign that he hasn't changed one bit. He knows you're here with me. That's the only reason why he approached you in the first place."

"And here I thought it was my sparkling wit that attracted him to me."

Connor stopped and stared at her. Then he rubbed his hand across his jawline. "Hell, Maggie. I'm sorry. I didn't mean it the way it came out. Any man in that room tonight would be damn lucky to breathe the same air as you."

"I was just teasing you." She beamed a smile at him and wound her arm through his. "Let's forget about Ted. I just want to go upstairs with you."

"Sounds good to me."

"Mm, and I can't wait to take off my shoes."

"This might help," Connor said, and swept her up in his arms.

"I could really get used to this," she murmured, wrapping her arms securely around his neck.

So could I, Connor thought, but didn't say the words aloud as he carried her snugly in his arms across the lobby to the elevators.

It was crazy, Maggie thought as they lay in bed together. They'd spent almost every night of the past week making love with each other, but still she wanted more. Would this need she felt for him ever diminish?

They'd raced from the elevator to the hotel suite, and after tearing off their clothes, they'd fallen into bed and immediately devoured each other.

Now, just as she was slipping into sleep, Connor reached for her again. And she couldn't resist him.

She stirred and saw him, saw the sweet desire reflected in his eyes and knew he could see it in hers, as well. Knew he wanted the same thing in that moment that she did. It awakened her, filling her with so much love she could barely wait to hold him inside her again.

Purely and simply, she had fallen irrevocably in love with him and there was no escaping the truth. Maybe she'd known all along that this was where she would end up from the first moment she walked into his office and saw him sitting at his desk.

She'd first gone to see him thinking she would be unfazed by his charm. She had known she was taking a risk but was certain she'd gotten over him years ago. But clearly, she was wrong. The passion was still there, as real and palpable as it ever had been, even after ten long years.

She adored Connor's hands, loved the way he touched her, the way he stroked her everywhere, the way he continuously awakened her body to such pleasure and desire. And she prayed he would never stop.

He slid lower to taste her and with the first sensation of his mouth on her, she gasped and arched into him. Then her mind emptied of all thought and she could only feel and enjoy. His fingers and lips brought her to the brink of ecstasy, only to reel her back and start all over again. When he swept in with his tongue and flicked at her very core, she shuddered as a sudden climax erupted, threatening to engulf her in a pool of need and yearning.

"Again," he murmured, his voice edgy with hunger.

"But…I don't…I can't…"

His gaze locked on hers and she shivered with need. "For me, Maggie."

"Yes," she whispered.

"I want to watch you," he said in a raw, throaty whisper. "I want to feel you tremble in my arms. I want to see your eyes turn dark with pleasure." And he moved his fingers in a staccato rhythm that drove her straight to the edge of rapture and then beyond as she shattered in his hands.

Seconds—or was it minutes—later, he eased her onto her stomach and covered her with his muscled body. His flesh pressed against hers as he kissed her shoulder. And in a heartbeat, she was enflamed with need. She wanted him, wanted everything he had to give her, almost as if she hadn't just fallen apart in his arms minutes earlier.

He trailed kisses along her spine, stroked her as he lowered himself down to plant kisses on her behind, then continued down her thighs, licking and nibbling and exploring every inch of skin until she was breathless again.

"Please, Connor." She wanted to see him, watch him, kiss him. She started to roll over, but he stroked her back, silently urging her to stay this way awhile longer. He kissed her again at the base of her neck and began the tender onslaught all over again.

Maggie sighed, then moaned as his fingers moved to stroke her more intimately again. Then he suddenly shifted, lifted her pelvis and shifted her hips to allow him entrance. When he thrust himself into her, she gasped for air. He was hard and solid as he delved deeper, filling her completely until she was sure he had touched her soul.

She met his urgent movements with her own, could hear him gasping for breath, could feel his heated body scorching her skin, and hoped this feeling would never go away, prayed that this moment would never end.

Suddenly he stopped and she almost collapsed, but he

held her steady. He pulled himself away from her and she almost cried until he gently rolled her over onto her back.

"I have to look at you," he said, simply, and instantly thrust himself inside her. She gasped, and then immediately felt complete again with him sheathed within her.

He moved faster now, plunging deeper, thrusting harder, taking her along on a frantic ride to an inexorable climax that had her screaming his name within mere seconds.

Connor tightened his hold on her, driving into her. She could feel the immense coil of tension rise within him and stretch to the breaking point. Only then did he shout out her name and follow her into blissful oblivion.

Ten

Connor woke up the next morning with a beautiful warm woman snuggled beside him. His first impulse was to wake her up slowly, kiss by kiss, touch by touch, until she welcomed him gladly into her heated core once again.

Despite his rampant erection, he couldn't do it. She looked so peaceful Connor didn't have the heart to wake her. And he figured, from now on, they had all the time in the world to spend pleasuring each other.

For now, he climbed out of bed, careful not to disturb her, and prepared for the day. The awards ceremony would be early this evening and he still had some final round judging to finish before noon.

He was reading the sports section and drinking his second cup of coffee from room service when he received a text from Jake. Emergency. Meet us in judges room immediately. Come alone.

Maggie awoke slowly, happy but exhausted from their lovemaking the night before. She glanced across the bed and found it empty, so Connor was already up and out of bed. She must have overslept, she thought, stretching languidly. Every muscle in her body was groaning, but it was so worth it. No pain, no gain, right? She chuckled lazily and glanced at the clock.

"Oh dear." She really had overslept. She didn't hear Connor in the bathroom, so she walked out into the living room to check whether he was still eating breakfast. The suite was deserted, so she knew he must have left for the festival floor.

It took her a few seconds to remember what day this was. Saturday. The day of the final judging. Tonight was the awards ceremony. She needed to kick herself into gear.

Today would also be the busiest day of the festival with members of the general public coming in droves. She would need extra energy to fight the crowds, but all that was left of Connor's breakfast was a piece of leftover toast and one last cup of coffee. She grabbed them both, then raced to shower and dry her hair. She decided to dress a little more casually in capris, a short linen jacket and a pair of colorful sneakers.

Still hungry, she stopped at the coffee kiosk in the lobby and bought herself a quick breakfast burrito and a latte.

Then she went directly down to the judges' room to find Connor. She knew she wouldn't be allowed inside during the final judging round, but she just hoped she could see his face.

The doors to the hall were closed and the outer foyer was deserted. Maggie glanced around, looking for Johnny, but he was nowhere to be found, either.

She finished her latte and tossed the cup in a trash can, then decided to make a run to the ladies' room while she had a few minutes.

She slipped into one of the stalls, hung her tote bag on the hook and had to smile. She'd been in here before, the other day when she'd been too afraid to confront Sarah. She had dashed to the safety of the bathroom stall like a helpless ninny, but never again, she vowed. She was fed up with being afraid. She would never hide from confrontation again.

Before she could exit the stall, the outer bathroom door opened with a bang. Two women entered and stopped at the bathroom mirror to talk. Some protective instinct convinced Maggie to wait inside the stall as the women chatted in front of the mirror.

So maybe she was still working out some of those *helpless ninny* issues, Maggie thought, shaking her head. Baby steps, after all.

"So, what happened?" the first one said, her voice low.

"Oh, my God, you won't believe it," the other one said, her inflection classic *Valley Girl*. She sounded about twelve years old. "One of their contest entries was tainted."

"That's terrible," the first woman said. "How?"

"Johnny said that someone broke into the storage room last night and tampered with the MacLaren entries. It wasn't discovered until this morning during the semifinal round of judging, about an hour ago. A couple of the judges tasted the MacLaren ale and a few minutes later, they lost their breakfasts. The head judge sampled it and declared it was ruined."

"But how'd anybody get into the storage room?"

Huddled behind the stall door, Maggie wanted to know the same thing. Who would do it? Why? And how?

And despite her lofty thoughts from a moment ago about facing confrontation, there was no way she was leaving her hiding place until she heard the whole story.

"I'm not sure," Valley Girl said. "They either found a key or just broke in. Johnny's mortified."

"Poor guy, it's not his fault," the first woman said. "Wow, so someone deliberately sabotaged the MacLarens. I wouldn't want to piss them off. Do they know who it is?"

"You have to ask?" Valley Girl said, her voice dripping sarcasm. "Who else could it be?"

There was a pause, and then the first woman whispered, "Oh, come on. You can't be serious."

"Connor is absolutely certain that she did it," Valley Girl said, her voice hushed but confident. "And look at the evidence. It happened during the dance last night. She arrived really late. And then later on, I saw her talking to Ted Blake. And it wasn't the first time, either. I've seen them together before. Connor saw them, too. They were very tight and cozy, if you know what I mean."

"Ted Blake?" the first woman whispered. "He hates the MacLarens. Do you think the two of them planned it together?"

Maggie's heart sank. She knew they were referring to her. And it was true that she'd talked to Ted Blake a few times, but she hadn't known what a rat he was until Connor told her. Her eyes narrowed in suspicion, almost certain she knew who "Valley Girl" was.

"Oh, absolutely," Valley Girl insisted, then fudged a bit. "Or she planned it alone. Either way, she's guilty as sin."

"But why would she do that to Connor?"

"She's jealous," Valley Girl hissed. "She'll do anything to win the competition, and that includes cheating."

"It doesn't make sense. Why would she sabotage Connor? She likes him."

"Because she can't have him back."

"News flash," the first woman said dryly. "She's sleeping in the same hotel room with him."

"That's only because he's paying her."

Maggie wondered if she had fallen down a rabbit hole. Their conversation sounded like a bad soap opera, and her head was starting to spin. And worst of all, she was sick to death of standing by idly while her reputation was being torn to shreds.

"He's paying her to sleep with him?"

"Yes, and I would've done it for free," Valley Girl whined.

"Lucinda, you're delusional," the first woman said. "You've had a crush on him since high school and he's never even looked at you. Face it, he's just not that into you."

"He would be if she would just go away."

Maggie's head was going to explode. She had to get out of here. It was time to take a risk, stop hiding, stop running from her mistakes. She had to fight for herself, for her reputation, for her life. And for Connor. Taking a deep breath, she gathered her strength and shoved the stall door open. "Hello, ladies."

Sarah saw her in the mirror and blinked in surprise.

Lucinda whirled around, then froze. Her face blanched and she stuttered in shock, "Wh-what are you…what… you…"

"Oh, shut up, Lucinda," Maggie said, dismissing her as she stepped up to the sink to wash her hands.

Sarah slowly shook her head. "Wow. I did not see that coming."

"Hello, Sarah," Maggie said pleasantly as she grabbed a towel from the dispenser.

Her old friend began to laugh. "Maggie, I was wondering how long it would take you to find your spine again."

Sarah was smiling in real pleasure and Maggie realized that maybe she hadn't lost all of her friends after all.

"Well, I've found it now, so look out." Maggie tossed the towel, then straightened her shoulders and shook her hair back defiantly as if she were about to go into battle. She looked at Sarah in the mirror. "You ain't seen nothin' yet."

"Go get 'em, Maggie," Sarah said, still laughing as Maggie stalked out of the bathroom.

Maggie stormed down the wide hallway to the judges' room entrance. She didn't much care what someone like Lucinda thought. What bothered her was that anyone else might think that she would resort to cheating. With a firm tug, she pulled the heavy door open. She no longer cared about contest rules and regulations. She had to find Connor and find out the truth. She wasn't about to take the word of a silly twit like Lucinda again.

The room was bustling. Dozens of judges sat at twenty

round tables scattered around the room. Each judge had at least five small glasses in front of them, each one marked with numbers only and filled with a different beer or ale. They were in various stages of tasting and studying and Maggie couldn't help being drawn into the process.

Each judge had a clipboard listing all of the categories used to judge the entries. Maggie knew them by heart. Appearance, aroma, flavor, balance, body and mouth feel, overall impression and flaws.

These judges took their job seriously, and the brewers who submitted their products to the competition were even more serious. Taking home these prizes could mean millions of dollars to the winner. The judges were trusted with making those critical decisions. And someone had destroyed that trust.

And they were blaming it on Maggie.

If Lucinda was to be believed, they'd already put her on trial and found her guilty.

But Lucinda was an idiot. Always had been. Would Connor actually take her word over Maggie's? It wasn't possible. She had to find Connor and hear the truth from him. After all this time they'd spent together, after all they'd shared, he had to realize that she would never do anything to hurt him. He had to know that she could be trusted with his heart.

She thought he already did. But now…was he still unsure of her feelings for him? Was he still holding on to the hurt he'd felt for so many years? They had talked about it over and over this week. How could he still believe she'd betrayed him back then?

She had to find him. But would he believe her? Would he trust her? Would he listen and believe it when she told him she'd never stopped loving him? That she loved him more than life itself?

She was confident that if she could just look into his

eyes, she would see the answers and know that he truly believed her, trusted her, loved her.

So where was he? The room was filled with people, but she could've picked him out of any crowd. And he was no-where to be found.

"Where are you, Connor?" she murmured anxiously.

At that very moment, as if he'd been summoned by tele-pathic command, Connor walked out of a smaller anteroom and into the larger judges' room. He was followed by his brothers, the three of them looking like warriors marching into battle. All that was missing was the blue war paint and their clan tartans wrapped around them.

Johnny and two older men she didn't recognize followed in the brothers' wake. Their expressions were all severe and Maggie wouldn't want to tangle with any of them. But it appeared that they were headed in her general direction.

Connor's face was stern and ashen. Jake stared ahead with fierce intent, and Ian was fuming, as well.

Her heart went out to them. They looked angry and ready to fight. Maggie could completely understand their feelings, especially after overhearing Lucinda's unfounded accusations in the bathroom.

Then Connor spotted her. He led the men straight to her, watching her the entire time as he walked closer. Maggie stared back at him, searching for that same spark of love she'd seen in his eyes the night before. But all she saw was…guilt?

Blame?

Censure?

She couldn't tell, but she backed away instinctively as they got closer.

"Maggie, wait," Connor said.

She stopped and straightened her shoulders. "For what?" Sarah was right, she thought. Maggie had found her spine and she wouldn't be treated like a criminal. "For you and your brothers to pronounce me guilty? No, thank you." She turned to leave and slammed right into Lucinda, who was standing inches behind her.

"Don't believe her, Connor," Lucinda shouted.

"Lucinda," Jake said. "We were just looking for you."

Lucinda shot Maggie a look of triumph. "I was just looking for you guys, too."

"Connor," Maggie said. "I just heard about the tainted beer. I'm so sorry." But Connor wouldn't meet Maggie's gaze.

Why? Wait. He didn't believe her? Couldn't even look at her? Without even listening to her side of the story? So this was it?

Instead of meeting Maggie's gaze, he was staring at Lucinda.

"Your entries weren't damaged, Red," Johnny chimed in reassuringly.

"Thanks, Johnny," Maggie said, not reassured at all.

"So you only care about your own entries," Lucinda taunted. "Kind of selfish if you ask me."

"Nobody asked you," Maggie said.

"That's enough, Lucinda," Jake muttered.

"Me?" Lucinda slapped her hands on her hips in outrage. "She's the one pretending to be innocent. I'm just trying to point out who's guilty here."

Maggie looked carefully at each of the men in front of her and saw nothing encouraging in their eyes. "So you believe her? You think I'm…guilty?" She almost choked on the words. "You really believe I could do this?"

But Lucinda wasn't about to let them talk. Instead she confronted Maggie face-to-face. "What time did you finally show up at the dance?"

"What does that matter?" she asked.

Lucinda whipped around to the men. "She was late because she was busy sneaking into the storage room. You saw her talking to Ted Blake, Connor, I know you did. And that wasn't the only time I've seen them together. They probably planned it from the start."

Maggie frowned. The men were all watching Lucinda. Were they actually taking her word for this? Connor still wouldn't look at her and Maggie felt as if she were facing another inquisition, as she used to call her confrontations with her ex-husband and his mother.

Well, screw that. That was the past, she reminded herself. She would never, ever put up with an unfair accusation from anyone, ever again.

She gazed up at Connor. "Do you think I would do this to you?"

He stared hard at her, then said, "No."

"Wow," she whispered. "It took you more than a few seconds to decide on your answer. So your first instinct was to believe I would hurt you that way?"

His jaw tightened. "No, Maggie, it wasn't."

But again there was that momentary pause and Maggie began to question everything. Did he believe her? Did he trust her? Did he honestly think she would do this to him? If he believed she was innocent, then why wasn't he grabbing her and kissing her and assuring her that he knew she would never hurt him again?

Because he didn't believe that.

Her heart was breaking and she wanted to cry, to scream and demand that he believe her, love her, trust her.

But that would give Lucinda too much satisfaction. So instead Maggie cast one more beseeching glance at Connor, and when she received nothing back from him, not even a glance her way, she couldn't remain there another second. She turned and walked away.

"Maggie, wait," Connor said.

She wanted more than anything to keep moving away

from him, but she'd just remembered something important. She whipped around and walked up to Johnny.

"I'm signing my three Redhead entries over to the Mac-Laren Brewery," she said tersely. "I owe them the formulas anyway, so now they officially belong to Connor and his brothers. If you need me to sign anything swearing to that, text me. You have my phone number on my entry form."

She cast one more glance at Connor. "Oh, and you should fire your secretary."

And then she walked away.

He fired their secretary.

It was a unanimous decision made by all three brothers, especially after they viewed the videotape that had caught the culprit red-handed, so to speak.

Luckily for everyone, the convention center had videotapes running twenty-four hours a day, in every single room of the massive structure, including the storage room. Who knew? Connor thought, giving thanks that the center was so security-minded.

Connor, Jake and Ian had viewed the tape with Johnny and the festival president, along with the local sheriff, who had shown up for the festival on his day off. They had all seen the moment when their secretary Lucinda had snuck into the storage room and tainted one of the MacLaren entries.

But even before Connor saw the evidence, he had known Maggie was innocent, although Lucinda had done everything she could to sway their judgment in Maggie's direction.

But when Maggie stomped back over to Johnny and told him she was signing over her entries to MacLaren, Connor felt his heart jump in his chest. He could swear he'd never seen anything so courageous in his life. He'd been ready to tear off after her, but Lucinda was still raving and the sheriff needed their united presence.

"Don't tell me you believe her!" Lucinda had cried after Maggie stormed off. "Just because she put on a show for all of you, it doesn't mean anything. She's still your most viable suspect."

"What's your problem, Lucinda?" Connor asked, fed up with the woman sniping at Maggie. "What do you have against Maggie?"

"She's trying to hurt you. I'm trying to help you, but you can just forget it. I'm through doing all your dirty work." She spun around and began to walk away quickly.

"Not so fast, young lady," the sheriff said, jogging after her and grabbing hold of her arm. She squirmed and twisted to escape, but it was no use.

"Something you want to tell us, Lucinda?" Ian had said.

She stomped her foot. "I don't know why you think I did something. Maggie was the one who was talking to Ted Blake. Didn't you see her? The two of them were probably plotting the whole thing together. And look how late she was for the dance. She had plenty of time to break in and destroy the entry."

"It's not Maggie," Connor had said decisively, putting an end to Lucinda's blathering.

But he knew the damage had been done. Maggie had arrived right after he and his brothers had viewed the tapes. They all knew who the guilty party was. The videotape was a powerful indictment. But the sheriff had suggested it would be easier to deal with Lucinda if she would just confess. Connor had been willing to go along with his request, but regretted it the second he saw Maggie's reaction to his silence.

"Damn it." Connor should've grabbed her in his arms the instant Lucinda began to spew her venomous accusations. He'd been glaring at Lucinda, but she'd been standing directly behind Maggie. So now he wondered if Maggie might've thought his glares had been aimed at her.

"No doubt," Connor muttered, and rubbed his jaw in frustration. Maggie would naturally default to the worst-case scenario, and he couldn't really blame her in this situation.

She'd been through enough trauma in her life. Connor was sick at the thought that he might've given her a reason to doubt that he was completely, utterly, irrevocably in love with her.

Now he needed to find her and convince her otherwise.

Maggie barely made it to the suite and got the door closed before the tears threatened to fall.

But she was sick to death of tears. Yes, her heart was breaking, but she refused to cry about it.

And to think that she'd gone downstairs to find Connor and tell him she'd fallen in love with him. She had foolishly thought he'd be happy to hear it and would respond by telling her how much he loved her, too.

How ironic. It seemed that circumstances had played a cruel joke on her. It wouldn't be the first time.

So much for taking risks.

"Now you're just feeling sorry for yourself," she muttered. "But don't you dare cry." She grabbed her suitcase and opened it on the bed. Then she began to toss her clothes into the open bag.

She couldn't wait to leave this damn hotel and go home to Grandpa and the goats.

"Goats? Really?" She sniffled a little at the thought of the goats, then rolled her eyes. How pathetic could she get? She was reduced to depending on goats to comfort and sympathize with her in her moment of misery. It just added to the misery.

She heard the suite door open and knew that Connor

had come back. Could things get any worse? She wanted to hide under the bed, but she'd been hiding for way too long. No more hiding, Maggie. She'd grown so much in the past few years, and these past few days had made her feel more powerful than she ever had.

Besides, it was a platform bed, so there was no place to hide anyway.

She really didn't want another confrontation with Connor, but she couldn't avoid it now and she figured it was long past due. But at least she knew that his last impression of her would not be of red-rimmed, swollen eyes and tear-drenched cheeks. Nope. She was not going to cry and look like some pathetic water rat.

But then, why would he care what she looked like? He thought she was a saboteur—or worse.

He stood in the doorway, watching her.

"Hello, Connor," she said, and dropped her shoes into the suitcase. "Did something else happen that you can accuse me of doing? Maybe I tainted the water supply? Released a dirty bomb? Stole your underwear? Take your best shot."

"I'm not here to accuse you of anything, Maggie."

"Good," she said, folding her arms across her chest defensively. "Because I'm not putting up with one more accusation from you or anyone else. If you honestly believe that I would ever do anything like that to hurt you, you're horribly mistaken." She grabbed another shirt from the closet and flung it into the suitcase. "My God, what you must think of me. One of those judges could've been killed. Do you really think I'm capable of that?"

"No."

"Right." She tossed a pair of pants into the suitcase. "Look, this has been fun. Well, most of it, anyway. The past hour or so, not so much. But other than that whole belittling, accusing thing that just happened downstairs, I had a really wonderful time and I'll always keep the memory of you in my heart."

And with those words said, she burst into tears. Damn it. She really didn't want to cry. She was stronger now. But the truth was bringing her to her knees. Connor had always been in her heart and he would remain there forever, even if they were apart.

Still, tears were not acceptable. She hastily brushed them away as she grabbed more clothes and threw them into the suitcase.

"I'm glad to hear it," he said, "because you'll always be in my heart, too."

"Thank you." She sniffled.

"And I owe you this," he said, handing her a piece of paper.

Her eyes were still a little blurry, but she could see it was a check with a lot of numbers written on it. He was paying her for her week of service. Another sob escaped and she had to struggle to speak. "Do you really think I'm going to take this?"

"That was the deal," he said.

She took a deep breath and wiped her eyes. Then she gazed at him for a long moment. "Forget the deal," she said finally, and tore the check in two.

"Maggie," he said softly.

"Connor, I saw that look of accusation in your eyes."

"That look you saw," he said with aggravating calmness, "was aimed at Lucinda, who was standing about two feet behind you the whole time."

"If you say so," she muttered.

"You know she was there, right?" Connor took one step into the room. "She was the one we were all looking at. We already knew she was guilty. We reviewed the videotapes a few minutes before you arrived. We saw her do it, Maggie."

"Videotapes?"

"Yeah. The center runs security videos in all the rooms," he explained. "So we knew Lucinda was guilty. But even before I saw the tape, it never crossed my mind to suspect you, Maggie. Why would I? You're in love with me. You would never hurt me."

She glared at him. "How do you know?"

He laughed, damn him. He wasn't playing fair. She'd wanted to be the one to tell him she loved him, had rushed downstairs to find him and let him know her feelings. But he'd guessed anyway before she could say the words. But wait, she thought. He hadn't said he loved her, too. Why? She knew he loved her. Or he *did,* before this day happened.

"You got caught in the cross fire," he continued. "The sheriff wanted her to confess, so he advised us not to say anything. But he finally got tired of her caterwauling and dragged her off to book her."

That got her attention. "Really? You had her arrested?"

"Hell, yes," he said, scowling. "You were right, Maggie. She could've killed one of those judges."

Her anger left her in a heartbeat and she had to lean against the dresser to steady her suddenly weak knees.

"So let me turn the question around on you," Connor said softly, taking another step farther into the room and disturbing what little equilibrium she had left.

"What question?" she asked warily.

He took a step closer. "Do you really think I'm capable of believing you could do such a horrible thing?"

"Oh." She stared at him in shock, then had to think about what he'd said. "No. Of course not, but we've had to overcome some history to—"

"I'd say we've overcome all that." Another step. "So now, do you really think I believe you could hurt me that way?"

She bit her lip. "When you put it like that, no. But I still think—"

"Don't think." He was inches away now, close enough to

reach out and tenderly sweep a strand of hair off her face. His fingers remained, lightly stroking her cheek. "Don't think, Maggie. Feel. Take a chance. Believe. In me. In us. I do."

"I do, too," she whispered. "I believe in us. I believe in taking a chance. Risking it all. For you."

He kissed the edge of her chin. "I'm so in love with you, Maggie."

"Oh." She had to catch her breath. "I—I love you so much, Connor. I don't think I've ever stopped loving you."

"I've never stopped loving you, either."

"I'm so sorry I wasted so much time being away from you."

"Let's make up for it now," he said. "Say you'll marry me, Maggie?"

"Oh, Connor," she said, staring up at him. Her heart filled with so much joy she wasn't sure she could hold it all. "Yes, of course I'll marry you."

"And love me always?" He kissed her cheek.

"You know I will," she whispered.

He nibbled her neck. "And have my children?"

"Oh, Connor." She blinked away more tears. "Yes. I would love to have children with you."

He licked her earlobe. "And pick out my clothes for me?"

She laughed and smacked his chest, then threw her arms around his neck. "Yes. Absolutely yes to all of the above."

"I'm glad you're packing your bags," he said, glancing around the room. "Let's go home right now and start our lives together."

"Please, Connor," she said as he swept her off her feet and into his arms. "Take me home."

Epilogue

"I heard from the Scottish lawyers again," Jake said, leaning back in his chair as he downed his beer. "They're getting more nervous about the property, so I told them that one of us would fly over to check things out."

Connor's brothers had come by his house to talk business and to try a taste of Maggie's latest award-winning ale. Connor had named it Maggie's Pride, a takeoff of their own MacLaren's Pride. "Ian's the logical choice to go."

Ian scowled. "Just because my ex-father-in-law lives there doesn't mean I'm the one who has to go. Forget it."

"Why not?" Jake asked.

Ian glared at him but said nothing. He'd been doing that a lot lately, Connor realized. Something had crawled up his butt, but he wasn't willing to talk about it. It wasn't too hard to figure out, though, since he and his wife, Samantha, were no longer living together.

"Well, don't look at me," Connor said. "I'm not leaving Maggie."

At that moment, Connor's beautiful wife walked into the room carrying two bowls of chips and salsa and set them on the table in front of the men. Her gaze went directly to Connor. "You're leaving me?"

Jake laughed. "No, he's not leaving you. He just married you. I haven't seen him wander more than five feet away from you since the wedding."

"Come here," Connor said, smiling up at Maggie. He grabbed her hand and pulled her gently onto his lap. Then he wrapped his arms around her waist and felt utterly content with life.

He hadn't announced the news to his brothers yet, but Maggie had been to the doctor yesterday, where they found out that she was pregnant. Connor wasn't sure he could contain all the love he had inside for his wife and the tiny baby growing within her belly.

It had barely been a month after the festival ended when he and Maggie were married on the beach with their family and a few trusted friends gathered around to celebrate. They had been apart for so many years that neither of them had wanted to wait any longer to begin their married life together. The small ceremony had suited Maggie perfectly. She'd already endured an extravagant society wedding with her ex-husband and didn't want to repeat the experience.

And speaking of her bizarre ex-husband, Connor had not been surprised to hear the news that Ashford had recently been arrested on suspicion of murdering his dear mother. According to the news reports Connor had seen, it appeared that the old woman hadn't died of natural causes after all. Her cantankerous butler had hounded the police until they agreed to investigate and finally discovered the truth.

Maggie snuggled closer and Connor kissed her neck, thankful again that she had come back home to him. The day she told him she was ready to take the biggest risk of her life and marry him, he knew he was the luckiest man alive.

"Jeez, you two," Ian groused. "Get a room."

Connor laughed, unfazed by his brother's bad mood. "Ignore him, he's jealous."

"He's especially cranky today," Jake said.

"Stop talking about me like I'm not in the room," Ian protested. "Besides, you would be cranky, too, if…never mind."

"If what?" Connor asked, growing concerned. He'd

never seen his brother more miserable. Ian had always been the most even-tempered of the three brothers, but ever since he'd separated from his wife, Samantha, he'd been unhappy.

Ian shoved his hand through his dark hair in frustration. "Never mind."

"Now you've got our curiosity piqued," Jake said mildly.

"You'll get over it," Ian muttered.

"I still don't see why you can't go to Scotland," Connor said, looking at Ian pointedly. "You loved it there last time. And Gordon is a great host."

"Yeah, well, last time I went, I was with Gordon's daughter," Ian reminded them. "Things have changed."

"No kidding," Jake said, took a last gulp of beer and set his glass on the table.

Maggie turned and gave Connor a look of concern, then glanced at his brother. "I'm sorry, Ian. Connor would go, but the timing—"

"No, love," Connor interrupted, not yet willing to share their baby news. He gave her a quick hug. "They understand that I won't be going this time."

Jake stood and stretched. "Fine, I'll go. I should've just agreed to go in the first place. Better than listening to Ian whine."

"I don't whine," Ian whined.

Maggie giggled.

"It's better if you go, anyway, Jake," Connor said. "You'll do the job quickly and get home."

"Yeah, I'll make it a fast trip, but I still want to stop in Kilmarnock for a day and visit Gordon. If Ian's really going to divorce Samantha, it's more important than ever to maintain a strong contact with her father."

"No," Ian said, more forcefully than usual.

"What do you mean, no?" Connor said. "Are you getting a divorce or not?"

Restless, Ian pushed his chair back from the table and stood. "I mean, no. You can't stop to see Gordon."

Jake whipped around. "Why the hell not?"

"Because he's disappeared," Ian said. "Nobody's seen him for days and they don't have a clue where he's gone." And with that bombshell dropped, he left the room abruptly.

Jake and Connor exchanged looks of apprehension. Then Jake shrugged. "You know Gordon. Chances are he slipped away to be with a woman. Let's not jump to conclusions."

"That's the most likely answer," Connor said, nodding in agreement. Right now he had to admit he was more concerned about his brother than Gordon McGregor's whereabouts. He wasn't sure what was going on with Ian and his in-laws, but it was something Connor would have to deal with later on. Much later, he thought, after he'd had more time to spend with his beautiful new wife and the unborn child they had created.

Maggie reach for his hand and whispered, "I love you."

"I know," Connor said, making her smile as he leaned over and kissed her with all his heart.

* * * * *

A sneaky peek at next month...

PASSIONATE AND DRAMATIC LOVE STORIES

My wish list for next month's titles...

In stores from 20th December 2013:

☐ Beneath the Stetson – Janice Maynard

& For the Sake of Their Son – Catherine Mann

☐ Pregnant by Morning – Kat Cantrell

& The Nanny's Secret – Elizabeth Lane

☐ At Odds with the Heiress – Cat Schield

& Project: Runaway Bride – Heidi Betts

2 stories in each book - only £5.49!

Available at WHSmith, Tesco, Asda, Eason, Amazon and Apple

Just can't wait?

Visit us Online

You can buy our books online a month before they hit the shops!

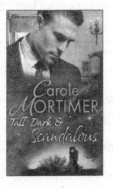

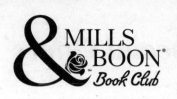

Join the Mills & Boon Book Club

Want to read more **Desire**™ books?
We're offering you **2 more** absolutely **FREE!**

We'll also treat you to these fabulous extras:

- 🌹 **Exclusive offers and much more!**

- 🌹 **FREE home delivery**

- 🌹 **FREE books and gifts with our special rewards scheme**

Get your free books now!

**visit www.millsandboon.co.uk/bookclub
or call Customer Relations on 020 8288 2888**